CARL JACOBI

Revelations in Black

I0612326

Introduction by
LUIGI MUSOLINO

VALANCOURT BOOKS

Revelations in Black by Carl Jacobi
Originally published by Arkham House in 1947
First Valancourt Books edition 2024

Published by Valancourt Books, Richmond, Virginia
http://www.valancourtbooks.com

ISBN 978-1-960241-15-3 (trade hardcover)
ISBN 978-1-960241-16-0 (trade paperback)
Also available as an electronic book.

Cover by M.S. Corley
Set in Dante MT

REVELATIONS IN BLACK

CARL JACOBI was born in Minneapolis in 1908. He attended the University of Minnesota, majoring in English literature and getting his start as a writer in the campus literary magazine. His story "Mive" first appeared in *The Minnesota Quarterly* before being picked up by *Weird Tales* in 1932, a sale that earned Jacobi twenty-five dollars. It was his first appearance in a professional magazine, but it would be far from the last: during the 1930s Jacobi was a mainstay of the pulps, producing dozens of stories in various popular genres from horror to science fiction to detective stories, including many contributions to the most famous of the horror pulps, *Weird Tales*.

With the collapse of the pulp market in the early 1940s, Jacobi was forced to take on a job at a local Honeywell plant working the night shift seven days a week, which had a severe effect on his health and his writing schedule. Nonetheless, he continued to produce high-quality supernatural tales, the first volume of which, *Revelations in Black*, appeared from Arkham House in 1947. He would go on to publish two more collections with Arkham House, *Portraits in Moonlight* (1964) and *Disclosures in Scarlet* (1972).

Though Jacobi continued to write and publish almost to the end of his life, in his later years he was greatly troubled by poor health, which limited his production but did not prevent him from collaborating with his literary agent R. Dixon Smith on two final collections of his stories, published in 1989 and 1994. Jacobi died in 1997.

Contents

Introduction

Carl Jacobi: A Forgotten Master of the Weird

It has been said that a writer's literary fortune doesn't necessarily depend on the quality of his art. Many authors of tales of the supernatural, science fiction, and adventure, especially those who lived during the Golden Age of pulp magazines between the First and Second World Wars, enjoyed a fleeting success tied to that specific moment in time, with the lucrative boom of the genre magazines, only then to fall into oblivion. Others, snubbed by the literary establishment, have subsequently been rediscovered and included among the pantheon of the greats, thanks to word of mouth from enthusiasts and the undeniable caliber of their work.

One of the last "survivors" of the pulp era, Carl Jacobi has received recognition and appreciation from genre aficionados, but probably not the attention he deserves. His production, fascinating and wide-ranging, spans more than half a century of speculative fiction. Esteemed by world-renowned authors like H.P. Lovecraft, Robert Bloch, Clifford D. Simak, Donald Wandrei, Robert E. Howard, Clark Ashton Smith, and Hugh B. Cave, Jacobi was a mild-mannered, versatile writer, a close friend of the founder of Arkham House, August Derleth, with whom he maintained an extensive correspondence for almost forty years.

Jacobi's work spans the various genres of popular fiction, ranging from horror and science fiction to adventure and detective stories, thriller, and mystery. Some of his stories have become cornerstones of supernatural short fiction (such as "Revelations in Black," a disturbing story of vampirism, and "Matthew South & Co.," a notable revisiting of the *doppelgänger* theme), and his contribution to the most famous American horror pulp, *Weird*

Tales, was substantial. Not to mention his numerous appearances in other legendary pulp magazines such as *Astounding Stories*, *Thrilling Mysteries*, *Comet*, *Strange Stories*, *Planet Stories*, etc.

Jacobi had a shy personality and was devoted to his parents, whom he would look after until their death, and to his typewriter, his only true companion in life; a life dedicated to the fantastic, spent almost entirely in his hometown.

Born in Minneapolis on July 10, 1908, Carl began writing very early, fascinated by the fiction of writers such as Jules Verne, Edgar Allan Poe, and Edward Bulwer Lytton. With his father's encouragement, young Jacobi began to experiment with words. His earliest literary efforts were published in the school newspaper at Central High, the high school he attended from 1924 to 1926. Around the same time Jacobi discovered *Weird Tales*:

> I believe I was introduced to *Weird Tales* by the issues which featured on their covers 'The Stolen Body' by H.G. Wells, 'Monsters of the Pit' by Paul S. Powers and 'The Werewolf of Ponkert' by H. Warner Munn.

After graduating in January 1927, Carl enrolled at the University of Minnesota, continuing to cultivate his passion for the Weird and writing. The *Minnesota Quarterly*, the university's literary magazine, published four of his stories between 1928 and 1930. The first was "Mive," a mature and evocative story, in which Jacobi seems to capture the sort of gloomy atmosphere so dear to Edgar Allan Poe, presenting the reader with a swamp infested with alien butterflies.

And it was "Mive" that helped Jacobi make the leap to the next level: *Weird Tales*, the magazine that had so fascinated the young Minneapolis student, accepted and published the story in 1932. True recognition of Jacobi's talent came not just from the magazine's decision to publish the story, but also from the numerous letters of praise from enthusiasts and fellow writers; a letter of appreciation from H.P. Lovecraft, always very critical of his own and other people's literary production, gives us an idea of the quality of the story: " 'Mive' pleased me immensely," writes Lovecraft at the beginning of his first letter to Jacobi. Clark

Ashton Smith, Robert E. Howard, and August Derleth would follow with their tributes.

The extraordinary success achieved by "Mive" was repeated, the following year, with "Revelations in Black," perhaps the author's best-known story. Jacobi began to consider the idea of dedicating himself to writing full time; he rented an office in Minneapolis, moved his desk and typewriter there, and began creating. It was the beginning of a career that, with ups and downs, would span almost sixty years.

Robert E. Howard, the famous creator of Conan and one of the "musketeers" of *Weird Tales*, in a letter sent to Jacobi in 1933 characterizes his style as *subtle*. It is a label that fits perfectly. Jacobi's stories instill unease in the reader through the sophisticated use of words, an accumulation of clues, and veiled hints that contribute to the crescendo typical of his stories, a gradual, almost surgical escalation of tension, which relies on atmosphere and psychological analysis of the protagonists, leading to explosive and revelatory endings. Carl Jacobi was an exacting wordsmith, a delicate chiseller of sentences. He firmly believed that the overall effect of a story could only be achieved through "the word that would hit home," as his friend Hugh B. Cave recalls. In fact, Carl revised his tales countless times, with obsessive care, thus giving life to fiction without frills, made up of concise and direct prose. A style that at times could be characterized as almost minimalist.

Another fundamental aspect of Jacobi's stories is their atmosphere, which often seems to be elevated to a character in and of itself. Whether the events take place in the rural Midwest or on a Caribbean island, the author's ability to depict disturbing landscapes and suggestive settings is one of the hallmarks of his work. To give greater realism to his stories, especially the "exotic" ones, Jacobi got in contact with a number of military detachments in Malaya, Borneo, and other remote regions of the globe, in order to obtain first-hand information from the officers in charge. The garden with the twenty-six jays in "Revelations in Black," the isolated manor in "The Unpleasantness at Carver House," or the disturbing exoticness of the island of Tortola in "An Incident at the Galloping Horse," are perfect examples of this conception of setting: not simply a backdrop for the characters' actions, but an active part of the story, sometimes even the protagonist of the story as the harbinger of the supernatural event.

In the best Weird tradition, Jacobi's work also includes a cursed tome, *The Restitution of Decayed Intelligence*, which, contrary to the myth of literary grimoires, is a volume that actually existed, written in 1605 by Richard Verstegan; the author would adopt its fascinating title to create his own grimoire.

There are times when Jacobi's fiction seems to anticipate that fringe of horror that would bring success to authors such as Richard Matheson, Stephen King, and others: the simple (but difficult to achieve) concept of "everything creeps," of the dark, strange, unexpected event that insinuates itself into the banal everyday life of reality and explodes with its disturbing charge of horrors and mysteries. And so the discovery of an old book in an antique dealer's shop is the prelude to a dizzying descent into madness and vampirism ("Revelations in Black"); two ordinary scarecrows come to life on an isolated Louisiana farm ("Witches in the Cornfield"); a simple wall dividing an estate becomes the last bulwark of defense against mythological horrors manifesting in nineteenth-century England ("The Singleton Barrier"). And then there is the fleeting parallel between horror (often embodied in objects, ancient manors, and dark events of the past) and the dormant madness of human beings, an ephemeral boundary that is difficult to grasp. As the protagonist of the celebrated story "Mive" wonders, "Where did the delirium fade into reality?"

Jacobi has a tendency to plant the seed of doubt in the reader that the supernatural story is attributable to a hallucination, an alteration of the senses, making the final effect of the story even more ambiguous and disturbing. Robert Bloch, the author of *Psycho*, a pupil of Lovecraft and an established writer of horror and the fantastic, seems to have fully grasped this aspect of Jacobi's work; as he wrote in the pages of *The Arkham Sampler*, reviewing *Revelations in Black*:

Carl Jacobi's concept is, at first glance, the velvet pall, the midnight moor, the unlit house, the *mysterioso* chord on the piano—in a word, the conventional, almost traditional "stage effect" or backdrop for the saga of the supernatural. It is the inevitable background for the mysterious veiled woman in "Revelations in Black," the genius recently released from the asylum in "The Satanic Piano," and the diabolical stranger of "The Coach on the Ring." Yet one cannot dismiss the Jacobi gambit quite this easily. On the surface, his use of "black" is proper to the atmosphere of "manors" and "lodgings" and "laboratories" so familiar to readers of the standard weird tale. But on closer examination of thematic material, one notes the peculiar correspondence of darkness in the background and mental disorder in the characters who emerge from that background. . . . It would seem, then, that to Carl Jacobi, "black" symbolizes the mental blackout of insanity.

And Jacobi's own words contain the key to the effectiveness of his tales, the ability to pull readers in and involve them in the stories:

> To me there is one unbreakable rule in successful fiction writing. If your chief character's actions are fantastic or removed from reality, then your background should be commonplace. If your backdrop is a strange world, a far distant planet or an antediluvian period of the Earth's past, then your protagonist should be an ordinary fellow with ordinary traits and characteristics. If you have both in the same story (as some sword and sorcery tales do) it is difficult for your reader to have something which he can relate to. (Jacobi, *The Derleth Connection*, p. 6).

Despite the enthusiasm of his readers, relying solely on the uncertain market of the pulp magazines was not an easy way of making ends meet. In 1942, Jacobi was forced to get a full-time job at a factory in the city; every night he sat in front of his typewriter, despite his fatigue and frustration, continuing to turn out little gems of the supernatural for his readers.

His physical decline began in the seventies, with a bad fall that left him hospitalized for months. But his passion for the fantastic was stronger than his illness. Carl continued to write and collaborated with R. Dixon Smith on the anthologies of his tales *East of Samarinda*, released in 1989, and *Smoke of the Snake*, published in 1994.

He passed away on August 25, 1997 in his Minneapolis home. With him went one of the last bastions of 1930s horror fiction, a writer who had fully experienced the unforgettable epic of the American pulp magazine, a historical period that made and continues to make legions of readers dream. Dreams (and nightmares) that Jacobi's narrative continues to fuel . . .

LUIGI MUSOLINO

LUIGI MUSOLINO was born in the Italian province of Turin, where he still lives and works. A specialist in Italian folklore, he is the author of several collections of tales of weird fiction, horror, and rural Gothic, including his English-language debut, *A Different Darkness and Other Abominations*, which was a finalist for the World Fantasy Award. He has translated into Italian works by Brian Keene, Lisa Mannetti, Michael Laimo, and the autobiographical writings of H. P. Lovecraft. He is currently at work on a new volume of short fiction to be published by Valancourt in 2025.

Revelations in Black

It was a dreary, forlorn establishment way down on Harbor Street. An old sign announced the legend: "Giovanni Larla— Antiques," and a dingy window revealed a display half masked in dust.

Even as I crossed the threshold that cheerless September afternoon, driven from the sidewalk by a gust of rain and perhaps a fascination for all antiques, the gloominess fell upon me like a material pall. Inside was half darkness, piled boxes and a monstrous tapestry, frayed with the warp showing in worn places. An Italian Renaissance wine cabinet shrank despondently in its corner and seemed to frown at me as I passed.

"Good afternoon, *Signor.* There is something you wish to buy? A picture, a ring, a vase perhaps?"

I peered at the squat bulk of the Italian proprietor there in the shadows and hesitated.

"Just looking around," I said, turning to the jumble about me. "Nothing in particular . . ."

The man's oily face moved in smile as though he had heard the remark a thousand times before. He sighed, stood there in thought a moment, the rain drumming and swishing against the outer pane. Then very deliberately he stepped to the shelves and glanced up and down them considering. At length he drew forth an object which I perceived to be a painted chalice.

"An authentic Sixteenth Century Tandart," he murmured. "A work of art, *Signor.*"

I shook my head. "No pottery," I said. "Books perhaps, but no pottery."

He frowned slowly. "I have books too," he replied, "rare books which nobody sells but me, Giovanni Larla. But you must look at my other treasures too."

There was, I found, no hurrying the man. A quarter of an hour passed during which I had to see a Glycon cameo brooch, a carved chair of some indeterminate style and period, and a muddle of yellowed statuettes, small oils and one or two dreary Portland vases. Several times I glanced at my watch impatiently, wondering how I might break away from this Italian and his gloomy shop. Already the fascination of its dust and shadows had begun to wear off, and I was anxious to reach the street.

But when he had conducted me well toward the rear of the shop, something caught my fancy. I drew then from the shelf the first book of horror. If I had but known the events that were to follow, if I could only have had a foresight into the future that September day, I swear I would have avoided the book like a leprous thing, would have shunned that wretched antique store and the very street it stood on like places accursed. A thousand times I have wished my eyes had never rested on that cover in black. What writhings of the soul, what terrors, what unrest, what madness would have been spared me!

But never dreaming the secret of its pages I fondled it casually and remarked:

"An unusual book. What is it?"

Larla glanced up and scowled.

"That is not for sale," he said quietly. "I don't know how it got on these shelves. It was my poor brother's."

The volume in my hand was indeed unusual in appearance. Measuring but four inches across and five inches in length and bound in black velvet with each outside corner protected with a triangle of ivory, it was the most beautiful piece of book-binding I had ever seen. In the center of the cover was mounted a tiny piece of ivory intricately cut in the shape of a skull. But it was the title of the book that excited my interest. Embroidered in gold braid, the title read:

"*Five Unicorns and a Pearl.*"

I looked at Larla. "How much?" I asked and reached for my wallet.

He shook his head. "No, it is not for sale. It is . . . it is the last work of my brother. He wrote it just before he died in the institution."

"The institution?"

Larla made no reply but stood staring at the book, his mind obviously drifting away in deep thought. A moment of silence dragged by. There was a strange gleam in his eyes when finally he spoke. And I thought I saw his fingers tremble slightly.

"My brother, Alessandro, was a fine man before he wrote that book," he said slowly. "He wrote beautifully, *Signor*, and he was strong and healthy. For hours I could sit while he read to me his poems. He was a dreamer, Alessandro; he loved everything beautiful, and the two of us were very happy.

"All . . . until that terrible night. Then he . . . but no . . . a year has passed now. It is best to forget." He passed his hand before his eyes and drew in his breath sharply.

"What happened?" I asked.

"Happened, *Signor*? I do not really know. It was all so confusing. He became suddenly ill, ill without reason. The flush of sunny Italy, which was always on his cheek, faded, and he grew white and drawn. His strength left him day by day. Doctors prescribed, gave medicines, but nothing helped. He grew steadily weaker until . . . until that night."

I looked at him curiously, impressed by his perturbation.

"And then—?"

Hands opening and closing, Larla seemed to sway unsteadily; his liquid eyes opened wide to the brows.

"And then . . . oh, if I could but forget! It was horrible. Poor Alessandro came home screaming, sobbing. He was . . . he was stark, raving mad!

"They took him to the institution for the insane and said he needed a complete rest, that he had suffered from some terrific mental shock. He . . . died three weeks later with the crucifix on his lips."

For a moment I stood there in silence, staring out at the falling rain. Then I said:

"He wrote this book while confined to the institution?"

Larla nodded absently.

"Three books," he replied. "Two others exactly like the one you have in your hand. The bindings he made, of course, when he was quite well. It was his original intention, I believe, to pen in them by hand the verses of Marini. He was very clever at such work. But the wanderings of his mind which filled the pages now, I have never read. Nor do I intend to. I want to keep with me the memory of him when he was happy. This book has come on these shelves by mistake. I shall put it with his other possessions."

My desire to read the few pages bound in velvet increased a thousandfold when I found they were unobtainable. I have always had an interest in abnormal psychology and have gone through a number of books on the subject. Here was the work of a man confined in the asylum for the insane. Here was the unexpurgated writing of an educated brain gone mad. And unless my intuition failed me, here was a suggestion of some deep mystery. My mind was made up. I must have it.

I turned to Larla and chose my words carefully.

"I can well appreciate your wish to keep the book," I said, "and since you refuse to sell, may I ask if you would consider lending it to me for just one night? If I promised to return it in the morning? . . ."

The Italian hesitated. He toyed undecidedly with a heavy gold watch chain.

"No, I am sorry . . ."

"Ten dollars and back tomorrow unharmed."

Larla studied his shoe.

"Very well, *Signor*, I will trust you. But please, I ask you, please be sure and return it."

That night in the quiet of my apartment I opened the book. Immediately my attention was drawn to three lines scrawled in a feminine hand across the inside of the front cover, lines written in a faded red solution that looked more like blood than ink. They read:

"*Revelations meant to destroy but only binding without the stake. Read, fool, and enter my field, for we are chained to the spot. Oh wo unto Larla.*"

I mused over these undecipherable sentences for some time without solving their meaning. At last, I turned to the first page and began the last work of Alessandro Larla, the strangest story I had ever in my years of browsing through old books, come upon.

"*On the evening of the fifteenth of October I turned my steps into the cold and walked until I was tired. The roar of the present was in the distance when I came to twenty-six bluejays silently contemplating the ruins. Passing in the midst of them I wandered by the skeleton trees and seated myself where I could watch the leering fish. A child worshipped. Glass threw the moon at me. Grass sang a litany at my feet. And the pointed shadow moved slowly to the left.*

"I walked along the silver gravel until I came to five unicorns gallop- ing beside water of the past. Here I found a pearl, a magnificent pearl, a pearl beautiful but black. Like a flower it carried a rich perfume, and once I thought the odor was but a mask, but why should such a perfect creation need a mask?

"I sat between the leering fish and the five galloping unicorns, and I fell madly in love with the pearl. The past lost itself in drabness and—"

I laid the book down and sat watching the smoke-curls from my pipe eddy ceilingward. There was much more, but I could make no sense to any of it. All was in that strange style and com- pletely incomprehensible. And yet it seemed the story was more than the mere wanderings of a madman. Behind it all seemed to lie a narrative cloaked in symbolism.

Something about the few sentences had cast an immediate spell of depression over me. The vague lines weighed upon my mind, and I felt myself slowly seized by a deep feeling of uneasi- ness.

The air of the room grew heavy and close. The open case- ment and the out-of-doors seemed to beckon to me. I walked to the window, thrust the curtain aside, stood there, smoking furiously. Let me say that regular habits have long been a part of my make-up. I am not addicted to nocturnal strolls or late mean- derings before seeking my bed; yet now, curiously enough, with the pages of the book still in my mind I suddenly experienced an indefinable urge to leave my apartment and walk the darkened streets.

I paced the room nervously. The clock on the mantel pushed its ticks slowly through the quiet. And at length I threw my pipe to the table, reached for my hat and coat and made for the door.

Ridiculous as it may sound, upon reaching the street I found that urge had increased to a distinct attraction. I felt that under no circumstances must I turn any direction but northward, and although this way led into a district quite unknown to me, I was in a moment pacing forward, choosing streets deliberately and heading without knowing why toward the outskirts of the city. It was a brilliant moonlight night in September. Summer had passed and already there was the smell of frosted vegetation in the air. The great chimes in Capitol tower were sounding midnight, and the buildings and shops and later the private houses were dark and silent as I passed.

Try as I would to erase from my memory the queer book which I had just read, the mystery of its pages hammered at me, arousing my curiosity. "Five Unicorns and a Pearl!" What did it all mean?

More and more I realized as I went on that a power other than my own will was leading my steps. Yet once when I did momentarily come to a halt that attraction swept upon me as inexorably as the desire for a narcotic.

It was far out on Easterly Street that I came upon a high stone wall flanking the sidewalk. Over its ornamented top I could see the shadows of a dark building set well back in the grounds. A wrought-iron gate in the wall opened upon a view of wild desertion and neglect. Swathed in the light of the moon, an old courtyard strewn with fountains, stone benches and statues lay tangled in rank weeds and undergrowth. The windows of the building, which evidently had once been a private dwelling, were boarded up, all except those on a little tower or cupola rising to a point in front. And here the glass caught the blue-gray light and refracted it into the shadows.

Before that gate my feet stopped like dead things. The psychic power which had been leading me had now become a reality. Directly from the courtyard it emanated, drawing me toward it with an intensity that smothered all reluctance.

Strangely enough, the gate was unlocked; and feeling like a man in a trance I swung the creaking hinges and entered, making my way along a grass-grown path to one of the benches. It seemed that once inside the court the distant sounds of the city died away, leaving a hollow silence broken only by the wind rustling through the tall dead weeds. Rearing up before me, the building with its dark wings, cupola and facade oddly resembled a colossal hound, crouched and ready to spring.

There were several fountains, weather-beaten and orna-mented with curious figures, to which at the time I paid only casual attention. Farther on, half hidden by the underbrush, was the life-size statue of a little child kneeling in position of prayer. Erosion on the soft stone had disfigured the face, and in the half-light the carved features presented an expression strangely gro-tesque and repelling.

How long I sat there in the quiet, I don't know. The surround-ings under the moonlight blended harmoniously with my mood. But more than that I seemed physically unable to rouse myself and pass on.

It was with a suddenness that brought me electrified to my feet that I became aware of the significance of the objects about me. Held motionless, I stood there running my eyes wildly from place to place, refusing to believe. Surely I must be dreaming. In the name of all that was unusual this . . . this absolutely couldn't be. And yet—

It was the fountain at my side that had caught my attention first. Across the top of the water basin were *five stone unicorns*, all identically carved, each seeming to follow the other in gal-loping procession. Looking farther, prompted now by a madly rising recollection, I saw that the cupola, towering high above the house, eclipsed the rays of the moon and threw *a long pointed shadow* across the ground *at my left*. The other fountain some distance away was ornamented with the figure of a stone fish, a *fish* whose empty eye-sockets *were leering* straight in my direc-tion. And the climax of it all—the wall! At intervals of every three feet on the top of the street expanse were mounted crude carven stone shapes of birds. And counting them I saw that *those birds were twenty-six bluejays*.

Unquestionably—startling and impossible as it seemed—I was in the same setting as described in Larla's book! It was a staggering revelation, and my mind reeled at the thought of it. How strange, how odd that I should be drawn to a portion of the city I had never before frequented and thrown into the midst of a narrative written almost a year before!

I saw now that Alessandro Larla, writing as a patient in the institution for the insane, had seized isolated details but neglected to explain them. Here was a problem for the psychologist, the mad, the symbolic, the incredible story of the dead Italian. I was bewildered and I pondered for an answer.

As if to soothe my perturbation there stole into the court then a faint odor of perfume. Pleasantly it touched my nostrils, seemed to blend with the moonlight. I breathed it in deeply as I stood there by the fountain. But slowly that odor became more noticeable, grew stronger, a sickish sweet smell that began to creep down my lungs like smoke. Heliotrope! The honeyed aroma blanketed the garden, thickened the air.

And then came my second surprise of the evening. Looking about to discover the source of the fragrance I saw opposite me, seated on another stone bench, a woman. She was dressed entirely in black, and her face was hidden by a veil. She seemed unaware of my presence. Her head was slightly bowed, and her whole position suggested a person in deep contemplation.

I noticed also the thing that crouched by her side. It was a dog, a tremendous brute with a head strangely out of proportion and eyes as large as the ends of big spoons. For several moments I stood staring at the two of them. Although the air was quite chilly, the woman wore no over-jacket, only the black dress relieved solely by the whiteness of her throat.

With a sigh of regret at having my pleasant solitude thus disturbed I moved across the court until I stood at her side. Still she showed no recognition of my presence, and clearing my throat I said hesitatingly:

"I suppose you are the owner here. I . . . I really didn't know the place was occupied, and the gate . . . well, the gate was unlocked. I'm sorry I trespassed."

She made no reply to that, and the dog merely gazed at me in dumb silence. No graceful words of polite departure came to my lips, and I moved hesitatingly toward the gate.

"Please don't go," she said suddenly, looking up. "I'm lonely. Oh, if you but knew how lonely I am!" She moved to one side on the bench and motioned that I sit beside her. The dog continued to examine me with its big eyes.

Whether it was the nearness of that odor of heliotrope, the suddenness of it all, or perhaps the moonlight, I did not know, but at her words a thrill of pleasure ran through me, and I accepted the proffered seat.

There followed an interval of silence, during which I puzzled for a means to start conversation. But abruptly she turned to the beast and said in German:

"*Fort mit dir, Johann!*"

The dog rose obediently to its feet and stole slowly off into the shadows. I watched it for a moment until it disappeared in the direction of the house. Then the woman said to me in English which was slightly stilted and marked with an accent:

"It has been ages since I have spoken to any one ... We are strangers. I do not know you, and you do not know me. Yet ... strangers sometimes find in each other a bond of interest. Supposing ... supposing we forget customs and formality of introduction? Shall we?"

For some reason I felt my pulse quicken as she said that. "Please do," I replied. "A spot like this is enough introduction in itself. Tell me, do you live here?"

She made no answer for a moment, and I began to fear I had taken her suggestion too quickly. Then she began slowly:

"My name is Perle von Mauren, and I am really a stranger to your country, though I have been here now more than a year. My home is in Austria near what is now the Czechoslovakian frontier. You see, it was to find my only brother that I came to the United States. During the war he was a lieutenant under General Mackensen, but in 1916, in April I believe it was, he ... he was reported missing.

"War is a cruel thing. It took our money; it took our castle on the Danube, and then—my brother. Those following years were horrible. We lived always in doubt, hoping against hope that he was still living.

"Then after the Armistice a fellow officer claimed to have served next to him on grave-digging detail at a French prison camp near Monpré. And later came a thin rumor that he was in the United States. I gathered together as much money as I could and came here in search of him."

Her voice dwindled off, and she sat in silence staring at the brown weeds. When she resumed, her voice was low and wavering.

"I . . . found him . . . but would to God I hadn't! He . . . he was no longer living."

I stared at her. "Dead?" I asked.

The veil trembled as though moved by a shudder, as though her thoughts had exhumed some terrible event of the past. Unconscious of my interruption she went on:

"Tonight I came here—I don't know why—merely because the gate was unlocked, and there was a place of quiet within. Now have I bored you with my confidences and personal history?"

"Not at all," I replied. "I came here by chance myself. Probably the beauty of the place attracted me. I dabble in amateur photography occasionally and react strongly to unusual scenes. Tonight I went for a midnight stroll to relieve my mind from the bad effect of a book I was reading."

She made a strange reply to that, a reply away from our line of thought and which seemed an interjection that escaped her involuntarily.

"Books," she said, "are powerful things. They can fetter one more than the walls of a prison."

She caught my puzzled stare at the remark and added hastily: "It is odd that we should meet here."

For a moment I didn't answer. I was thinking of her heliotrope perfume, which for a woman of her apparent culture was applied in far too great a quantity to show good taste. The impression stole upon me that the perfume cloaked some secret, that if it were removed I should find . . . but what?

The hours passed, and still we sat there talking, enjoying each other's companionship. She did not remove her veil, and though I was burning with a desire to see her features, I had not dared ask her to. A strange nervousness had slowly seized me. The woman was a charming conversationalist, but there was about her an indefinable something which produced in me a distinct feeling of unease.

It was, I should judge, but a few moments before the first streaks of a dawn when it happened. As I look back now, even with mundane objects and thoughts on every side, it is not difficult to realize the significance of that vision. But at the time my brain was too much in a whirl to understand.

A thin shadow moving across the garden attracted my gaze once again into the night about me. I looked up over the spire of the deserted house and started as if struck by a blow. For a moment I thought I had seen a curious cloud formation racing low directly above me, a cloud black and impenetrable with two wing-like ends strangely in the shape of a monstrous flying bat.

I blinked my eyes hard and looked again.

"That cloud!" I exclaimed, "that strange cloud! ... Did you see—"

I stopped and stared dumbly.

The bench at my side was empty. The woman had disappeared.

During the next day I went about my professional duties in the law office with only half interest, and my business partner looked at me queerly several times when he came upon me mumbling to myself. The incidents of the evening before were rushing through my mind. Questions unanswerable hammered at me. That I should have come upon the very details described by mad Larla in his strange book: the leering fish, the praying child, the twenty-six bluejays, the pointed shadow of the cupola—it was unexplainable; it was weird.

"Five Unicorns and a Pearl." The unicorns were the stone statues ornamenting the old fountain, yes—but the pearl? With a start I suddenly recalled the name of the woman in black: *Perle* von Mauren. What did it all mean?

Dinner had little attraction for me that evening. Earlier I had gone to the antique-dealer and begged him to loan me the sequel, the second volume of his brother Alessandro. When he had refused, objected because I had not yet returned the first book, my nerves had suddenly jumped on edge. I felt like a narcotic fiend faced with the realization that he could not procure the desired drug. In desperation, yet hardly knowing why, I offered the man more money, until at length I had come away, my powers of persuasion and my pocket-book successful.

The second volume was identical in outward respects to its predecessor except that it bore no title. But if I was expecting more disclosures in symbolism I was doomed to disappointment. Vague as "Five Unicorns and a Pearl" had been, the text of the sequel was even more wandering and was obviously only the ramblings of a mad brain. By watching the sentences closely I did gather that Alessandro Larla had made a second trip to his court of the twenty-six bluejays and met there again his "pearl."

There was the paragraph toward the end that puzzled me. It read:

"Can it possibly be? I pray that it is not. And yet I have seen it and heard it snarl. Oh, the loathsome creature! I will not, I will not believe it."

I closed the book and tried to divert my attention elsewhere by polishing the lens of my newest portable camera. But again, as before, that same urge stole upon me, that same desire to visit the garden. I confess that I had watched the intervening hours until I would meet the woman in black again; for strangely enough, in spite of her abrupt exit before, I never doubted that she would be there waiting for me.

I wanted her to lift the veil. I wanted to talk with her. I wanted to throw myself once again into the narrative of Larla's book.

Yet the whole thing seemed preposterous, and I fought the sensation with every ounce of will-power I could call to mind. Then it suddenly occurred to me what a remarkable picture she would make, sitting there on the stone bench, clothed in black, with the classic background of the old courtyard. If I could but catch the scene on a photographic plate. . . .

I halted my polishing and mused a moment. With a new electric flash-lamp, that handy invention which has supplanted the old mussy flash-powder, I could illuminate the garden and snap the picture with ease. And if the result were satisfactory it would make a worthy contribution to the International Camera Contest at Geneva next month.

The idea appealed to me, and gathering together the necessary equipment I drew on an ulster (for it was a wet, chilly night) and slipped out of my rooms and headed northward. Mad, unseeing fool that I was! If only I had stopped then and there, returned the book to the antique-dealer and closed the incident! But the strange magnetic attraction had gripped me in earnest, and I rushed headlong into the horror.

A fall rain was drumming the pavement, and the streets were

deserted. Off to the east, however, the heavy blanket of clouds glowed with a soft radiance where the moon was trying to break through, and a strong wind from the south gave promise of clearing the skies before long. With my coat collar turned well up at the throat I passed once again into the older section of the town and down forgotten Easterly Street. I found the gate to the grounds unlocked as before, and the garden a dripping place masked in shadow.

The woman was not there. Still the hour was early, and I did not for a moment doubt that she would appear later. Gripped now with the enthusiasm of my plan, I set the camera carefully on the stone fountain, training the lens as well as I could on the bench where we had sat the previous evening. The flash-lamp with its battery handle I laid within easy reach.

Scarcely had I finished my arrangements when the crunch of gravel on the path caused me to turn. She was approaching the stone bench, heavily veiled as before and with the same sweeping black dress.

"You have come again," she said as I took my place beside her.

"Yes," I replied. "I could not stay away."

Our conversation that night gradually centered about her dead brother, although I thought several times that the woman tried to avoid the subject. He had been, it seemed, the black sheep of the family, had led more or less of a dissolute life and had been expelled from the University of Vienna not only because of his lack of respect for the pedagogues of the various sciences but also because of his queer unorthodox papers on philosophy. His sufferings in the war prison camp must have been intense. With a kind of grim delight she dwelt on his horrible experiences in the grave-digging detail which had been related to her by the fellow officer. But of the manner in which he had met his death she would say absolutely nothing.

Stronger than on the night before was the sweet smell of heliotrope. And again as the fumes crept nauseatingly down my lungs there came that same sense of nervousness, that same feeling that the perfume was hiding something I should know. The desire to see beneath the veil had become maddening by this time, but still I lacked the boldness to ask her to lift it.

Toward midnight the heavens cleared and the moon in splendid contrast shone high in the sky. The time had come for my picture.

"Sit where you are," I said. "I'll be back in a moment."

Stepping to the fountain I grasped the flash-lamp, held it aloft for an instant and placed my finger on the shutter lever of the camera. The woman remained motionless on the bench, evidently puzzled as to the meaning of my movements. The range was perfect. A click, and a dazzling white light enveloped the courtyard about us. For a brief second she was outlined there against the old wall. Then the blue moonlight returned, and I was smiling in satisfaction.

"It ought to make a beautiful picture," I said.

She leaped to her feet.

"Fool!" she cried hoarsely. "Blundering fool! What have you done?"

Even though the veil was there to hide her face I got the instant impression that her eyes were glaring at me, smouldering with hatred. I gazed at her curiously as she stood erect, head thrown back, body apparently taut as wire, and a slow shudder crept down my spine. Then without warning she gathered up her dress and ran down the path toward the deserted house. A moment later she had disappeared somewhere in the shadows of the giant bushes.

I stood there by the fountain, staring after her in a daze. Suddenly, off in the umbra of the house's facade there rose a low animal snarl.

And then before I could move, a huge gray shape came hurtling through the long weeds, bounding in great leaps straight toward me. It was the woman's dog, which I had seen with her the night before. But no longer was it a beast passive and silent. Its face was contorted in diabolic fury, and its jaws were dripping slaver. Even in that moment of terror as I stood frozen before it, the sight of those white nostrils and those black hyalescent eyes emblazoned itself on my mind, never to be forgotten.

Then with a lunge it was upon me. I had only time to thrust the flash-lamp upward in half protection and throw my weight to the side. My arm jumped in recoil. The bulb exploded, and I could feel those teeth clamp down hard on the handle. Backward

I fell, a scream gurgling to my lips, a terrific heaviness surging upon my body.

I struck out frantically, beat my fists into that growling face. My fingers groped blindly for its throat, sank deep into the hairy flesh. I could feel its very breath mingling with my own now, but desperately I hung on.

The pressure of my hands told. The dog coughed and fell back. And seizing that instant I struggled to my feet, jumped forward and planted a terrific kick straight into the brute's middle.

"*Fort mit dir, Johann!*" I cried, remembering the woman's German command.

It leaped back and, fangs bared, glared at me motionless for a moment. Then abruptly it turned and slunk off through the weeds.

Weak and trembling, I drew myself together, picked up my camera and passed through the gate toward home.

Three days passed. Those endless hours I spent confined to my apartment suffering the tortures of the damned.

On the day following the night of my terrible experience with the dog I realized I was in no condition to go to work. I drank two cups of strong black coffee and then forced myself to sit quietly in a chair, hoping to soothe my nerves. But the sight of the camera there on the table excited me to action. Five minutes later I was in the dark room arranged as my studio, developing the picture I had taken the night before. I worked feverishly, urged on by the thought of what an unusual contribution it would make for the amateur contest next month at Geneva, should the result be successful.

An exclamation burst from my lips as I stared at the still-wet print. There was the old garden clear and sharp with the bushes, the statue of the child, the fountain and the wall in the background, but the bench—the stone bench was empty. There was no sign, not even a blur of the woman in black.

I rushed the negative through a saturated solution of mercuric chloride in water, then treated it with ferrous oxalate. But even after this intensifying process the second print was like the first, focused in every detail, the bench standing in the foreground in sharp relief, but no trace of the woman.

She had been in plain view when I snapped the shutter. Of that

I was positive. And my camera was in perfect condition. What then was wrong? Not until I had looked at the print hard in the daylight would I believe my eyes. No explanation offered itself, none at all; and at length, confused, I returned to my bed and fell into a heavy sleep.

Straight through the day I slept. Hours later I seemed to wake from a vague nightmare, and had not strength to rise from my pillow. A great physical faintness had overwhelmed me. My arms, my legs, lay like dead things. My heart was fluttering weakly. All was quiet, so still that the clock on my bureau ticked distinctly each passing second. The curtain billowed in the night breeze, though I was positive I had closed the casement when I entered the room.

And then suddenly I threw back my head and screamed! For slowly, slowly creeping down my lungs was that detestable odor of heliotrope!

Morning, and I found all was not a dream. My head was ring-ing, my hands trembling, and I was so weak I could hardly stand. The doctor I called in looked grave as he felt my pulse.

"You are on the verge of a complete collapse," he said. "If you do not allow yourself a rest it may permanently affect your mind. Take things easy for a while. And if you don't mind, I'll cauterize those two little cuts on your neck. They're rather raw wounds. What caused them?"

I moved my fingers to my throat and drew them away again tipped with blood.

"I . . . I don't know," I faltered.

He busied himself with his medicines, and a few minutes later reached for his hat.

"I advise that you don't leave your bed for a week at least," he said. "I'll give you a thorough examination then and see if there are any signs of anemia." But as he went out the door I thought I saw a puzzled look on his face.

Those subsequent hours allowed my thoughts to run wild once more. I vowed I would forget it all, go back to my work and never look upon the books again. But I knew I could not. The woman in black persisted in my mind, and each minute away from her became a torture. But more than that, if there had been a decided urge to continue my reading in the second book, the desire to see the third book, the last of the trilogy, was slowly increasing to an obsession.

At length I could stand it no longer, and on the morning of the third day I took a cab to the antique store and tried to persuade Larla to give me the third volume of his brother. But the Italian was firm. I had already taken two books, neither of which I had returned. Until I brought them back he would not listen. Vainly I tried to explain that one was of no value without the sequel and that I wanted to read the entire narrative as a unit. He merely shrugged his shoulders.

Cold perspiration broke out on my forehead as I heard my desire disregarded. I argued. I pleaded. But to no avail.

At length when Larla had turned the other way I seized the third book as I saw it lying on the shelf, slid it into my pocket and walked guiltily out. I make no apologies for my action. In the light of what developed later it may be considered a temptation inspired, for my will at the time was a conquered thing blanketed by that strange lure.

Back in my apartment I dropped into a chair and hastened to open the velvet cover. Here was the last chronicling of that strange series of events which had so completely become a part of my life during the past five days. Larla's volume three. Would all be explained in its pages? If so, what secret would be revealed?

With the light from a reading-lamp glaring full over my shoulder I opened the book, thumbed through it slowly, marveling again at the exquisite hand-printing. It seemed then as I sat there that an almost palpable cloud of quiet settled over me, muffling the distant sounds of the street. Something indefinable seemed to forbid me to read farther. Curiosity, that queer urge told me to go on. Slowly, I began to turn the pages, one at a time, from back to front.

Symbolism again. Vague wanderings with no sane meaning.

But suddenly my fingers stopped! My eyes had caught sight of the last paragraph on the last page, the final pennings of Alessandro Larla. I read, re-read, and read again those blasphemous words. I traced each word in the lamplight, slowly, carefully, letter for letter. Then the horror of it burst within me.

In blood-red ink the lines read:

"What shall I do? She has drained my blood and rotted my soul. My pearl is black as all evil. The curse be upon her brother, for it is he who made her thus. I pray the truth in these pages will destroy them for ever.

"Heaven help me, Perle von Mauren and her brother, Johann, are vampires!"

I leaped to my feet.

"Vampires!"

I clutched at the edge of the table and stood there swaying. Vampires! Those horrible creatures with a lust for human blood, taking the shape of men, of bats, of dogs.

The events of the past days rose before me in all their horror now, and I could see the black significance of every detail.

The brother, Johann—some time since the war he had become a vampire. When the woman sought him out years later he had forced this terrible existence upon her too.

With the garden as their lair the two of them had entangled poor Alessandro Larla in their serpentine coils a year before. He had loved the woman, had worshipped her. And then he had found the awful truth that had sent him stumbling home, raving mad.

Mad, yes, but not mad enough to keep him from writing the facts in his three velvet-bound books. He had hoped the disclosures would dispatch the woman and her brother for ever. But it was not enough.

I whipped the first book from the table and opened the cover. There again I saw those scrawled lines which had meant nothing to me before.

"Revelations meant to destroy but only binding without the stake. Read, fool, and enter my field, for we are chained to the spot. Oh, wo unto Larla!"

Perle von Mauren had written that. The books had not put an end to the evil life of her or her brother. No, only one thing could do that. Yet the exposures had not been written in vain. They were recorded for mortal posterity to see.

Those books bound the two vampires, Perle von Mauren, Johann, to the old garden, kept them from roaming the night streets in search of victims. Only him who had once passed through the gate could they pursue and attack.

It was the old metaphysical law: evil shrinking in the face of truth.

Yet if the books had bound their power in chains they had also opened a new avenue for their attacks. Once immersed in the pages of the trilogy, the reader fell helplessly into their clutches. Those printed lines had become the outer reaches of their web. They were an entrapping net within which the power of the vampires always crouched.

That was why my life had blended so strangely with the story of Larla. The moment I had cast my eyes on the opening paragraph I had fallen into their coils to do with as they had done with Larla a year before. I had been drawn relentlessly into the tentacles of the woman in black. Once I was past the garden gate the binding spell of the books was gone, and they were free to pursue me and to—

A giddy sensation rose within me. Now I saw why the doctor had been puzzled. Now I saw the reason for my physical weakness. She had been—feasting on my blood! But if Larla had been ignorant of the one way to dispose of such a creature, I was not. I had not vacationed in south Europe without learning something of these ancient evils.

Frantically I looked about the room. A chair, a table, one of my cameras with its long tripod. I seized one of the wooden legs of the tripod in my hands, snapped it across my knee. Then, grasping the two broken pieces, both now with sharp splintered ends, I rushed hatless out of the door to the street.

A moment later I was racing northward in a cab bound for Easterly Street.

"Hurry!" I cried to the driver as I glanced at the westering sun. "Faster, do you hear?"

We shot along the cross-streets, into the old suburbs and toward the outskirts of town. Every traffic halt found me fuming at the delay. But at length we drew up before the wall of the garden.

I swung the wrought-iron gate open and with the wooden pieces of the tripod still under my arm, rushed in. The courtyard was a place of reality in the daylight, but the moldering masonry and tangled weeds were steeped in silence as before.

Straight for the house I made, climbing the rotten steps to the front entrance. The door was boarded up and locked. I retraced my steps and began to circle the south wall of the building. It was this direction I had seen the woman take when she had fled after I had tried to snap her picture. Well toward the rear of the building I reached a small half-open door leading to the cellar. Inside, cloaked in gloom, a narrow corridor stretched before me. The floor was littered with rubble and fallen masonry, the ceiling interlaced with a thousand cobwebs.

I stumbled forward, my eyes quickly accustoming themselves to the half-light from the almost opaque windows.

At the end of the corridor a second door barred my passage. I thrust it open—and stood swaying there on the sill staring inward.

Beyond was a small room, barely ten feet square, with a low-raftered ceiling. And by the light of the open door I saw side by side in the center of the floor—two white wood coffins.

How long I stood there leaning weakly against the stone wall I don't know. There was an odor drifting from out of that chamber. Heliotrope! But heliotrope defiled by the rotting smell of an ancient grave.

Then suddenly I leaped to the nearest coffin, seized its cover and ripped it open.

Would to heaven I could forget that sight that met my eyes. There lay the woman in black—unveiled.

That face—it was divinely beautiful, the hair black as sable, the cheeks a classic white. But the lips—! I grew suddenly sick as I looked upon them. They were scarlet . . . and sticky with human blood.

I reached for one of the tripod stakes, seized a flagstone from the floor and with the pointed end of the wood resting directly over the woman's heart, struck a crashing blow. The stake jumped downward. A violent contortion shook the coffin. Up to my face rushed a warm, nauseating breath of decay.

I wheeled and hurled open the lid of her brother's coffin. With only a glance at the young masculine Teutonic face I raised the other stake high in the air and brought it stabbing down with all the strength in my right arm.

In the coffins now, staring up at me from eyeless sockets, were two gray and moldering skeletons.

The rest is but a vague dream. I remember rushing outside, along the path to the gate and down Easterly, away from that accursed garden of the jays.

At length, utterly exhausted, I reached my apartment. Those mundane surroundings that confronted me were like balm to my eyes. But there centered into my gaze three objects lying where I had left them, the three volumes of Larla.

I turned to the grate on the other side of the room and flung the three of them onto the still glowing coals.

There was an instant hiss, and yellow flame streaked upward and began eating into the velvet. The fire grew higher . . . higher . . . and diminished slowly.

And as the last glowing spark died into a blackened ash there swept over me a mighty feeling of quiet and relief.

Phantom Brass

Rock River. A water tower, an abandoned freight shed, and a dingy box-like station huddling against the granite wall in the September dusk. Two switch lights gleaming dismally, one at the east, one at the west end of the siding. And telegraph poles diminishing down the long, eastern grade toward Flume, thirty miles beyond.

Inside the little station McFee leaned back in his swivel chair and idly turned the pages of a last week's newspaper. On the instrument desk the train wire sounder rattled incessantly, clicking out an endless chatter into the sultry heat of the room. It was routine stuff. Garnet, the graveyard-trick dispatcher, was talking to some station farther down the line. But abruptly it hesitated, stopped, and then began spelling out call letters:

RR—RR—RR—RR—DS

Quickly McFee reached over, opened the switch, and hammered back:

I—I—RR

Then he poised a pencil over a pad of paper and began copying down a train order. But he did it without interest, scribbling rapidly and finishing long before the sounder had stopped. It was the same old 11.15 order: No. 7, eastbound freight, to wait here in the passing track until the "Coast Limited" roared through. McFee had worked two years in this lonely hole, and he knew in advance what was expected of him.

He set the light against No. 7 and strolled out through the door to the edge of the platform. The glare in the eastern sky was still there, all right. It had grown from a pale yellow to a deep orange in the intervening hour since he had last looked at it. Bad business. If a wind sprang up, there'd be the devil to pay down in the valley.

It had been going on for a week or more, this forest fire. Eating a trail of desolation through some of the finest forest country in the state. Henderson, the young op at Flume, had kept him posted of its steady advance. And messages had come through from the dispatcher, tightening up the schedule because no lumber trains could get through on the inland timber spur.

McFee stepped back into the station, got a package of cigarettes out of the desk drawer and sat down again.

"Wonder how Henderson likes it down there that close to the hot country?" he mused. "He's a funny kid."

The cigarette smoke coiled ceiling-ward, and McFee closed his eyes a moment in retrospection. Yes, Henderson was a funny kid. Came from Montreal. A month ago, before his transfer to Flume, he had worked the day shift here at Rock River. A steady and ambitious operator, scarcely in his twenties, he had an engaging smile and a touch to the key that was clear and precise. McFee liked him, even though he couldn't quite understand the kid's ideas.

Spiritualism. That was Henderson's faith. He became interested in the subject just after the death of his sweetheart—a lovely French-Canadian girl, judging from the snapshot he always carried in his wallet along with his O.R.T. card. The kid must have loved her a lot; he wore on his little finger the engagement ring he'd given her.

Henderson had brought a lot of books along when he came to Rock River—books by Sir Oliver Lodge and other writers—and subscribed to a little paper called *The Doorway* that was tossed off the 2.15 local on the first of each month.

Queer stuff. At first McFee thought it the worst bunk he'd ever set eyes upon. All about communications with our loved ones who were dead and waiting to talk to us from the world beyond. But Henderson seemed to accept it all, and tried to convince McFee. The way he put it did sound logical.

"Everything in this world," Henderson explained with a strange light in his eyes, "leads us to believe that life does not end with the material death of the body, but goes on into some higher and finer existence. You believe that, don't you?" he asked earnestly.

"Sure," McFee agreed. "I been to church."

"The world to which the dead depart is, of course, a spiritual world," the kid went on. "Yet it is close to our own. The boundary wall is thin and can be crossed. Who knows?"

McFee missed the boy when he left. The new day man was a cold and taciturn Scot, a fundamental Presbyterian, not a spiritualist; and the loneliness and monotony of the Rock River station had become a reality once more.

Only one bright spot remained in the recent turn of events. Henderson had been assigned the same trick as McFee's at the Flume Station. Which meant that when things were quiet they could utilize the station-wire to exchange scraps of conversation.

No. 7 arrived on time and waited, puffing impatiently until the "Coast Limited" roared around the curve, screeched a greeting with a blast of its whistle, and disappeared down the grade.

A moment later the freight, too, was only a winking tail-light, and McFee stood alone. Nothing more, he reflected, until 12.26 when that crack "varnish," No. 12, the "Pacific Mail," would shoot by like a flaming rocket.

But the fire down in the valley must be getting worse. Standing there on the platform, McFee looked into a sky that was flushed and sullen. From north to south, high over the horizon, stretched a lurid crimson glare like the advance of a premature dawn. And sweeping to his nostrils came that same pungent smell that had been growing steadily for days. Smoke!

Inside the station once again McFee switched in the station-wire and called Flume. When Henderson replied, he asked:

How's the fire?

The sounder immediately broke into a terse description of the conflagration. And as he listened McFee slowly tightened his lips into a grim frown.

The increasing glow in the sky had told a true story then. The fire was worse. It was sweeping, a raging inferno, on a thirty-mile front, devouring virgin timber and jumping the cut-over open spots as if they had been only a yard wide. The whole western ridge had been wiped out, and the citizens of Flume were making a frantic exodus for safety.

When the sound finally came to a halt McFee queried hurriedly:

> U think fire will get far as Flume?

The reply shot back:

> No. River too big a gap. Nm. Nw. (no more now)

For a long time after that McFee sat smoking and listening to the flow of conversation over the train-wire. At 11.55 he heard the Rockport man, thirty miles north, report to the dispatcher. The "Pacific Mail" was "by" there. McFee peered absently out of the bay window and made sure the light was green.

And then, without warning, the one kind of hell feared by all railroad men broke loose. The wire suddenly went dead! West, it was all right. But east, where it ran through the fire district, there was no communication. Poles burned down. *Half of the division was running blind!*

McFee swore and called Henderson immediately. If there were any news, Flume was the place to get it.

A moment later the sounder began its chatter, and the Rock River operator was mentally decoding Morse. It came in Henderson's smooth style.

But halfway through the first sentence McFee sat rigid and stared in astonishment. Good Lord, something was wrong with the kid. He must be drunk—or something. Nobody in his right mind would dare to send such stuff over the wire.

All the familiar "box-car abbreviations" were missing. Henderson was spelling out his message word for word, an insane message, an impossible message that seemed to shout its way into the room as it rattled out of the sounder:

> Death is a beautiful thing. It is merely a transition from this life to the spirit world beyond. One should not fear it. Those who have lived on this earth are living again. They are waiting for us just beyond the doorway. They try to speak with us but we do not listen. We are foolish not to listen. They

could tell us many things and advise us as to the future.
Death is not horrible. It is but a natural . . .

McFee slammed open the switch, began pounding his own key:

> Stop it! U gone nuts? Don't send that stuff over the wire.
> Cut it!

A few more meaningless words rattled in; then the sounder
stopped abruptly. Henderson put his "sine" on the message without further explanation.

The Rock River operator slumped backward in his chair. His
cigarette slipped unnoticed from his lips and dropped to the
floor. It was bad business letting an irresponsible person like that
handle a key. Damn fool must be off his nut.

A crazy operator at Flume and the wires down beyond, cutting
off all messages from the dispatcher's office. This was a night!

Abruptly McFee got to his feet and paced back and forth the
length of the room. Everything was quiet now; no sound save
the old alarm clock as it pushed its ticks slowly through the heat.
Outside, the darkness seemed to gather around the open door
and window like a velvet curtain.

All this talk about death and life in the other world—it was
enough to give one the creeps. Made a man shudder when he
heard it come over the wire like that. Yep, the kid must have taken
his girl's death pretty hard, to act that way. In a way you couldn't
blame him.

A long drawn-out whistle sounded suddenly from far off.
McFee glanced absently out of the open doorway. No. 12, the
"Pacific Mail," was entering the hairpin bend five miles north-
west on the canyon rim.

It would be roaring by the station any moment now.

Funny about Henderson. He seemed so sober and sincere
most of the time. It was only occasionally when he gave in to that
bug of his and babbled spiritualism that he seemed to lose his balance. Henderson could believe what he wanted to believe, but he
had no business sending such drivel over the line. It would serve
him right if some other operator reported it to the dispatcher,
and the kid lost his job.

Once again that whistle came, nearer now, shrieking high in the air like the discordant wail of a giant violin.

And then McFee stiffened as though shot. The sounder on the instrument desk had suddenly leaped into life. It was sputtering, hammering like mad, repeating call letters over and over:

RR—RR—RR—RR

McFee flung over the switch and quickly pounded out his reply:

I—I—RR

Then came the question:

No 12 by thr. yet?

There was a strange gleam of bewilderment in the Rock River operator's eyes as he listened to the question. That touch on the brass was familiar. It was evenly-spaced and precise in the Henderson manner he knew well. Yet it didn't seem to be Henderson. It had a curious staccato-like crackle like bottles breaking under heat. McFee raced his answer:

No. 12 due hr 1 min. Wo R U?

The brass chattered back:

> Henderson, of course. For God's sake stop No. 12! River trestle burned out by advancing forest fire. Stop her! Stop her!
> Stop . . .

The last words were still pounding into the room when McFee leaped across to the other wall and pulled the red signal on the outside semaphore.

He was barely in time. Even as the connecting rod groaned under the movement, a shaft of white light wheeled around the canyon and transformed the rails into twin ribbons of silver. Came the bark of the exhaust, the roaring of steel against the rail joints, the thunder of the big 2-8-2.

McFee snatched up a lantern and ran out on the platform. But the engineer of the oncoming Mail had seen the signal against him and answered with two short screams of his whistle.

A moment later the train was stopped at the station, and McFee was shouting the news into the ears of an excited conductor and engineer.

Superintendent Winter looked across his flat-topped desk and toyed with a pencil.

"You are deserving of special citation, Operator McFee," he said. "Had it not been for your excellent foresightedness when the wires on the eastern half of the division were down, the Pacific Mail and everyone aboard would have gone into the river. That means a great deal to the road, and we are proud to thank you."

McFee squirmed uneasily. "But I don't deserve any credit, sir," he said. "I only obeyed orders from the kid down in Flume."

"Flume? I don't understand."

"Why"—McFee cleared his throat—"it's simple enough, sir. Henderson, the operator at Flume, warned me just before the Mail arrived at Rock River that the trestle was down. He ordered Number Twelve stopped, and I simply obeyed orders."

For a moment Winter sat silent in his chair, gazing at the man before him. Then he rose to his feet and moved around to the front of the desk.

"You say you received a call from Flume, informing you of the destruction of the trestle? I didn't know that. When did you receive that message?"

"At twelve twenty-five," McFee replied without hesitation. "Number Twelve was due at Rock River at twelve twenty-six."

The superintendent stood motionless, eyes gradually narrowing to slits. He got a cigar out of his pocket.

"Twelve twenty-five?" he said slowly. "Are you sure?"

"Positive. Why, sir?"

"Listen, McFee," Mr. Winter explained, "the forest fire swept into Flume with the speed of an express train, but because of a cross wind it struck only the tail end of the town. Only two buildings were in its path, and one of those buildings was the station. Henderson was caught in that burning matchbox before he knew what was happening. The fire destroyed the trestle a few minutes later. But when the villagers finally fought their way in to the station, they found a beam from the falling roof had struck the operator on the head and apparently killed him instantly."

McFee nodded soberly. "I know."

"I have the boy's personal effects here, sent to me to forward to his relatives in Canada—a wallet, some letters, a girl's picture, a diamond ring and a watch. The blow from the crashing beam shattered that watch at the same moment it killed Henderson."

The superintendent crossed back to the desk, opened the drawer and drew forth a blackened timepiece with a cracked crystal and broken stem. For a moment he stared down at it.

"Considering what you've told me," he said solemnly, "it's very strange. As you know, an operator's watch should always be correct to the split second. That's a rule this road has always upheld. But according to the hands he was killed at exactly twelve fifteen. At twelve fifteen, do you understand? That would mean the last message you received was sent *ten minutes after the operator was dead!*"

The Cane

Mr. James Grenning, retired senior partner in the firm of Bay, Halstead & Grenning, Lincoln's Inn Fields, was a most punctual person. It was his custom to leave his residence in Bloomsbury each morning save Sunday, walk past High Holborn, down Kingsway as far as Great Queen Street and return by way of Drury Lane. He left at precisely ten o'clock. At eleven he stopped in a small tobacconist's shop to purchase a Rosa Trofero cigar. And his steps were so regulated as to bring him back to his door just as the hands of the hallway clock pointed to the hour of noon.

During these morning promenades, which were undertaken at the advice of a physician, Mr. Grenning always carried a cane. He neither needed the wooden support nor cared for the traditional modish effect it added to a masculine costume. He merely liked canes.

The odd part of it was, however, that each day was carefully observed with a different stick. Monday, he carried a black Malacca. Tuesday, it was a thin shaft of rosewood. Wednesday, a heavier length of oak. Thursday, ebony. Friday, a strip of mahogany topped with an ivory handle. And Saturday, a delicately formed piece of walnut, very plain and very simple.

Apart from canes, Mr. Grenning was not in the slightest given to shows of temperament. And absurd though it may sound, his only reason for this one discrepancy was to remind him in his rather drab existence, of the exact day of the week.

It was on Thursday, a gray morning which had been preceded by a night of chilling rain, that Mr. Grenning left his residence as usual promptly at ten o'clock. At twelve o'clock the tobacconist was quite surprised that his regular customer had not appeared. And at one Mr. Grenning's housekeeper stood astounded in the hallway when she observed by the vacant hat-tree that her lodger had not yet returned.

Obviously only an incident distinctly apart from the commonplace could have caused Mr. Grenning to interrupt his careful routine in such a manner. For no other reason would he have taken it upon himself to dash wildly down Clarges Street and enter without knocking the luxurious apartment of his old friend, Sir Hugh Stanway.

Sir Hugh sat slumped in a huge, over-stuffed chair and gazed with curious eyes at the ashen face of his unexpected visitor.

"Now, Grenning," he said firmly but soothingly, "stop all this wild babbling and start from the beginning. I haven't the slightest idea what you're talking about."

With shaking hands Mr. Grenning helped himself to the decanter on the table, poured out a stiff portion of brandy and drank it at a swallow.

"Do you see anything wrong with this cane?" he asked tremulously, handing the stick across.

Sir Hugh reached for the smooth shaft, turned it over and over in his thin, graceful hands, balanced it on one knee and squinted down its wooden length to see if it were warped. Then he held it out before him, gripped at each end in the manner of a swordsman testing the strength of a blade.

It was not an unusual cane. Fashioned of a heavy, grainless wood, topped with a small cap of gold, and weathered and battered from long use, it looked the typical walking-stick of an unassuming gentleman of the middle class. Sir Hugh handed it back to its owner and raised his eyes inquiringly.

"It isn't one of the six you usually carry," he said. "Other than that, I see nothing wrong with it. Why?"

"Stanway," said Mr. Grenning, swallowing hard, "that cane is haunted! Haunted, I say! And if I don't get rid of it, I'll go mad. I'd have broken it into kindling hours ago if something, some inner force, hadn't prevented me."

"Ghosts?" asked Sir Hugh dryly, a suggestion of a smile at his lips.

"I've had it only since yesterday," continued Grenning, unmindful of the interruption. "Bought it at an auction for eight shillings to replace the one I broke last week. Today I carried it for the first time on my usual morning walk.

"It happened on Great Queen Street, shortly before eleven o'clock. There are several oldish houses in the block, you may remember. Freemason's Hall is just beyond. Well, a funeral was leaving one of the buildings, and I had to stop a moment before I could go on. Six pall-bearers were carrying the casket out of the doorway to the waiting hearse just as I came up.

"Curious how the sight of a funeral immediately sobers one. I stood there, trying hard not to stare. And yet I remember casually noticing the pall-bearer nearest me, the man who supported the right rear corner of the casket. He was a tall, dark-haired individual of about thirty years of age; his profile stood forth strikingly handsome, but as he turned, I couldn't help musing over the expression that twisted the line of his lips. Almost a smirk, it was, as if he were enjoying the whole affair.

"From then on, Stanway, I can't be sure what happened. It was horrible, revolting, and to my dying day I'll never forget it. My cane—this cane—was propped at an angle at my side, slightly supporting me as I stood waiting for the procession to pass. Suddenly I felt a distinct tremor pass up the wood through the handle. It was a vibration, a shock as if ... well, as if the metal cap at the bottom had come into contact with an electric current.

"For a moment I thought the aged wood must be breaking. Then that tremor changed to a violent jerk. I felt the cane pull my hand upward, high over my head, poise there for an instant, and then lash back and forth through the air like a whip.

"With that stick raised above me, something seemed to snap in my brain. I felt as if my head were clamped in a vise, as if some power other than my own were controlling my thoughts. I believe I shouted some terrible oath, something at any rate that turned the surrounding crowd around to stare at me. Then I ran forward like a beast, seized that last pall bearer by the shoulder, spun him around and—God help me!—brought the cane crashing down full upon his head.

"Oh, I know it sounds common enough in these modern times of ours, simply beating a man on the head. But it was hellish to do, hellish to realize that I couldn't help myself. It was like some damned Juggernaut striking the first thing in its path. And coupled with the fact that the man was part of a funeral procession, which is macabre even in itself, the effect was hideous.

"I had one look at him as he fell away from the coffin and collapsed on the sidewalk, blood streaming down his forehead. Then I turned and ran."

Mr. Grenning slumped back in his chair and stared helplessly across the table. "Since then I've been wandering the streets with the fear and desperation of a hunted animal. I didn't kill the man, Stanway. I saw him stumble to his feet—thank Heaven!—just as I raced around the corner. But the stark horror lies in the fact that I'm not responsible, that I can't explain why I did it. My will was controlled by some power from without, and absurd as it may sound, that power came unmistakably from—this cane!"

The clock on the mantel ticked off a minute before Sir Hugh broke the silence.

"The man you struck, you're quite sure he was a stranger?"

Mr. Grenning nodded vehemently. "I never saw him in my life before."

"And your health during, say the last few weeks, it has been quite all right?"

"Health?" Mr. Grenning bristled. "Damme, Stanway, are you trying to—"

"I'm merely asking questions," interposed Sir Hugh. "You can answer them or not as you see fit. You say you bought this cane at an auction?"

"Yes, at Carter's, yesterday. I paid eight shillings for it."

"Any idea who was its former owner?"

"No. Hold on. Yes, I believe I do. The last part of the auction dealt entirely with the property of a man by the name of Wells, Stephen Wells. I remember reading of his death in the *Times*. I don't know *him* either."

Sir Hugh nodded. "One thing more," he said, choosing his words with care. "Were there any queer circumstances surrounding the sale?"

Mr. Grenning hesitated a moment in retrospection. When he looked up, there was a frown of puzzlement lined across his brow. "Now that you speak of it," he replied, "there was. I wasn't the highest bidder. The bidding started at three shillings. It worked up to six. I offered eight. But the man behind me called out ten almost immediately after I had spoken. I thought it odd that the auctioneer accepted my price instead of the higher amount, which he most certainly had heard; odd, too, that the man behind me made no objection when I moved forward to complete the sale."

Into Sir Hugh's eyes there was slowly creeping a gleam of interest. He rose to his feet, strode across to the window and stood staring out into the gray, cheerless street. Absently he drew a pipe from his pocket and rattled the stem against his teeth.

"Grenning," he said suddenly, returning to the table, "if anyone but you had told me this story I'd say he was a crazy fool. But I've known you for a good many years, and I know you're telling the truth. Have I your permission to look into this?"

Mr. Grenning looked up dully. "Yes, of course," he said. "That's why I came here. But how—"

"There's something wrong here, believe me, something decidedly wrong. I'm going out—going to see if I can unearth a few facts. Wait here for me, Grenning. It would be better you didn't appear on the streets for a while. Your room is first along the right hall."

"But haven't you anything to say at all?" snapped Mr. Grenning. "Haven't you any ideas?"

"Not now," replied Sir Hugh, reaching for his hat and gloves. The gleam in his eyes had increased to an excited glitter. "I want to look around a bit before I make any comments. Only this I can tell you quite positively: the funeral you interrupted so rudely was that of Stephen Wells, the former owner of the cane."

The afternoon passed for Mr. Grenning with maddening slowness. Again and again he attempted to thrust himself in the pages of a book and forget his thoughts. But each time the print blurred and a vision of the afternoon's horrible experience formed like an optic scar before his eyes. Evening came, and still Sir Hugh did not return. Mr. Grenning barely tasted the food served by Stanway's man-servant. He continued to pace back and forth the length of the library until a nervous drowsiness slowly settled over him. At length, brain in a whirl, he went to his bed and stared at the designs on the wallpaper until the very concentration threw him into a fitful sleep.

He dreamed wild dreams of running through the streets of London, caning every pedestrian within reach and leaving a trail of horribly mutilated dead behind him. At two o'clock by the radium clock on the bureau he awoke abruptly, sat up in bed, trembling in every nerve and muscle.

The room was hot and suffocating. The wind had died down, and the whole world seemed steeped in a great ringing silence. For a moment Mr. Grenning was puzzled as to what had happened. After all, he reasoned sleepily, it was foolish to let such a small incident bother him. He hadn't killed the man, had merely struck him a blow on the head, and by tomorrow the few who had chanced to see the action would have forgotten. The daily history of London must be filled with such things.

Yet as he sat there, now fully awake, he realized his brain was slowly giving way to an overpowering sensation. It was an urge, a definite, irresistible urge, that he dress, go out and walk once again those same streets down which he passed every morning.

Mr. Grenning had long been a man of habit, but he gave in to routine only through the process of time. To submit to a mere mental suggestion, especially a wild one like this, seemed the act of a weakling. He called to arm every ounce of will-power he possessed to fight it.

As the clock ticked on and on, however, the sensation grew stronger. He felt as if his entire body were encased in a suit of iron, and outside his window some powerful magnet had swept him into its field.

At length he could stand it no longer, and with a little whimper of submission, he leaped from bed, turned on the light, and proceeded to don his clothes. Dressed, he moved to the door, only to hesitate on the sill, staring back over his shoulder.

His cane! It stood there, propped up against the chair where he had left it. Slowly Mr. Grenning paced back the length of the room and halted a few feet away, staring down at the heavy stick. He clenched his fists, tried to turn in his tracks and swayed weakly. When a moment later he slipped out the front door and made his way to the street, the cane was clenched hard under one arm.

A late cab cruising along Piccadilly carried him down Coventry, Cranburn, Long Acre and finally to Great Queen Street. He realized now, as he paid the driver, that the unexplainable psychic urge which had forced him on this mad adventure was sweeping him not only into the general district of his afternoon walks, but toward one house in particular, the Wells residence from which he had seen Mr. Wells' funeral leave.

And presently he stood before it, a once-fashionable residence, made gaunt and somber by the passing years, set flush with the sidewalk. Up to this point, Mr. Grenning had been a man puzzled and bewildered, responding to something he didn't understand. Now as he glanced down the silent thoroughfare and then at the brooding mass of gables at his side, he suddenly changed.

The look of bewilderment gave way to one of craft. His head shrank lower into the protecting collar of his coat, and he moved cautiously into the shadows as if afraid of being seen. Five minutes he waited while the bobby on the opposite side of the street whistled his way around the corner. Then he stole silently up the steps of the dark house, fumbled at the latch, inserted one of his own keys in the antiquated lock, and after a moment of twisting, slipped inside.

A long hallway, dimly illuminated by a single night-light, confronted him. Without hesitation, Mr. Grenning crept to the first door on his right, opened it, and passed into a room that was a pit of darkness. He was moving forward steadily now, deliberately, treading unfamiliar ground, yet avoiding table, desk, and chairs with an uncanny sense of direction.

At the farther wall a third door barred his passage, and he halted momentarily to get a firmer grip on the cane. Then he pushed open this last barrier and stared within. A shaft of yellow light from the street lamp outside filtered through the huge bay window of the room and disclosed directly before him the heavy bulk of an old-fashioned canopied bed.

For a moment Mr. Grenning stood there, head erect, shoulders thrown stiffly back like some strange automaton. Then slowly in measured pace he stepped forward, advancing on his shadow.

A young woman lay sleeping in the bed, a woman whose tousled black hair and closed eyes did not conceal the fine molding and delicate beauty of her features. She was breathing deeply and regularly, one arm folded above her head, covers drawn slightly away from her throat.

Not a line of expression found its way into Mr. Grenning's face. He surveyed the woman coldly as the silence of the old house hung like a pall about him. He continued to stand motionless as hollowly from a distant street came the roar and clatter of a far-away tram-car.

Then with the relentless motion of a machine his right hand raised his cane swiftly until it hung poised high over his head. Deliberately he moved closer, estimated his aim, and brought the heavy stick crashing down upon the head of his victim.

A single, penetrating scream came from the woman's lips as she rose up, clawed wildly at the bedclothes and then with a low gurgle slumped back against the pillow.

Mr. Grenning looked down at her. A tremor swept through his frame as he stared at the silent, bloody form. A short dry gasp slid through his clenched teeth. Then with a smothered sob he turned and moved slowly toward the door.

A voice from an upper room called down fearfully: "Mrs. Wells! Are you all right?"

With machine-like pace Mr. Grenning continued his way through an adjoining room. Not until he reached the outer hallway and a rush of feet sounded behind him, did he alter his speed. Then with a hideous cry of defiance, which seemed to come from another throat than his own, he lurched into a run, threw open the door and staggered forth into the dark street.

Sir Hugh Stanway flung the latest edition of the Friday *Times* on his library table and looked across at the silent figure opposite him. If Grenning had been frightened and bewildered when he appeared at the door of Sir Hugh's rooms the night before, he presented a picture of absolute despair now. His gray hair was clawed into wild disarray, his eyes gleamed hard and feverish, and his hands as he gripped the arms of his chair opened and closed convulsively.

"I'm a murderer!" he moaned aloud for the tenth time.

Sir Hugh frowned perplexedly. "How many times must I tell you, Grenning, that you're nothing of the sort? The paper here gives a full account of last night's happenings. Mrs. Wells suffered only lacerations of the scalp. The pillow, it seems, partly protected her. It is very strange though that you should choose as your second victim the widow of the man whose funeral you interrupted the day before."

"Stanway," said Mr. Grenning, "if you don't do something to help me, I'll go mad. Realize—can't you?—that during the entire event, from the moment I entered the house, I absolutely couldn't help myself. Another will was controlling me, and yet I was horribly conscious of everything that was done. Beating that defenseless woman as she lay there—God, it was terrible!"

For a moment Sir Hugh studied his friend in silence. Then he settled back in his chair.

"I went to considerable trouble to unearth facts," he said. "But the information I have gathered offers nothing in the way of explanation that a sane brain can understand.

"You bought this cane at an auction. It was formerly the property of a Stephen Wells, now deceased. So much, you know already. Wells was a very rich man, Grenning. He was sole owner of the Wells East Indies Products Company, and when he died he left a considerable fortune to his wife. But whereas he had been a success financially, his marriage had been a complete failure. I've heard of antipathy between man and wife before, but never anything like this. That woman was so relieved at her husband's death that she had the unparalleled audacity to dispose of his possessions at public auction even before he was decently buried."

Mr. Grenning looked up slowly. "What has all that to do with my cane?" he queried.

"Very much. Those articles of Wells' that were offered for sale included some of his most personal possessions, and among them was your cane. Now the cane has quite a story connected with it that is rather generally known among Wells' friends.

"Wells, it seems, was in the yearly habit of taking business trips through the East Indies to look over some of his company's property. It was in North Borneo, inland from Sandakan, that he saved a Dyak witch-doctor from death. He shot a king cobra only a few inches from the native's foot. The witch-doctor was so filled with gratitude he presented Wells with a strange gift.

"It was a shaft of wood, fashioned from the branch of a death-tree. If you are at all acquainted with the customs of those natives of Borneo, Grenning, you will know that some tribes have a most peculiar practice in the burying of their dead. They choose a large tree, hollow out an aperture in the trunk, insert the corpse in an erect position and then seal the opening. The tree continues to grow, a living tomb, and is from then on an object of religious veneration.

"This particular piece of wood came from the branch of a tree in which had been buried the body of the witch-doctor's predecessor, a Dyak priest. The wood was therefore supposed to be endowed with the power of protecting one in case of danger and working revenge on one's enemies.

"Two days later, while Wells was returning down-river in a native dugout, his party was attacked from ambush. Poisonous darts from *sumpitan* blow-guns killed three native guides and one other white man. Wells experienced a marvelous escape. The piece of wood given him by the witch-doctor happened to be propped up against his equipment before him. One of the darts, which would have found its mark in his throat, struck the wood and was deflected to the side.

"Arriving at the coast, Wells had the shaft made into a cane and vowed it would never leave his side. He seemed to have kept this promise, for wherever he went, that cane was always with him."

The narrative ceased for a moment, and Mr. Grenning stirred restlessly. "I still don't see—" he began.

"There are just a few things more," interrupted Sir Hugh. "The man you struck yesterday while he carried the coffin of Stephen Wells was Philip Garn, a well-known idler in gambling circles, and he represents the third part of the triangle in Wells' unhappy marriage. It is open gossip that Mrs. Wells was in love with him, wanted to marry him, and sought by every means to force her husband to grant a divorce, an action which he refused to take. It seems a cruel gesture on her part to have chosen Garn as one of the pall-bearers.

"Now then"—Sir Hugh drummed his finger reflectively on the arm of the chair—"I offer no conclusions. The whole thing looks impossible from start to finish. All I can say is that it would seem by your recounting of the odd way in which you purchased the cane at the auction, it was foreordained that you, who are known always to carry a cane and to walk daily past that Wells house on Great Queen Street, should be its new owner."

Curiously enough, Mr. Grenning had almost the same dreams that night as he had the night before. But there was one vision in addition, a most vivid one that so stayed by him, he couldn't refrain from telling it in detail to Sir Hugh over the breakfast table.

"It seemed that the ringing of the doorbell roused me in the middle of the night," he began. "I could have sworn that I was awake, that I got out of bed, put on the dressing-gown you loaned me, and hurried down the hall to answer it.

"When I opened the door and stood shivering on the threshold, two men confronted me. And they were the strangest pair I had ever seen. The one on the right was a tall, spare-looking Englishman, a common enough fellow, I suppose, if he had worn regular clothes. But what did he have on but a suit of white duck and a pith helmet! There wasn't a trace of color in his face. It was white as lime. And his eyes! God, Stanway, they seemed nothing more than two black holes. I started backward and stared. The other looked even more like a page out of a book. He was a native of some kind, stark naked save for a loin-cloth and a cap of queer-looking feathers on his head. Over his left arm he carried the dried and stiffened body of a dead snake.

"They stepped in, and the white man said, as if it were the most ordinary thing in the world: 'We've come for the cane!'"

Sir Hugh laid down his tea-cup sharply. His gray eyes slowly widened.

"And in this dream," he asked, "did you see yourself giving the men the cane?"

"Yes, I—"

With a start Sir Hugh kicked back his chair, jumped to his feet and ran to the umbrella cabinet in the outer room. He thrust the little door open and peered inside. The rack, which the night before had held the cane, was now empty!

Whirling, Sir Hugh leaped across the room and made his way quickly to the hallway. Here he bent down on his knees, examined the rug and the uncovered floor before the door. And an instant later, a smothered exclamation burst from his lips.

Clearly outlined on the maple parquet was the muddy outline of a naked human foot!

"Quick, Grenning!" Sir Hugh turned on his stupefied guest who stood staring at the mark on the floor. "There's not a moment to lose. Come on."

As their cab sped down Piccadilly, Stanway sat silently, unrelaxed, staring with impatient eyes at the flying streets. Only once did he break his silence, and that was to urge the driver to greater speed.

Along Great Queen Street through a maze of traffic they raced. Then, framed like a photograph in the windshield, their destination loomed up before them. It was the Wells house, and before it was collected a milling crowd.

Sir Hugh looked out before him, took in the scene at a glance and struck his fist sharply on the leather upholstery.

"Too late, Grenning," he said.

They left the cab and began shouldering their way through the crowd, Stanway opening up a lane for Grenning to follow. And abruptly a moment later at a point half-way between the curb and the steps they reached the inner edge of the silent crowd and stood staring at the gruesome spectacle before them. Mr. Grenning felt suddenly faint.

Lying on the sidewalk were two blood spattered figures, a man and a woman. The man was Philip Garn, whom Mr. Grenning had struck during the funeral procession. The woman was Mrs. Wells. It did not need a medical examiner to see that both had been instantly killed. Their heads were horribly crushed and battered.

Stanway turned away to a tall, lean man who was standing to one side, a notebook in his hand.

"Good morning, Inspector Melton, do you remember me?"

The man looked up and then stared in recognition. "I should say I do. I—"

"Tell me," Stanway broke in hurriedly, "how did this dreadful thing happen?"

Inspector Melton frowned. "Double murder," he said shortly,

"and it's the strangest case I've ever come upon, if we can believe everything we've heard."

"Murder?"

"Yes. The man is Philip Garn, you know. He was Mrs. Wells' lover, I guess, now that Mr. Wells is dead. The two of them were just returning to London from a day out in Sussex. Somebody had a score to settle apparently and waited for them. A moment after they stepped out of the cab they were both struck over the head from behind with a cane. We've got the cane inside. But the queer part is that the cabby swears he didn't see a soul on the street. Says he had driven the cab only a few yards after leaving when he heard two screams and turned just in time to see them fall to the sidewalk. Nobody else, he claims, was anywhere in sight. It's mighty strange."

Stanway nodded slowly. "Thank you, Inspector," he said. "Come, Grenning, we may as well go."

On Monday, October the 12th, the evening edition of the *London News-Chronicle* carried the following small account on the bottom of its third page:

> A strange and ironic sidelight was added by officials of Scotland Yard today to the yet unsolved tragedy which occurred on Great Queen Street. The victims, it will be remembered, were Mrs. Stephen Wells and Mr. Philip Garn, both of whom were killed by heavy blows from a cane wielded by an unknown assailant.
>
> Mrs. Wells was the recent widow of the late Stephen W. Wells, owner of the Wells East Indies Products Company, who died early last week. Since his death rumors have been current among Mr. Wells' friends that there must have been a grave mistake in the report that he died from carditis, as he was known to enjoy perfect health. So far-reaching were these rumors that officials of Scotland Yard had the body of Mr. Wells exhumed and a complete autopsy performed. The result, made public for the first time today, was that Mr. Wells had died of poison.
>
> After a thorough search it was found that a vial of strychnin had been purchased by Mrs. Wells at a neighboring apothecary shop. Mrs. Wells was to have been called for legal questioning when her sudden death occurred.

The Coach on the Ring

I met him in the *Zum schwarzen Rosz,* a lonely inn somewhere on the forgotten Castle Road in the heart of the Imperial Forest, East Prussia.

Outside, the storm which had been gathering over the trees all day lashed the casements and old stone walls of the hostelry with wild fury. Thunder boomed under the night sky at intervals, and although the heavy, oaken door was tightly closed behind me, I could hear the wind racing through leaves and branches of the surrounding woods.

The tavern in which I had sought shelter was deserted save for the innkeeper, a heavy-jowled Teuton, and the man who sat alone at a table in one of the far corners of the room. So strange was the dress of the latter that my first glance lengthened into a rude stare, and a full moment passed before I finally turned and stepped to the high, carved counter in the rear.

"A room for the night, please," I said to the innkeeper, "and a light supper with a little wine."

He bowed, *"Ja, mein Herr.* If you will choose a table, you may sup immediately."

I removed my dripping hat and coat, sat down at a near table, and after surveying the confines of my temporary haven with a brief glance, peered across the room at the only other visible guest. He was quite old, and yet as I looked, I saw that his age was most deceiving. It was not so much that his features or body were old; it was his dress that gave the appearance of antiquity. Almost theatrical were his clothes. They dated back a full two centuries and were the type worn by the nobility in times long past. He wore high boots of black leather, ornate with gilded tracery and spurs on the heels. His waist cuffs hung rakishly long with flowing lace. A coat of blue velvet was unbuttoned carelessly, and he wore a plumed hat. His hair was an iron grey and worn very long.

Presently he became aware of my gaze, looked at me sharply, and then rousing himself, walked across to my table.

"Guten abend," he greeted. His voice was cold and arrogant with a certain hollow quality that began deep in the throat.

"Good evening," I replied at length. "Or rather a bad evening, a very bad evening, we should say," and I smiled.

He nodded, his black eyes continuing to bore me through and through. "We seem alone in the inn. Would you not care to join me at my table?"

I accepted the invitation gladly. The inn was not a cheerful place. It was dimly lighted by several hanging, sooty lanterns which flickered and flared most unpleasantly, and in the half-glow under the beamed ceiling threw long, disproportionate shadows on the floor.

A large, unframed painting was mounted on one wall, a picture of the head of a black horse, representative, no doubt of the establishment's name. It had been done by some artless painter. The work was insufferably crude, yet whether it was intentional, or only the result of a lack of skill in forming the animal's eyes, there was a wildness, a sense of unrest that emanated from it and permeated the entire room. Added to the howling of the storm, everything went to urge companionship.

"You are a stranger here?" the man asked when we were finally seated and the *Gastwirt* had brought me a tray of steaming dishes.

"Yes," I said, "though I was in Danzig three years ago. I'm bound for Schlossberg. Is it far?"

"Not far," he said, pouring out two glasses of white wine, "not far and not large either. Why do you go there—if I may ask?"

"Relatives there, distant relatives. I'm American by birth, but of German descent. I'm a tourist, you see."

He lifted his glass to me in a toast. *"Prosit,"* he said as the tumblers clinked.

"Your health," I replied. It was excellent wine—*Liebfraumilch* I believe—though rather strong, for it brought a warm flush to my head. "I'm here in Europe with five friends," I continued. "They flew direct to Berlin where I am to meet them in a week or so. I wanted to see the village of my ancestors, so decided upon the longer way."

"Flew?" he repeated, raising his eyebrows.

"By plane," I said in explanation and looked sharply at him. Oddly, he didn't seem to understand. Was it possible a man could live such a rural life as to not be aware of the popularity of modern aviation? I glanced again at his ancient attire and fell into a puzzled thought. The man was evidently a frequent visitor of the inn, accounting, I concluded, for the innkeeper's passive acceptance of his old-fashioned clothes. That I was right in this assumption was soon proved when the innkeeper, bringing more dishes, said to him respectfully: "You are late tonight, *mein Herr.*"

"It storms," the man replied shortly. Then again turning to me, he said casually: "These relatives, they are merchants?"

"I think not," I answered, "though I really don't know what their occupation is now. Years ago, I believe, they were gold-smiths. Perhaps you know the name? Hess—Johann Hess. We've Americanized it in the States to John Hess."

"Hess?" he repeated, "Johann Hess!" And in his apparent excitement his voice became tense and strained. He leaned across the table, his eyes gleaming under heavy brows as he said very slowly, his words rising in gradual crescendo:

"*Mein Herr,* do you know anything of a ring that belongs to the family of Hess, a gold ring with a large cameo upon which is carved a coach and six horses?"

I jumped back in my chair. It was only then that I realized that I had kept my left hand hidden from him. That I should meet an utter stranger in the heart of the Imperial Forest who should question me about my personal jewelry, was startling to say the least. And yet as I thought it over, it was not odd at all. The ring had been in my family for generations. This country was the home of my people. Why shouldn't a native of the district be aware of its existence? I extended my left hand, half-smiling.

"Is this it?" I asked, showing my fourth finger.

He grasped my hand in a vise-like grip. A shudder crept slowly down my spine. His hands were clammy and cold as ice.

With an apparent effort he sought to restrain himself.

"I beg your pardon," he said, "but this ring—do you know about it?"

I had always treasured that ring. It had come to me as a trivial part of my uncle's estate, and because of its oddness, its genuine appearance of antiquity, and its rare beauty, I had worn it constantly and on all occasions.

The carving on the gold setting was the most intricate I have ever seen, but it was the cameo that attracted one. The once white face, which was indeed unusually large, had turned almost yellow with age, but carved deeply upon it was a strange old royal coach drawn by six horses, horses running at a full gallop. The maker had put more than craftsmanship in the work. The horses seemed singularly endowed with speed. The coach gave the impression of flying along at a frightful rate. I had often examined it closely, sometimes even under a magnifying glass, and the effect was always the same.

"Yes," I said, answering his question. "It is a Spanish ring."

He looked up. "What makes you say that?"

"Because," I replied, "that coach is a type used several hundred years ago by the nobility of Spain."

"You are right," he agreed. "The coach is Spanish, but the ring is German, and it was made in Schlossberg, the town to which you are going. It is odd—very odd that you should come here just to-night." He took out a heavy old watch and consulted it. "In three quarters of an hour that ring will be precisely two hundred years old. Two hundred years—it is an eternity."

I said nothing. I was strangely impressed with the man before me. His peculiar attire, his queer German—which frequently included words or phrases unfamiliar to me and which seemed to belong to an older day, his perturbation, and his whole singular manner of bearing, had all aroused me to the highest point of interest.

He poured himself another glass of wine, apparently calmer now, but I could see that his hand trembled slightly and that he was making an effort to mask his emotions. "Would you care to hear that ring's history?" he suddenly asked.

"Indeed I should," I replied, leaning forward in my chair. The storm instead of lessening was growing in fury. The shutters, driven back and forth by the moaning wind, rattled hollowly throughout the old inn. Rain pounded steadily the wet earth outside; great flares of lightning occasionally transformed the room into a grotto of leaping shadows, and thunder crashed over the forest in long, rolling repercussions. The innkeeper had gone to bed now after giving me a key and instructions as how to find my room.

I scrutinized my companion with greater care. His skin was unnaturally fair, and the pallor brought into prominence the dark, sunken eyes with their long lashes, and the lips which were thin and colorless. Accentuated by the small close ears, the face was round and full, yet strangely enough, the cheek bones projected quite noticeably.

He wore a large military moustache, which in contrast to his iron-grey hair, was an absolute white. His fingers were long and bony, and I was rather horrified to see that they were quite without nails. And as I sat there before him, a vague, indescribable sense of uneasiness stole over me.

He rose from his chair and stepped to a near window, motioning that I follow. "Look!" he said, drawing aside the curtain.

I stared out into the darkness and was about to say that I saw nothing, when a sudden flash of lightning dimly lit up the forest around. Then I glimpsed far to the south high above the waving trees, a towering cliff and upon it the great grey walls of an old feudal castle. For a brief instant its towers and turrets were silhouetted against the driven cloud. Then blackness thicker than before swept down about us, and the vision was gone. We returned to our chairs.

"That," said my companion when we were again at the table, "is the Castle of Hensdorf. At the foot of the cliff lies the village of Schlossberg." He was calmer now, but I saw that he was staring again at my ring.

"In the days when Germany was composed of many tiny principalities, this district was under the rule of the princes of Hensdorf. From 1691 to 1730 Hans, the blackest, cruelest tyrant of them all was in power, a man who cared no more for his subjects than he did for the pebbles under his feet, a cold arrogant ruler who was hated even by his royal guards, a crafty, scheming blackguard who sought only to bleed his country for its wealth. During his reign, the people were held under a grinding heel of taxation and oppression. They looked with embittered eyes at the splendor and pomp of those at the castle, at the extravagant balls, the drunken orgies, and mad fetes, and the luxury of the court.

"Hans had a sister, Wilhelmina, who for diplomatic reason was married to a prince of Spain, Jose de Isle, ruler of the province of Luego. The marriage was a great success, and as a token of thanks, good-will, and friendship, the Spaniard sent his Prussian brother-in-law a gift of a splendid royal coach, a coach to be drawn by six horses.

"The coach reached Hans von Hensdorf's pride. He was as happy as a child with a new toy and spent months sending envoys all over Europe to procure for him the finest thoroughbred horses. He saw to it that its scarlet sides were kept in a state of gleaming polish. Not a fleck of dust did he allow on the harness. And alongside the Spanish coat-of-arms in gold on each door was emblazoned the escutcheon of the House of Hensdorf.

"Each evening the six prancing horses would be harnessed to the vehicle, the postillion take his place, and Prince Hans in magnificent array would dash down the steep winding road from the castle and into the village of Schlossberg. At first the peasants and villagers were terrified by the sight of the red coach thundering by them in the shadows of the dusk. They called it a devil-cart and ran frightened to their homes. They soon learned, however, that it was owned by their overlord and that he always appeared in the streets at the same time. At that hour, therefore, the children were kept at home, the cobblestones cleared of people, and the village took on an aspect of desertion.

"This did not please von Hensdorf at all. With his Prussian pride, he enjoyed making a dramatic entrance, seeing the inhabitants flee for their lives, and carts overturn in a mad attempt to gain safety. So he changed his hours. The carriage thundered through the town without warning. The people begged him to slow down in their streets. The lives of their children were endangered, they said. But Hensdorf only laughed drunkenly, told them to keep their brats at home.

"At length one evening in early autumn the coach came later

than usual. It raced around a corner and bore down upon a group of children playing in the street. The coachman stood up by his high seat and sawed on the reins.

"Von Hensdorf thrust his head out of one of the carriage windows and shouted to his driver: 'What are you stopping for? The whip—the whip!'

"The driver obeyed. He seized the whip and lashed the foaming horses mercilessly. Straight toward the children raced the coach—"

The man across the table stopped speaking abruptly as though lost in recollection. He left his chair and walked silently to the window where he stood staring out into the darkness.

"What happened?" I broke out impatiently.

A moment dragged by without answer. Slowly he returned to the table, reached for the bottle of wine, and filled our two glasses. In the sudden quiet, the wind screamed wildly round the corners of the outside walls. A lamp hanging above us sputtered and flickered its flame.

His voice was filled with emotion when he continued:

"All reached safety save one. A little girl was killed beneath the wheels. Her name was Olga Hess, and she was the daughter of Johann Hess, goldsmith of Schlossberg."

And now the man leaned across the table, his black eyes blazing wildly, his hands trembling.

"Johann Hess," he said, "led more than the simple life of a goldsmith. Unknown to the villagers he was a student of black art and alchemy. He spent his days poring over rare books of magic that he had come upon among the wares of an old wandering Italian curio peddler. There were dark whispers about him throughout the town. Some claimed to have seen him prowling through the graveyard in the light of the moon. Others had heard him talking to bats as if they could understand. The people would have shuddered had they known that within his shop he spent most of his time studying the evil practices of unholy magicians who had gone before him. The black names of Cornelius, of Alburtis, of Cagliostro were his idols. From old papyri and ancient cabalistic writings, he read in the forbidden arts of sorcery and necromancy.

"Only one human interest did he have, and that was his love for his daughter, Olga. Years before his wife had died, and it was the resultant grief that drove him into the sullen isolation from society that now formed his life. The little girl became his sole comfort, his only contact with the world about him, and he worshipped her madly.

"And now when the news of her death beneath the Hensdorf carriage was brought to him, all his emotions burst forth without restraint. Insane with grief, he swore revenge.

"It was an oath Schlossberg would never forget. Pushing aside the neighbors who tried to comfort him, Hess staggered drunkenly out into the street. In the shadows by the side of his shop he waited until the coach would make its return.

"When at last it came, rattling, rocking abreast of him, he leaped, climbed up to the coachman's seat, strangled the driver and flung him lifeless to the street. He grasped the reins and pulled the horses to a stop. And then while the rest of the populace stood aghast, he tore open the door of the carriage and dragged the cowering Hensdorf to the cobblestones.

" 'You murderer!' he shouted. 'You have killed my child! Killed her with your fine, gilded coach. Ride, must you? Well, ride you shall!'

"The voice of the goldsmith had risen to a scream now.

" 'Do you hear, Hensdorf,' he cried, 'you are going to die! And by the kingdoms of Styx, of Acheron, and the fiery lake of Phlegethon, by the flaming powers of Belzebub and Lucifer, *may your soul find no rest but ride this road each midnight henceforward in that accursed coach for two hundred years!'*

"The hands of Johann Hess clamped around the throat of the gasping nobleman, held there until they clutched only lifeless flesh. There were no cries on the street around them. The townspeople gazed on the scene silent and horrified.

"Hess raised the corpse, staggered forward, and threw it into the coach on the upholstered seat. Then running to the horses, he wheeled them around, seized the whip from its socket and lashed them furiously. With snorts of fear the six beasts lunged off into the forest, the coach and its awful burden following.

"And as it disappeared in the trees, Hess shouted after it: 'The curse be upon you! For two hundred years shall you ride in your coach!'

"All that night the goldsmith worked in his shop behind drawn blinds. Villagers who hovered near heard fearful incantations, and invocations to the prince of darkness, saw the spasmodic flame of his crucible, caught the strange odors of magic perfumes of the East. By morning his work was done. He had fashioned a gold ring, a ring with a cameo upon which was carved the hated coach and six horses, *a ring that would seal the curse on the soul of Hans von Hensdorf.*

"The castle guards found Hess raving mad. Without compunction they dragged him to the village square and before the hushed populace burned him at the stake.

"With the rest of the goldsmith's property, the ring fell into the hands of another branch of the family. A search was begun for the body of the dead nobleman, but although the guards questioned everybody, although they scoured the forest for leagues in every direction, not a trace did they find of the coach, the six horses, or the dead prince Hans."

The voice before me hesitated a moment and then continued slowly as though lost in thought: "All that happened two hundred years ago. Times have changed, yet Schlossberg has not forgotten the curse. It is the eighth generation now, but the story has been told from father to son, and each midnight the old castle road is deserted, avoided by all who know, for it is a place accursed. The ghost of Hensdorf haunts it, the soul that can find no rest but must ride through the forest and up to the ruined castle, jolted in a coach drawn by six horses.

"But tonight, *mein Herr*, the two hundred years are over; tonight the curse is at an end, and tonight is the last ride."

He stopped talking and began filling his glass with the last of the wine. A clock somewhere struck slowly, twelve times. He listened. At the last stroke he muttered an exclamation, threw his glass to the table, rose and lurched to the door.

"One moment," I cried as he placed his hand on the latch. "Who are you?"

He turned, his eyes seeming to bore me through to the soul.

"I am Hans von Hensdorf," he said, and the words floated hollowly through the room.

He opened the door and staggered out. As if bidding him

welcome, the storm burst forth in an even greater roar. From its mounting on the opposite wall, the horse with its savage eyes leered at me.

And then suddenly from afar off there came a low rumble, the sound of a pounding upon the wet earth—in the distance—nearer—approaching the inn. The rumble grew into a roaring clatter, louder and louder, rising over the jealous howl of the wind.

With a crash I threw back my chair and tore open the door.

For a moment I stood there, the rain lashing my face, my eyes seeing only a wall of blackness. And then with a roar and a clatter a great bulk swept out of the storm toward me. The darkness was softening now, and in the light of the plunging lanterns back in the inn I saw—an ancient Spanish coach, a crimson coach, rocking, swaying down the road with six mad black horses racing forward at full gallop. I had but a fleeting glimpse of it, yet high on the coachman's seat I beheld a cloaked and hooded figure. He leered at me as the coach shot past. His face was that of a white, grinning skull.

And in that instant before it disappeared a head was thrust out of the carriage windows—

"Hans von Hensdorf!" I cried.

The coach swept on into the blackness and was devoured by the storm. In a daze I stood at the doorway staring after it, the rain running down my face in rivulets, the thunder booming over the Imperial Forest, the wind laughing mockingly.

Then flooding the heavens with white light came a tremendous flash of lightning. In its instantaneous splendor it revealed the old road lined on both sides by the boles of giant trees and far to the south silhouetted against the sky the Castle of Hensdorf with its towers, its turrets, and its broken battlements. There was no sign of the coach!

"The two hundred years are over," I said aloud to the storm; "the curse is ended. That was the last ride!"

And suddenly I looked at my ring. *The coach and six horses upon it had disappeared,* and there was left only a white, blank cameo.

The Kite

Tuesday being Christmas, I slept late, worked until noon on my paper for the *Batavia Medical Journal*, then headed for the waterfront to arrange passage on the next K. P. M. boat for Singapore. It was the anniversary of my six years' practice in Samarinda, and I was glad to be leaving Borneo for good.

I returned to my quarters in the European district and began immediately the long job of packing. At two P.M. suddenly and without warning a strange nervousness seized me. At the very moment the last strokes of the clock died into silence a nameless fear swept through my brain, quickening my pulse.

I lay no claim to being psychic. Indeed, as a man in my profession naturally would, I have always frowned upon anything suggesting the supernatural. But I have learned by past experience that such a feeling as I now experienced invariably presaged some black event, some tragedy within my own circle of acquaintanceship.

A quarter of an hour later I received that strange message from Corlin. The message was delivered by a Cantonese boy, and it read as follows:

> DEAR DR. VAN RUELLER:
>
> Since Alice was to see you last, her illness, which you diagnosed as a touch of fever, has grown steadily worse. If you can possibly make the trip upriver before you leave Samarinda, I would be much indebted to you.
>
> I must warn you of one thing, however. If you do come and you see a kite flying over the jungle near my place, on your life make no attempt to pull it down.
>
> Faithfully,
> Edward Corlin.

I read that letter twice before I looked up. I hadn't known Corlin long. A year ago he had wandered down from British North Borneo where he had held the post of Conservator of Forests. Following him on a later steamer had come his lovely wife, Alice, and his daughter, Fay.

There were ugly stories about Corlin. Rumor had it that the British Government had requested his resignation after his cruelty to the Dyaks had caused a native outbreak in one of the forest preserves.

Shortly after his arrival in Samarinda, the man took over an old rest-house a short distance up the Mahakam river. There he had made his home, and there his wife and daughter were forced to accept the loneliness and the jungle with him.

As the Cantonese boy stood there I felt a strong desire to refuse the call. Frankly, I didn't like Corlin. But what I didn't understand was the mention of the kite.

"Kang Chow," I said, for I had spoken to Corlin's "boy" several times before, "have the Dyaks in your district taken over the Malay practice of kite flying?"

The boy shook his head.

"The Malays are doing it then?"

"No Malays there. Only one Dyak village. You come?"

I hesitated.

"Yes, I'll come," I said at length. "Have your boatmen and sampan ready in half an hour. I'll meet you at the river jetty."

My usual procedure during a trip upriver is to sit back in the shade of the thatch-cabin, puff a pipe and wait until the chanting Dyaks pole the sampan to my destination. Today, however, I squatted tense in the bow, under the hot sun, and gazed at the steaming shores.

For two hours nothing happened. Then, as we approached the last turn before Corlin's place, Kang Chow pointed up into the sky, said:

"See? Kite. Big kite."

The kite was there, and I could see it clearly from the river. There was nothing strange about it—an enormous cross fashioned of two pieces of bamboo and red rice paper, the tail cut to resemble a dragon.

But suddenly I caught the sunlight at a new angle, and I gave a sharp exclamation. The line which held the kite was not native hemp but wire. Copper wire! I could see it glinting like a slender strand of gold. The wire slanted down from the sky and disappeared in the jungle.

"Inshore, Kang Chow," I snapped. "Inshore."

Minutes later I was fighting my way through the bush, fighting off a horde of insects. The wire ended abruptly at a large *palapak* tree. It was wound several times around the bole and spliced.

What was a kite doing here, flying without human guidance? A native kite and yet held down by white men's wire.

Troubled, I headed back for the sampan. Ten minutes later the boat slipped to a mooring beside the Corlin wharf, and I followed Kang Chow to the clearing and the house.

Corlin met me at the door, shook hands and ushered me into the central room.

"Glad you could make it, Doctor," he said. "It's been hell waiting to see if you'd come. Alice is in the back room. My daughter, Fay, is attending her."

"How is the patient?" I asked.

"She's no better," Corlin replied. "I've kept her dosed with quinine, as you suggested. But it isn't fever that's troubling her. It's . . . In God's name, Doctor, did you see the kite?"

I stared at the man. Corlin was hawk-faced with little pig eyes and a skin insect-bitten from years in the tropics. But something was troubling him.

"Perhaps you'd better look her over first," he said. He led the way to a room in the rear.

It was a small chamber with a single bed, the window shutters partially closed, and a definite smothering odor of sickness. Corlin's wife lay motionless on the bed. In a chair by her side sat the daughter, Fay.

I felt the woman's pulse, took her temperature. The heart action was rapid, but the thermometer showed below normal.

Abruptly Corlin stepped forward and drew me to the window. He pointed out into the sky.

"Look!" he whispered hoarsely. "Do you see it?"

My gaze followed his hand, and again I saw that kite. It was still as high, but much closer, blown by the rising wind. The red rice paper glowed like a fever spot against the blue.

"Yes, I see it," I said. "A kite. But what . . . ?"

Corlin snapped at me before I could finish. "I want you to watch that kite, Van Rueller. Keep looking."

Staring upward, I felt my own heart begin to hammer in my throat.

"Now feel her pulse and keep watching that kite," Corlin directed. He lit a cigarette with shaking hands and leaned against the wall.

For a long time I kept my hand pressed to the limp wrist, while I watched the kite, motionless, high over the jungle. Abruptly the dragon tail sagged in a slackening of the wind, and the kite settled fifty feet downward.

I whirled to the woman in the bed. Her breath was coming in short gasps. Her pulse was only a feeble flutter.

But even as I ripped open my case and reached for a capsule of amyl nitrite, the sinking spell passed. The heart returned to normal. Outside the kite was leaping, climbing like a frightened bird to new altitudes.

But it was a quarter of an hour before I realized the hideous significance of it. With shaking fingers I gave the woman a dose of strychnine. Stepping to the door I motioned Corlin to follow.

Back in the central room I poured myself a glass of whiskey and faced the ex-Conservator across the table.

"Corlin," I said, trying to control my voice, "I've been in Borneo six years. I've treated everything from yellow jack to the bite of a hamadryad. But I never came upon anything like this before. It's—it's—Good Lord, it isn't possible!"

"I'm not crazy then?" Corlin drummed his fingers.

"You saw—?"

"I saw," I replied, "and impossible as it may sound, it's true. In some unholy way your wife's physical condition is linked with the movements of that kite. When the kite is stationary or climbing, her pulse is normal.

"But the moment the thing begins to fall, her heart slows, and death is close. How long has it been there?"

"Since yesterday afternoon," Corlin replied. "I noticed it

shortly after Alice became so weak she was forced to bed. The first thought that came to me was to pull the kite down.

"I tried it, and I almost killed her. Went over to that tree and began to pull it in slowly. Fay was to fire a revolver the moment she noticed any ill-effect. The shot came almost at once."

He paced over to me. "In heaven's name, what are we up against?"

I moved toward another doorway leading into a side chamber. Inside I could see several cases, an array of curious objects on the wall.

"Show me your collection," I said at length. "Perhaps it will give me time to think."

Corlin's collection was well known through the district. Gathering it had been his one intense interest for many years. The man turned his head now, called:

"Kang Chow. Here, damn you. Chop-chop."

The Cantonese boy came on the run, surmised Corlin's orders and quickly drew the shades in the other room.

"Some one broke in here a couple of nights ago," Corlin said. "Tried to steal my things. I fired a shot at the sneak, but I missed."

Most of Corlin's collection was Borneo stuff from the deep interior. There were also articles from Java, the Celebes and China. I saw *parangs,* blow-pipes and pottery. But my eyes lingered on a case in a corner within which was an enormous piece of crimson silk.

"That silk is pure Tibetan work," Corlin said, noting my interest. "Comes from the forbidden temple of Po Yun Kwan, the headquarters of the Nepahte sect in North India. When I obtained it, it was adorning the Supreme Fire Altar in what was known as the Sacred Flame Room.

"I—er—well, to be frank, I climbed up an outer wall, sneaked through an unbarred window and lifted it when the priests were sleeping."

"You stole it?" I exclaimed.

Corlin nodded. "One has to do such things if he's going to have a collection. This silk has some mystic significance to a Tibetan. The priests called it the cloth of the Fire-God, and all the terrors of seven hells are supposed to follow anyone who defiles it.

"The beauty of the piece is the dragon design in the center. I don't know for sure, but I understand all sorts of evil obscene rites have been practiced in its name. This is the least understood religion of Asia. It is steeped in Black Magic and . . ."

I stepped closer and examined the cloth. The lower right corner ended in a ragged edge where a section had been torn off.

"The thief who broke in here did that," Corlin snarled. "I surprised him before he could rip it completely out of the case, and he got away in the darkness— What is it, Fay?"

The Conservator's daughter had entered the room. Her face was white as lime.

"Quick, Doctor," she cried. "My mother . . ."

In ten strides I was into the other room. But the moment I knelt at the woman's side I realized she was beyond human aid. There was practically no pulse. An instant later the death-rattle sounded. Alice Corlin was dead!

Still holding the lifeless wrist I looked through the window up into the sky. My eyes filled with horror. Even as I watched, the kite slowly settled downward. It fell into the jungle and disappeared.

Impatient as I was to leave Samarinda, the curious facts surrounding the death of Alice Corlin led me to postpone my departure. My certificate attributed her death to congestive malarial fever. But I knew—only too well—the cause went deeper than that.

I had the kite. River Dyaks near Corlin's house had brought it to me in return for a quantity of tobacco. It was made of bamboo sticks and rice paper, as I had suspected. But glued to the surface was a small remnant of red silk—a fragment from Corlin's Fire-God altar cloth.

Exactly a week later Corlin came to my quarters. He entered my veranda and faced me with haggard eyes.

"Van Rueller," he said. "There's another kite."

"What?" I cried.

He nodded. "Exactly like the first. Same size, same color, same kind of wire. It's been up two days now, but it seems to disappear each night. And my daughter Fay . . ."

"It isn't affecting her too?" A feeling of helpless horror swept over me.

Corlin clenched his fists.

"Not physically the way it did Alice, but mentally. Something unspeakably evil is slowly claiming her soul."

By this time I was tense with excitement. Dislike Corlin I did, but the events combined to draw me on with a hypnotic attraction. I told Corlin I'd go upriver in an hour.

It had rained during the night, and as we paddled up the Mahakam the sky was a leprous grey. Again Kang Chow sat stiffly in the stern directing the Dyak boatmen.

The kite came into view in almost identically the same spot I had seen its predecessor. I watched it until the sampan thumped against the wharf, but I made no comment.

A moment later in the house I came upon Fay Corlin. She sat in a chair in the center of the room, rigid, eyes fixed ahead. There was a drawn look of terror in her face; her lips were white.

For five minutes I spoke to her soothingly. She did not respond. Instead, abruptly and without warning, she leaped to her feet and gave a choking cry. Then like a lifeless thing she slumped to the floor. Even as I bent over her I knew my worst fears were realized.

The kite was working again!

But this time I had no intention of standing by without intervention. The girl's physical condition was linked with the movements of that kite. Impossible as it seemed, I knew that was true. The kite could not be pulled down, or Fay Corlin would die. *It must be destroyed in mid-air.*

I seized my medicine case and ran out. I dashed along the jungle path and down to the jetty. I leaped into the sampan and paddled furiously for the opposite shore.

Overhead low-bellied storm clouds were racing in from the horizon. The sky to the east was a sickly green. Following the copper wire, I reached the far bank and plunged into the bush.

The wire was fastened to the same *palapak* tree. I opened my case and fell to work.

From one compartment I drew forth a quantity of pyroxylin, spread it before me. Forty grams of pyroxylin mixed with ether and alcohol make collodion, which is useful in treating small wounds. But pyroxylin is nothing more than gun cotton.

I had in my case also a brass tube, capped at both ends to carry matches. Tearing off the caps, I inserted the gun cotton. Next, from an inner pocket I drew forth a large piece of paper, then ripped free my watch chain.

You've seen a boy send a message up a kite string, driven upward by the wind? I was doing much the same, only my "message" was a charge of inflammable gun cotton.

The slightest charge of lightning from the oncoming storm would be sufficient to ignite the pyroxylin and destroy the kite in mid-air. I re-fastened the wire to the tree again, then threaded the paper up the wire.

As I worked, the storm raced nearer. The kite rode high above the undulating roof of the jungle.

I released it. For a moment the "message" hung motionless. Then with a low hum it began to mount upward along the wire. I rushed back to the sampan and paddled back across the river.

Back in the house I found Fay unconscious on the cot in the collection room where Corlin had carried her. At the far side of the room, peering out the window, stood the Cantonese boy, Kang Chow.

I waited. One hand clamped to the girl's wrist, I knelt there. Corlin paced back and forth across the room. If he saw Kang Chow, he gave no sign. The room was half-masked in shadows.

In the corner the crimson silk, the Fire-God cloth from the Tibet temple shown luridly in its bamboo case. Its scarlet surface seemed enlarged a hundred times.

The storm drew nearer. From out of the east a blacker cloud raced over the jungle. And then, knifing down, a jagged fork of lightning shot toward the kite. A roar of thunder trembled the very piles of the house.

Five seconds later a sheet of flame burst out into the sky, high above the open window. The fire swept down the dragon tail like a devouring monster, and the wire dropped earthward like a writhing snake. The kite was gone!

Instantly a violent tremor shot through the stricken girl. A gasp came to her lips. The pulse became a pounding hammer. Then the beats slowed to normal, and I leaned back with a cry of exultation.

But at that instant any thought of success was thrust from

my mind. A muffled cry from Kang Chow spun me around. The Cantonese boy stood rigid, eyes fastened on the crimson silk in the case beside him.

And it was that silk that held by own gaze. Even as I watched, a streamer of smoke appeared over the design of the Fire-God. A tongue of flame shot outward.

Corlin whirled. One instant he stood motionless. Then the door of the case shot open. And slowly, a fraction of an inch at a time, the flaming silk began to move outward. Of its own accord, without support, it moved, lifted into the air, began to float across the room.

Relentlessly it closed in on Corlin. The Conservator's face was ashen. He tried to turn, but seemed riveted to the spot. Horrified, I watched the flaming silk lessen the intervening distance. Then with a final jerk it leaped forward.

The burning mass dropped over Corlin's head, tightened like a shroud!

I swear I was powerless to move. For an instant I vow some outer power prevented me from taking a single step.

Screaming hideously, Corlin fell to the floor. A curtain of smoke rolled over him. Into my nostrils swept the odor of burning flesh.

I broke the spell then, ran forward. I snatched at the cloth with both hands. It resisted all efforts. I seized a rattan rug, attempted to smother the flames. But the fire only flared higher.

At last Corlin's hands flailed wildly in a last death agony. He sank downward and lay still.

Fay Corlin left Samarinda on the 29th of January. My own passage to Singapore and thence to home was scheduled for a week later. But Kang Chow disappeared.

I might have explained the Cantonese boy's part in the death of Edward Corlin to the Dutch authorities. Or I might have asked for an inquest and testified to all that I knew. Yet somehow those facts, if brought to light in a colonial court of law, would have seemed even more impossible.

I can offset the whole thing by cataloguing a few of my subsequent findings. There was for example, the can of gasoline which I discovered under Corlin's house.

There was the spool of wire, a section of which had been stretched across the collection room, presumably as a supporting line for a bamboo curtain. Such a wire might conceivably have served as a track for the floating, flaming silk.

And there was my own knowledge that the Chinese will sacrifice anything to attain the proper theatrical effect. For Kang Chow, as was later revealed was not a Cantonese coolie.

He was a Tibetan, a former priest of the forbidden temple of Po Yun Kwan, from which the cloth of the Fire-God had been stolen!

And yet there was the kite, the death of Corlin's wife and the strange effect on the life of the daughter, Fay. Perhaps it was fever that caused these things. But I do not think so.

Canal

At the top of the stairs Kramer stood still a long moment, listening. The road behind him was empty and desolate, stretching off into the red-rimmed horizon like a crayon streak on a piece of cardboard. Up above in the dry motionless air a lone Kiloto wheeled and soared, searching for prey. There was no sign of pursuit.

Mentally Kramer checked over his equipment: canteen, food concentrate envelope, sand mask, and most precious of all, the map. The official Martian Cartographic Folio 654, direct from its glass case in the FaGanda Bureau of Standards. The map still lay in its oilskin pouch, and the archaic printing thrilled him as he stared down upon it.

It was Monday morning, 11:14 Earth time; he checked with his watch. In exactly eleven days, assuming all went well, he should be entering Canal 28 Northwest and coming down the homestretch. After that it would be easy. His forged passports would give him easy access to the Crater City port. The regular Earth Express would take off at high noon. Not even Blanchard would suspect him of escaping in this direction. Since Kramer had first conceived the plan a month ago, he had studied each detail, accounted for each contingency, and everything had worked like clockwork.

He began to descend the steps, absently counting them as he went down: fifty-six, fifty-seven, fifty-eight. Level One. Here the first sign, almost illegible from age, met his gaze:

IT IS ABSOLUTELY FORBIDDEN

TO ENTER THESE CANALS

BY ORDER OF

ZARA

It seemed strange seeing that name, Zara, there out of a history book. The last Martian monarchy had passed on into the limbo ages ago. And Kramer remembered that even during the last three—or was it four?—dynasties the canals had been closed.

One twenty-eight, one twenty-nine. Third, fourth, fifth level. Kramer drew up before a massive door, fashioned of arelium steel. A second sign stood out mockingly in the light of his torch:

IT IS ABSOLUTELY FORBIDDEN . . .

Without hesitation he reached into his pocket and drew forth a key. He removed the royal seal with the utmost care, inserted the key in the lock and twisted. The door swung open slowly of its own accord.

Even then with virtual success just within his grasp, he did not forget himself. He replaced the seal in such a way that the closed door would show no signs of passage. Then he broke into a low laugh.

There it was—Canal Grand, the master artery that linked North Mars with South Mars, the single avenue that crossed the Void, and offered a possible means of escape. No Earth men, no living Martian had ever penetrated the Void and returned. Planes, expeditions, rocket ships had taken off time and time again, only to disappear without trace. In their wake superstition had flowered, rumor had multiplied, until today the Void stood, a chasm of isolation, effectually slicing the red planet into two parts.

Kramer strode boldly forward, warm and comfortable in his space suit and hextar helmet. For the first twenty yards alluvial drift impeded his progress, and he swore to himself as he thought of his early schooling that had taught him there was no wind on Mars.

Then he reached the hard-packed center of the canal, and the ground here was firm and level as a pavement.

The frowning walls, towering sheer on either side, were as oppressive as a tunnel at first. The geometric desolation fatigued the eye. But after he had gone a mile Kramer swung along rapidly, immune to these irritations.

Queer how things worked out in one's life. A month ago he

had been an ordinary salvage ratio clerk at the Metropolitan Power Unit in FaGanda. His life had been routine, with only a few petty thieveries and unimportant swindlings to break the monotony. Then, quite by accident, he had hit upon the plan.

The plan had as its nucleus the secret of the Void which had baffled mankind for so many years. In 3091 the historian, Stola, had written:

> I am convinced that the great catastrophe which caused the complete dehydration of the canals and began the rapid decline of the early Martians under the monarchy is linked in some unexplainable way with that corridor which we know today as the Void.
>
> We know of a certainty that Canal Grand was unquestionably the only passage which crossed that corridor even in those early times, and we know by spectroscopic analysis that somewhere along that canal lies a deposit of retnite, now catalogued as Chemical X. Since Chemical X is the most desired thing by Earthmen today, there is no doubt in my mind but that eventually the lode will be tapped and the mysteries of the Void explored.

Stola had written that, and he had been conservative. In the entire System, Kramer knew, there were but fourteen kilograms of retnite known to exist. That was reserved for the nine members of the Interplanetary Council and their elected successors.

But retnite was in reality nothing more than a drug, a mental stimulant which, when taken correctly, could amplify the thought processes of the brain a thousandfold. A retniter carried with ease, not only the heritage of his ancestors but viewed the panorama of life intelligently. A retniter, in other words, was a super intellect.

Kramer wanted that elixir. He wanted it because it would open the door for him to success. No more petty swindlings then, no more trickster schemes with constant fear of the police. He could tell Blanchard and the law to go to blazes.

Inside his helmet he pressed his chin against a stud, and automatically a Martian cheroot dropped out of a rack and slipped between his lips. A tiny heat unit swung over to ignite it, and the exhaust valve behind his neck increased its pulsations to expel the smoke. He walked on . . .

Kramer's introduction to the plan had come about in an odd way. In a small curio shop in FaGanda he had purchased an old vase, marked with a mixture of curious hieroglyphics on one side and some doggerel Martian verse on the other. Now Kramer was no student of languages, but in order to quicken his wits he had frequently pored over early Martian.

He was astounded to discover that the hieroglyphics and the verse keyed the two languages and offered the first translation of the ancient parchments in the Bureau of Standards.

The rest was a matter of detail. Kramer had managed to hide in the gallery at night. Alone, behind locked doors, he had selected one folio of the hundred and twenty-six in the glass cases. It was that one, he knew, which held the secret of the Void.

There remained then but one thing to do. Hom Valla, the Martian philologist, must be removed. Hom Valla had announced only recently that, after years of study, he was finally on the verge of deciphering early Martian and the folios.

Kramer had taken his time. He waited until Hom Valla was known to be leaving on a trip up-country. Then he had entered his apartment, fired one shot with a heat gun and fed the body into the city's refuse tubes.

Blanchard? Yes, Blanchard would probably couple the three details: the stolen folio, the death of Hom Valla, and Kramer's disappearance. But it would take time, and during that time Kramer would be increasing the distance between himself and the law.

He began to study the canal as he paced along. Straight as a knife blade, it stretched before him to the vanishing point. The walls were sheer, dug out of the red rock by a means that so far had baffled archaeologists. Three-quarters of the way up he could see a series of darker serrated lines, and he knew these were the ancient water marks.

How many hundreds of explorers had started this way, hoping to penetrate the secret of the Void, only to disappear completely. And what was the Void? If it held retnite at its core, what power did it wield to entrap all trespassers?

The stolen folio in this respect had been oddly disappointing. It had charted the location of the lode, in such a way that only a person able to decipher ancient Martian could read it. It had mapped a route through the labyrinth of canals, but it had made no mention of the mystery that lay ahead.

At noon, by his Earth watch, Kramer halted for a rest. After a half hour he set off again, walking at that same mechanical pace that ate up the miles.

The red ditch faded out of his thoughts now. He saw the canals as they were of old, as the Chronicles had described them. Luxurious waterways clogged with commercial shipping, with tapestried gondolas and canopied barges. He saw the gigantic locks and the way stations where swashbuckling pilots drank genith and watched South Martian girls writhe and sway to the rhythm of the Ucatel drums.

It was at that moment that preceded the sudden advance of night that Kramer found himself rudely torn back to reality. He had kept his visa set turned on, and now a low magnetic hum told him that its finder was in operation. The vision plate above his eyes began to glow with a dull light.

Abruptly a violent shock swept through him!

In the plate he saw a section of red wall and the huge studded entrance door through which he had recently passed. As he watched, that door opened, and a man appeared clad in a space suit. Through the crystal helmet his features revealed themselves clearly. It was Blanchard!

The I. P. man was on his hands and knees, examining the sand on the floor of the canal. Presently he straightened and began to stride forward rapidly.

Kramer swore. Only a few hours had elapsed since he had dispatched Hom Valla. How could Blanchard possibly have picked up the trail so quickly? In some way he, Kramer, must have erred, must have left a clue.

For a moment panic swept over the former salvage ratio clerk. Then quickly he was in control of himself again. He lay down on the sand, swallowed a few food concentrate pellets and in a moment was asleep.

Awakening before dawn, he pushed on again in the darkness.

But with the coming of the sun the first of the three quanthrows swooped down to attack him.

The quanthrows were far south for this time of year, but their ferocity was no less great. Strangely resembling swordfish, but with octagon-shaped heads and curious square wingspreads, they wheeled out of the saffron sky with rasping squawks that vibrated the earphones in Kramer's helmet.

He killed the first with a single shot, managed to wound fatally the second with a double charge from his heat pistol. The third, a colossus of avian strength, shot toward him, its steel-like proboscis thrust straight for his throat.

Kramer escaped the murderous attack by inches. Even so, before he could whip out his knife and jam it upward, the "sword" penetrated his suit and bit deep in his shoulder.

Breathing hard, he stood there looking down at the three lifeless bodies. And then, with that sudden clarity which physical action always brought him, Kramer thought of something.

If there were three quanthrows, there must be ninety-seven more close by. It was one of the peculiarities of this creature to travel always in flocks of a hundred. Also—and here in spite of the pain in his shoulder, Kramer permitted himself to indulge in a broad smile, the one thing which would attract a quanthrow was salt.

In an instant he was ripping open his haversack, pouring the white crystals on the three dead bodies.

With their strange clannishness, the quanthrows would miss these members of their flock shortly and would return to investigate their absence. When they found the salt they would linger there for hours. And Blanchard ... ! Kramer walked on again with new vigor.

The sword cut in his suit was easily repaired. Duoresilient tape fixed that. To his dismay, however, Kramer found that the attack by the quanthrows had damaged the delicate wiring of his visa set. Several times he switched it on, expecting to see the oncoming Blanchard. But the vision plate remained blurred.

At nightfall of the second day he reached the first way station. Stumbling in the doorless cubicle, Kramer threw himself prone on the debris-covered floor, panting with exhaustion.

Here at least he could rest a while, free from the incredible dangers of this world.

The cubicle ages ago had housed the air filtration apparatus and heat control units of the way station. This machinery had weathered to a pile of oxidized metal. But in a hermetically sealed cabinet mounted on one wall Kramer found a spanner glass still in usable operation.

He pursed his lips in satisfaction, quickly transferred the battery connections of his suit to the device and tripped over the vernier.

For a long moment the cracked screen showed a blank surface. Then, with an oath, Kramer drove his clenched fist into the panel, shattering pintax tubes in a shower of fragments.

He had seen enough. Clearly outlined in the screen the figure of Blanchard could be seen, plodding doggedly through the sand. Kramer dropped into a ruined settee and chinned the stud feeding a lighted cheroot to his lips. He inhaled the rank smoke savagely.

He stood up and began a careful survey of the cubicle's interior. Nothing at all which might serve to entrap the oncoming I. P. man. Kramer went outside and began to pace along the short narrow street.

On the right was the matrilated dome where canaleers passed the night so long ago. On the left stood the remnants of the harthode tower where first, second and third Monarchy Martian dispatchers had pored over their charts and lock controls, guiding the network of traffic in and out of Canal Grand.

The last structure was still in fairly good preservation. It was a canalserai, and Kramer's heart leaped as his gaze took it in. Even pilots in those days had not lacked for entertainment. This was their pleasure palace where gambling and dancing had taken place.

The door to this building had long since vanished and five feet over the threshold was a small mound of drifted sand. Inside, however, Kramer, found the rarefied air had kept things in pretty good trim.

The long demdem bar still stood before one wall. Farther on he saw the little alcoves where incoming pilots had drowsed under the effect of the forbidden electro-hypnotic machines.

The dismantled parts of one of these machines still stood in a corner, and he paused to examine it. Self applied hypnotism was one of the accomplishments of the early Martians. This device was simple. It consisted of two prism-shaped pieces of translucent metal, mounted on brackets in front of a many-side panel of refracto-glass. Seated before the instrument, under a powerful ato-light, the imbiber found his gaze drawn toward a single perspective, where the reflection of his own eyes was transmitted back to him.

Abruptly Kramer seized the instrument and carried it to the doorway of the room, scooped the drifted sand into a higher mound, and placed the machine upon it.

Directly above a stone girder hung precariously, balanced by the jammed key stone in the archway. Kramer dug toe holes in the crumbling masonry, mounted to that key stone and loosened it with his knife blade. An instant later only a few chips of stone kept the massive girder from plunging downward.

Back on the floor level again, he whipped out his electric stylus and wrote the following words across the refracto-glass panel:

> Blanchard: I know you're after me, but our trails part here.
> If you want to know which canal I've taken, the secret lies in the glass.

He signed his name and smiled quietly. It was a rather complicated trap, but if he knew the I. P. man, it was a good one. Blanchard would enter here, searching for clues. He would see the hypnosis machine, and he would read the message.

From the moment he looked into the refracto glass, the machine would begin its spell. Blanchard would be lulled into a quick, deep sleep, and as he slumped backward against the wall, the dislodged girder above would complete the story.

Five minor canals angled off Canal Grand at this way station. But Kramer's original plan of taking one of these to throw his pursuer off the track was gone now. Sure of himself, he continued almost light-heartedly down Canal Grand.

As he went on, he worked at the wiring of his visa set. Once he got it in partial operation, but then it blurred again, and refused to respond to the controls. The pain in his shoulder was a dull throb now; his whole arm felt numb and feverish, and there was a growing lump in the gland under his armpit.

By noon he was aware of a subtle change in the scene about him. The canal's walls seemed to draw closer together and become deeper. The sides of the great ditch took on a deeper brownish red hue that caught the glare of the sun and refracted it back into his eyeballs.

Abruptly Kramer halted, staring with wide-open eyes. A quarter mile ahead a large black mound barred his path.

Rocks! As he drew nearer he could see the outlines of gargantuan boulders piled high in a grotesque cairn. But how had they come here? They had not rolled down from the top of the canal, for no whim of nature could have constructed such a regular formation.

Kramer approached with caution. Twenty yards away he stopped again, and a wave of fear swept over him. There was something curiously life-like about those stones. He received the impression they were watching him with unseen eyes.

Then suppressing the scream which arose in his throat, he turned and ran. Simultaneously he looked over his shoulder, and an incredible sight met his eyes.

The "stones" had left their mound and were now deploying over the hard-packed ground and slowly, but unmistakably, pursuing him.

Not until that moment did Kramer realize what he had blundered into. They were the horrors of the canals—the *kanal-bras*, Mars' link between organic and inorganic life.

At first he outdistanced them easily. Then, as they increased their locomotion, he seemed to be running on a treadmill with painted scenery unrolling on either side. The *kanal-bras* came on with no apparent effort, gliding across the surface of the sand as if they weighed nothing at all. Looking back, Kramer thought he could see cavernous mouths and multiple eyes.

He understood their purpose. They were inorganic, yes, but they were also omnivorous. That is, feeding on organic matter, they permitted that matter to adhere to their surfaces and slowly petrify like a coal deposit.

They were close upon him now. Kramer's breath was searing his lungs, and he could hear the exhaust valve in the back of his helmet rattle open and shut like a shuttlecock.

And then once again his reading background came to the aid of the former salvage ratio clerk. Somewhere he remembered that a *kanal-bra* reacted to sub-sonic vibrations. They alone could penetrate their metal-stone bodies.

He had no vibrator, but he did have his heat pistol. Frantically he clawed the weapon out of its holster and twisted the control stud to its farthest marking. From a heat ray to an infra-red ray to a sub-sonic ray was but a step. He turned and fired.

Even then he was not prepared for the results. As the single blast pulsed out of the barrel, the *kanal-bras* lost their forward momentum and halted. Like a slow motion camera turned backward, they slowly retreated across the sand. Reaching their former position, they mounted one upon the other, until they formed the identical mound Kramer had seen before.

He stood still a long moment, staring in amazement. Then boldly he tried an experiment. The heat pistol was of the latest Gan-Larkington type, and the tiny rheostat was capable of controlling vibrations almost the entire breadth of the vibratory scale. Super-sonic charges, though rare with most weapons, were included in the Gan-Larkington.

If a sub-sonic charge would thus stultify the *kanal-bras* would not a super-sonic or ultra-sonic wave tend to release them?

Kramer tried it. He adjusted the weapon, fired a shot and saw the stony creatures immediately erupt into life. A sub-sonic blast sent them returning in that curious retrogressive action to their former position.

He smoked a cigarette over the discovery. A quarter of an hour later he had set his third trap. Beyond a doubt there wasn't the slightest need for it. But with the stakes he had, there was no use taking chances.

He buried the heat gun in the sand, leaving only the barrel and the trigger exposed. He stretched a cord tightly for twenty yards across the canal floor, connecting one end to the trigger. The barrel he aimed directly at the motionless *kanal-bras*.

"Now," he muttered, "if Blanchard does get by the way station, he'll get a surprise. All you need, these days, is brains."

With a quick step he skirted the living rock cairn and headed down the canal.

Within a quarter mile he found it necessary to consult the stolen map. And a mile farther on found him clutching the folio in one hand, gazing at it constantly as he walked.

At intervals of every few hundred yards other tributary canals branched off the main stem. Some of these were equally as large and impressive as Canal Grand, and shortly it dawned upon Kramer that he might be lost.

The map was clearly enough marked, but apparently new waterways had been dug since those ancient cartographers had penned the manuscript. Kramer swore but did not slow his pace. He still had his magno compass. He might wander off the main artery, but sooner or later he should be able to place his position and swing back into it.

Faded hieroglyphics began to make their appearance now, stenciled deeply in colossal letters above the water marks on the canal's sides. Some of them were undecipherable. Others, Kramer tried to ease his growing tension by translating.

"Praise to Zara," one of them read. Another: "Calthedra five hundred legaros." There was one in larger marking that caused Kramer to knit his brows in puzzlement. Translated freely, it read: "Beware of the Echo."

He forgot the hieroglyphics abruptly when he tripped over a heavier mound of sand and fell sprawling. The sudden shock did something to his visa set. It crackled, hummed, began operation, then went dead again.

But that momentary glimpse in the vision plate was enough. Kramer had seen Blanchard plodding forward relentlessly through the drifted sand. He had safely passed both traps.

Was there no stopping the man?

Kramer lurched to his feet and began to walk at a faster pace, though the pain in his shoulder had increased a hundredfold.

He noticed now that the red banks of the canal had given way to a kind of lustreless, metallic wall. Slate gray in color, they towered even higher than before, and they seemed to converge at the top like a tunnel. Simultaneously he felt a cloud of mental uneasiness sweep over him, accompanied by an overpowering desire to break the brooding oppressive silence.

Twenty yards forward, and that desire had become maddening. The utter quiet pressed against his ears. Against his will he found his steps drawn toward the nearer wall. And here, like a crazed man, he seized a heavy rock fragment and began dashing it again and again against the metallic bank.

He could feel the snapping recoil as the blow traveled up his arm. The hum in his headset told him there was nothing wrong with his audiphone.

But the blows produced no sound.

It was as if he had struck a mallet into a pile of cotton. And then he went rigid. Out of the corner of his eye he had seen something leap up from the rock fragment even as he hit it and race outward across the canal with incredible speed. A shadow, it seemed to be, and yet a shadow that possessed a certain miniature form with moving ghost legs and arms and a tiny button knob that might have been a head.

Again he struck the rock and again a shadow leaped up and sped away. An instant later Kramer threw himself flat upon the sand, groveling in agony. The shadows, a dozen of them, had formed a phalanx at the opposite wall of the canal, and had raced back upon him.

As they came, they carried the delayed sound of Kramer's blows upon the stone.

Delayed, but multiplied and amplified a thousand times. The concentrated roar was agonizing. Vainly he thumbed the switch, disconnecting the headset. But the vibration pulsed relentlessly through the space suit and hextar helmet. He thought he felt the shadow bodies leaping upon him, striking his skull with tiny invisible hammers.

Were they sound shadows, some mixture of light and sound waves possessing the ability to travel through space and time, a mutant echo that had the dominant characteristics of living matter?

Or was the whole thing a vagary of his brain, the result of a mounting fever from his infected arm? He did not know.

Kramer sat there a long time, mulling over the situation, as the vibration finally ceased. He wondered if there were any possibility of using the phenomena as a trap. A last and final trap that would forestall Blanchard for once and for all.

But he had no time for further thought. His gaze had turned idly to that length of canal down which he had just passed. And far off, almost at the limit of his vision he saw something which made his mouth suddenly fall slack.

A man was toiling through the sand, slowly advancing toward him. Blanchard!

Leaping to his feet, he raced away, fleeing madly at top speed. Nor, thereafter, did he relax for an instant his frenzied efforts to escape.

Six days later Kramer entered the last lap of his trek. He knew it was the last lap because the way station at the confluence of the two mighty canals was clearly marked and described on the map. Any moment now he should be sighting the cavern mouth that led to the retnite deposit.

After that his worries would be over. He would extract a quantity of the deposit—the folio gave a detailed account of the method to obtain and purify it. He would swing into Canal 28 Northwest and manage somehow to reach Crater City. Blanchard was close on his heels, yes. But in some way he would take care of Blanchard.

Give him a year then—six months, and success would be his. The mental doors that would be flung open to him would eliminate all necessity of subsistence worry, and the law would be a trivial thing which he could dispense with.

Remained only one item unanswered—the Void. Since he had entered Canal Grand, Kramer had tried to put that mystery out of his thoughts. It had persisted, however, and now that he was nearing his goal, he thought about it more and more.

It lay ahead somewhere, a gulf which he must cross. Not until he had reached it would he know the answer.

He began to study the canal sides now with care. The hieroglyphics had long since disappeared, and there was utterly no sign of life.

All that long Martian day he walked steadily onward. His throat was dry; his arm and shoulder felt strange and numb like alien parts of his body; at intervals reddish spots danced before his eyes.

At three o'clock by his Earth watch Kramer was startled to see the left canal wall swing outward on a tangent, forming a vast ellipse before him. Simultaneously the sand floor began to descend, deeper and deeper, until he could no longer discern the tops of the banks.

An hour later a cry of amazement escaped his lips.

Scattered across the canal floor a quarter mile ahead was an array of incredible objects. He saw modern rocket ships; he saw thirtieth century stepto planes with their curious elongated wing exhaust jets. All of them lay there in the oppressive silence, conning doors open as if their crews had left only a moment before and would shortly return.

But as he passed them at closer range, he saw, too, that they had been there a long time. The hulls were half buried in the sand. The glassite ports were yellowish and opaque with the peculiar dull hue brought about by long exposure to the Martian atmosphere.

There were some twenty ships of types and manufacture he recognized. One of them was the ill-fated *Goliath,* whose disappearance, he vaguely remembered, had caused a furor when he was a child. Older vessels loomed as he walked on, some of them antedating the ancient models he had seen in his history books.

Kramer did not have to be told that this was the end of the trail for these ships. They too had come this far, hoping to probe the Void. But what had become of their crews? Why had they not returned?

He passed the last vessel at length and reached a point where the view before him was unrestricted. Here he halted, oppressed by an inner sense of unease. He drew out the oilskin pouch and began a close survey of the folio.

Almost at once a cry of triumph came to his lips. It seemed queer he had not noticed it before, but this widening point of the canal was marked on the map. More than that, the map also showed the retnite deposit to lie in the center of the huge bowl.

Two trails leading to the lode were shown. One of them a narrow, round-about route was marked with a dotted line. The other trail, larger, shorter bore two words in early Martian at its entrance. A-krey menarga, it read.

Kramer stood up and walked a hundred yards east. He saw no trail. Nothing but trackless sand. And then abruptly, as he turned his eyes slightly upward, he did see it.

Extending before him was a narrow corridor where the sand floor somehow seemed tilted at a different angle and where the atmosphere bore a curious glazed effect, as if he were looking through a double thickness of glass. Also, he thought he saw a row of black spots, like a dotted line, stretching into space before him.

But even at that moment with success at his finger tips, Kramer did not forget himself—or Blanchard. Two trails were marked on the map, this one and another farther on. He threw the map to the sand, grinding it under his heel to give the impression it had been dropped there accidentally.

Then he continued walking east. And shortly afterward his efforts were rewarded. The second trail was larger, more inviting. A stone floor stretched out before him across the sand. But here, too, he received the impression he was looking at it through imperfect plates of glass.

Without hesitation Kramer swung into it. Almost at once he had a feeling of exhilaration, of mental buoyancy. Mingled with it was a feeling that the way behind him was closing up.

The stone floorway led up. And that was odd. For Kramer could have sworn that the sand bowl was flat as a vast die. As he went on, however, he thought less about his surroundings and more about the stolen folio.

A-krey menarga? What did those words mean? Menar, he knew, was an early Martian prefix, meaning bent or twisted. And the only logical definite of krey was space.

Kramer stopped while an icy chill crawled up his spine. Into the space warp! ... Of course, that was what the secret of the Void was. A space warp would account for everything: the eternal division of North and South Mars, the disappearance of the various expeditions, the dehydration of the canals. It meant that another world—another dimension—was impinged at this point and whoever blundered into it would be lost forever!

Quite slowly, Kramer began to walk again.

He forced his eyes ahead where the usual perspective was supplanted by a jumble of angles, tilted ellipses and quadrants. But at length he could stand it no longer, and he turned.

Nothing! There was nothing behind him at all. Only the way ahead, stretching like a forsaken causeway into measureless distances.

The Satanic Piano

Midnight, and I was seated at the old concert grand in my study, running my fingers over the keys to the wild melody of Saint-Saëns' *Danse Macabre.* Outside the fog like some toothless centenarian peered in at the glowing electroliers and drooled mist and greenish drizzle on the window panes. Hollow and muffled through the thick air, Big Ben boomed its chimes of the hour.

I was restless. The night was hardly conducive to sleep. The empty weeks in London with Martha, my fiancée, gone for an extended visit up-country, had reached a climax of loneliness in the preceding solitary hours at the theater. And above all, that puzzling message which had come to my door a few moments past still lay there on the chair, leering up at me with the insistence of a spoken command. It read:

> Come at once to 94 Milford Lane. I have something of the utmost importance to show you. It concerns your music.
> > Wilson Farber.

For a moment as I stared down upon the black card with the peculiar writing in white ink, I was almost inclined to smile. Farber, eh? Wilson Farber. Yes, I remembered the man, remembered the day I had first come upon him in his dirty little music shop on lower Telling Street. I had gone there in search of some old collection of Russian folk-dances, and he, sitting amid his jumble of tarnished horns and battered violins, had led me into a conversation. And I remembered his book, which had attracted such wide interest and which psychology professors had been forced to admit opened new fields for thought in the subjects of hypnotism and telepathy.

Once again after that I had visited his shop, and while I must confess I was impressed by the man's queer erudition, still I had been only too glad to remove myself from his presence. There was something disturbing about the way he stared into your eyes, seemed to plumb your very soul. Nor did I like the silent way he glided about dragging his thick ebony cane, or that high-pitched laugh that sounded like the mirthless squeak of a ventriloquist.

Tall and gaunt, with a shock of sable hair and a ragged beard the color of slate, he was at once a commanding and repelling figure. There were rumors about the man, rumors that came into existence when his unorthodox book first appeared in the stalls. Was it the work of a trained or a neurotic brain? And was there any significance in the fact that a *James Wilson Farber* had been released from St. Mary's Institution for the Insane some nine months before?

I say now that had that last line, "it concerns your music," not been included in the missive, I should probably have dismissed the matter entirely from my mind. But the thought stole upon me that perhaps back in the shadows of his shop he had come upon some rare old music composition and was offering it for sale. Farber knew my weakness. He knew that for years I have amused myself by collecting original manuscripts and unknown works of forgotten composers. This hobby has brought me almost as much enjoyment as my own creation for the piano, and I hated to let any valuable work slip through my fingers.

Yet even music compositions were not so important but that they could wait until the morrow.

I moved to my favorite armchair, and tried to immerse myself in the pages of a half-read novel. For a time the movements of the characters attracted my full attention, and the disturbing message of Farber faded slowly out of my thoughts. But when in the course of a quarter-hour the narrative before me began to lag, I found my eyes inadvertently returning to the bit of paper there on the chair.

For the third time I read its imperative lines. And suddenly I gave in to impulse.

Five minutes later, clad in trench-coat and cap, I was rolling across the wet streets in an east-bound cab past Piccadilly Circus down Haymarket and through a world of white to the Strand.

The fog was even thicker here by the Embankment and it seemed to increase as we sped onward.

Milford Lane was almost a half-hour's drive from my apartment. It was close to one o'clock by my watch when I stood before the frowning door of number 94, and by the light of a single street lamp, gazed upon the gigantic jumble of brick and wrought iron that formed the ancient edifice. I hesitated there, the fog and drizzle pressing close against my face like wet gauze, the rumble of a distant tram reaching my ears hollowly as if from some lower world. Then I stepped forward and rattled the knocker.

The sounds had but died away into silence when the door opened, and I found myself staring once again into the iron countenance of Wilson Farber. Even though I had known what to expect, I confess I recoiled slightly before those black eyes.

"You sent for me—?" I began.

He nodded. "I'm glad you've come, Bancroft. I think you'll find it well worth your trouble. This way, please."

He conducted me through a dark corridor to a brilliantly lighted room in the rear of the house, thrust forward a chair, and bade me sit down. Slowly unbuttoning my coat, I glanced at my surroundings. Glanced, I say—then stared. Without fear of contradiction, I believe I can safely put down that room to be the strangest chamber in all London.

The four walls had been painted or frescoed a dead white, and over this in black, beginning from the ceiling and continuing down to the very floor, were a series of five lines of the musical scale, adorned with notes—full notes, half notes, and flagged eighths and sixteenths. At two-foot intervals on the wall with no show of artistic placement, hung a line of musical instruments, the choice of which seemed to have been guided by a bizarre taste rather than a love for harmony. There were several lutes, battered and ornate, an oboe, a mandolin, a Javanese drum, and a number of queer elongated horns. Over in a far corner stood a harpsichord dating to an early period. Heavy black drapes curtained the two windows, and a white porcelain operating table stood under the glare of a green-shaded lamp in the center of the room.

There was a desk at my side, the top littered with manuscript, chemical vials and tubes, and a disorderly array of books. Some of the volumes, I saw by the titles, were technical studies of music composers and their various works, but the majority dealt with such subjects as hypnotism, experiments of Doctor Mesmer and telepathy.

Farber was leaning forward now, placing before me a glass and a decanter, and motioning that I help myself.

I shook my head. "It's late," I said, "and I live a long way from here. What do you want with me?"

He settled in his chair, hooked his thumbs in the vest of his black suit and studied me closely.

"Bancroft," he said, "you're a concert pianist and a composer. Are you not?"

I looked at him carefully before I made my answer. There was power in that face. Every line suggested cruel determination as if once he were moving toward an end, nothing could stop him. The mouth with its thin bluish lips was fixed in that characteristic half smile, half sneer. The eyes under their heavy brows gleamed like separate entities.

"I suppose you might call me that," I replied. "My public appearances have been a source of livelihood for some years now. But although I've written a lot, only one number of mine ever acquired much notice."

He nodded slowly. "I know," he said. "*Satanic Dance.* It has been acclaimed one of the finest examples of modern music in the last decade. And at present you are working on a sonata which you plan to present at your next concert at Kensington Hall."

"Will you kindly tell me where you obtained that information?" I inquired coldly. "That sonata was to come as a complete surprise."

With a gesture of his hand he waved my question aside. "That is beside the point," he said. "I am in possession of a number of facts this blundering world will some day be surprised to learn about. When the time comes . . . but never mind. What I want to know now is this: What, exactly, is your method of composing music?"

"Method?" I repeated.

"Yes. For example, how did you go about writing *Satanic Dance*? What was your procedure?"

The question was so prosaic, so matter of fact, that I leaned back in disappointment. To be drawn out of one's apartment at such an hour, led to a distant point of the city, and then amid such surroundings, asked a simple detail about my bread-earning profession—as I have rationally come to look upon it—was indeed disillusioning.

"Basically speaking," I replied, "the composing of music is no different from the writing of, well ... say fiction. Half inspiration, half craftsmanship, I suppose. A central theme, a strain of melody courses through my mind. I immediately go to the piano, play as much of it as I can—play it several times, in fact—and then put the proper notes as far as my memory permits, on paper. Is that what you mean?"

The thin lips twisted into a smile of satisfaction. "Yes," he said. "And what do you find to be your greatest difficulties in this method?"

"That," I replied, " is obvious. In transposing from the mind to the keys of the piano, and then to the printed notes on the page, much of the original inspiration is lost. It cannot be otherwise."

He reached for the decanter, poured himself a glassful and sipped it slowly.

"Suppose," he said "an instrument were to be placed at your disposal—a machine, let us call it—which under certain conditions would seize this musical inspiration that courses through your brain and transform it of its own accord into the actual living sound, a device so delicate that it would record permanently, note for note, the very melody that exists in your thoughts. How valuable do you think it would be?"

"If such an instrument could be created," I said slowly, "it would bring fame to its musical owner in twenty-four hours. It would make a mere writer of songs a master musician, and it would make a great musician a genius. But it's impossible. I know something of science, and I know that telepathy—if that's what you're driving at—has never been acknowledged. Oh, I'm aware there are so-called mind-reading machines in use in criminal courts, but they are mere lie-detectors and show only the presence or absence of emotion."

Without further word he got to his feet, stepped to the door leading to the adjoining room and disappeared. Silence swept down upon me as I found myself alone. What on earth was this Farber person driving at? What was the significance of all the conversation regarding the composition of music? And why had I of all people been summoned here to be a party to it? As my wrist-watch ticked off the passing seconds, a mounting sense of uneasiness welled up within me.

At length, impatiently, I stepped across to one of the heavily curtained windows at the far side of the room, thrust the drapes aside and peered out into the pool of drifting fog. But my vision was interrupted. Heavy iron bars were there, preventing access either to or from the street. A wild sudden thought that I might be a prisoner here whipped me about. The sight of the open door, however, reassured me, and when Farber put in his appearance a moment later, I chided myself for being a nervous fool.

He was staggering forward, arms strained and bent under the weight of a large object shrouded in a black cloth covering. Reaching the operating-table, he set the square-shaped thing under the glare of the suspended light, then turned and carefully placed my chair on a parallel five feet away.

"Bancroft," he said as I sat down, "I want you to listen and obey instructions very closely. Keep perfectly quiet, fasten your eyes on the object on the table and concentrate your mind upon it as much as you possibly can."

He turned and whipped off the cloth covering. I stared in astonishment. There before me was a midget piano, the shape of a concert grand, three feet in width and about eighteen inches high. Its sides were painted a lurid crimson, and at a glance I saw that from the ivory keys of its little keyboard to the tiny strings revealed by the open sounding-top, it was a piano complete in every detail. The carving on the diminutive legs was as intricate as that on the huge Lonway in my study, the entire woodwork perfectly formed. A thick hard-rubber base-board served as a mounting for the instrument, and at one extreme end of this was a small box with a glass panel. The panel bore a single black-faced dial, but within I could see a world of wires, coils, queer-shaped bulbs and a thick glass winding tube filled with some black liquid.

Farber busied himself for some moments, adjusting and

readjusting the dial. Presently the black liquid in the glass tube began to surge back and forth like a steam pressure gauge. Then as my concentration grew more intense, there came a slight hiss, and the fluid raced through the tube, boiling and bubbling like lava. One of the bulbs began to glow cherry red.

At last Farber looked up. "For ten years," he said, "I have worked on the instrument you see here on the table. Until tonight I have had only ridicule and failure for my reward. But tonight, a few hours before you came, chance showed me where I had erred. There was only a slight correction to be made, but it changed the principle of the entire working mechanism."

He turned to the dial again and began moving it slowly.

"You will in a moment find yourself in complete operation of one of the most drastic inventions science has ever known," he said. He was speaking quickly and loudly now, running his words together and almost gasping for breath. "Up until now genius has been vested in only a few persons, and those persons have been hailed as leaders in their field. The truth is that there is genius in many of us, but it is unable to find its proper expression outlet. It is born and dies in the brain without ever seeing the light of the world.

"Psychology has known for a long time that the nervous impulses which course through the brain are electro-chemical in nature, but that these impulses while in action set up a wave motion, psychology has steadfastly refused to admit.

"Call it telepathy, if you need a term, but my postulation was that each thought, each idea, and particularly each strain of melody which passes through the brain sets up a distinct field of motion as existent as the field of an electro magnet, and that if an instrument could be made delicate enough, it would seize those waves and transform them into their actual sound.

"You know yourself how clearly a certain bit of music will pass through and linger in your mind. The very orchestra, instrument, or voice seems to live there in your brain. In your case, perhaps, this is accentuated a thousand times because you are a trained musician.

"Very well, Bancroft, I want you to think back, remember some one of your music numbers, some piece which you have played and heard many times and which you can recall note for note. Keep your attention upon this piano, and *think of that music!*"

It was with a curious mixture of emotions that I sat there listening to him. The little crimson piano rested on the table before me like some elaborate toy. The black liquid in the glass tube pulsed steadily upward. And Farber's face was contorted now into an expression of delirious absorption. His hands were opening and closing convulsively.

I tried to guide my mind backward into the maze of piano compositions I have committed to memory. Names of titles, of composers, spun through my head: waltzes, scherzoes, caprices—what was it I had been playing when Farber's message arrived at my door? ... Saint-Saëns' *Danse Macabre*. The weird melody seemed a fitting one for the occasion. I puzzled my brain as to how the composition began. A moment of seeking a mental impression of the opening chord; and then, simultaneously with that instant when the train of melody entered my mind, an astounding thing happened. The piano, five feet away, trembled violently. The light in the queer shaped bulb increased from a cherry red to a brilliant flaming orange, and the keyboard—as though controlled by invisible hands—that keyboard leaped into motion and began to play—the very music of which I was thinking!

I turned and stared at Farber. He was watching the instrument of his making with dilated eyes.

"It's ... it's reading my mind!" I cried.

On played the piano, the little keys pressing downward to form the chords and racing along the octaves with lightning speed—faster and faster as my brain ran over the familiar melody. It was *Danse Macabre*—the *Dance of Death*—Saint-Saëns' masterpiece, and it was filling the room with all the tone and depth of a standard-size instrument.

Suddenly, however, as the utter singularity of it claimed my full attention, the tones of the piano dwindled off, and the keys came to a standstill.

Farber turned abruptly. "The music is no longer passing through your brain," he said. "The musical thought-waves have ceased, given way, I presume, to your complete surprise. You are wondering at the natural tone coming from an instrument of such small size. This is accomplished by a sound-chamber beneath the strings, made of *zyziphus* wood, an importation from central Baluchistan. A rotating light ray is sent through the sound-chamber which automatically brings the reborn tones to their proper vibration. But see if you can concentrate again. Try another composition, one of your own, if you wish, and keep your eyes on the piano."

In a moment I was intoxicated with the strangeness of it. Sitting there tensely, my palms cold with perspiration, I ran my mind through the opening strains of my own fantasy, *Satanic Dance,* and from that with a rush into the middle of Rachmaninoff's *Prelude in C Sharp Minor,* and then, not waiting an instant, into the slow tempo of a Chopin lullaby. The piano did not falter. Even as the chords entered my mind they were born into sound on the keyboard. In full obedience the instrument played a few bars of one selection, then leaped to another.

It was weird, and as I sat there I found it difficult to repress an actual shudder. Yet the moment I submitted to incredulity, and my thoughts, as a result, slipped away from the remembered music—that moment the piano, finding no stimuli, fell into a sudden silence. I saw that in order to make it continue smoothly, I must call every bit of concentration I could to mind, that I must control my thoughts to an absolute chronological succession of the notes and chords of any certain composition. To do this through an entire piece, keyed to fever pitch as I was, was almost an impossibility, and the piano consequently raced from the work of one composer to another in a mad, chaotic fashion.

At last, when it seemed I could think no more, I sank back into my chair and stared speechless at Farber. He too appeared strangely affected by the performance and for a moment said nothing. There was a deep flush of victory slowly mounting in his cheeks, and there was a wild stare of suppressed emotions in his eyes.

"You see, Bancroft," he said, "the piano proves my theory and opens a new world for research. This is only the beginning. But let me show you another feature of the instrument, the one probably that will be the greatest aid in the art of composing."

He reached for a second knob, which I had not seen before, and turned it with a snap. The piano began again, this time with no effort on my part. Then in an instant I understood. It was repeating all that it had received, playing it all a second time exactly as it had before. It was not hard to recognize the significance of this act. Once born into sound, the musical inspiration was recorded permanently, could be played as many times as one wished, and then set down on paper at leisure.

All my desire to have that machine on the table as my own personal possession burst forth within me.

"Is it for sale?" I asked hoarsely. "Will you part with it? Will you make me a duplicate? You can name your price—any price!"

He surveyed me in silence, apparently weighing his answer.

"The piano is still incomplete," he said. "There are other features, additional mechanism, I plan to add. But it will take me three weeks or more to get it ready. During that time I am willing to lend you the instrument for work on your new sonata, provided"—his lineaments hardened suddenly—"provided you will agree to one thing.

"If your composition is pronounced a success, you must declare to the world that it was conceived—from your own brain, of course—but by the sole means of this piano. You can readily see that my invention can be introduced only by a great musician. In my own hands it would be the mere recorder of simple tunes. Do you agree?"

"Yes," I said.

"Then I will have the piano expressed to your apartment early tomorrow. It is, of course, much too heavy for you to carry with you."

I nodded and followed him out of the door and through the dark hallway. At the street entrance I paused.

"May I ask," I inquired, "the nature of the mechanism you plan to add? The instrument seems very complete."

His face was a study in black and white there in the corridor's gloom. The dark eyes stared past me into the street of drizzle and fog.

"Now it is only a servant of the will," he said in a low voice. "It can only receive and bring forth what it receives into sound. Perhaps some day it may create and compose itself."

For two weeks the piano had been mine, two delirious weeks with the door of my apartment locked to the world. During that time I had worked like a creature bewitched, composing, buried deep in the ecstasy of new creative music.

During those fourteen days I brought into creation *Valse du Diable, Idyls to Martha, Mountain Caprice,* and *The March of the Cannoneers,* all of which compositions I knew to be the best I had ever accomplished. It was a tremendous amount of work, yet more than that I wove to a sublime finis the thing I had been laboring on for so many months, my *Sonata in B Flat Minor.*

As Farber had said, the repeat device of the instrument was its chief asset. There was no more toiling through the octaves, bar by bar, line by line. I let my brain run unhampered through as much of the passing fancy as I could, then turned the little second knob on the instrument panel and recorded the notes on paper as the piano repeated the strains a second, a third or a fourth time.

I became intoxicated with the spell of it. I sat there hour in and hour out, searching for a basic theme that was original. The piano's uncanny reaction to the slightest stimulus my brain chose to give it, its apparently effortless operation, affected me like drafts of old wine. Like some instrument of Satan it stood there on my library table, the little white keys leaping erratically, feverishly, from chord to chord.

And yet I lived under a distinct feeling of unease. The impression stole upon me that the piano was a living thing, that it was watching through hidden eyes my every move.

On the fifteenth day Martha returned from her visit up Cheshire way, and I hurried over to her apartment. Martha Fleming was the girl I was engaged to marry, and during her long absence from London I had almost died of lonesomeness. I had met her a year before in the course of some musical contact, a common interest in the piano bringing us together. She was an accomplished pianist herself, and I have always maintained that her rendition of Brahms was far more intelligent than my own.

I found Martha's face darkened with a troubled frown when I arrived. There was anxiety in her eyes, and when I took her in my arms, her usual joviality seemed missing.

"Martha," I said at last, "what's wrong?"

She sat staring out through the open window into the humming traffic of St. Anne's Court.

"It's Kari again," she said slowly.

"Kari?" I glanced at the door of the opposite room, but the maid was not in sight. A year ago Martha had toured and visited the various beauty spots of the West Indies. And it was somewhere in Jamaica that she had found Kari, and still living a life steeped in the black rites her slave-trade ancestors had brought from Africa.

She was an *obea* woman, a performer of *obi*, that sorcery still practiced by inland West Indian negroes, which the most rigid British law enforcement has failed to suppress. I had heard of this weird form of black magic before, had read somewhere how the unfortunate victims would fall into a morbid state which would finally terminate in a slow unexplainable death, or how the *obea* woman would reveal the events that awaited one in the future.

For some reason Martha had been attracted to Kari there in Jamaica. Her heart had gone out to the negro girl when she saw the squalor and superstition under which the poor creature was living, and when she had returned to England, she had contrived to take Kari along as her maid.

I remembered the day Martha had first brought the young dark-faced woman forward and smilingly introduced me to her. "The poor thing's life would have been a sordid thing," Martha had said. "I couldn't bear to leave her there to practice her evil worship."

But she hadn't made a perfect maid. Although Martha had drilled her in the customs of European etiquette, Kari still clung to her black background. Several times she had given in to her inborn desire for mumbled incantations, and several times she had persisted in foretelling events of the future.

In this respect, I confess my skepticism regarding such matters suffered a severe blow. On three occasions, once in my presence, the negro girl had seemed to throw herself into a trance and slowly chanted a prophecy of what lay ahead. And strangely enough, three times she had been correct almost to every detail.

"What has she told you now?" I asked Martha.

For a moment the girl who was to be my wife said nothing.

Then she sketched briefly Kari's latest psychic introspection.

At intervals during the train ride from Cheshire, the negro girl had lapsed into fits of crying and had begged Martha to exercise the utmost caution in everything she did for the next few days. The immediate future, she declared, was very black, and a terrible misfortune lay in store for both of them.

"You shouldn't let such throw-backs to superstition bother you," I said. "They mean nothing at all."

"There was a time when I would have thought the same," she answered slowly, "but you—you don't know Kari. Sometimes I almost believe *obi* to be an actual power, something fundamental and primitive which we cannot understand."

I talked to destroy her fears, and in the end we left for my apartment, where I was anxious to show her the powers of Farber's strange invention.

While we walked I enumerated the compositions I had written in the past few days and waxed enthusiastic over them separately. The strange instrument I described in detail.

Finally we reached the door of my study. I thrust it open and strode ahead toward the table. Two feet away I stopped.

The piano was gone! Only empty space on the walnut table met my eyes. For a moment I stood there, motionless, disappointment sweeping over me. Then I saw the slip of paper lying on the floor where the draft had evidently blown it, and picking it up, I read the following:

> Bancroft:
>
> I am very sorry, but the changes I have planned to include in the piano are almost ready, and I shall have to take the instrument back sooner than I expected. I trust that in the short time you have had it, you have found it the means of bringing forth some excellent compositions. If they are favorably received, remember your promise to give the piano its full credit. Possibly when the new additions are fully completed, I may permit you to operate it again.
>
> Wilson Farber.

The adventure was at an end. Those hours which had seemed

like an excerpt from the *Arabian Nights* had run to their close. Well, at least I had not wasted the opportunity. Through the instrument's powers I had finished my *Sonata in B Flat Minor*.

An urgent request that I go to Chatham Downs to the country manor of my old friend, Major Alden, and play for a group of weekend guests came early next morning. Alden was prominent behind one of the largest music-publishing houses in all Britain. To strain his friendship, if only from a monetary standpoint, would be foolhardy. I telephoned Martha and caught the first train.

Three days later, bored with an interlude of playing before an audience that thought more of cricket than of music, and horribly lonesome, I arrived back in London. But the instant I stepped into the station, tragedy fell upon me. Even after its full significance had been brought to me by the pages of the *Times* I found myself walking the streets sick with despair, helpless as to what I should do next.

The disappearance of Martha Fleming caused a furor in music circles. A member of the Saturday Musicale and the Etude Society, she had countless friends who were shocked at the thought that anything had happened to her. Scotland Yard raced to the case.

From the landlord of her apartment building I gathered only the feeblest of information. Martha had left her rooms about eight o'clock in the evening apparently bound for the little sweet shop around the corner. The landlord had noticed her exit on this evening because of the strange action of Kari, her West Indian negro maid. Scarcely had the street door closed behind Martha, he said, when the negro girl slipped stealthily down the hall and followed her.

The two of them had failed to return!

As my bewilderment slowly settled into cold reasoning I became frantic for Martha's safety. I questioned the other occupants of the building. I searched her apartment trying to find some clue. But I found nothing. Nor did Scotland Yard have any better results. Martha and her negro maid had disappeared as completely as if they had fallen into another dimension.

I paced along the night streets, searching the face of every passerby. Hopelessly I offered a reward for information as to her whereabouts.

There seemed no reason. If it had been kidnapping, there would have been a ransom note; and if murder—I shuddered— some traces of the crime. There was nothing, nothing save Kari's black prophecy to stand out in an otherwise clueless mystery.

At last one night I returned to my study, utterly discouraged.

I sat there slumped in the chair, brooding with my thoughts. Then, as if to add to my unpleasantness, came—Wilson Farber. He entered my apartment without knocking, and almost before I was aware of it, he was pushing me out of the door and into the hallway.

"I tell you I'm not interested in your piano," I said. "I don't care how much you've improved it. I have other things on my mind. Please go away and leave me alone."

"I know, Bancroft," he said. "But I must have a man who is musically trained inspect the instrument in its new form. I—"

"Get someone else then," I snapped. "You can throw the thing into the Thames for all I care."

"You are the only man I can trust, Bancroft, the only one I've told my secret. Come. It can do no harm. Perhaps it may freshen your mind and give you new vigor in continuing your search."

Almost as in a dream I permitted Farber to lead me into a waiting cab. Then once again I was gliding toward that fantastic room in Milford Lane.

I found that wild music chamber with its note decorations, aged instruments and black drapes the same as before. But I looked vainly for the midget piano. The operating-table was empty. Then, following Farber's gaze, I saw the thing.

It was mounted on a small extending shelf high up on the right wall at a point just below the ceiling. And as I looked upon it, there came that same feeling that it was watching me.

"I have placed the instrument up there," explained Farber, "because I find it is more susceptible to the thought waves if at a higher position than the level of the operator's eyes. Now your full attention, please, while I adjust its tuning."

He propped a chair against the wall, stood on it and began to turn the little dial on the instrument panel. Five seconds later I saw the little bulb within glow cherry red and the black liquid in the glass tube bubble and mount slowly upward.

"I shall leave you to yourself now," said Farber, stepping down.

He strode to the door, pulled it open, then slowly turned and faced me again. "I think, Bancroft," he said softly, "I think you will agree that the improvements I have added are very much worth while."

Moments dragged by. As before, that same sense of uneasiness, that seemed to fill the room whenever I was in the piano's presence stole over me. Mingled with it now was a curious impression that the pulsations of the liquid in the glass tube were following the rhythmic cadence of a human heart.

But suddenly I roused myself, and tried to guide my thoughts to the opening chords of my *Sonata in B Flat Minor*. The instrument was changed, eh? Well, I would operate it once more, and then I would tell Farber I was through with the thing.

Abruptly as the first strains of my sonata flashed upon my brain, the piano up on the shelf quivered and broke out into the familiar sounds. I leaned forward in my chair, that queer exhilaration rushing over me. But something was wrong. I sensed it, felt it with every nerve of my body. Something like an impalpable miasma was rising from the scarlet instrument and contaminating the air about me.

It happened without warning! For a few bars the midget piano followed my thought waves and played the sonata note for note exactly as I had composed it. Then suddenly it lapsed into silence. There was an instant's hesitation. And then with a leap downward the keys burst forth into a crash of discord. The piano began again, swung wildly into the middle of my sonata, and I stiffened in horror.

It was my sonata, yes. It was my own composition, the work which I knew to be my masterpiece, and the chords were manipulated by my own brain. But oh, how changed, how different! They were rotten with malignity; they were obscene with basic evil. Like a screech from the grave they crashed into sound, searing their way into my eardrums in grinding cacophony. My sonata, which had once been an idyllic interpretation of a peaceful sea, now shrieked at me a threnody of despair, a dirge of horror. Quivering, vibrating, the piano pounded insane harmony, defiling the composition with music of the damned.

It was diabolical—that music, befouled, sullied by every repulsive sound from the depths, played in a pitch insufferable to the human organism.

And as I sat there, the painted notes on the frescoed walls seemed to reel before my eyes in bacchanalian accompaniment. The mounted mandolins and lutes cried out in an obbligato of sympathetic vibration. On and on through the second and third movements the piano raced, faster and faster as though drunk with its power.

Trained musician though I am, with years of experience in searching through all the intricate combinations known to the laws of harmony, I was hearing now for the first time a melody from an unknown register, from unexplored octaves in black.

The third movement ended in the climax of the composition. It was here that the sonata pounded into a dramatic crescendo of booming chords, descriptive of storm waves lashing the Irish coast. And it was here that the midget piano suddenly crashed out in demoniac fury.

An instant I stood it—no longer. Then with a wild cry I was out of that chair and lunging for the door. Blindly through the gloom of the outer hall I ran.

I reached the door, leaped down the steps to the sidewalk. There I halted, trembling. My heart was pounding, my ears throbbing. And then as the silence of the deserted street gathered to soothe me I turned and began to walk slowly toward the Strand. But from behind, from the huge dark house to the rear, a sound swept through the night air to follow me. It was a laugh filled with mockery.

I spent the next day combing London once more in a determined search for Martha. I wandered through Limehouse; I visited filthy grog shops and sailors' hangouts, engaging in conversation all who were willing to talk. And I beseeched Scotland Yard to continue their hunt.

Nightfall found me plodding wearily along Essex Street, despondent after having run down the last vague rumor to a futile end. A cab-driver had reported he had driven two women, who he vaguely thought answered the description, to an address somewhere in this district. But just where, he had forgotten, and the scant information was of little value.

The fog was rolling in from the river again, thick and moist. And the darkness behind it hung close upon the yellow glare of the street lamps like a curtain.

At first I walked aimlessly. But gradually there came the impression that my steps were not altogether haphazard. I was entering a part of the city I seldom frequented.

Strangely enough, as I stopped to consider it, a distinct urge that I continue stole over me.

I was on Milford Lane, and the black bulk brooding there just ahead I recognized as number 94, the house of Wilson Farber. I shuddered as I recalled the wild events which had sent me running down those steps the night before.

There was something strangely magnetic about that dark building, something that drew me toward its portals and at the same time seemed to warn me away. And then . . .

A sound emerged from somewhere in the depths of that house, a sound that penetrated the silence of the street like a muted tocsin. It was a woman's scream. And distorted though it was, I knew that voice!

With a cry I leaped up those steps, wrenched open the door and plunged into the blackness of the inner corridor. The way before me was steeped in silence, sounding only to my footsteps.

At the far end of the hall I came upon that door leading to the music room. A pencil of light filtered under the sill, but within was dead quiet. I waited an instant, listening. Then I grasped the knob and pushed the door open. The sight that met my eyes flung me backward.

The room was dazzling in its brilliance. Farber was there, bending over the lighted operating-table in the center of the room. And upon that operating-table, stretched out as in death, lay the figure of Martha Fleming!

Exactly what happened after that I can not be sure. I remember standing there framed in the doorway, staring at Farber, who was still unaware of my presence. I remember growing suddenly sick as I saw him unfasten her dress at the throat and, bending down, mumble some words of incantation.

Then I lunged forward, leaped upon the man and struck him with every ounce of strength I could call to arm.

It was a tiger that whipped around to face me. Farber's face was contorted into a mask of rage and hate.

"So you've come, Bancroft?" he said. "Well, I expected you. Even a fool will blunder into the truth, and you had plenty of time. Had you arrived a few moments later you would have missed a very rare operation."

I seized him by the arm. "If you have harmed that girl, I'll—"

"She is in a state of hypnotic trance," he said. "But in a few moments she will be dead. I shall take her soul and—"

With a crashing blow to his jaw I closed in. Back and forth across the floor of that fantastic room we struggled, pounding each other mercilessly. There was power and physical strength in those gaunt arms, and in a moment I realized I had more than met my match.

We crashed to the floor and rolled over and over. His knee lashed out into my abdomen. And then all at once I grew faint. One of those hands seized my wrist and was slowly twisting my arm backward to the breaking point.

With a jerk he raised me from the floor higher and higher until I lay squirming in his hands two feet over his head. Then his arms shot forward, and I felt myself catapulted into space. The wall leaped to meet me; my head seemed to split open with a dull roar. A wall of flame and dancing lights broiled in my vision, and I sank into a cloud of oblivion.

I was conscious that but a few minutes had elapsed when I opened my eyes. My temple throbbed and as I struggled to rise I found that my hands and feet had been tightly lashed behind me. Two feet away stood Farber, swaying sardonically on the balls of his feet.

"I have delayed the operation for your sake, Bancroft," he said. "I knew you wouldn't have wanted to miss it."

"In God's name," I cried, "what are you going to do?"

He stared at me silently a moment, then turned and pointed high up on the wall at his right. There, on the overhanging shelf, was the midget piano.

"The piano, Bancroft," he said. "I'm going to make my dream

of ten years come true. I am going to do something no man has done before. As it stands the instrument will receive your musical thought-waves and transpose them into the actual sound. But I want it to do more than that. I want to make it compose.... Create ... play music of its own making without anyone's help."

"You're mad!"

He shrugged. "Madness? It is only a relative state. Perhaps I am mad. But if I am, so were the old alchemists of the Middle Ages. Have you ever studied alchemy, Bancroft? The learning of those sorcerers is a lost art. They made gold out of lead, and the one necessary essence of their mixture was the soul of a young maiden.

"It is obvious no cold mechanical thing could create music. No, it must be an object of warmth; must have a woman's soul. And more than that, the soul of one who has lived a life of music. Are you following me, Bancroft? Martha Fleming is such a woman."

He removed his coat and began to roll back his sleeves.

"When I lured her here by telling her you were taken suddenly ill in my apartment, I did not expect the negro maid to come along. But Kari was a most interesting person. I found to my surprise that she was an *obea* woman from the West Indies. *Obi*— an admirable system of sorcery, Bancroft. The civilized world would do well to study it. I thus had two totally different yet ideal subjects for my experiment. I tried the native girl first."

"You mean—"

"I mean that while Kari was not musically trained, her occult background made her worthy of the experiment. You perhaps noticed last night her heart pulsing in the glass tube in the piano. She—"

"You murdered her!"

"In the interests of science," he said. "The piano still would not compose, but it was no longer a cold, inanimate thing. The powers of *obi* had been woven into it. It was that that rose up and colored your sonata last night."

He stepped across to the operating-table and adjusted carefully the powerful light suspended over it.

A sense of utter helplessness swept over me. Motionless she lay there on the operating-table, face white under the glaring light.

Farber left the operating-table now and moved toward the farther wall. My eyes never left him. Directly under the shelf that held the midget piano was a built-in wall cabinet, and opening the door the bearded man drew forth a white enameled tray.

As if measured into focus, a single object took form in my vision—the midget piano up on the shelf. There was that damnable creation that had thrown me into this well of terror. There it stood, tuned to my thought-wave as on the night before. All my loathing and hatred for it rose up within me.

Then suddenly it happened! As I gazed with utter abhorrence upon it, as my concentration increased a thousandfold, the little bulb within the glass panel flared into orange brilliancy. The ivory keys trembled, and an electric shock swept through me from head to foot. An invisible bond seemed to connect my brain with that piano.

And somehow I understood. It was not music that was sweeping from my mind to the inner vitals of that instrument. *It was hate!* Hate—and the piano was reacting to it in a manner which Farber had never dared dream was within its scope. Hate—a thought-wave a thousand times more potent than any musical fancy.

Up there on the shelf the keys were trembling violently. Abruptly they came to a standstill. Then with a soul-rending thunder of discord those keys surged downward in unison. The piano shook and swayed, and the strings under the open sound-top screeched forth a chord.

Farber, at the wall cabinet directly beneath, stared with astonishment. The tray of knives slipped from his hand and clattered to the floor.

The chord passed on, and there came now from somewhere within the piano's sides a low, humming sound, as of a distant electric motor.

Louder and louder, growing into a subdued roar, it filled the room. The ivory keys began again, quivered in rotation down the octaves. Back and forth in trembling vibration the instrument swayed, rocked on its hard-rubber base.

And then—a single repercussion burst forth from the bowels of that piano. To the edge of the shelf the piano toppled, hung there, the strings screeching that symphony of horror.

Farber came to life too late. With one mad lunge he sought to throw himself out of the instrument's reach.

The piano fell. Straight toward that upturned bearded face it hurtled—struck with a sickening thud. There was a single shriek of agony, a rending of wood and broken bone, and I turned my eyes away.

It is Martha, not I, who remembers the happenings of the next few moments. The death of Farber released her from her hypnotic trance. She came to her senses slowly, looked about her as if awakening from some wild dream, and then stumbled from the operating-table. It was she who released me from my bonds. Then we passed out the door and through the black corridor to the street. I looked back when I reached the walk.

There was that huge disproportionate building with the three bulging colonnades rising to form a claw of granite before the black facade. There were the dark eye-like windows staring sullenly.

I passed my arm around Martha, and led her gently toward the Strand.

The Last Drive

It was a cold wind that whipped across the hills that November evening. There was snow in the air, and Jeb Waters in the cab of his jolting van shivered and drew the collar of his sheepskin higher about the throat. All day endless masses of white cumulus cloud had raced across a cheerless sky. They were gray now, those clouds, leaden gray, and so low-hanging they seemed to lie like a pall on the crest of each distant hillock. Off to the right, stern and majestic, like a great parade of H. G. Wells' Martian creatures, marched the towers of the Eastern States Power lines, the only evidence here of present-day civilization. A low humming whine rose from the taut wires now as the mounting wind twanged them in defiance.

Through the windshield Jeb Waters scanned the sky anxiously.

"It's going to be a cold trip back," he muttered to himself. "Looks mighty like a blizzard startin'."

He gave the engine a bit more gas and tightened his grasp on the wheel as a sharper curve loomed up suddenly before him. For a time he drove in silence, his mind fixed only on the barrenness of the hills on all sides. Marchester lay thirty miles ahead, thirty long, rolling miles. Littleton was just behind. If there were going to be a storm, perhaps it would be wise to return and wait until morning before making the trip. It would be bad to get stuck out here tonight, especially with the kind of load he was delivering. Enough to give one the creeps even in the daytime.

Marchester with its few hundred souls, hopelessly lost in the hills, too small or perhaps too lazy to incorporate itself, had been passed by without a glance when the railroad officials distributed spurs leading from the main line. As a result all freight had to be trucked thirty miles across the country from Littleton, the nearest town on trackage. But there wasn't much freight, as the officials had suspected, and although Jeb Waters drove the distance only twice a week, he rarely returned with more than a single package.

Today, however, the load had stunned him with its importance. In the van, back of him, separated by only the wooden wall of the cab, lay a coffin, and in that coffin was the body of Philip Carr, Marchester's most promising son. Philip Carr—Race Carr they had called him because he was such a driving fool—was the only man who could have brought the town to fame. With his queer-looking Speed Empress, the racing-car which was a product of his own invention and three years' work, he had hoped to lower the automobile speed record on the sand track of Daytona Beach, Florida. He had clocked an unofficial 300 miles an hour in a practice attempt, and the world had sat up and taken notice.

On the fatal day, however, a tire had failed to stand the centrifugal force, and in a trice the car had twisted itself into a lump of steel. Philip Carr had been instantly killed. There was talk of burying him in Florida, but Marchester, his home town, had absolutely refused. And so the body had been shipped back to Littleton, the nearest point on rails, and Jeb Waters had been sent to bring it from there to Marchester.

Jeb hadn't liked the idea. There was nothing to be afraid of, he knew, but somehow when he was alone in these Rentharpian Hills, even though he had known no other home since a child, he always felt depressed and anxious for companionship. A coffin would hardly serve to ease his mind.

The wind was mounting steadily, and now the first swirls of snow began to appear. The cab of the van was anything but warm. A corner of the windshield was broken out, and the rags Jeb had stuffed in the hole failed to keep out the cold.

Premature darkness had swooped down under the lowering clouds, and Jeb turned on the lights. The van was a very old one, and the lights worked on the magneto. As the snow became thicker and thicker, Jeb was forced to reduce his speed, and the lights, deprived of the most of their current, dimmed to only a low dismal glow, illuminating but little of the road ahead.

Yet the miles rolled slowly by. The snow was piling in drifts now. It rolled across the hills, a great sweeping blanket of white and swirled like powder through the crevices of the cab. And it was growing colder.

Frome's Hill, the steepest rise on the road, loomed up abruptly, and Jeb roared the rickety motor into a running start. The van lurched up the ascent, back wheels spinning in the soft snow, seeking traction. The engine hammered its protest. The transmission groaned as if in pain. Up, up climbed the truck until at length it reached the very top.

"Now it's clear sailing," said Jeb aloud.

But he had spoken too soon. With a sigh as if the feat had been too great, the motor lapsed into sudden silence. The lights blinked out, and there was only the gray darkness of the hills and the swishing of the snow on the sides of the cab.

For a full moment Jeb sat there motionless as the horror of the situation fell upon him. Snowbound with a corpse! Twenty miles from the nearest habitation and alone with a coffin! A cold sweat burst out on his forehead at the realization of the predicament.

But he was acting like a child. It was ridiculous to let his nerves run away with him like that. If he could only keep from freezing there would be no danger. In the morning when it was found he hadn't reached Marchester the people would send help. Probably Ethan would come. Old Ethan. He would come in that funny sleigh of his. And he would say:

"Well Jeb, howdja like spending the night with a dead 'un?"

And then they would both laugh and drive back to town.... But that was tomorrow. Tonight there was the storm—and the corpse.

He set the spark, got out, and cranked the engine. But he did it half-heartedly. He knew by the tone of the engine when it had stopped that it would be a long time before it would resume revolutions.

At length he resigned himself to his plight, returned to the cab and tried to keep warm. But the cab was old and badly built. The wind blew through chinks and holes in great drafts, and snow sifted down his neck. It suddenly occurred to him that the back part of the van, which had been repaired recently, would give better protection against the blizzard than the cab. There were robes back there too, robes used to keep packages from being broken. If only the coffin weren't there! One couldn't sleep next to a coffin.

Another thought followed. Why not put the coffin in the cab? There was nothing else in the van, and he would then have the back of it to himself. He could lie down too and with the robes manage to keep warm somehow.

In a moment his mind was made up, and he set about to accomplish his task. It was hard, slow work. The coffin was heavy, the cab small and the steering-post in the way. Finally by shoving it in end up he managed it successfully, and then going to the back of the van, he went in, closed the door, rolled up like a ball in the robes and lay down to sleep.

Sleep proved elusive. He stirred restlessly, listening to the sounds of the storm. Occasionally the truck trembled as a stronger gust of wind struck it. Occasionally he could hear the mournful Eolian whine of the power lines. Powdery snow rustled along the roof of the van. And the iron exhaust pipe cracked loudly as the heat left it. Minutes dragged by, slowly, interminably.

And then suddenly Jeb Waters sat bolt upright. Whether or not he had dozed off into a fitful sleep he did not know, but at any rate he was wide awake now.

The van was moving! He could hear the tires crunching in the snow, could feel the slight swaying as the car gained momentum. He leaped to his feet and pressed his eyes against the little window that connected the back of the van with the cab.

For a moment he saw nothing. A strip of black velvet seemed pasted before the glass. Then the darkness softened. A soft glow seemed to form in the cab, and vaguely he seemed to see the figure of a man hunched over the wheel in the driver's position.

The van was going faster now. It creaked and swayed, and the wheels rumbled hollowly. Yet strangely enough there was no sound of the engine. Jeb hammered on the little pane of glass.

"Hey!" he cried. "Get away from that wheel! Stop!"

The figure seemed not to hear. With his hands grasping the wheel tightly, elbows far out, shoulders hunched low, he appeared aware of nothing but the dark road ahead of him. Faster and faster sped the van.

Frantically Jeb rammed his clenched fist through the window. The glass broke into a thousand fragments.

"Do you hear?" he cried. "Stop, blast you! Stop!"

The man turned and leered at him. Even in the half-glow Jeb recognized the features—that deathly white face, the black glassy eyes.

"Oh, my God," he screamed. *"It's Philip Carr!"* His voice rose to a hysterical laughing sob. His hands trembled as he clutched the careening walls, striving to keep his balance.

"Philip Carr," he shouted. "You're dead. You're dead, do you hear? You can't drive any more."

A horrible gurgling laugh came from the man at the wheel. The figure bent lower as if to urge the van to a greater speed. And the van answered as if to a magic touch. On it raced into the storm, rocking and swaying like a thing accursed. Snow whirled past in great white clouds. The wind howled in fanatical accompaniment.

Suddenly with a lurch the van left the road and leaped toward the blacker shadows of a gully. A giant tree, its branches gesticulating wildly in the wind, reared up just ahead.

There came a crash!

* * * *

"It's odd," said the coroner, and frowned.

Old Ethan scratched his chin.

"It 'pears," he said, "as if that danged van engine went and stopped right on the top of that hill. Then Jeb, he musta gone into the back of the van to keep warm, and durin' the night the wind started the thing a-rollin'. It come tearin' down the hill, jumped into this here gully and ran smash agin the tree. That's the way I figure it. Poor old Jeb!"

"Yes," replied the coroner, "but there doesn't seem to be the slightest injury on Jeb's body. Apparently he died of heart failure. And the corpse of Philip Carr! . . . The crash might have ripped open the coffin. But that doesn't explain why the body although set in rigor mortis is in a sitting position. The way his arms are extended, it looks almost as though he were driving once more."

The Spectral Pistol

As I look back, my friendship with Hugh Trevellan seems to have been inevitable. Our ages were near, we were both bachelors, and our avocational interests were much the same. Instilled deeply in both of us was that fascination for art and craftsmanship that has been mellowed and made attractive by time.

I had gone in for books, and my shelves were filled with rare volumes, the result of years of collecting and considerable expense. But Trevellan had done his browsing along a different line. I remember the night Major Lodge brought us together.

"Idiot, meet idiot," he had introduced jokingly. "You two must know each other.

"The antique bug has got you both. McKay here knows all there is to know about books, and Trevellan's case of pistols would make a gunsmith turn green with envy."

"Pistols?" I had repeated, shaking the thin hand and scrutinizing the gaunt form before me.

And Hugh Trevellan had smiled. His pale blue eyes twinkled pleasantly. "Yes," he replied, "revolvers of all kinds: wheel-locks, flint-locks, muzzle-loaders, and even those absurd modern automatics. Would you care to see them?"

It is strange how inborn in every man is the collecting instinct. I have heard that even a savage will hoard colored pebbles, and I know that as a boy my greatest disappointment came when I lost my book of foreign stamps. Trevellan's pistols were his life. He stood before their heavy mahogany case and admired them at least once every day. He dusted them. He polished their scroll-work. And he searched constantly for more.

There were, in truth, a masterly assortment. Ranging from the earliest mid-Fourteenth Century hand-cannon on the top shelf to a modern long-barreled Luger automatic on the bottom, the case displayed all the gradual developments conceived by man in the making of light fire-arms.

"This one I picked up only yesterday at the Meldrow sales," said Trevellan, taking out one of the weapons. "It's an Italian Snaphaunce pistol, and I'm not sure yet whether it's forgery, though I paid a price for it. Here are a pair of flint-locks by Lazarino Comminazzo. Note the double-necked hammers. This is an old arquebus, and this a French wheel-lock with the royal shield in gilt and damascened with gold."

Even my books on which I had prided myself for so long seemed to fade and lose some of their glamour as I stared down upon these beautiful relics. I said as much to Trevellan, and he smiled graciously.

"I should like to see your books," he replied. "I have a few volumes on munitions that are rather old, but from a standpoint of binding or edition I'm afraid they are of little importance. Unfortunately I'm leaving for the country tomorrow, so I'll have to postpone the visit."

"How long are you going to stay?"

He shrugged. "Rented a secluded place down Arronshire way, and I may stay all summer. Doctor's orders, you know. Says I'm all on edge and need solitude. It'll be a miserable nuisance, but still I don't mind. I can finish a paper on Scotch pistols I started a month ago. But say . . . why not motor down and stay a fortnight or so? We could have a royal time."

Early in July, when my business permitted, I had "motored down," but I had cut my stay short and actually breathed a sigh of relief when I was back in Bloomsbury. Why? The reason is hardly a tangible one. And yet now, seen retrospectively, it seems a psychic warning of what was to follow.

I found Arronshire a district quite distinct and separate from its neighbors, both from a philologist's and a cartographer's point of view. The people were a rough, burly type, and the characteristic voice inflection was harsh and unpleasant. The country was extremely wild and rugged. And a general air of neglect seemed to pervade everywhere. The hedges had grown rank and untrimmed. Road markings had fallen to decay, bridges rattled ominously as my car rolled over them, and the villages seemed to shrink back despondently as I passed.

For a solid two miles the lane which led to the manor was lined with gnarled old apple trees. But it was the sign on the post-box that drew me up short. "Blueker House," it read. "Ludwig Blueker, Undertaker."

The house was one of those monstrosities of the Victorian age, ornate and sadly in want of paint. The lawn before it was overrun with weeds, and a general air of neglect was over all.

"How do you like it?" Trevellan hailed from the veranda.

"Why on earth don't you take away that undertaker's sign?" I replied in question. "This place is about as cheerful as a grave-yard."

He had moved into the house furnished, bringing with him a single trunk and, of course, his beloved pistols. The weapon case he had placed by the big bay window, opening on the front lawn. The huge mahogany cabinet seemed strangely out of place there, and so did Trevellan himself. As I sat across from him, his delicate face glowed in the lamplight like tinted wax, and I could not help thinking of an old painting, a portrait of a French court-ier that hung in my rooms.

But while I could not point my finger at any one feature of the house that was in itself distasteful, there was something utterly somber and depressing about the architecture that crushed all buoyancy of feeling and left me in a state of deep melancholia. I stayed only two days, then headed back for London.

The rest of the summer passed with only an occasional letter from Trevellan. He had grown accustomed to the solitude, he said, and was really enjoying his convalescence. August dragged into September, and his letters grew fewer, and finally stopped altogether.

Then one day in Charing Cross I stumbled upon a book that brought Trevellan back to mind. It was an old volume, once finely bound, with the title, *Historie of Certayne Small Fire Arms*, stenciled deeply in a brass plate on the cover. It contained some exquisite colored drawings of old pistols. I knew how eagerly my friend would welcome the sight of such a work.

Accordingly, the next day I headed toward Arronshire and

Hugh Trevellan. A week before, the countryside had been a mael-strom of autumn color, but now, as I drove along, I found only a graveyard of naked trees and drab bracken. The strong winds which had whipped in from the south during the past few days had removed every leaf, the advance warning of an early winter.

By nightfall I was nearing the manor. Again, as in early summer, I felt an increasing heaviness of spirit as I entered the district. Black storm clouds were pouring into the sky when I reached the village of Darset. Dust and old leaves swirled into the car, and a drop of rain spattered on the windshield. But my attention was drawn to the state of general excitement which had seized the townfolk.

Knots of them stood in the light of shop windows, talking ear-nestly. Several rickety cars tore by, loaded with men armed with hunting-rifles. And in the doorway of one house several persons were trying to console a woman who was crying bitterly.

"What's wrong?" I asked the garage man, as he began filling my car with petrol.

"Wolves," he replied, and looked frightened as he said it.

"Wolves," I told him rather coldly, "have been extinct in England since the Fifteenth Century."

He looked at me queerly and spilled a quart of petrol on the mudguards. "Have they, sir?" he said. "Then it's a wild dog it must be, or something worse."

"Did it attack somebody?"

The man's hand shook as he took the money. "That's what it did, sir. Carried off the widow Chase's youngest, the sweetest girl you've ever seen."

I stared. "You mean a wild dog actually killed a child?"

"And she's not the first, sir. Only a fortnight ago, Johnny, the cobbler's son, was taken from almost under his mother's eyes. It comes at night, alone, a big, gray brute, with fiery eyes, they say. Jeff Twillger took a shot at him from his bedroom window. Jeff can hit a shilling every time from here to that tree, but he missed. A reward be posted too: fifty pounds for the man who brings in his pelt. I'll be bringin' down my gun, I think. It's nice earnin's."

I took note of the threatening heavens now, and with the garage man's help, put up the tonneau top of the car. The distant rolling of thunder was in my ears as I headed down the winding road, and the headlights showed the rain coming down in earnest. In a quarter of an hour the road was in bad condition, and I was forced to reduce speed.

I came to Blueker House lane at last and the next moment was shaking hands with Hugh Trevellan.

The house looked even gloomier than before, but when my friend offered me a glass of Liebfraumilch, I was almost glad I had come.

"It *is* good wine," agreed Trevellan. "It was left here by the old Austrian who formerly owned the place. He died, you know, and the house was offered completely furnished. I saw the ad and leased it before even seeing it. Not so bad, eh?"

I smiled and set down my glass. "I've got something to show you," I said, reaching for my grip-sack.

He was up and out of his chair at that with the exuberance of a child suddenly reminded of a toy. "And I've got something to show you."

He stepped quickly to his pistol case and returned with an oblong box of tarnished silver. Placing it on the table before me, he opened it and stood back proudly. "The masterpiece of them all," he said. "And where do you think I found it? In Darset, of all places."

Resting on its cushion of dark velvet, gleaming in the lamplight, was a beautiful long-barreled pistol. The butt was made of ivory, yellowed now like an ancient cameo, and adorned with an intricate network of silver filigree. Mosaic inlays formed queer designs above the trigger, and the barrel, which was trim and graceful as a poised lance, glittered with engraved gold spirals. A small gold cross was upraised at one end. But it was the hammer that attracted my attention. Of blackened steel, it had been fashioned into a perfect death's-head.

"Isn't it a beauty?" Trevellan said, leaning over my shoulder.

"And you bought it in Darset?" I said, unbelievingly.

He smiled in delight. "By a sheer piece of luck. It belonged to one of the villagers, and when he found I was interested in old weapons, he offered to sell it to me. I gave him twice what he asked."

I took the pistol from its case and fondled it. "Italian?"

Trevellan frowned. "You've got me there. I really don't know what it is. I don't believe it's Italian, and nothing about it suggests the Germanic. The man said it had been in his family for years."

We lit our pipes after that, and Trevellan went into a lengthy dissertation on the artistry of ancient weapons in general. At length I brought out the book which had really been the incentive for my visit. Trevellan thumbed through its pages carefully and looked a long time at the illustrations.

"It's an excellent work," he said. "I—"

His voice trailed off; his eyes suddenly riveted themselves on the book. With a low exclamation he pushed the table lamp nearer the printed page.

"Look here, McKay," he cried hoarsely. "Read this."

The volume was turned to the chapter, Early Eighteenth Century, and in the center of the page I read the following paragraph:

"The moste skillful worke of the master craftsmanne, Johann Stiffter of Prague, was a holstre pistol made for a subject of England, Sir William Kingston, in the yeare of our Lord, 1712. This weapon was fashioned in certayne unusual ways, being made to fire a silver bullet, being blessed by seven priests with holy water, and having the crucifix carved upon the barrel. Sir William, it was said, was wont to travel often in the southerne countrys, and while on one of his journeys was attacked by werewolves and other daemons. The witch-wolves, who were really human creatures in league with Satan, carried off his little daughter, Julie, and left Sir William sore hurte. Whereupon the Englishmanne swore vengeance upon all like fiends of hell and ordered the pistol made, combining all knowne methods by which they could be killed."

And following these startling words came an illustration and a detailed description of none other than the ivory pistol Trevellan had shown me only a short while before.

There was no mistaking the fact. No pistol of similar craftsmanship could have been created. But there was one way to prove absolutely its authenticity. The description mentioned five words carved upon the weapon by the gunsmith: *Tod dem Wehr-wolf schwöre Ich* (Death to the Werewolf I swear).

"Have you a magnifying glass?" I asked Trevellan. And then I stared as I saw my friend's consternation. The man was almost beside himself. His hands were opening and closing convulsively; his face had grown white, and a strange frightened look had stolen into his eyes. He got up, swaying.

"There's one here some place. I'll—I'll see if I can find it."

A moment later we were scrutinizing the pistol through the glass. Tiny lettering appeared on the barrel.

"There it is!" I cried. "It's the same pistol."

There was no answer. I turned and stared at Trevellan. He was leaning heavily against the table, lips twitching. Abruptly he seized the pistol from my hands, thrust it back in its box and replaced it in the mahogany case.

"Are you ill?" I said.

"Yes," he replied jerkily. "I—I feel a bit faint. That long walk I took today must have done me up. If you don't mind, I think I'll go to bed."

I nodded and regarded him curiously as he left the room. What on earth had come over the man? He had been perfectly normal until reading that paragraph about the pistol. I lit my pipe and sat there, musing over his strange actions. And as the tobacco smoke drifted ceilingward, I suddenly became aware of the storm again.

The rain was swishing against the big bay window now. Thunder boomed steadily overhead as if some giant rolling-pin were being moved back and forth across the roof.

For a time I was content to sit there, listening to the wild night so near, yet so far. But as my mind began a train of thought suggested by that queer paragraph, a decided sense of unease came over me.

Werewolves! What strange horrors man will mentally create for himself. It was a queer belief, this idea that a man will adopt a taste for human blood and will change into a lower animal, a wolf, to obtain it. Stranger still the legend that holy water, the sight of the crucifix, or a silver bullet will kill such a demon. And yet I knew such superstitions were still current in south Europe.

Suddenly my pipe slipped from my teeth, and I sat bolt

upright. The words of the garage man in Darset suddenly flashed back to me. He had spoken of a wolf or wild dog that had entered the town and made off with a child on two separate occasions.

I tried vainly to ward off the absurd question that was stealing into my brain. Might not this big gray brute be a werewolf? I forced a laugh. But the thought persisted, and more details arose to defeat my better judgment.

Was it not true that wolves had been extinct in England since the Fifteenth Century? Yes, of course; but the beast might have been a wild dog. But if it were a wild dog, would there not be some record of its once being tame? I frowned. Not necessarily. The animal might have come from a distance, left there by its owner when he had vacated. But still a wild dog would make for the poultry coops. No matter how long it had been wild, human flesh would be repugnant to it, would it not? I stared into the bowl of my pipe. To this question I could offer no answer at all.

A shelf of books on the other side of the room caught my eyes, and thinking perhaps to steer my mind into more pleasant channels I crossed over and let my gaze pass along the titles. I saw with astonishment that all of the two dozen volumes dealt with lycanthropy, sorcery, black art, and the occult. Richard Verstegan's *Restitution of Decayed Intelligence*, strange names of long-dead authors, rare works whose publication had been banned by God-fearing people lay there on the shelf before me. There was Le Loyer's *Book of Spectres*, the sixth edition of *De Praestigies Daemonun et Incantationibus*, printed at Basle, and that hellish writing of Milo Calument, *I Am a Werewolf*, all copies of which I remembered were supposed to have been cast in Hoxton marsh.

It was odd that Trevellan had not mentioned these books to me when he knew nothing could have delighted me more. And it was odd, I suddenly thought, that Trevellan should be reading them himself. One would find nothing in the line of pistols in these pages.

But when I looked at one of the volumes I found the reason. They were not Trevellan's property. They belonged to Ludwig Blueker, the former resident of the house, as attested by the name scrawled on the flyleaf. Yet the books had not passed Trevellan's notice. Throughout the pages I found queer notations in his writing. There was no mistaking his peculiar scrawl.

One particular group of sentences caught my eye. It read:

"July 31. I followed all the rituals tonight and found that I have the power. I can hardly realize it, but it's true. Something seemed to draw me toward the village, but I dared not venture from the grounds. One must grow accustomed to such a terrific change."

Far back in my brain a lurking suspicion was beginning to grow, and I thumbed through the pages for more notations. But beyond a few meaningless jumbles of words, the rest was in Latin, which I did not understand.

Puzzled, I made my way up the stairs to my bedroom, undressed and went to bed.

Sleep has always come readily in my life, yet now with the rain surging at the windows, and the lightning flares drawing drunken shadows along the wall, I lay awake, listening to the slow ticking of the hall clock.

Midnight came with the slow striking of the clock chimes. And then I heard the door of Trevellan's bedroom creak open and footsteps pass softly down the hall. I sat up. I slipped to the door, opened it a crevice and peered out.

A dim nightlight burned at the far end of the hall. In its feeble glow I saw Trevellan, fully dressed, moving toward the staircase. But his actions were not those of a man in his own home. He was skulking forward, stopping every few steps to listen carefully. As he reached the first stair I caught a glimpse of his face.

A wild, insane look contorted his features. The eyes bulged in their sockets; the mouth sagged downward in an empty grin. For an instant he stared unseeingly toward my door; then he began to descend.

For a moment I knelt there, staring into empty darkness, my mind whirling madly. Had the man been sleepwalking? But there was nothing of the somnambulist in Trevellan's actions. Where then was he going stealing out of his house like a hunted criminal?

On impulse I darted down the stairs, ripped open the door. A sheet of rain slapped my face. The grounds loomed dark before me. Then a fork of lightning streaked down from the heavens, and I saw it. Bounding along the path, heading toward the road was a great gray dog-shaped wolf! It turned in that instant of electrical flash, and the sight of those fiendish, fiery eyes was something I would never forget.

Then darkness returned, and for many moments I stood there, motionless. Chilled, I slowly returned to my room, sank into a chair by the window and watched the rain trickle down the glass. Questions unanswerable pounded at my brain.

Hours dragged by, and gradually I lapsed into a fitful slumber.

When I awoke the gray dawn was stealing into my room. The wind had gone, and outside the water puddles lay motionless, like strips of iron under the leaden sky. All was strangely still. Through the open casement came the smell of wet earth and moldering leaves.

I listened. From far off in the direction of the village came a long mournful howl. Again it sounded, louder, more distinct. Years before I had heard such a cry when I had ridden through Royalwoods in pursuit of the fox. But it was not the baying of hounds I heard now. It was the cry of a wolf, and it was approaching the manor at lightning speed.

Fists clenched, I waited. And then a moment later it bounded into sight directly beneath my window. A feeling of loathing swept over me as my gaze fell on that gray shaggy body. The wolf looked around with a snarl, then moved out of my sight toward the other side of the house.

An interval of silence, and then I heard the door unlatch softly. Footsteps sounded on the carpeted stairs. I strode across the room, opened the door.

Hugh Trevellan was entering the hall. No longer was he skulking as though afraid of being seen. He was erect now, and he turned and cast a last look over his shoulder before entering his room.

Suddenly a giddy sensation rose within me. A scream gurgled unsounded to my lips. I had seen the mouth, the lips of Trevellan in that instant before he entered his room, and God help me, they were slobbered with thick red blood!

Those intervening hours until I stumbled down to breakfast were an eternity. When I sat down at the table my hands were trembling perceptibly.

"Good morning, McKay," Trevellan said. "Hope you had a good night's sleep in spite of the storm."

The silky satisfaction of the man sent a wave of nausea through me. But he did not seem to notice the fact that I made no reply. Keeping up a steady conversation, he laughed and joked, and I could not help thinking his actions were those of a man living the after effect of a powerful drug.

I studied him closely as he sipped his tea. His cheeks glowed with a brightness of almost super-health. And yet he seemed to have changed. Not greatly. The features were the same and the pale, blue eyes still gave him that look of doll-like fragility. But about his head there were certain alterations that destroyed the classic moulding I had always admired. The ears were more prominent, longer and pointed in shape. The nose, I'm sure, was larger, with dilated nostrils.

"Trevellan," I said when breakfast was over, "who was Ludwig Blueker?"

He frowned. "The former owner of the manor," he replied. "Shall we go for a walk down the road a bit?"

"I know he was the former owner," I said as we went out the door, "but was he a farmer or an undertaker?"

"Both, I believe," Trevellan answered. "He eked out a mean existence from the soil, and he made a few pounds now and then by doing the occasional funeral work for the people of Darset."

It was plain that Trevellan did not care to discuss the matter with me further.

"I was looking at some of his books last night," I said, "and what a collection! Blueker must have been a superstitious fool!"

Trevellan turned on me almost with a snarl.

"He was a great man," he cried. "Those villagers laughed at him because he preferred to stay in solitude and study things which they could not understand. Blueker took years to gather those books."

We were nearing the end of the lane now, weaving our way in and out among the pools of water. Emerging on the post road, we drew up as two men on horseback clattered up beside us.

"Good mornin'," said the nearest, a tall fellow I remembered seeing in the village.

"But a wet, chilly one."

He nodded. "You haven't been seeing a wolf or wild dog about, have ye?" The voice was stern and filled with determination.

I could feel myself swaying slightly. "It didn't attack someone in Darset again?"

He shifted in his saddle. "It did. Broke into a house last night. It's getting more courage every time. The mothers be watching their children like hawks today, and there's ten parties out hunting the brute."

"How many last night?" I waited his reply with an inner terror.

"Two. The Jepson twins. It's 'orrible, sir."

"If he comes around here," I said, "he'll leave his pelt."

The man smiled grimly. "There'll be a hundred pounds in it if ye do, sir. And the personal thanks of every mother in Darset."

He dug his knees into the horse's flank, and the two of them rode off at a fast trot.

Trevellan stared at me dumbly. The jovial mood had left him, and in its place was a look of unmistakable fear.

"I—I think we'd better be getting back," he said. "I've got some writing to do."

In Blueker House once again Trevellan excused himself and went to his room. Left alone, I wandered into the library.

The moment I entered that chamber I felt the presence of some unseen power! Like a great lodestone I felt myself drawn toward Trevellan's pistol case. As I stood there, gazing through the glass doors, a single object centered into my vision: the silver box that contained Trevellan's latest ivory pistol.

Impulsively I opened the case and took out the weapon. The sight of that relic there affected me like old wine. I turned it over and over, but I offer no explanation for what I did a moment later. In slots on the velvet-lined box lay the weapon's charge, three silver bullets, and loading equipment. Hesitating a moment I picked up one of the silver balls, inserted it in the gun and poured in powder from the little horn. I rammed the charge home. Then with an effort I replaced the weapon in the mahogany case.

Not until it was quite dark outside did Trevellan come downstairs.

"I'm sorry, McKay," he said, "but I've got to go to the village.

You'll find some cold food in the kitchen. I may be back late, so don't wait up for me."

The door slammed, and his footsteps died away on the gravel.

And then a slow feeling of dread rose up within me. I fell to pacing the room nervously. Outside a flotilla of velvet clouds was creeping across the sky, but off to the east a darker blot glowed with a soft radiance where the moon was trying to break through.

More hours snailed past; the ticking of the pendulum clock pounded through the rooms like the blows of a mallet. Stranger than before came that strange psychic urge to open again Trevellan's gun case and take into my hands that ivory pistol.

Then suddenly there floated to my ears a far-off ringing sound. I listened. It came from the direction of the village, swept forward by a wind, a deep bong, bong that penetrated every corner of the manor like a tocsin. The blood rushed to my head. It was a tocsin! They were ringing it to awaken the village. The horror had begun!

And as I listened, another sound rose over the bell—the long wailing cry of a wolf.

I stood by the big bay window, staring out into the grounds. The moon rode in and out through thick clouds. Giant disproportionate shadows staggered across the lawn.

Abruptly the clouds parted, and I saw the beast in the full light of the moon. It was the wolf, and its mouth was smeared crimson.

A scream rose to my lips. I felt myself turn like a puppet on a wire. My gaze centered on the weapon case, and its magnetic lure increased a hundredfold. An inner power, a psychic will drew me toward it.

My hands moved forward. I opened the glass door.

"Trevellan!" I cried. "Trevellan! Go back!"

The wolf stopped short and peered upward. Like lightning my hand leaped to the case. My fingers closed over the ivory pistol, snatched it from its velvet mounting. My thumb reached for the death's-head hammer, pulled it to full cock. My forefinger tightened on the trigger.

"Trevellan!" I cried. "Good God, I can't help myself!"

There was a crashing report. Glass shattered and fell to the floor. From out on the lawn below me came a hoarse cry of pain.

Then I was released. Turning, I flung the pistol to a far corner, raced out into the grounds. I found him there, sprawled on the grass, his shirt marked with a growing circle of red. He rose up as I lifted his head in my arms.

"Thanks, McKay," he said, his voice a whisper. "It was—it was the only way."

He fell back with a sigh, and I was alone with the corpse of Hugh Trevellan.

On October second, the evening edition of the *London Chronicle* published the following item:

"Reports of an unfortunate tragedy in north Arronshire, near the village of Darset, were made known today by police of the district. The body of Mr. Hugh Trevellan, noted antiquarian and authority on ancient firearms, was found in his summer home by a close friend, Mr. Martin McKay of Russel Square, Bloomsbury, who had come from London to visit him. After examining the body, the district doctor expressed the opinion that death had come accidentally when a weapon Mr. Trevellan was cleaning was discharged. The bullet, curiously, was found to be made of silver."

Sagasta's Last

The package arrived on the fifteenth of August. I had given Martin Crade's West-Starling house as a forwarding address on my departure from London, but I had instructed my servant to trouble me with only imperative communications.

In this case the servant had acted with full appreciation for my avocational whims. The package was from the Bristol Optical Company, Southampton, and it contained a three foot, thirty-power telescope, for which I had paid the sum of twelve pounds.

There was an accompanying letter which somewhat detracted from my expectations.

It read:

> Dear Mr. Brockton:
>
> In response to your order for one of our French LeGare scopes, we are sorry to inform you that our supply of this glass has been exhausted. We are substituting on approval a sample telescope of similar measurements which is not a part of our general line.
>
> This scope was manufactured by Jose Sagasta, the well known optician of Lisbon, and represents the last of his work before his death. We sincerely hope the product will meet with your approval.
>
> Bristol Optical Co., Ltd.

Martin Crade took the letter as I handed it to him, read it casually and tossed it to the table.

"Still at it, eh, Brockton? You must have three dozen of the things by now. What do you do with them?"

I smiled. "Collect them. The science of optics is really a fascinating one. And all of my glasses aren't telescopes," I went on.

"I have a pair of stero-prism binoculars which are just about as perfect as modern science can make them. I have a Seventeenth Century Lippershey, a—"

Martin Crade wasn't listening. He crossed to a chair and slumped into it with an air of boredom. Crade was like that, unemotional, self-centered. Tall and thin, with a hawk face and a shock of black hair, there was a sinister something about his eyes that seemed to penetrate to the depths of one's soul. I knew I could expect but the briefest hospitality from him.

Crade had married my sister Louise a year before. Always delicate, Louise had steadily languished in the gloom of this West-Starling moor country. I had feared for her health and stood out against the marriage from the beginning. But her infatuation had known no barriers.

Even the appeals of her childhood sweetheart, young Clay Stewart, had fallen on unheeding ears. After a hurried wedding and a trip through France, she had taken up her residence in this house. And then on January last, suddenly and without warning, Crade had written me of her illness and death.

It was primarily, therefore, to cherish my sister's memory that I had accepted his invitation to visit him during the last part of August.

Yet all the way from London I had looked toward my destination with a sense of foreboding. Twice before I had been here, and then as now I had been utterly depressed by the bleak moor on all sides.

Dinner over, Crade showed me to my room on the second floor.

"I'm afraid you'll have to amuse yourself, Brockton," he said. "I'm a solitary sort of person and a devil of a poor host. But if you want anything, let me know."

Like the rest of the house, my chamber was painfully severe, with dark and heavy furnishings. Overlooking the south sweep of the moor were two French windows, opening onto a small balcony.

At the sight of that balcony I nodded in satisfaction. I took up the telescope and stepped outside. I placed the tube to my eye and focused it.

Dusk had not yet fallen, and the heath below extended from horizon to horizon, the dark moor-grass undulating like water in the chill wind. For several minutes I looked through that scope, moving it from left to right. Then I lowered it with a frown of disappointment.

The 31mm. achromatic objective lens was strong and clear, but something was wrong with the instrument. I got the impression that a whitish blur was fogging the vision somewhere near the limit of the range.

Dusting the glass, I tried again. When at length I returned to the inner room I was puzzled.

Turned to the west, to the south, the telescope revealed only the monotonous stretches of the moor. But to the east something focused itself in the lens that defied explanation. It was as if a compact wall of white fog hung there, a tall surface like the front of a ruined building.

Yet it was past that spot I had walked on my way from the village. I was positive no structure of any kind was there.

A quarter of an hour later I heard Crade leave his room and descend to the floor below. But when I came upon him in the library and told him what I had seen, he could offer no explanation.

"To the east? No, Brockton, you must be mistaken. My house is quite alone here. The nearest building of any kind is at Glover, and since the village lies in the depression of the river, you couldn't possibly see it."

"And there are no chalk cliffs, no Roman ruins in that direction?" I persisted.

Crade's black eyes surveyed me curiously as he shook his head.

Next morning I looked again, and although a drizzling rain and a leaden sky considerably lessened the scope's vision range, I saw as before that same wall.

But after a moment of scrutiny, it seemed the color had altered. The wall had changed from a white to a light pink. Also it had moved. It was nearer now. Studying it, I thought I could discern its slow division into two separate sections.

Rain and wind drove me from the balcony at length. I dressed and went down to the dining room.

It was there that Crade revealed his true reason for inviting me here. Prior to her marriage, Louise had obtained considerable property near Harwich. The property had increased multifold in value, but in several cases the abstracts had been written in joint name with me. Crade asked if I was prepared to relinquish my claims.

The unmasked avarice and lack of tact in the question staggered me. I stared at Crade, studied his hawk-face, his deep-set eyes as he awaited my answer. It was through my influence that Louise had purchased that property, and I was tempted to give him a cold negative. Yet in all fairness, inasmuch as my sister had paid for the land with her own money, and had been the wife of this man, I should, I realized, waive my rights.

A smile of complete satisfaction turned Crade's lips as I agreed reluctantly.

"I felt sure you'd see it that way," he nodded. "We can walk to the village tomorrow and sign the necessary papers."

Without further word he got up, drew on a heavy rain coat and went out. Through the window I watched him. He moved slowly through the rain heading east in a general direction toward Glover.

Alone now in the house, I climbed the staircase toward my room. Hand on the latch, I hesitated.

As yet I had not told Crade of my intention to take back with me any of those possessions which my sister, Louise, had treasured, and which Crade would permit me to remove. There was in particular a valuable signet ring with the letter "L" upraised in jade which she had worn constantly and which I had given her. I saw no reason why I should not find it now.

I continued down the corridor to the door of Louise's room and stopped abruptly.

The door was double locked. A chain was stretched across from a staple on the frame, and attached to it was a heavy padlock.

For a full minute I stood there, staring. Back in my own room I slumped in a chair and attempted to see through the growing puzzle.

It would have been a logical, a pardonable move on the part

of Crade to close forever the room of his dead wife, assuming his grief had been deep and sincere. But paradoxically, from the last letters of Louise, I was inclined to believe otherwise. From time to time she had written that Crade treated her cruelly, that her life was no longer a happy one.

A growing feeling of unease began to rise up within me. I took up the telescope, hoping to divert my mind into other channels, went out on the little balcony and looked to the east.

The wall was still there. But it was ten times closer, ten times magnified in size.

As I looked, I saw that it was no longer a vague thing of one part. It was divided completely into two sections, one above the other, extending horizontally. There was something oddly familiar about the shape of those two objects. Absurd though it seemed, I thought they resembled arms and hands.

I turned the scope in a quick circle. Then I saw something else.

The figure of Martin Crade could be seen, walking slowly across the moor. Shoulders hunched into the wind, he was advancing directly upon that double wall.

But an instant later I jerked rigid in every nerve and muscle of my body. Crade stopped a few yards away from the walls and looked back. Then he went on, apparently unaware of the objects in his path.

The walls offered no resistance to his passage. Like a man moving across a shadow, Crade passed through them and continued on the other side.

I adjusted the focus a fraction. The twin walls were steadily growing larger. Stereoscopically clear they became, as if I had trained the scope upon an object close at hand.

And then a mounting sense of horror began to creep upon me. Viselike I held the telescope balanced on the balcony rail.

They *were* hands! The thin, delicately-formed hands, wrists and forearms of a woman. They hung there in mid-air, swaying gently back and forth like some flesh-colored marine serpents. The fingers opened and closed gently. The nails caught the gray light of the moor and glittered perceptibly.

For a quarter of an hour I knelt there, watching them. During that time the hands continued their slow oscillation, but did not move from the spot. And then once more Crade came into sight, toiling across the moor. With his appearance the hands abruptly disappeared.

I spent the rest of the morning trying to collect my chaotic thoughts. Fear for my very sanity oppressed me. What was the meaning, the cause of it all? Into what world was my new tele-scope seeing? Not this world—not this place of earth and flesh! But how could it see into any other, enabling me to see too? Had the science of optics, by some miraculous accident, created a lens no mortal mechanic had wittingly ground?

Shortly before noon, as I sat there, turning the telescope over and over in my hands, a thought came suddenly to me. The wrap-pings in which the glass had arrived—had I destroyed them—

The pasteboard box still lay undisturbed in the wastebasket. I crossed the room and with trembling fingers examined it.

But when I had found what I was looking for and when I had read the cryptic words, the mystery only became deeper. Glued to the inside of the box-cover was a small card, bearing words in a spidery hand-writing. The first part was a technical description of the telescope, the type of glass, the quality of grinding, notes such as usually accompany a manufacturer's product. The last part was puzzling:

> . . . glass formed from sand found in eastern Kurdistan, near the lost Yezidee city of Chaldabad. Although undoubtedly of a finer quality, rich in silicates, it is to be regretted that this sand was utilized in the making of the scope.
>
> The Yezidees are the devil-worshipers of Asia, and the sand was taken from a site close to one of their temples. I do not know, but I sometimes suspect this fact played a part in the manufacture of this glass.
>
> Lisbon, May 24th.
>
> Jose Sagasta.

The tinkling of a bell below advised me I was wanted for luncheon. Putting aside the box, I descended the stairs. But not until the meal was over did I tell Crade what I had seen. Then I described the vision of the hands.

It was remarkable the effect those details had upon the man. His face went white, his black eyes swiveled, bored into mine with piercing intensity.

"Hands, Brockton?" he repeated hoarsely. "Are you sure they were hands?"

I nodded. I had not been mistaken. I had seen them clearly.

Crade rose to his feet, paced unsteadily across the room. Suddenly he whirled.

"I'd like to look through that glass of yours."

"Of course," I assented. "It's in my room. But the vision disappeared an hour ago."

Unleashed fear seemed to dominate the man. He clawed his fingers through his hair, gaped at me wildly. Turning, he almost ran from the room.

I stared after him, perplexed and a little frightened. At last I got up and strolled into the library. I was troubled more than I care to admit, and the silence and gloom of that vast chamber did not lighten my feelings. Slowly I moved past the bookshelves, glancing absently at the titles.

In my present mood none of the titles offered any interest. A spell of depression seeming to emanate from the shadow-filled ceiling pressed down upon me. Tables and chairs were gaunt silhouettes in the gray light.

And then abruptly I came upon a book almost hidden on a lower shelf, and different from the others. Leatherbound, it was filled with Crade's writing in pencil. I moved quickly to put it back, when the cover fell open, revealing the following passage.

> Monday, Dec. 6th. She does not suspect I know, and I have given her no reason to believe otherwise. Yet since the day young Clay Stewart visited us, I am positive she has been in love with him. Stewart is younger than I, but he is a callow fool. I must watch this and see if there are any developments.

I read this twice. Curiosity, a rising suspicion, prompted me to continue:

12th Dec. Stewart called on us again today. He came supposedly for the loan of my rifle, but I know this was but an excuse. The moment I left the room I am positive Louise was in his arms. The situation is developing faster than I had expected. But as yet I see no reason for concern. She is quite within my reach.

17th Dec. Stewart left this morning for London. There remains now to see what effect this will have on Louise. I will watch carefully. . . .

Beads of cold perspiration gathered on my forehead. I turned the page and hurried on.

24th Dec. She has not forgotten. She sits in her room, night after night, writing letters. Letters to him!

27th Dec. She scarcely speaks to me. She stays in her room. Tonight I saw part of one of the letters she was writing. She is going to run off with him. My plans are complete. *I must and will kill her!*

The writing ended here. Mechanically I closed the book, replaced it on the shelf. Rigid, I stood there while the huge pendulum clock on the farther wall ticked off the passing seconds. Then I swung about and headed slowly for my own room.

The events that followed after that are a bit confused in my memory. I remember sitting stiffly in a chair, staring at the table and the telescope upon it. Presently, hardly knowing why, I got up, took the glass and strode out onto the balcony.

The hands were there again, graceful and feminine, swaying lightly in the air. Long and intently I stared, the scope carefully focused. With almost microscopic clarity I could see the tapering fingers, the pink skin.

There was something infinitely horrible about those bodyless members suspended there before me. Slowly, inexorably they were drawing closer; the intervening space lessened until they occupied the entire width of the glass. About me, all was deathly stillness. I could hear the wild hammering of my heart.

Larger they grew. The moor background faded away, and my

eyes, held by a hypnotic attraction, watched feverishly.

Suddenly the hair rose on my head. A violent contortion had seized the hands. As if startled, as if taken unawares by some unseen thing which had come within their reach, they recoiled, leaped backward. A perceptible tremor of expectancy passed through them. The cords of the arms stood out.

And then with a jerk and a twist of the wrists, they lunged forward, fingers outstretched . . . clawing. . . .

Simultaneously, filtering through the walls of that house, a piercing scream split the air. It was the scream of Martin Crade. Again it came, ricocheting down the corridor, filling every corner in a voice of agony.

I dropped the scope, leaped to the door and raced down the hall. Silence greeted me as I flung open the door to Crade's room. The man was not there. I ran on down the corridor to Louise's chamber.

The door here stood open. I pushed inside, stood stock still, frozen by what I saw.

In the center of the room slumped back in a chair, was the motionless figure of Martin Crade. His head was tilted far back, his eyes were staring upward. His hands hung at his sides. I saw at a glance that he was dead.

There was no sign of wound on his body. No weapon or person was visible in the room. Fighting back the horror that was overwhelming me, I stepped closer.

No wound, no. Only Crade's throat bore marks of violence. There were prints there on the skin just above the unbuttoned collar of his shirt—deeply indented fingerprints that had undoubtedly caused strangulation. They were the marks of a woman's hands. But the prints of the fourth finger bore an additional mark in the deeply discolored flesh. Staring at it, I felt a slow scream rise to my lips!

It was the mark of Louise's signet ring, round and symmetric, with an upraised letter "L."

The Tomb from Beyond

It was in late September, while in the employ of Payne, Largarten and Company, land agents, Boston, that I first came into that district known as the Opal Lake country. The thirty-five miles from Pine Island to Flume I had found necessary to travel by car, no trains making the run on the inland spur for the past six years, or since the cessation of the lumbering industry.

I was tired from a two-day trip and six-hour ride on the jerking, creeping local, and my spirits fell even lower as I sat hunched back in the rear seat of the old Ford and surveyed the forlorn aspect of the region that stretched away on all sides.

I was aware that my destination was one of those depressing oddities that one finds occasionally in the wake of American enthusiasm—a deserted town. But if the conclusion to my trip was to be an inglorious one, the approach was no less depressing. The spent day was chilly and gloomy, a raw wind whining past the windshield from the north, and the tortuous road, unrepaired since its years of unuse, wound in and out through a gaunt graveyard of second growth. To the side, fallen in various angles of despair, stumbled the rotting poles of the abandoned telegraph line, the wires dangling in ensnarled coils like some gigantic grape-vine withered in decay.

Nor was the somberness of my trip made any more pleasant by the personality of my driver. A stolid and taciturn Finn, he answered my questions with nods or unintelligible gutturals around the stem of his pipe and confined his entire attention to the uneven way ahead.

It was when we had reached a higher eminence, a point where the road mounted an old terminal moraine, that I, sweeping my gaze below me, remarked to the driver:

"Opal lake, eh?"

He grunted an agreement, and I stared down upon that perfect circle embedded there in the growth. Farther on, near the point where I judged the abandoned town of Flume to be, was a much smaller lake, this one curiously in the shape of a half moon.

"And the other . . . ?" I asked, looking up once more. "The little lake off to the right . . . what is it called?"

The driver drew on his pipe, and a cloud of blue smoke, strong with perique, swirled back into my face. Somehow I got the impression that my question had disturbed him. He turned, glanced down at the crescent-shaped strip of water, and his lips tightened.

"That isn't a lake," he said shortly.

The man wasn't joking. As I reached for a cigarette and cupped my hands around the match, I was about to reply that my vision, in spite of a need for reading glasses, was still unimpaired. But at that moment, the car struck a deep gash in the road, tilted sharply, and I was forced to clutch hard to keep from being thrown from the seat. When the road had resumed a comparatively even plane again, the thought had passed on.

Nightfall had gathered upon us when half an hour later we swept around a curve and drove into the empty street of Flume. It was here, according to our correspondence arrangement, that I was to meet my client, Julian Trenard. For a moment, as we drove slowly forward, I thought he had forgotten about it. Then we came abreast of the boarded-up building that had once housed the town's furniture store, and I saw him.

In the gloom, he seemed at first only a blacker shadow standing there motionless, hands hanging at his sides. He was tall, and his height was even more accentuated by the long black rain-poncho that draped loosely from his shoulders. He gave no sign of recognition as we clattered to a halt before him, until I climbed out of the car and stepped forward.

"Are you Mr. Trenard?" I asked hesitatingly.

My voice sent a visible shock through him, and he started to attention abruptly as though he had been immersed in his thoughts.

"I'm Arnold," I continued, "John Arnold of Payne, Largarten and Company. You received my letter?"

"Yes." He nodded slowly and after a moment extended his hand. "You may dismiss your driver, Arnold. It is only a short distance to my place, and we can talk as we walk."

The fact that he neither wished me welcome nor expressed a thankfulness that I had come, even as a matter of courtesy, took me a bit back, and I stood studying the man in silence. In the gathering darkness, the evidences of years spent under a tropical sun were clearly apparent. He stood noticeably erect, shoulders wide and square, marking, it seemed, a man of determination and strength. Yet the left side of his lips twitched constantly, and there was a furtive stare in his eyes that suggested fear.

I paid the driver, who, still in silence, handed out my grip-sack, then whirled the car around in the center of the street and raced off in the direction from which he had come.

"There are two roads," Trenard said abruptly, after the driver had gone, "one skirting the lake and a shorter one through the woods. Which do you prefer?"

"There is a lake, then?" I asked, remembering the queer remark of the driver.

For a moment Trenard made no answer. He stared straight ahead of him and walked forward a couple of paces. "A lake, yes," he said slowly.

We reached the edge of town and entered the remnants of an old logging road, merely two ruts in most places, necessitating my walking on one side and Trenard four feet away on the other. The man gave no indication of commencing that conversation which he had declared the march to his house would permit, and we paced along in silence.

It was quite dark now, the way before us walled in by two lines of towering trees. Up above, thick velvet clouds swept across the low-hanging sky, but off to the east, a growing circle of radiance showed where the moon was trying to break through.

As the man continued to say nothing and I could think of nothing worthy of disturbing his study, I fell into a deep thought myself, musing on all his colorful history which had so intrigued the world a year before.

Here, then, was the leader of that epoch-making Trenard-Fielding expedition, which, in the face of all scientific ridicule, had discovered off the coast of British North Borneo, the remnants of a hitherto unknown civilization: the unchronicled, unfabled city of Dras. I remembered the lengthy newspaper accounts that had been devoted to the finding of the submerged city and the queer artifacts brought back to New York. Down there on the sea floor, Trenard had walked the streets of a city buried under water for centuries. He had found marble buildings, architecture unaffected by Roman or Arab invasion, statues of deities of a distinct and separate religion, and carven hieroglyphics that were as yet undecipherable. It was indeed a success.

But Fielding had not fared so well. His sudden death had been a shock to the entire country, and especially to his colleagues back in the University of Virginia. There were queer rumors about his being killed by some unseen sea monster which lurked there in the depths, rumors that had been partially verified by other members of the expedition, but in all cases stoutly denied by Trenard.

In the exact center of the water-covered city, according to Trenard's popular book, *The Mysteries of Sunken Dras*, which I had browsed through, he had found a large mausoleum where apparently were entombed the five kings of the last dynasty. And for some reason, Trenard had been so taken up by either the architectural beauty or the regal associations of this edifice, that he had raised it to the surface, segment by segment, and shipped it back to the United States. It was a tremendous undertaking, involving the use of costly derricks and equipment and endangering the lives of the men. Why Trenard should have chosen this one building to raise rather than the many others, and why indeed he should have sacrificed further exploration and the removal of other objects to raise any at all, was, to the popular mind, a mystery.

It was said, of course, that the touch of fever, which had delayed him for three weeks at Kuching on the west coast of Borneo, had left his mind unbalanced. It was said also that the radiogram which had come to him out there in the Java sea, telling of the sudden death of his sister, Sylvia, had left him half mad and brought about a strange obsession.

At any rate, Trenard had taken the mausoleum back with him to New York. Then at further expense, he had conveyed it by train and motor truck to his wilderness home near the town of Flume. That was a year ago.

Flume at that time was only a monument of past industry. Only some seventy-five persons remained in the village. But I had heard or read somewhere that three months after the mausoleum had been set up in the town's cemetery and the body of his deceased sister, Sylvia, entombed in it, every one of those seventy-five had packed up and left en masse.

My reverie suddenly came to an end, when Trenard, grasping my arm, spoke for the first time in many moments.

"The road forks here. Let us take the wood path. The lake road is considerably longer."

I nodded in agreement, and increased my pace to keep up with him. Abruptly, the way before us opened upon a large glade, and there, fifty yards ahead, loomed the walls of a huge, oblong house. I stared at it coldly. Even in the half-darkness, the simple, the severe style of its architecture was apparent. The building, though frame, had not the slightest suggestion of gable or ornamentation, and rose straight up and across like an enormous packing case.

Trenard led the way to a small door, unlatched it with a key, and ushered me inside.

To the interior decorator, I presume, that chamber would have appealed as being furnished in good taste. But to me, depressed already by the somberness of my passage through the September woods, it seemed even more austere than the building's outside.

The white walls ran up two stories to an arched ceiling of a sickly-hued blue. On the side opposite me, half-way up, extended a small gallery swerving out over the room in a wide curve and terminating in a steep staircase, the balustrade fashioned of polished silver. There was a white porcelain bookcase in one corner, and on its top stood two curious ebony figures. One was in the likeness of a large deep-sea fish, with huge scales and a bloated middle portion. The other, complete in every detail, was a carving of a diver with helmet and full equipment. All in all, the room gave the impression of utter coldness, and my eyes moved from side to side, searching for a bit of red or brown to break the frigid monotony.

Trenard had removed his hat and coat now. He moved toward a connecting door, saying:

"Make yourself comfortable for a few moments, Arnold. I'll get you a little refreshment. I have no servants. I've lived here alone since the death of my sister, you know."

Before I could explain that I had eaten heartily in Pine Island, he had gone, and I was left to my thoughts.

I stood there a moment musing over the strange ways a man's ornamental fancies will manifest themselves. Then, lighting a cigarette, I tossed my hat and coat to a chair and strolled over to the bookcase. There were the volumes I had expected to find; altases, travel accounts, texts on deep-sea diving. Wallace's *Malay Archipelago*, and one or two technical works on ancient civilizations. But my attention was attracted abruptly from the bookshelves to a large framed picture hanging on the white wall.

It was an enlarged photograph, a scene taken under water by a submerged camera. It presented, I realized instantly, a street view of the sunken city of Dras. Vaguely, through the blur of the water and under the glare of what apparently was the submarine's beam light, had been snapped a formless mass of ornate buildings, shadowy columns and capitals. It was indistinct, yet that very lack of line and boundary increased its mystery and appeal. In the foreground could be distinguished a school of fish, and at a point in the rear, above the city, hung a black shapeless mass, which apparently had failed to register in the lens of the camera.

Toward this latter object I suddenly found my gaze attracted. For an instant I stood there wondering what could have caused this blotch on an otherwise almost incredibly perfect photograph. Then slowly there came a singular sensation that my eyes were being held in focus, that another will stronger than my own would not permit them to turn away. It was inexplicable, that feeling. It seemed as though some hidden eye were looking from beneath that discoloration on the print, gazing at me with the controlling stare of a hypnotist.

A moment later, I thought that formless shadow had begun to move—to creep slowly toward me with the sluggish wavering movement of a heavy body in deep water.

Heavy steps and a slamming door broke the spell abruptly, and

I turned to meet Trenard approaching with a tray of china. He sat across from me, lit an old meerschaum pipe and proceeded to lose himself amid clouds of tobacco smoke.

"Mr. Trenard," I said at length, my repast finished, "if we can agree on one subject, that of price, I believe my business may be concluded here with as little trouble and as quickly as possible. We have found a potential purchaser of your property. You must realize, however, that because of the inconveniences caused by the abandonment of the town of Flume, you cannot command a very high price."

He seemed noticeably relieved at this information, and laying aside his pipe, replied quickly.

"Then I will accept the offer, whatever it is. I've got to get away from here, and I can't do it until I've realized the money invested on the property."

I nodded, puzzled at his marked vehemence. "My company will live up to its reputation of fairness," I assured him. "As your agent, we will ask only the customary commission for finding a purchaser and completing the transaction. Shall we draw up the papers now, then, and I will leave in the morning?"

"The papers can wait," Trenard replied. "It will be easier to write by daylight. And if you will pardon me, I am in the custom of retiring early. You may stay here and read, if you like. Your room is reached by the staircase and is the second door to the right."

I nodded silently and watched him as he climbed the staircase with my grip-sack and disappeared somewhere in the darkness of the gallery above. Again he was either thoughtless, disturbed or characteristically impolite, for he made no offer to bid me good-night.

After my refreshment, the profound weariness which had so dulled me since my arrival in Pine Island had gradually left, and I now experienced no desire for sleep. I picked up a leather-bound copy of Trenard's book, *The Mysteries of Sunken Dras*, and absently opened it. A clock ticked slowly, steadily, somewhere, as I glanced at random through the pages. Presently I came to several passages which had been underlined with pencil, and before them my eyes hesitated long enough to read:

"A careful study of the hieroglyphics on the tomb has led me to the belief that the inhabitants of Dras had reached an intelligence considerably higher than the average observer would gather by merely examining the artifacts brought to the surface. I am of the opinion that the scholars and wise men at the courts of the five kings of the last dynasty had probed to a remarkable degree the most profound depths of abstract mathematical calculation and theoretical physics."

And again:

"The Drasian theology seems to have been an unexplainable combination of the vilest forms of demonology and a scientific concept of the relation between time and space, or to be exact, a religious intellection based on the belief that the four-dimensional continuum, as we would term it today, is teeming with gargoyle horrors, the foulness of which the finite mind cannot even conceive. In this respect, I am almost led to believe that Einstein was crudely antedated thousands of years."

Dry and bookish as these statements were, I gave them considerable thought. Toward the end of the volume, thrust in the pages, I came upon a scrap of paper covered with penciled writing. Let me say that ordinarily I am not addicted to reading other people's personal notations, but almost before I realized it, I was staring at the following:

"Can it be possible that the mausoleum's space interior itself constitutes a disruption of the space-time coordinates, a channel, so to speak, an opening formed in some unknown way by the priests of Dras which leads from our own three dimensional world into the fourth dimension? It is a thought which seems unbelievable. Yet the strange tales the villagers told and their frantic exodus from Flume would confirm it. Surely Fielding's story which he told before he went down the last time was untrue. But even if true, it would be mad to think it has followed me and is out there now—out there, God forbid, with poor Sylvia. What does it all mean?

"Today, one of the forest rangers from the district north of here passed through and confirmed what I had already guessed to be true. The government-made dike constructed to keep Opal Lake at its level on the north shore has been wearing away, and there is danger of inundation. How high the water will rise if it breaks through, I can't imagine. But I must get away from here. I shall go mad if I stay."

I sat back and stared at these enigmatic lines, frowning. Undoubtedly it was Trenard's handwriting, but what, in the note's own words, did it all mean?

At length, shrugging, I closed the book, tossed it to the table, and rose to my feet. There was a small half-sized door just before me, and if nothing else, it offered a way out of my thoughts. I longed to get out of the room. Its cold, white walls, blue ceiling and bleak furnishings produced in me that same sense of cheerlessness one finds in the interior of a hospital. I opened the door and stepped out under the night sky.

It was a small balcony that extended over the rear of the house. Even as I walked to the edge of the railing, the moon suddenly broke through a last rift of clouds, and I saw below me, like a sheath of ribbed silver, a long and narrow lake, the water swashing against the bushes almost at the building's foundation, the farther shores hidden by an intervening fringe of trees. Straight ahead, the gently rising surface was unbroken, but off to the left, toward the abandoned town of Flume, the water was dotted with orderly rows of white objects, which at that distance appeared to be pieces of anchored chalk. Farther on huddled a heavy shadow, the outlines of some huge building.

For a moment, I stood there musing. Then, as my eyes were drawn once again to those rows of white things, a little thrill of understanding swept through me.

The driver who had brought me from Pine Island had been right. This wasn't a lake. Those even files of white blocks were—tombstones! Tombstones, and the expanse of water before me must be a development of recent months, an inundated grave-yard. The dike on Opal Lake's northern shore had finally worn away, and the water, seeking its own level, had flowed here, flooding without respect the last resting-place of Flume's dead.

Looking directly below me now, I saw half in the moonlight, half in the shadow, a small flat-bottom duck-boat, drawn up on the bush-lined shore. Why, indeed, my host should have wished to row out on such a body of water struck me as most singular. And yet, as I gazed at the little craft and the short stubby oars thrown carelessly beside it, there came a distinct impulse that I myself go out on the moonlit water. I debated a moment, then lifting myself over the railing, dropped the short distance to the ground below. There was a certain macabre attraction to the scene before me.

Five seconds later I had adjusted the oars in the locks and shoved the boat gently into the lapping waves. Without knowing why, I headed due east, following the line of the shore. The moon, though high in the indigo heavens, seemed strangely bloated and out of proportion. As I rowed farther and farther, the white blank wall that marked Trenard's house fell back deeper into the gloom of foliage and looked out at me like an eyeless face swathed in a cowl. At intervals, I rested my oars across the thwart and sat surveying the scene.

Presently I was in that part of the lake that was directly over the old graveyard, and looking over my shoulder, I could see, some distance ahead, Trenard's mausoleum. There, within its ancient walls, was entombed the man's sister, Sylvia, buried in a monument that had once held the five kings of Dras. I pulled harder on my left oar and headed toward it.

The lake was even narrower here, the banks close, and I could see row on row of white tombstones and tilting crosses rising above the water. Waves swashed against them in a low liquid dirge. The water, too, seemed clearer than that fronting Trenard's house. Looking down over the boat's gunwales, I thought I saw more gravestones and crosses far below in the dark depths, gleaming white like scattered mounds of bleached bones.

Then the shadowy mass of the mausoleum rose like a curtain before me. To a general appearance, the architecture might be classed as Oriental, the domed roof rising gracefully like a Mohammedan mosque. Above the doorway, a hideous gargoyle perched on a block of stone.

I dipped my oars and brought the boat around to the other side, dark there with the shadow of the hidden moonlight, but still revealing a small iron-barred window that had been cut through the wall. With the boat bobbing close to the stone side, I steadied myself, reached up and strove to see into the interior.

My curiosity was disappointed. I saw nothing. Only a well of blackness met my eyes. For a moment, I remained in that perilous position, staring between the bars. And then—my head jerked back with revulsion.

Sweeping to my nostrils from the inner recesses of that vault had come a horrible fetid smell, a loathsome odor of unutterable filth. It surged out upon me like a putrescent blanket of green mold.

I clung there gasping. For an instant, there was only silence and that festering breath. Then, without warning, there came from within those walls a prolonged hiss like escaping steam and a heavy sluggish splashing in the interior water. Something cold and clammy slid across my hands clenched there on the iron bars, and I whipped them away dripping with blood, gashed to the bone.

I did not cry out: only dropped back into the boat and began to row furiously for the shore. I worked the paddles with might and main until my shoulders ached in their sockets.

Back in my own room in Trenard's house, I sat down on the edge of the bed and stared at my hands. Both were marked with deep ragged gashes between the wrist and first knuckle. Blood gushing from the wounds dyed the fingers crimson.

Confused, bewildered, I poured a quantity of water and carefully bathed the injured members. Then, utilizing the little first-aid kit I always carry in my grip-sack, I carefully bathed the gashes in iodine, then applied gauze and adhesive tape.

How long I lay there awake, I cannot tell: My brain was whirling, seeking an answer to it all. But at length I lapsed into a fitful slumber.

The rumble of thunder was in my ears when I awoke. Rain

was slashing the pane of my bedroom window, and in the early morning gloom, a wall of trees, just beyond, was bending double in the face of a raging wind.

I jumped to my feet with an exclamation. Bad weather meant bad roads, and, considering the disrepair of the Flume-Pine Island trail, this unexpected storm might cause an enforced stay in Trenard's house, an outlook which, as I considered it, rose to appalling proportions.

Dressed, I made my way downstairs to find my worst fears realized. The rain was slanting down in torrents, and the path that led across the glade into the woods was a swirling river of mud and water.

The little door leading to the balcony that faced the lake was open, and stepping to the sill, I paused and looked out.

Julian Trenard was standing at the railing, staring out ahead of him at the foaming lake. He was drenched to the skin, and the water was running down his face in tiny rivulets. Suddenly he became aware of my presence, whirled around and stepped back into the room. I watched him as he moved to a chair and sank into it with a low moan.

"Arnold," he said, "have you ever gone into the theory of relativity? Do you know anything of the principles of space-time, of the fourth dimension? Do you believe there are other worlds around us, worlds which, because of our limited three-dimensional senses, we cannot see or understand?"

I took out a cigarette, lit it twice before I made my reply.

"Yes, of course," I said. "I'm not so strong on my science, but I've read the usual articles. Why?"

The nerve near Trenard's mouth was twitching violently now. He got up, paced to the farther wall and back again, then hesitated before me, leaning hard on the table top.

"And do you believe it to be true that in that other fourth dimensional world there exist forms of life entirely removed from our own evolutionary scale, creatures horrible beyond the farthest reaches of our imagination? Do you believe that?"

"Who knows?" I replied. "It's logical, I suppose. But the unknown is always popularly embodied with strange terrors. So far we have only a tangle of mathematical calculations to go by."

He turned away without listening, and as I looked after him curiously, I thought I saw his lips form the words over and over again: "Oh Sylvia, Sylvia!"

Both breakfast and the subsequent business formalities were dismal affairs. The storm, instead of dying down, grew steadily in fury, and we sat in that cheerless room with the thunder hammering overhead, and the wind rushed by the outer walls. Noon came and passed, with Trenard making no suggestion of a lunch. Curiously enough, the man had not seemed to notice the fact that both my hands were thickly bound in bandages; or if he did, he asked no questions. The wounds, incidentally, were causing me constant worry. Though I had not inspected them since the night before, they felt hot and feverish, and an unpleasant sensation of a pulse, beating deep in the gashes, made me resolve to visit a doctor immediately upon my return to Boston. But the unexplainable events, of which those hurts were a climax, I deliberately thrust from my mind. That was something I could not think of without trembling in horror.

Abruptly at five o'clock the rain and the wind came to an end, and there was left only an occasional sullen delayed burst of thunder. The storm had passed on.

With the quieting of the elements, Trenard suddenly roused himself. A tremor seemed to pass through him from head to foot, and he called softly:

"I'm coming, Sylvia. I'll take you away."

He ran across the room, flung open the outer door and disappeared. Moments dragged by as I stood looking after him. Had the man reached the climax of some mental malady? Were his queer actions, his apparent obsession, the result of a diseased brain?

I waited in indecision an instant. Then, as the cold gloominess of that room slowly gathered around me, I strode to the door and followed him. His footprints were embedded there in the wet loam, and slowly, half held back by some inner dread, I traced them around the outer wall of the house. At first I thought he was making for the little duck-boat I had used the night before, but the trail led farther on, through a dense thicket, down into a low marshy section of land, and finally to the edge of the lake.

I drew up behind the bole of a tree and peered ahead of me. Trenard was there, up to his knees in water, dragging a huge flat-bottomed barge to the shore from its anchoring buoy. Along the strip of beach stood seven steel drums, black barrels of apparently fifty gallon capacity. I could not even guess at their contents.

As I watched, Trenard began to roll the barrels one by one onto the barge. They were terrifically heavy, it seemed, the man apparently using every ounce of his strength in the task. The barge itself was a strange affair. Half raft, half boat, it was made of untrimmed logs, bound together with wire and rope of every size and description.

Puzzled I kept in the protective shadow of the tree and watched the work slowly being completed. Trenard was laboring like a madman now. Sweat was streaming from his forehead. He had thrown off his coat, and hatless, his hair hung wildly over his eyes.

At length, the last barrel was moved from the beach to the barge. Without a glance behind, Trenard leaped aboard, seized a long wooden staff, and began poling out into the lake. Fifty feet from the shore the depth became too great for the use of the pole, and he discarded it for a crude, square-bladed paddle arrangement which he operated from a socket in the bow.

For a long while, I watched him as he worked the clumsy craft slowly into the upper reaches of the lake. Then, when an intervening fringe of trees hid him from sight, I turned, ran back to the little duck-boat, threw in the oars, and shoved off in pursuit. Curiosity once more had got the better of me.

The lake lay as flat and motionless as a great mirror, and the tombstones ahead seemed only lighter reflections of the leaden sky. Ahead, the domed mausoleum reared itself above the colorless water.

But Trenard did not steer directly for the tomb. Carefully, as one proceeding under a long premeditated plan, he maneuvered the barge to a point some forty or fifty feet from the vault's entrance, and there, halting his paddling, seized one of the steel barrels and rolled it to the boat's edge. Gradually lessening the intervening space, I rowed my own craft parallel to the bank, watching him.

He had resumed his paddling again now, moving slowly forward with that one barrel still lying at the edge of the barge, almost touching the water. From that barrel a dark heavy liquid was pouring onto the lake, coloring the surface with a gleaming purple black, thickening in an ever-widening circle.

It was oil! No other fluid would act in like manner when in contact with water.

Round and round the mausoleum Trenard directed the barge. I was quite near now, and I could see the mingled expression of fear and determination in the man's face; the wild stare in his black eyes. Back and forth he worked the enormous socket paddle, and in his wake grew a steadily widening trail of oil. When the steel drum was emptied, Trenard shoved it into the water and rolled another into position. And thus he repeated the process; circumnavigating the tomb again and again until the surface of the lake was black with petroleum.

At length, the contents of the seven barrels were emptied, and Trenard headed for the vault entrance. He lashed the mooring rope around one of the narrow stone columns, leaped out, and waded over the water-covered stairs to the door. A moment later I heard the iron barrier clang open and saw him disappear into the interior.

Five minutes passed, an eternity with only the gentle lapping of the water on the surrounding masonry. Then, as I leaned over the gunwale watching, Trenard reappeared, and I started as if struck by a blow. From the entrance of the vault he was dragging a heavy, oblong shape, struggling to slide it onto the barge. A black wooden box, it was . . . a coffin . . . the carved and ornamented casket of his sister, Sylvia.

But something was wrong. The man was making frantic efforts to close the iron door behind him. He was straining backward, arms bent double, exerting all his strength to force it into position. There was but a foot separating it from the latch, yet some interior force seemed holding it open.

Suddenly Trenard threw back his hands and uttered a shriek of horror. He released the door and with one wild lunge threw himself onto the barge, unfastened the mooring rope and seized the paddle arm. Back and forth he moved the blade, churning through the thick water. The clumsy craft began to move slowly away from the tomb.

And then—I can only chronicle the events that followed from the nightmare train of horror images that remain engraved on my mind. From the entrance of the domed mausoleum there emerged a thing which sent a wave of terror over me.

It was utterly bestial. It was a sight so indescribably loathsome and repulsive that it held me there in the boat, rigid and unable to believe my eyes, doubting my very sanity.

Creeping over the water-covered steps, past the carved columns, came a huge, bloated, semi-saurian monster, a giant sea serpent, an enormous water reptile, and yet a creature with eight jointed, hairy spider-legs like some hybrid insect from the canvas of the mad August Schlegel. The body, sliding endlessly from the inner recesses of the vault, was a gleaming black, the head, a flat, pointed, featureless mass. As I stared out upon it and a great nausea rose up within me, I subconsciously catalogued it, in spite of those hairy spider-like appendages, as something akin to a Mosasaur, the giant sea snake that infested the prehistoric seas of the later Mesozoic. And yet, though I am neither biologist nor student of paleontology, though I have never beyond casual browsing, delved into the little-known subject of deep-pressure marine life, I knew it to be no naturally evolved form of life of my own mundane world.

Head and three long, undulations above the surface, it poised there, then suddenly lunged straight at Trenard. Again the man screamed, and the cry shot over the lake, wailing to the farthest shore. He was working like a madman at the socket oar now, churning the oily water in great foaming waves, and the barge, with the coffin in its center, moved sluggishly forward.

And as I sat, transfixed, in the boat, I thought I understood. The interior of that mausoleum, where once had been entombed the five kings of Dras, constituted a channel, an opening in space, formed in some strange way by the priests of that ancient city, leading from our own three-dimensional world to that of the fourth dimension. When Trenard had raised the tomb to the surface from the sea-floor, transported it here to the Flume cemetery, the passage through space-time had not disturbed that opening. It still existed in the vault's interior, a door to the world beyond.

I saw now the reason for Trenard's actions. He had guessed all this too, long before. He had lived a life of constant growing dread in his lonely home, and had gradually become obsessed with the horrible thought that the body of his sister, Sylvia, was out there with the monster. Was not death in our plane but a process of transmutation, of metempsychosis into another world? And would not that creature drag her into a pit of deepest corruption where she would be imprisoned forever?

The huge thing, hairy appendages slowly treading water, was moving forward in pursuit of the barge. And Trenard was struggling at the oar, casting frantic glances behind him.

On swept the barge, the square prow turning the oily surface of the lake into a river of creaming ink. Behind, and scattered at intervals near the mausoleum, floated the seven empty steel drums, half submerged, like so many black porpoises.

Scarcely ten yards apart, they were now, and even from where I sat in the duck-boat, I could see the veins on Trenard's brow extend, as he worked the huge paddle. Mercifully, perhaps, the occurrences of the next few instants have been blurred in my memory.

There it was, poised on the surface of the lake, a creation from the inner reaches of a geometric hell, python body stretched flat downward now, hairy spider-legs motionless. Then, it closed in on him.

Trenard had only an instant. With a leap, he whirled away from the arm of the socket paddle and clawed madly at his pockets. Then a pinpoint of orange flame flared up, and with a start I understood.

Trenard meant to ignite the heavy film of oil that covered the surface of the water. He had planned this carefully as the one and only means of self-preservation. Now he turned the flame of the match to the box itself and flung the flaming missile out before him. Then with a scream, he looked over his shoulder.

The thing was upon him. Trenard lurched to the opposite end of the barge and flung himself wide and clear into the thick water.

Even as his body momentarily disappeared beneath the surface, a wall of flame shot up over the spot, raced toward the monster and the barge. I can tell little more. I saw the whole tableau
before me transform into a roaring cauldron. There came a violent lashing and floundering as the monster found itself caught
in the center of it. One after another, I saw the spider-legs burst
into flame. Up from the cremating body rose a thick, greenish
miasma.

The lake was singing with flame now. Red reflections stabbed
deep into the water depths. The barge and its coffin cargo were a
floating funeral pyre. Of Trenard, there was no sign. Only flaming oil, leaping higher and higher, swirled over the spot where
he had disappeared. Abruptly, a dense billow of black smoke
belched upward and hid it all in a thick curtain.

But I had no wish to see more. I seized the oars of the duck-
boat and rowed madly to the beach. Five feet from the shore I
leaped into the water and ran—through the dripping woods,
down the old logging road and into the abandoned town of
Flume.

To this day, my passage from the lake across the long tortuous
miles to Pine Island remains a blank spot in my memory. There
is but a single instant during the endless hours of that advance
which I can recall with any degree of clarity, a moment when I
reached a higher, open point on the old road and looked out upon
a scene that probed its gloom into the lowest reaches of my soul.

The lowering sky was deepening into dusk, and the wilderness
stretched below me, a dark carpet of undulating green. In its
center, like a leaden wedge, lay the elliptical expanse of that lake.
Off to the side brooded a heavier shadow, which I knew to be
the Dras mausoleum, and over all, from shore to shore, hung a
slowly diminishing cloud of smoke.

The Digging at Pistol Key

Although he had lived in Trinidad for more than fifteen years, Jason Cunard might as well have remained in Devonshire, his original home, for all the local background he had absorbed. He read only British newspapers, the *Times* and the *Daily Mail*, which he received by weekly post, and he even had his tea sent him from a shop in Southampton, unmindful of the fact that he could have obtained the same brand, minus the heavy tax, at the local importer in Port-of-Spain.

Of course, Cunard got into town only once a month, and then his time was pretty well occupied with business matters concerning his sugar plantation. He had a house on a narrow promontory midway between Port-of-Spain and San Fernando which was known as Pistol Key. But his plantation sprawled over a large tract in the center of the island.

Cunard frankly admitted there was nothing about Trinidad he liked. He thought the climate insufferable, the people—the Britishers, that is—provincial, and the rest of the population, a polyglot of races that could be grouped collectively as "natives and foreigners." He dreamed constantly of Devonshire, though he knew of course he would never go back.

Whether it was due to this brooding or his savage temper, the fact remained that he had the greatest difficulty in keeping house-servants. Since his wife had died two years ago, he had had no less than seven: Caribs, quadroons, and Creoles of one sort or another. His latest, a lean, gangly black boy, went by the name of Christopher, and was undoubtedly the worst of the lot.

As Cunard entered the house now, he was in a distinctly bad frame of mind. Coming down the coast highway, he had had the misfortune to have a flat tire and had damaged his clothes considerably in changing it. He rang the antiquated bell-pull savagely.

Presently Christopher shambled through the connecting doorway.

"Put the car in the garage," Cunard said tersely. "And after dinner repair the spare tire. Some fool left a broken bottle on the road."

The Negro remained standing where he was, and Cunard saw then that he was trembling with fear.

"Well, what the devil's the matter?"

Christopher ran his tongue over his upper lip. "Can't go out dere, sar," he said.

"Can't . . . Why not?"

"De holes in de yard. Der dere again."

For the first time in more than an hour Cunard permitted himself to smile. While he was totally without sympathy for the superstitions of these blacks, he found the intermittent reoccurrence of these holes in his property amusing. For he knew quite well that superstition had nothing to do with them.

It all went back to that most diabolical of buccaneers, Francis L'Ollonais and his voyage to the Gulf of Venezuela in the middle of the seventeenth century. After sacking Maracaibo, L'Ollonais sailed with his murderous crew for Tortuga. He ran into heavy storms and was forced to put back in here at Trinidad.

Three or four years ago some idiot by the idiotic name of Arlanpeel had written and published a pamphlet entitled *Fifty Thousand Pieces of Eight* in which he sought to prove by various references that L'Ollonais had buried a portion of his pirate booty on Pistol Key. The pamphlet had sold out its small edition, and Cunard was aware that copies had now become a collector's item. As a result, Pistol Key had come into considerable fame. Tourists stopping off at Port-of-Spain frequently telephoned Cunard, asking permission to visit his property, a request which of course he always refused.

And the holes! From time to time during the night Cunard would be awakened by the sound of a spade grating against gravel, and looking out his bedroom window, he would see a carefully shielded lantern down among the cabbage palms. In the morning there would be a shallow excavation several feet across with the dirt heaped hastily on all four sides.

The thought of persons less fortunate than himself making clandestine efforts to capture a mythical fortune dating to the seventeenth century touched Cunard's sense of humor.

"You heard me, Christopher," he snapped to the houseboy, "put the car in the garage."

But the black remained cowering by the door until Cunard, his patience exhausted, dealt him a sharp slap across the face with the flat of his hand. The boy's eyes kindled, and he went out silently.

Cunard went up to his bathroom and washed the road grime from his hands. Then he proceeded to dress for his solitary dinner, a custom which he never neglected. Downstairs, he got to thinking again about those holes in his yard and decided to have a look at them. He took a flashlight and went out the rear entrance and under the cabbage palms. Fireflies in the darkness and a belated Qu'-est-ce-qu'il-dit bird asked its eternal question.

Forty yards from the house he came upon the diggings Christopher had reported. That they were the work of some ambitious fortune hunter was made doubly apparent by the discarded tape-measure and the cheap compass which lay beside the newly turned earth.

Again Cunard smiled. It would be "forty paces from this point to the north end of a shadow cast by a man fifteen hands high," or some such fiddle faddle. Even if L'Ollonais had ever buried money here—and there was no direct evidence that he had—it had probably been carted away long years ago.

He saw Christopher returning from the garage then. The houseboy was walking swiftly, mumbling a low litany to himself. In his right hand he held a small cross fashioned of two bent twigs.

Back in the house, Cunard told himself irritably that Christopher was a fool. After all, he had seen his mother come into plenty of trouble because of her insistence on practicing *obeah*. She had professed to be an *obeah*-woman and was forever speaking incantations over broken eggshells, bones, tufts of hair and other disagreeable objects. Employed as a laundress by Cunard, he had discovered her one day dropping a white powder into his tea cup, and unmindful of her plea that it was merely a good-health charm designed to cure his recurrent spells of malaria, he had turned her over to the Constabulary. He had pressed charges too, testifying that the woman had attempted to poison him. Largely because of his influence, she had been convicted and sent to the Convict Depot at Tobago. Christopher had stayed on because he had no other place to go.

The meal over, Cunard went into the library with the intention of reading for several hours. Although the *Times* and the *Daily Mail* reached him in bundles of six copies a fortnight or so after they were published, he made it a practice to read only Monday's copy on Monday and so on through the week, thus preserving the impression that he was still in England.

But this night as he strode across to his favorite chair, he drew up short with a gasp. The complete week's bundle of newspapers had been torn open and their contents scattered about in a wild and disorganized pile. To add to this sacrilege, one of the sheets had a ragged hole in it where an entire column had been torn out. For an instant Cunard was speechless. Then he wheeled on Christopher.

"Come here," he roared. "Did you do this?"

The houseboy looked puzzled.

"No, sar," he said.

"Don't lie to me. How dare you open my papers?"

But Christopher insisted he knew nothing of the matter. He had placed the papers on their arrival in the library and had not touched them since.

Cunard's rage was mounting steadily. A mistake he might have excused, but an out-and-out lie. . . .

"Come with me," he said in a cold voice.

Deliberately he led the way into the kitchen, looked about him carefully. Nothing there. He went back across the little corridor to the houseboy's small room under the stairway. While Christopher stood protesting in the doorway, Cunard marched across to the table and silently picked up a torn section of a newspaper.

"So you did lie!" he snarled.

The sight of the houseboy with his perpetual grin there in the doorway was too much for the planter. His rage beyond control, he seized the first object within reach—a heavy length of wood resting on a little bracket mounted on the wall—and threw it with all his strength.

The missile struck Christopher squarely on the temple. He uttered no cry, but remained motionless a moment, the grin frozen on his face. Then his legs buckled and he slumped slowly to the floor.

Cunard's fists clenched. "That'll teach you to respect other people's property," he said. His anger, swift to come, was receding as quickly, and noting that the houseboy lay utterly still, he stepped forward and stirred him with his foot.

Christopher's head rolled horribly.

Quickly Cunard stooped and felt for a pulse. None was discernible. With trembling fingers he drew out a pocket mirror and placed it by the boy's lips. For a long moment he held it there, but there was no resultant cloud of moisture. Christopher was dead!

Cunard staggered across to the chair and sat down. Christopher's death was one thing and one thing only—murder! The fact that he was a man of color and Cunard an influential planter would mean nothing in Crown court of law. He could see the bewigged magistrate now; he could hear the evidence of island witnesses, testifying as to his uncontrollable temper, his savage treatment of servants.

Even if there were not actual danger of incarceration—and he knew there was—it would mean the loss of his social position and prestige.

And then Cunard happened to think of the holes in his yard. A new one—a grave for the dead houseboy—would never be noticed, and he could always improvise some sort of story that the boy had run off. As far as Cunard knew, other than the old crone who was his mother, Christopher had no other kin, having come originally from Jamaica.

The planter was quite calm now. He went to his room, changed to a suit of old clothes and a pair of rubber-soled shoes. Then, returning to the little room under the stairs, he rolled the body of the houseboy into a piece of sailcloth and carried it out into the yard.

He chose a spot near the far corner of his property where a clump of bamboo grew wild and would effectually shield him from any prying eyes. But there were no prying eyes, and half an hour later Cunard returned to the house. There he carefully cleaned the clinging loam from the garden spade, washed his shoes and brushed his trousers.

It was when he went again to the room under the stairs to gather together Christopher's few possessions that he saw the piece of wood that had served as the death missile. Cunard picked it up and frowned. The thing was an *obeah* fetish apparently, an ugly little carving with a crude likeness of an animal head and a squat human body. The lower half of the image ended in a flat panel, the surface of which was covered with wavy lines, so that the prostrate figure looked as if it were partially immersed in water. Out of that carved water two arms extended upward, as in supplication, and they were arms that were strangely reminiscent for Cunard. Christopher's mother had had arms like that, smooth and strangely youthful for a person of her age. There was even a chip of white coral on one of the fingers like the coral ring the old woman always wore.

Cunard threw the thing onto the pile of other objects he had gathered: spare clothes, several bright colored scarves, a sack of cheap tobacco, made a bundle of them and burned them in the old-fashioned cook stove with which the kitchen was equipped.

The last object to go into the fire was the newspaper clipping, and the planter saw then with a kind of grim horror that Christopher had not lied at all, that the top of the paper in fact bore a date-line several months old and was one of a lot he had given to the houseboy "to look at de pictures."

For several days after that Cunard did not leave his house. He felt nervous and ill-at-ease, and he caught himself looking out the window toward the bamboo thicket on more than one occasion. Curiously too, there was an odd murmuring in his ears like the sound of distant water flowing.

On the third day, however, he was sufficiently himself to make a trip to town. He drove the car at a fast clip to Port-of-Spain, parked on Marine Square and went about his business. He was walking down Frederick Street half an hour later when he suddenly became aware that an aged Negro woman with head tied in a red kerchief was following him.

Cunard didn't have a direct view of her until just as he turned a corner, and then only a glance, but his heart stopped dead still for an instant. Surely that black woman was Christopher's mother whom he had sent to prison. True, her face was almost hidden by the folds of the loosely-draped kerchief, but he had seen her hand, and there was the coral ring on it. Wild thoughts rushed to Cunard's head. Had the woman been released then? Had she missed her son, and did she suspect what had happened?

Cunard drew up in a doorway, but the old crone did not pass him, and when he looked back down the street, she was nowhere in sight.

Nevertheless the incident unnerved him. When, later in the day, he met Inspector Bainley of the Constabulary, he seized the opportunity to ask several questions that would ease his mind.

"Where have you been keeping yourself?" Bainley asked. "I haven't seen much of you lately."

Cunard lit a cigar with what he hoped was a certain amount of casualness.

"I've been pretty busy," he replied. "My houseboy skipped, you know. The blighter simply packed off without warning."

"So?" said Bainley. "I thought Christopher was a pretty steady chap."

"In a way," said Cunard. "And in a way he wasn't." And then: "By the way, do you remember his mother? I was wondering whether she had been released. I thought I saw her a moment ago on the street."

The Inspector smiled a thin smile. "Then you were seeing things," he said. "She committed suicide over at the Convict Depot at Tobago two months ago."

Cunard stared.

"At least we called it suicide," Inspector Bainley went on. "She took some sort of an *obeah* potion when she found we weren't going to let her go, and simply lay back and died. It was rather odd that the medico couldn't find any trace of poison though."

Cunard was rather vague about the rest of the day's events. He recalled making some trifling purchases, but his mind was wandering, and twice he had to be reminded to pick up his change. At four o'clock he abruptly found himself thinking of his old friend,

Hugh Donay, and the fact that Donay had employed Christopher's mother a year or so before she had entered Cunard's services. Donay had a villa just outside of town, and it would take only a few moments to see him. Of course there was no reason to see him. If Bainley said the old woman had committed suicide, that settled it. Yet Cunard told himself the Inspector might have been mistaken or perhaps joking. He himself was a strong believer in his powers of observation, and it bothered him to have doubts cast upon them.

The planter drove through the St. Clair district and turned into a driveway before a sprawling house with roof of red tile. Donay, a thin waspish man, was lounging in a hammock and greeted Cunard effusively.

"Tried to get you by phone the other day," he said, "but you weren't at home. Had something I wanted to tell you. About that L'Ollonais treasure that's supposed to be buried on your property."

Cunard frowned. "Have you started believing that too?"

"This was an article in the *Daily Mail,* and it had some new angles that were rather interesting. I get my paper here in town before you do out there on Pistol Key, you know."

Cunard attempted to swing the conversation into other channels, but Donay was persistent.

"Funny thing about that article," he said. "I read it the same day the burglar was here."

"Burglar?" Cunard lifted his eyes.

"Well," Donay said, "Jim Barrett was over here, and I showed him the paper. Barrett said it was the first description he had read that sounded logical and that the directions given for locating the treasure were very clear and concise. Just at that moment there was a sound in the corridor, and Barrett leaped up and made a dash for the kitchen.

"I might tell you that for several days I thought prowlers were about. The lock on the cellar door was found broken, and several times I'd heard footsteps in the laundry-room. Several things were out of place in the laundry-room too, though what anyone would want there is more than I can see.

"Anyway, Barrett shouted that someone was in the house. We

followed the sounds down into the cellar, and just as we entered the door into the laundry-room, there was a crash and the sound of glass breaking."

Donay smiled sheepishly as if to excuse all these details.

"It was only a bottle of bluing," he went on, "but what I can't figure out is how the prowler got in and out of that room without our seeing anyone pass. There's only one door, you know, and the windows are all high up."

"Was anything stolen?" Cunard asked.

"Nothing that I'm aware of. That bluing though was running across the floor toward a hamper of clean linen, and without thinking I used the first thing handy to wipe it up. It happened to be the newspaper with that treasure article in it. So I'm afraid . . ."

"It doesn't matter. I can read it in my copy," Cunard said. But even as he spoke, a vision of his own torn paper flashed to him.

"That isn't quite all," Donay said. "The next day I found every blessed wastebasket in the house turned upside down and their contents scattered about. Queer, isn't it?"

The conversation changed after that, and they talked of idle things. But just before he left Cunard said casually.

"By the way, my houseboy, Christopher's run off. Didn't his mother work for you as a laundress or something?"

"That's right," Donay said, "I turned her over to you when I took a trip up to the States. Don't you remember?"

Cunard drove through town again, heading for the highway to Pistol Key. He had just turned off Marine Square when he suddenly slammed down hard on the brakes. The woman darted from the curb directly into his path, and with the lowering sun in his eyes, he did not see her until it was too late. Cunard got out of the car, shaking like a leaf, fully expecting to find a crumpled body on the bumper.

But there was no one there, and a group of Portuguese street laborers eyed him curiously as he peered around and under the car. He was almost overcome with relief, but at the same time he was disturbed. For in that flash he had seen of the woman against the sun, he was almost sure he had seen the youthful dark-skinned arms of Christopher's mother.

Back at Pistol Key Cunard spent the night. The sensation of distant running water was stronger in his ears now. "Too much quinine," he told himself. "I'll have to cut down on the stuff."

He lay awake for some time, thinking of the day's events. But as his brain went over the major details in retrospection, he found himself supplying the missing minor details and so fell into a haze of peaceful drowsiness.

At two o'clock by the radium clock on the chiffonier, he awoke abruptly. The house was utterly still, but through the open window came an intermittent metallic sound. It died away, returned after an interval of several minutes. Cunard got out of bed, put on his brocaded dressing robe and strode to the window. A full moon illumined the grounds save where the palmistes cast their darker shadow, and there was no living person in evidence.

Below him and slightly to the left there was a freshly dug hole. But it was not that that caused Cunard to pass his hands before his eyes as if he had been dreaming. It was the sight of a spade alternately disappearing in the hole and reappearing to pile the loosened soil on the growing mound. A spade that moved slowly, controlled by aged yet youthful appearing arms and hands, but arms unattached to any human body.

In the morning Cunard called the Port-of-Spain *Journal,* instructing them to run an advertisement for a houseboy, a task which he had neglected the day before. Then he went out to his post box to get the mail.

The morning mist had not yet cleared. It hung over the hibiscus hedges like an endless line of white shrouds. As he reached the end of the lane, Cunard thought he saw a figure turn from the post box and move quickly toward a grove of ceiba trees. He thought nothing of it at first, for those trees flanked the main road which was traveled by residents of the little native settlement at the far end of Pistol Key. But then he realized that the figure had moved away from the road, in a direction leading obliquely toward his own house.

Still the matter did not concern him particularly until he opened the post box. There was a single letter there, and it had not come by regular mail; the dirty brown envelope bore neither stamp nor cancellation mark. Inside was a torn piece of newspaper.

Cunard realized at once that it was the missing piece from his *Daily Mail.* But who besides Christopher could have had access to the house and who would steal a newspaper column and return it in the post box?

It was like him that he made no attempt to read the paper until he had returned to the library. Then he matched it with the torn sheet still on his desk. The two pieces fitted exactly. He sat back and began to read.

The first part was a commonplace enough account of the opening of new auction parlors in Southwick Street, London, and a description of some of the more unusual articles that had been placed for sale there. Cunard, reading swiftly, found his eye attracted to the following:

> Among the afternoon offerings was the library of the late Sir Adrian Fell of Queen Anne's Court, which included an authentic first edition of McNair's *Bottle of Heliotrope* and a rare quarto volume of *Lucri Causa*. There was also a curious volume which purported to be the diary of the Caribbean buccaneer, Francis L'Ollonais, written while under the protection of the French West India Company at Tortuga.
>
> This correspondent had opportunity to examine the latter book and found some interesting passages. According to the executors of the estate, it had been obtained by Sir Adrian on his trip to Kingston in 1904, and so far as is known, is the only copy in existence.
>
> Under the heading, "The Maracaibo Voyage," L'Ollonais describes his destruction of that town, of his escape with an enormous booty, and of the storms which beset him on his return trip to Tortuga. It is here that the diary ceases to be a chronological date-book and becomes instead a romantic narrative.
>
> L'Ollonais, driven southward, managed to land on Trinidad, on a promontory known as Pistol Key. There "By a greate pile of stones whiche looked fair like two horses running," he buried the equivalent of fifty thousand pieces of eight. His directions for locating the treasure are worth quoting:

"Sixty paces from the south forward angle of the horse rock to the crossing of a line west by south west by the compass from a black pointed stone shaped like a broken needle near the shore. At this point if a man will stand in the light of a full moon at the eleventh hour, the shadow of his head will fall upon the place."

Cunard lowered the paper and thoughtfully got a cigar out of the silver humidor on the table. So there was truth in that story of hidden treasure after all. Perhaps the money was still there, and he had been a fool to ridicule the motive behind those holes in his yard. He smoked in silence.

How many persons, he wondered, had seen that newspaper story. There was Hugh Donay and Jim Barrett, of course, but they didn't count. Few others here subscribed to the *Daily Mail*. Of those that did, the odds were against any of them wading through such a dull account. The fact remained, however, that someone had read it in his own copy and had been sufficiently interested to tear it from the sheet. Who was that person? And why had they seen fit to return it by way of his post box?

The landmarks he knew only too well. He had often remarked that that stone near the end of his property resembled two galloping horses. And the black stone "like a broken needle" was still there, a rod or two from shore.

Suddenly fear struck Cunard—fear that he might already be too late. He leaped from his chair and ran out into the grounds.

There were four holes and the beginning of a fifth in evidence. But, moving quickly from one to another, the planter saw with relief that all were shallow and showed no traces of any object having been taken from them.

Cunard hastened back to the house where he procured a small but accurate compass and a ball of twine. Then he went into the tool-house and brought out a pair of oars for the dory that was moored at the water's edge on a little spit of sand.

An hour later his work was finished. He had rowed the dory out to the needle point of rock and fastened one end of the twine to it. The other end he stretched across to the horse rock in the corner of his property. Then he counted off the required sixty paces and planted a stick in the ground to mark the spot. After that there was nothing he could do until night. He hoped there would be no clouds to obstruct the moon.

Still there was the possibility someone might blunder here while he was in the house, and after a moment's thought Cunard returned to the tool-house and rummaged through the mass of odds and ends that had collected there through the years. He found an old doorbell that had been discarded when the more musical chimes had been installed in the house, also several batteries and a coil of wire.

During the war Cunard had made a superficial study of electricity and wireless as part of what he considered his patriotic duties, and he now proceeded to wire a crude but efficient alarm system around the general area where he conceived the treasure to be.

Back in the house, he settled himself to wait the long hours until moon-rise. In the quiet of inactivity he was conscious again of that sound of distant water flowing. He made a round of all taps in the house, but none was leaking.

During his solitary dinner he caught himself glancing out the window into the grounds, and once he thought he saw a shadow move across the lawn and into the trees. But it must have been a passing cloud, for he didn't see it again.

At two P.M. a knock sounded on the door. Cunard was surprised and somewhat disconcerted to see Inspector Bainley standing on the veranda.

"Just passing by," Bainley said, smiling genially. "Had a sudden call from the native village out on the Key. Seems a black boy got into some trouble out there. Thought it might be your Christopher."

"But that's impos—" Cunard checked himself. "I hardly think it likely," he amended. "Christopher would probably go as far as he could, once he started."

They drank rum. The Inspector seemed in no hurry to leave, and Cunard was torn between two desires, not to be alone and to be free from Bainley's gimlet eyes which always seemed to be moving about restlessly.

Finally he did go, however. The throb of his car was just dying off down the road when Cunard heard a new sound which electrified him to attention. The alarm bell!

Yet there was no one in the grounds. The wires were undisturbed, and the makeshift switch he had fashioned was still open. The bell was silent when he reached it.

With the moon high over his shoulder Cunard wielded his spade rapidly. The spot where the shadow of his head fell was disagreeably close to the bamboo thicket where he had buried Christopher, but as a matter of fact, he wasn't quite sure where that grave was, so cleverly had he hidden all traces of his work.

The hole had now been dug to a depth of four feet, but there was no indication anything had been buried there. Cunard toiled strenuously another half hour. And then quite suddenly his spade struck something hard and metallic. A wave of excitement swept over him. He switched on his flashlight and turned it in the hole. Yes, there it was, the rusted top of a large iron chest—the treasure of L'Ollonais.

He resumed digging, but as he dug, he became aware that the sand, at first dry and hard, had grown moist and soggy. The spade became increasingly heavy with each scoop, and presently water was running off it, glistening in the moonlight. Water began to fill the bottom of the hole too, making it difficult for Cunard to work.

But it was not until ten minutes later that he saw something protruding from the water. In the moonlight two slender dark objects were reaching outward, a pair of Negro feminine arms gently weaving to and fro.

Cunard stiffened while a wave of horror swept over him. They were dark-skinned arms of an aged Negress, yet somehow they were smooth and youthful. The middle finger of the left hand bore a ring of white coral.

Cunard screamed and lunged backward. Too late, one of those grasping hands encircled his ankle and jerked him forward. And as he fell across the hole, those hands wrapped themselves about his throat and drew his head slowly but deliberately downward. . . .

"Yes, it's a queer case," Inspector Bainley said, tamping tobacco into his pipe. "But then of course no more queer than a lot of things that happen here in the islands."

"You say this fellow, Cunard, murdered his houseboy, Christopher?" the Warrant-Officer said.

Bainley nodded. "I knew his savage temper would get the better of him some day. He buried the body in the yard and apparently rigged up that alarm arrangement to warn him of any trespassers. Then he contrived that story which he told me, that Christopher had run off.

"Of course we know now that Cunard was trying to find that buried treasure by following the directions given in that newspaper clipping. But that doesn't explain why he disregarded those directions and attempted to dig open the houseboy's grave again. Or why, before he had finished, he thrust his head into the shallow hole and lay in the little pool of seepage water until he drowned."

Moss Island

Fifteen miles off the New Brunswick coast, to the south of Marchester yet north of Lamont, lies a great timber-covered rock which has become known as Moss Island. With its endless chain of reefs, its frowning sheer walls, and its bastions of dense underbrush and giant trees, the island has remained untrespassed and primeval. Fishermen fear its jagged sides and keep well away. And as far as I have been able to learn, I am the only human being, or at least the only one for years, who has cared to visit its Eden shores.

For the sum of ten dollars, a little fishing smack had brought me out, had carefully threaded its way to a bit of beach on the western side.

"You're a fool," the rather deaf owner of the boat had growled when we arrived. "I'm givin' you fair warnin'. I'll keep my part of the bargain and come back for you at five o'clock, but only if the weather permits. I'm not so crazy about the looks of that sky over there, and if there's anythin' stronger'n a breeze comes up—well, you can figure on stayin' here 'til it calms down. I ain't a-goin' through that bunch of saw-teeth in a wind for the fun of it. Not with *my* boat. Anyway, what's interestin' here? Nothin' on Moss Island but trees and rocks. Not even any moss no more. Somethin' killed it," and he pointed to a smooth expanse of black rock, in places covered by a mass of last year's vines, dead and brown colored. One slab high above me looked like a woman with long, flowing hair, a great embossed Medusa, it seemed, when the wind ruffled the withered grasses.

"That's Mape vine, not moss," I corrected him. "There's probably lots of moss farther in where there's damp shade." I picked up my hammer, my chart-drawing board and my knapsack and stepped from the boat, adding in explanation: "I'm going to do a little geological survey work, examine the rock formations, you know; and I don't think we'll have a storm. The weather report didn't say so."

He gave a derisive humph, whether at the nature of my work or my remark about meteorology I was left wondering, for without another word he shoved off. For a while I watched the boat bobbing away through the white caps, the little sail growing smaller and smaller and showing clean white in contrast to the green water and the blue sky. Then I turned to my surroundings.

I was still below the island proper, the cliff running some thirty to fifty feet up to the edge of the woods. In some places the wall was almost perpendicular, and I looked about for means of climbing it. Farther on along the beach I came upon a break and a series of jags which, with a little maneuvering, would serve as a staircase. I began my ascent. It was hard, slow work. Gulls whirled about me at my interruption, filling the air with their clamor. Ensnarled Mape vine impeded my progress and clumps of scarlet bush, which seemed to thrive on the scant nourishment it found in soil-filled crevices, dug its thorns relentlessly into my hands. Upon a little jutting shelf I saw a dead snake, its head hanging into space as though watching something below.

At length I reached the top, which I found to be flat as a pla- teau, the surface from the edge of the cliff quite void of vege- tation for a distance of about five yards, when abruptly began a wall of trees, the outer ones bearing evidence of the ravages of the elements. Peering off to sea again, I tried to catch sight of the boat that had brought me, but though I looked until the air before my eyes appeared porous, I could see no sign of it.

Striving to throw off a growing feeling of depression, I broke out into a loud whistle, following any tune my lips desired. The whistle seemed to travel for miles in the clear air. It rose above the trees and went far over the island. There was no echo. Only the waves swashed over rocks below me, and as I walked along the screaming cries of a solitary gull fell perfectly into the rhythmic cadence of my steps.

I kept close to the edge of the cliff. To have attempted pene- trating that jungle of growth would have been foolhardy. So I watched for a place where the trees might thin, reflecting idly that the glacial drift must be of a considerable depth to support such extensive vegetation. About half a mile onward I found some pieces of shale with a few shell fossils and a small slab of limestone with remarkably clear impressions of crinoids. These ancient forms of marine life I determined to be of the Mississippian geologic period.

But for some reason I lost interest in my work. The very solitude of the island seemed to have crept into me and dulled my senses. Occasionally I was forced to enter the wood to circle a mound of larger rocks that defied ascent. Occasionally I caught the glint of the sun shining upon the bloated body of a dead fish lying far below on the little stretch of sand. And although I had gone only a short distance, all the while the weight of my knapsack seemed steadily increasing.

By three o'clock I had almost reached the opposite side of the island. It was there on the eastern exposure that I came upon a sheer wall, a rock formation that would have delighted the most experienced geologist. Here with the Pennsylvania strata folded and resting upon the eroded edges of the Mississippian was a great sedimentary history of geologic time.

For a long while I examined the wall—from its base upward as high as I could reach. At length, taking my hammer, I began working on a rather peculiar outcropping vein or slight discoloration on the rock. Strangely enough, as I went deeper the color changed: from a dark brown at the surface to a reddish brown and from a reddish brown to a deep scarlet. If this were oxidation . . . but no . . . And then suddenly my hammer broke through—into a cavity in the limestone, a large hole which had been hollowed out by the ground water slowly filtering through the rock crevices and in the course of time dissolving the soluble parts. Such cavities are common to limestone, I knew, but sometimes rather interesting phenomena accompanies them. And so with a feeling of expectation I went to work with a will, enlarging the aperture until it was wide enough to thrust in my hand.

I extended my arm into the opening gently, felt a cold, sticky liquid touch the fingers. Hastily I drew my hand to sight. It was dripping with a brownish, viscous solution that had a musty odor. I stared in amazement. Pockets of mineral water are not uncommon in this district, but always it is clear and transparent.

The thought of oil flashed across my mind. But there is no oil on the New Brunswick coast nor for thousands of miles in any direction. And this brownish mass in no way resembled crude petroleum. It was very odd.

And then quite suddenly I remembered a recent conversation with Professor Monroe at the University of Rentharp, where I am doing graduate work in geology and mineralogy.

"Phillip," he had said when I came upon him in one of the laboratories, "I believe I've made a discovery." And while he worked he had told me about muscivol, the name which he had given to his find. "It is very rare," he had said, "rarer than radium."

I have always been interested in botany and I have a fair knowledge of the subject, but I confess some of his scientific explanation went over my head. This much, however, I roughly gathered:

In northern climates, under favorable conditions, can be found a rare moss which resembles and yet fundamentally differs from the common *Saelania* moss. After living in great luxuriance for a number of seasons, this *Musci* plant will suddenly die. If the diseased plant is examined just before its death, it will be found that almost a reversal of the natural processes of growth is going on.

A month earlier a small blister or pouch develops just above the rootlets. And for some unknown reason most of the food elements which the plant obtains from the soil and from the air, instead of serving to nourish the whole plant, gather and centralize in this pouch in liquid form. The rest of the plant is thus robbed of its food; it can no longer live healthily, and growing in damp places as it does, it is slowly overcome by rot.

The decay affects the contents of the pouch. The liquid goes through a process of fermentation. At length, the pouch bursts and the liquid soaks into the soil.

If a large number of these diseased moss plants are present, the ground will be almost saturated with the liquid. In time—always under favorable conditions—the liquid will soak down until it reaches and becomes a part of the ground-water—that is: the water in the solid rock below the surface which one taps when digging a well.

Limestone is full of subterranean cavities. The water carrying this plant-liquid in solution may find one of these, enter it, and become stagnant. Gradually the cavity deep down in the rock will be filled with the pouch-liquid of hundreds of these diseased mosses. And what is equally important with it will be certain amounts of mineral matter which is always present in the ground-water.

"Nowhere can it be found in the same intensity," Professor Monroe had said, "and in no two places is it really the same, for the mineral matter in the solution will always vary."

"Well, what good is it?" I had asked, rather bored by his long explanation.

The professor put down his test tube, leaned across the laboratory table: "I have discovered by accident that sometimes this liquid—Muscivol, I have called it—sometimes contains all the elements of growth."

"What do you mean?"

"I mean that if I apply a small quantity of it that has the right amount of mineral matter in solution to the original moss plant, one in healthy condition, its rate of growth will be speeded up tremendously. I mean that the few drops of Muscivol I have been able to find when placed on the stalk of a moss plant caused it to leap upward to twice its original size in a few seconds."

And as I stood there on the cliff, staring at my dripping fingers, it all came back to me. With a start I realized that this must be a vug of Muscivol, that rarest of liquids, the essence of moss growth. I emptied the coffee from my thermos bottle and, using the cover as a cup, carefully reached into the cavity and with the utmost care began the process of capturing as much of the sticky fluid as I could. I smiled to myself as I pictured Professor Monroe's surprise and delight when I brought him this find. The most he had been able to discover was a few drops, while here was almost a quart. True, I did not know as yet if it contained the necessary mineral matter to make it potent. That I must leave to the professor and his test tubes. When I had filled the thermos bottle, I carefully closed it and placed it in my knapsack.

The next hour I spent in making a rough chart of the sedimentary wall before me and writing in my notebook a brief geologic description of the island. All this, of course, was part

of my university work. At length, the brief survey complete, it
occurred to me that I still had time for further exploration before
the boatman would return, and so shouldering my knapsack, I
headed into the interior.

In a moment, as though a mighty door were shut, the woods
closed dark upon me, and I found myself in a jungle of growth
that discouraged further penetration. Gradually, however, as I
struggled forward, the underbrush, finding insufficient sunlight
to exist, thinned down until there were left only trees and moss.
The strange luxuriant abundance of the latter accounted, I saw,
for the island's name. Fern moss, Long moss, Urn and Cord moss,
Catharinaea angustata, Polytrichum strictum, and tree moss—in
every division common to the northeastern United States the
Musci order here was represented.

On rotting logs, at the foot of trees, in parasitical clumps upon
the trunks, and on the ground as a soft carpet of damp green—
everywhere was moss. With its perpetual damp and shade and
its moist sea air, the island seemed to present strangely perfect
conditions for this plant.

The wood was silent about me now, and occasionally, when
the tessellation of verdure above became less dense, could I see
the light of the sky. As I went deeper, the trees seemed to take
definite positions in the forest about me, to form long, dark corridors with winding turns. The mosses lost their dark greenish
hue and developed into a bluish yellow in the gloom. The air was
moist and warm. It weighed heavily upon my lungs. The island,
it appeared, was infested with blue jays, jays strangely fat and
over-nourished. Great flocks of them rose up at my approach,
their screaming cries filtering slowly through the sodden air like
the wails of a thousand drowning cats.

But as I went farther and farther, even they disappeared, and
I was left with only the walls of trees, the floor of moss and the
gloom. I saw more varieties now: Shaggy moss, Hooked moss,
and Hair-capped moss. Yellowish plants, they were, sickly and
flaccid in the half light.

At random I chose one of the corridors through the trees
and made my way slowly forward, my steps velveted in the soft
grasses. Winding, yet ever going deeper into the interior, the

walled lane stretched before me like a gallery. The intertangle-
ment of foliage far above was heavy and dense, admitting no light
but only a strange green glow.

It was a quarter after four by my watch when I reached a point
where the trees opened abruptly onto a little glade. Roughly
estimating this to be about the heart, the center of the island, I
was about to turn and retrace my steps when a mass of white at
the far side of the open space caught my eye. I stepped forward
and found myself gazing at a great circle of densely packed *White
Moss.* For some moments I stood there, looking down at the
cushion-like tufts.

The species I had recognized as *Leucobryum glaucum,* a *Musci*
plant common enough in moist woods, but for some reason,
whether because of its contrast to the green and yellow moss on
all sides or the anemic pallor of its gray whiteness, I viewed it here
with a feeling of utter revulsion. There was something repulsive
about the very way it sprawled across the glade.

During all this time, with the enthusiasm of exploration, I had
almost forgotten my finding of the liquid in the limestone cavity.
Now, however, I felt a sudden desire to prove to myself beyond a
doubt that the solution really was Muscivol, by observing how
this moss plant would react to a few drops. Quickly I unfastened
my knapsack, drew forth the thermos bottle, and unscrewed the
cap. Then carefully tilting it over the matted circle of white moss,
I let a small amount of the brownish liquid fall.

The result was amazing. The plant quivered a half moment,
then shot upward with terrific growth rate. Unconsciously
I jumped back. My foot caught in a bramble, I lost my balance
and fell full length. The thermos bottle bounced from my hand,
rolled across the ground straight into the White Moss plant, and
there the viscous contents began to pour forth.

With a cry of dismay I realized what had happened. A quart
of Muscivol was upon the plant, a quart where a few drops had
been multipotent. A great shudder ran through the moss. A sobbing sigh came from its grasses. And then with a roar, the rootlets
gouged down into the ground, tore at the soil, and the plant
with a mighty hiss raced upward, five feet, ten feet. The tendrils
swelled as though filled with pressure, became fat, octopus folds.

Like the undulations of some titanic marine plant the white coils waved and lashed the air. Up they lunged, the growth rate multiplied ten thousand times.

A tentacle in its mad gyrations brushed my face. I turned to the wood and ran—down the long corridors, through the trees. Behind me the roar rose into a great thunder; the hissing stabbed the air like escaping steam. On through the dark woods I raced. Looking over my shoulder, I could see the white moss with coils like cables now, climbing over the trees, advancing with frightful velocity. Muscivol! What chemical was this that could destroy the very laws of nature? A great wail rose up as a thousand terrified blue jays flapped away in a mad hegira for safety. The forest was endless. Miles I seemed to have run, but I tore on even faster toward the cliff.

At length I reached it, emerged into the open air, but found the day not as I had left it. A heavy fog had rolled in from the sea, had thrown a veil over the entire coast.

I did not stop. To the rear the wall of white was lunging over the island now like a tidal wave. Came the repercussions of the crashing of trees, snapping under the great weight of the moss. The growth fulminations pounded against my ear drums. Along the cliff, through the thickening fog, I ran. And suddenly a fearful thought came to me. Suppose the boatman had not returned?

Again I looked back. With frightful rapidity the advancing moss was gaining on me. Like an octopus the tentacles were clawing the sky, engulfing the whole island. And now the ground beneath my feet, torn and ruptured by the distant moss roots, began to shake in cataclysmic convulsions.

But at length I reached the break in the cliff where I had made my ascent from the beach. I ran to the edge and peered over. The boat was there! Through the haze of the fog I could see it drawn up on the sand, the boatman waiting. I leaped to the jags in the rock sides and began my descent.

How I ever reached the bottom I don't know. I remember running wildly across the beach to the boat, climbing in, and shouting something unintelligible to the boatman. And then we were out on the water, heading into the fog, the cool salt air fanning my face.

I came to my senses finding the old man chafing my wrists.

"What in thunder happened?" he asked.

I stood up in the rocking boat. Vaguely, through the haze I could see the great bulk of the island a half mile to our lea.

"That moss!" I cried, "that wall of white moss! Don't you see it?"

He stared over the water, squinting his eyes. "Moss?" he repeated slowly. "Did you say moss?" and he turned to me with a queer look.

"I don't see no moss," he said. "All I can see is fog, white fog."

Carnaby's Fish

Mr. Jason Carnaby was a man of medium height, medium features, and medium habits. At forty-six he was one of those bachelors who, having passed from youth well into middle age, would have attracted no comment other than a casual query as to why he had never married. He operated a small real-estate business with rather shabby offices in the town of La Plante and, with the exception of a stenographer who came in two days a week, he worked quite alone.

Inasmuch as La Plante was located near the Atlantic coast, much of his business had to do with shore property, summer homes and cottages. These holdings moved fairly fast, but occasionally he acquired a home which refused to attract a buyer.

Of all these, the Dumont place was undoubtedly the most difficult to move. While it was listed as "shore property," it was actually on Philip's Lake, a short distance inland. It was part of an estate which had passed through probate, old Captain Dumont having died more than five years ago. Since that time it had had but one occupant, a Dr. Septimus Levaseur, who had lived there almost a year and a half before his death, which had come about suddenly and somewhat obscurely.

The death of the doctor, who had been an amiable fellow, if somewhat distant and hazy at times, had given rise to some of the rumors which had become attached to the Dumont place and made it so difficult to sell or rent.

Dr. Levaseur had died of a heart attack, apparently brought on by over-exertion. He had been found on the East road the night of a big storm half-clad, a crucifix clutched in his hand. Mr. Carnaby, who was the soul of the conventional, had always regarded the doctor as somewhat queer, but, in final analysis, Mr. Carnaby's judgment was circumscribed by the question of rent, and Dr. Levaseur had always paid his rent promptly.

Nevertheless, his strange death had doubtless been the basis for the rumors that there was something odd about the house, that the whole property was damned, and that finally Philip's Lake was "queer." Mr. Carnaby was admittedly at a loss as to how these stories had got started; the circumstance of Dr. Levaseur's having been found clasping a crucifix and but half-clad on the East road might have excited the superstitious, but Mr. Carnaby failed to discover how the lake came to be implicated. Since other property in Mr. Carnaby's hands adjoined the lake, he was irritated, lest some stigma similar to that attaching to the Dumont place should likewise become attached to other properties. He made some effort to isolate rumors concerning Philip's Lake, and finally got down to two basic tales.

Three cottage residents on the opposite shore from the Dumont place said that a small area of water far out toward the center of Philip's Lake was frequently rough and white-capped, when not a breath of wind was stirring. Mr. Carnaby's very reasonable suggestion that the lake might be connected to the ocean by underground channels opening off from the vicinity of the disturbed area was brushed aside. The cottagers countered with an additional tale to the effect of a pale light or a shimmering radiance which sometimes wafted over the lake like a will-o'-the-wisp. And finally, old John Bainley told of hearing on several occasions a melodious singing far out from shore, singing which was so wonderfully lovely he wanted to swim out to it, though he hadn't been in the water "for nigh unto sixty years." Whatever the source of these old wives' tales, they played their part in the failure of the Dumont house to attract a renter.

After repeated efforts to dispose of the property, all of which came to nothing, Mr. Carnaby decided one morning in July that something final should be done about the Dumont place. Accordingly, he gave the keys of his office to his stenographer, hitched his horse to the buck-board, and headed down the East road.

In due time he reached Gail's Corners, where he rested the horse and refreshed himself with a soft drink at the settlement's only store, through the display windows of which he could see across the summer landscape to the circle of drab gray water which was Philip's Lake. He knew that this body of water was only by courtesy called a lake, for it was merely a small quay from which on occasion a neck of water afforded an outlet to the Atlantic.

As he stood there, gazing out at its surface, it occurred to him that he had never, after all, actually examined the lake; that is, he had not gone out on it, though he handled property touching upon it on all sides. There was something strangely melancholy and at the same time somberly attractive about Philip's Lake, and it might well be worth while to row out on to it, provided the flat-bottomed rowboat which had always laid along the shore of the Dumont place was still there. At the same time, it might not be amiss to idle away a little time in fishing, a recreation for which Mr. Carnaby had found all too little time. Acting on this impulse, he bought a cane pole, a spool of line, and several varieties of artificial bait, and resumed his journey.

He reached the property at length: an old style Cape Cod house, rectangular in shape, with a narrow veranda and an acre of surrounding ground. It seemed, as he stood in the weed-grown yard, that the house had a detached look, as if in some way it did not belong there. Gazing at the lake again, he had the rather uncomfortable impression that it too had been super-imposed upon the landscape like a double exposure photograph. He entered the house and went through the building room by room, making notes on the back of an old envelope as to repairs that should be made, their approximate cost and other items.

Finished, he locked the door and passed down the path toward the lake. A dozen yards from the house stood a stone well with a pagoda roof over it. At the shore he mused for some time over an old harpoon which Captain Dumont apparently had cast there in an idle moment. The weapon reminded him that Captain Dumont had served on a whaler in his younger days.

The flat-bottomed rowboat was still there. Mr. Carnaby bailed out the rain water with some effort, threw his new fishing tackle across the thwart and pushed out on to the lake. On the water the impression that the closely-wooded shores were somehow out of proportion came again, and he took off his spectacles and rubbed them with a polishing cloth. He began to feel that he had come here not of his own will but in response to an indefinable and growing attraction emanating from the depths of the green waves. What a queer creature man is, Mr. Carnaby thought, to create a fascination for the unpleasant. He thrust away a desire to leap overboard and, with an effort, began to arrange his tackle.

For an hour he fished. Having no leader, he fastened the plug directly to the line and proceeded to throw the bait as far out as he could with the aid of the pole, and then jerk it gently along through the water.

Tiring of his fruitless efforts at length, and wanting to rest his eyes from the glare of the sunlight on the water, Mr. Carnaby leaned back and lowered his lids. The day was drowsy, and so, too was he. When he awoke, the sun had gone down and the gloom of late twilight was dropping upon the lake. In his boat, Mr. Carnaby was far out from shore, drifting aimlessly.

Indeed, he was approximately in the center of the lake, and a little wind was rippling the water there. Suddenly conscious of the time, Mr. Carnaby took up the oars and began to row hard. It did not occur to him that his fish-pole was propped under one thwart with the line trailing behind the boat in the water until in the half-darkness he saw the pole abruptly bend almost double. He barely had time to grab it and pull with all his strength.

The fish came through the water slowly, heavily. As it drew closer, Carnaby could sense rather than see it weaving to and fro in the black water, not so much struggling to free itself as reluctant to come with the line, though his catch did not seem to come willingly. It was somewhat awkward to handle the cane-pole in his cramped quarters, but at last Carnaby got his catch alongside, and reached down to complete his capture.

His first impression was that he had caught a catfish. His second was of something so infinitely more horrible that an involuntary exclamation of horror escaped him.

But the twilight, surely, played his eyes tricks. He had now laid his pole down, and still holding the line, though with uncertain eyes averted from his catch, he slipped a small flashlight from his pocket, switched it on, and turned the comparatively feeble ray on to his catch.

A woman's head drifted there, looking up at him—an exquisite feminine face with long blond hair trailing in the water, which, rippling over the countenance white in that darkness, revealed teeth bared in an expression of unutterable malignance. The barbs of one of the gang hooks had bitten deep into the red mouth, and from it flowed a thin stream of blood.

It was alive, a perfectly moulded human head—but the body was that of a fish, with tail and fins!

For several seconds Mr. Carnaby sat frozen to immobility. Then the flashlight slipped from his hands; he dropped the line and began to row wildly for shore.

He beached the boat and staggered unsteadily up the path. When he reached the house he halted breathlessly, overcome by nervous reaction. The shadow of his patiently waiting horse and buckboard loomed beyond the gate, but in spite of this bewildering horror, he did not feel up to driving the lonely road back just yet. He climbed the stoop, inserted his key into the lock with trembling hands, and re-entered the house.

The stillness of the long-closed interior closed about him like a cloak, soothing his troubled nerves. He lit a lamp, carried it into the living room and placed it on the table. Then he got out his pipe and began to smoke slowly and deliberately.

Was he mad, he wondered, or was the thing he had seen only the after-effect of a latent dream? Had he witnessed some phantasmagoria, created by water and darkness which his numbed senses had reformed into a vagary of the subconscious? One thing was certain. Tell his experience to the townsfolk of La Plante, and he might as well write a no-sale ticket for the property. Once such a story got around, no amount of advertising would be able to overcome the superstitious aura that had already begun to gather around the Dumont place.

It came to him that certain rumors concerning Dr. Levaseur and his strange death had been bruited about with raised eyebrows—vague, formless whisperings. Certainly the man had been odd, and the oddity of his character was brought home to Carnaby now as he looked upon the room in which he stood.

The walls had been done over in a shade of bluish green that was dark and cheerless. The rug was a light brown, and the border design resembled thick layers of pebbles interlaced with sand. On one wall was an old print of Heinrich Heine; near it hung a faded etching of a sailing vessel in a storm; and in one corner stood a bookcase filled with large and heavy volumes.

Still smoking and somewhat calmer now, Mr. Carnaby crossed to the books. *Loreleysage in Dichtung und Musik. Mysteries of the Sea,* by Cornelius Van de Mar. *The History of Atlantis,* by Lewis Spence. As he stood looking at these titles, Carnaby became aware again, by a process of idea-association, of the nature of Dr. Levaseur's curious obsession. He was instantly apprehensive again, and curiously disturbed, for his memory brought back vividly that strange and horrible experience on the lake.

Dr. Levaseur had claimed to be an authority on loreleis, on marine lures of legend and mythology, and he had written several papers on these old beliefs. Surely these were somewhere available, thought Carnaby. Yet he was briefly reluctant to look for them, a little afraid of what he might find. However, after but a few moments of hesitation, he set about searching for Dr. Levaseur's papers among the publications in the bookcase, and in a short time found a thick sheaf of dusty foolscap, closely written in a fine precise hand.

This he carried to a chair and read.

At first, in his nervous haste, he found it difficult to keep his attention to the pages, but gradually the brooding silence of the house drifted out of his consciousness. He read for an hour, and at the end of that time he sat back in silent amazement. Dr. Levaseur had apparently been not only an authority on loreleis and ancient allied folklore, but he had also been versed in a myriad of psychic phenomena which had any kind of marine background. And, incredible as it seemed, the doctor apparently had accepted many of these tales as factual accounts.

He had written at some length the account of the Tsiang Lora siren which hardened Dutch sailors had reported dwelt near an islet off the southeast coast of Java. Seen only at night, cloaked in bluish-white radiance, this siren, like her many mythological counterparts, took the form of a woman, lovely and ethereal, whose whispered plea for help drifted across the water with all the power of a lodestone. Dr. Levaseur had added to this narrative the factual results of several geodetic surveys made by the

Netherlands East Indies Hydrographical Department, pointing out that the sea floor at this point of latitude and longitude sloped sharply upward and formed a shallow reef or submerged tableland. In addition, the doctor recounted the foundering of a Dutch brigantine near this location in the early sixties. This ship had carried a passenger, a rich Malay woman, who was suspected of being a priestess of the *dularna* sect.

He had carefully chronicled the tale of Dabra Khan in the Arabian Gulf, a masculine lorelei who supposedly shouted false commands in the helmsman's ears during a storm; of McClannon's Folly, a needle spire of rock off the Cornish coast which changed to a voluptuous maiden clinging to a spar when viewed through a lane of fog, each case described with scholarly directness.

But toward the end of the manuscript there was an underlined paragraph that Mr. Carnaby read several times.

It is now four months since I have come here. Yesterday I went out upon Philip's Lake for the first time, and I know now that I was not wrong in my judgment. It is there, it called out to me, and for a moment I thought I saw it in all its malevolent beauty.

I cannot wait until I have seen it again. Tomorrow, taking full precautions, and using all the powers at my disposal, I shall strive to entice it from its lair. The desire is almost overwhelming.

Mr. Carnaby sat looking off into space for a long time. At length he put his pipe into his pocket and returned the manuscript to the bookcase. He blew out the lamp and made his way out of the house to the buckboard. He was in deep, perturbed thought as he drove slowly home.

Thereafter, Mr. Carnaby made no further attempt to find a renter for the Dumont place. He filed the deed and abstract away in an old shoebox, marked: *Miscellaneous N.G.*, and he went about his business, saying nothing to anyone about his experience on the lake.

In this manner fall passed into winter, and the town of La Plante went about its routine in its usual fashion. It was the following spring, a balmy day in early May, that Mr. Carnaby chanced to meet his old friend, Lawyer Herrick, as the latter was emerging from the courthouse.

"Well, how's business?" Herrick inquired politely, accepting

Mr. Carnaby's cigar. "Should be a run on shore property this summer, what with that new pike cut through from Kenleyville."

"Yes, there should," Mr. Carnaby agreed.

"I see you've got the Dumont place rented again," Herrick continued. "I thought you would in time. It's a nice place."

Mr. Carnaby looked at the lawyer sharply. "Why no, it's not rented. What ever made you think it was?"

Herrick flicked his cigar ash into the wind and frowned slightly. "I drove by there yesterday, and I thought I saw a woman sitting on the shore, sunning herself. A woman with blond hair."

"Is that so?" said the real estate man. "That's odd."

It was so odd that he decided to visit the property the next day. He could, he told himself, kill two birds with one stone. A tenant farther down the East road had complained of a bad roof, and Mr. Carnaby had put off for some time the task of inspecting it.

When he turned into the lane leading to the Dumont house, Mr. Carnaby cast a quick glance at the shore. The westering sun was in his eyes, and the fire-like reflection from one of the windows blinded him, but for a moment he fancied he saw a woman sitting on the shore. But at second glance, somewhat out of range of the sun's reflection, he saw nothing; the place bore the unmistakable appearance of desertion—not alone the house, in its aloof desolation, but all the land belonging to it.

Mr. Carnaby opened the house and went into the living room. With all his experience in entering long-closed houses, he could never repress the initial spell of depression which swept over him as his nostrils caught the smell of dust and stale air. Nothing was changed from his visit of six months before. Yet he had, however, curiously, expected change; the casual suggestion inherent in Herrick's brief conversation had affected him most disagreeably; it had caused him to think again of that horrible experience on the lake, of Dr. Levaseur's pursuits and death, of the tales concerning the Dumont place.

He lit the lamp, for daylight was fading outside, and already the room was hazed with early twilight. He lit his pipe, too, and as usual, the tobacco smoke soothed him somewhat. Now that he was here, his thoughts returned again to Dr. Levaseur's manuscript; he took it from the bookcase where he had left it, and sat down to glance through it again. This time, however, he could find no attraction in the written words—the paragraphs seemed stilted, disconnected, even absurd. Nevertheless, cold as he remained to Dr. Levaseur's thesis of the reality of loreleis and similar creatures, he was most unpleasantly impressed by the scholarly, almost dryly erudite weight of evidence which the doctor had adduced to sustain certain half-hinted beliefs. And there was that curious reference to "something" in Philip's Lake.

Something like an hour passed before he heard the singing. Even then he was hardly aware of it, so soft was the voice and so far off. But presently he looked up from the manuscript and listened. Almost at the limit of his hearing range it sounded, the overtones blending into the sighing of the wind.

Definitely it was a woman's voice, singing a strange lilting melody. It grew louder, and, despite an apprehensive hesitation, Carnaby strode to the window and opened it. It was a song such as he had never heard before, sung in a contralto, wandering up and down the octaves in an aimless yet appealing way. Through the window he could see no living person, only the shadowy lombardies that marched down the slope to the shore of the lake.

The singing grew louder until it seemed to resound from the walls of the room. And now as he listened, Mr. Carnaby experienced a strange sensation. It was as if every nerve and fiber of his body responded to that voice and urged him to go to its source. It was a lure, and with his bucolic matter-of-factness the real estate man unconsciously fought it with all his will.

He might as well have been fastened to a steel cable. Step by step he found himself drawn across the room to the door and out on to the veranda. There he halted again, all but overcome by that voice.

On feet that were dead things Mr. Carnaby strode down the steps and down the path. He passed the well and continued to the shore of the lake. Black water rippled at his feet.

And then he saw her. She was twenty yards from shore, waist deep in the water, moving slowly toward him. In the moonlight he could see her carmine lips as she sang her golden song. He could see her dripping tresses coiling about her nude shoulders. On she came, and still he stood there transfixed, held by some alien power.

Suddenly the singing ceased. Mr. Carnaby felt something snap in his consciousness like a clipped wire. The woman was directly before him now, and as she advanced, the lower portion of her body came clear of the water. A greenish scaled body edged with white. The body of a fish! The head and breasts were those of a woman, but even as he watched, he saw that head bloat and swell, lose its features, change to a horrible reptilian mass that gazed upon him with diabolic fury!

He turned, the spell broken, and the thing lunged toward him, seeming to move through the air. Down the beach Mr. Carnaby ran, a mighty horror assailing him, but his steps were turned to lead. Then, even as he faltered, he caught the glint of moonlight on a shaft in the sand. Old Captain Dumont's harpoon.

Driven by the wild impulse to save himself, he bent down, seized it and turned to face the monster. His heart stood still. There it was directly before him, an horrendous, loathsome beast with slavering lips and blazing, hyalescent eyes. It closed in, and as it did, Mr. Carnaby drove the harpoon before him with every ounce of strength he possessed. He felt the stinging recoil, but whether it was merely his arm reaching the limit of its range he did not know. Things became vague and indistinct for Mr. Carnaby then. A piercing scream seared into his ears. The monster wavered and sank backward. Then, uttering low, mewling cries, it turned and scrabbled down the beach. Simultaneously the surface of the black lake seemed to rear upward and boil in a great cauldron of lashing waves and foam.

The thing reeled into the water. Twenty yards from shore it fell forward like a spent juggernaut. For a moment it lay there, body awash, heaving up and down. Then slowly it sank from sight.

Mr. Carnaby spent eleven days in the La Plante hospital under the close surveillance of his physician. Upon his release, he forced himself, however reluctantly, to return to the Dumont place and make a thorough investigation. He found the harpoon on the beach, where he had left it; he found also the indentations of his footprints. He found nothing more. Moreover, the house seemed exceedingly pleasant, even inviting. He could discover but one somewhat odd fact, and this mattered hardly at all—the report of the governmental meteorological station at the county seat nine miles east stated that, from May seventh to May sixteenth inclusive, wind velocities in the La Plante district were at the lowest point they had been for the entire year. Yet, during that time Philip's Lake remained in a turbulent state, white-capped and sullen with angry waves.

The effect of all this was to inspire Mr. Carnaby with the conviction that, in time, the Dumont place might after all be made to pay. He paid it another visit and found nothing altered; he took time to make a few repairs and had the house cleaned up a little. In a fortnight he managed to find a young couple who wanted the house, and rented it forthwith.

He waited uneasily for several weeks for any word of trouble, but nothing came from the Dumont place but the rent, with pleasant regularity, and presently Mr. Carnaby began to look back upon his experience as a kind of neurotic condition which had given him unhealthy hallucinations.

It was ten months before he visited Gail's Corners again. On that occasion he had to pay a visit to the village doctor concerning a property he was handling for him. He found the doctor just back from the country, offered him a cigar, and lit one for himself.

"It's a coincidence seeing you, Carnaby," said Dr. Holmes. "I've just come from one of your tenants—and I need a drink, bad. Just get that bottle and the glasses from that cupboard, will you?"

Carnaby did so, his eyebrows raised. "Which tenants?"

"The Plaisiers. They're on the Dumont place."

A ball of alarm exploded inside Carnaby; he sat down, feeling his mouth going dry. "Nothing wrong, is there?"

"Wrong? God knows what you'd call it, Carnaby." He shook his head and poured himself a drink. "I delivered her baby all right—usually have trouble with the first, you know—but I didn't have any trouble with the delivery. But the baby! My God, Carnaby!—I never saw a baby that looked so much like a fish in all my life!"

He poured a drink for Carnaby and looked up to hand it to him. He was not across the desk from him where but a moment before he had been. Quietly, without a sound, Mr. Carnaby had fainted.

The King and the Knave

The man accosted Sargent at the intersection of Charing Cross and Oxford. He was tall, with a long black rain-cape, an oddly-shaped alpine hat, and a cane. He said:

"I beg pardon, sir. But do you play cards?"

Sargent turned up his collar against the drizzle and shivered. For an hour he had known he was being followed. From Russell Square to the British Museum to Dyott Street, while fog swept steadily in from the Embankment, he had gradually increased his pace, aware of the muffled steps behind.

"Cards?" he asked. "What do you mean?"

The man extended a claw-like hand. "I am Doctor Paul Losada. You have perhaps heard of me . . ."

A little shock darted up Sargent's spine.

". . . And you are Basil Sargent, the man who won thirty thousand pounds at Monte Carlo, who broke the bank at Wang Tau's in Singapore, playing *main-po* three years ago. In short, you are, unless I am mistaken, the most well-informed person on games of chance in London at the present time."

"I am Basil Sargent, yes," Sargent replied coldly.

"Then, *Señor*,"—the stranger's pallid face seemed to swirl uncertainly in the fog—"may I ask a favor of you? I live but a short distance from here. Would you do me the honor of coming to my apartment? My wife and I are looking for a fourth at whist. But more than that, I have something I would like to show you, something which I believe you will appreciate more than anyone else."

"And what," Sargent asked uneasily, "do you wish to show me?"

A gleam leaped into the man's black eyes. "A deck of cards, *Señor*, bearing neither hearts, clubs, spades, nor diamonds—the strangest and perhaps the oldest deck in existence."

Sargent was expecting another answer, and his relief in not getting it left him cold for a moment. For a long time he stood there in silence. Then he smiled. Losada, eh? Inez Losada's impossible husband. The man must take him for a fool.

But why not? The situation which, to a less handsome, less confident man, might have loomed dangerous seemed only amusing to the gambler.

"I'll go," he said.

Rumbling down Charing Cross, their cab turned right at Old Compton Street and headed into Soho. Doctor Losada's residence was on Rupert Street, a huge stone pile that seemed to shrink back despondently in the shadows.

The doctor led the way down a gas-lit corridor to a door on the second floor back. Inside, he disappeared for a moment, then returned, followed by a man and a woman.

"My wife, Inez," he said. "Her brother, Ricardo."

Sargent bowed. "I have met the *Señora* once before," he smirked. "Wasn't it at Covent Garden?"

She was black-haired and strikingly beautiful, and there was a ghost of a smile about her reddened lips as she replied:

"Perhaps. I go to the opera frequently."

Doctor Losada opened a card table, placed four chairs around it.

"We will begin with whist," he said. "But first let me show you the cards."

He opened a small ivory box, took out a deck and spread it on the table top.

Sargent stared.

For twenty years as a professional card sharp he had earned his living by his wits. For twenty years he had wandered from city to city, winning games of chance by his own trickery and cunning, taking fortunes from the gullible. But never had he seen a deck like the one before him.

As Losada had said, the suits were distinguished by neither hearts, diamonds, clubs, nor spades. The two black suits were snakes and harpies, with a knave, a queen, a king, and ten pip-cards, including an ace. The two red suits were the same, except that their markings were spiders and moonflowers. In spite of the cards' apparent age, they were in remarkably preserved condition.

But most unusual of all was the joker. The very presence of this card seemed to constrict Sargent's lungs with a feeling of suffocation. Blackly marked on a white surface, it showed a small skull, a death's-head.

"Where did you get them?" Sargent asked, looking up.

Doctor Losada smiled. "The pack was sent me by a friend in Seville. As it happened, they were almost lost before they arrived."

"Lost?"

"They were sent by plane," Losada explained. "The pilot was stricken ill, en route to Croydon, and the ship crashed. Only part of the mail was recovered."

Losada now took the deck and shuffled it. "High card deals," he said, motioning Sargent to draw.

Sargent drew the knave and laid it down before him. And then a curious coincidence occurred. Losada's wife, Inez, drew the queen. Losada took the king. Knave, queen, king in direct rotation. Ricardo's card was a low number.

Losada cut and began to deal. A moment later play started. The game was a close one, and for a while, although there were no stakes, Sargent's old interest held him to each move. Gradually, however, other thoughts began to invade his brain, and he took and lost tricks mechanically.

Did Doctor Losada know him by name only? Had he chosen him for a fourth simply because he desired a person of his reputation to examine his antique deck?

Or was he aware of the clandestine affair between Sargent and the *Señora*, Inez? Did the doctor know that during the many nights his practice took him from his apartment, Sargent had visited his wife in secret?

There was no doubt that Inez was a beautiful woman. Her eyes were large. Her skin was like tinted satin, and her figure, as she sat there, was little concealed by her low-cut gown.

In the center of the table, next to the trump card, the joker still lay, face up. Looking at it, Sargent again got the impression that something about the card was affecting his breathing. It seemed as if an invisible dust fog were passing from that tiny death's-head into his nostrils.

The game centered down to the last trick. Again that coincidence occurred. Sargent's card was the knave. Inez played the queen, and Losada without the slightest show of emotion took the trick with his king. Once more rotation had been knave, queen, king—with king the winner.

At one A.M. Sargent took his leave. He expressed his thanks and pleasure for the evening. But as he descended to the street, some inner urge prompted him to look back over his shoulder.

Rupert Street lay dark and deserted, with only an occasional street lamp to light the oldish buildings on either side. But directly above the apartment he had just left, a solid, compact cloud-mass hung low in the night sky. He shuddered. For as he looked, it seemed to Sargent that that cloud bore the same design as the joker card of Losada's deck, and that something, dry and smothering like smoke, was creeping down from the death's-head in the heavens into his lungs.

The telephone in his Bloomsbury hotel woke Sargent early next morning.

"This is Doctor Losada," came the voice on the wire. "I'm sorry to trouble you again, but after you left last night I was unable to locate one of the cards of my deck. I desire very much to keep that deck intact, and I am wondering if you would mind looking to see if it attached itself unnoticed to your clothes."

"Just a minute," Sargent said.

He opened his wardrobe closet, searched quickly through the clothes he had worn the previous evening. In the rain-jacket, in the torn lower hem—sure enough, there was the card, the knave of snakes.

"The card is here," he said into the phone. "I'll mail it to you at once, doctor."

"Why not bring it yourself, *Señor*? Say tonight at nine, and we can have another game."

That night Sargent again stood before the gloomy corridor door of Doctor Losada's apartment on Rupert Street. All day the events of the night before had lingered in his brain, troubling him. Try though he would to fight it off, a distinct sense of terror seemed closing in on him. He felt as if he were gradually being drawn into a web from which he could not keep away, and from which there was no escape.

No response came to his pull at the bell. He tried the latch, opened the door and entered. The apartment was lighted but empty. Then he saw the note on the table.

> Señor Sargent:
>
> A thousand pardons, but neither my wife, Ricardo nor I will be able to be with you at the agreed hour. An urgent matter has come up, requiring our presence elsewhere.
>
> You may amuse yourself, if you wish, until we return, with the cards. They are in the lower right compartment of the wall cabinet.
>
> Losada

Sargent scowled and nervously lighted a cigarette. He turned toward the door. But the desire to view that deck once more became overpowering.

A moment later, hat and coat removed, he opened the little ivory box and took out the cards. In the droning solitude of the room he shuffled and re-shuffled—then mechanically began to play solitaire.

There are many ways to play solitaire. Sargent's game was quite simple. A cross was made of five cards. On the cross, cards were played in *down* rotation without regard to suit. The corner cards finished out the square and were played upon in *up* rotation, according to suit. The object was to build these corners into complete sets of thirteen each.

Rapidly he played. He was on the verge of winning when he saw that his last card, the queen, could not be played. The king had gone into the discard pile, and he was unable to retrieve it.

He shuffled and tried again. But at the end of half an hour he stood again blocked. In three games, each with the queen in the corner, a king prevented him from winning.

Sargent felt a bead of cold sweat stand out on his brow. Terror, an invisible, nameless thing, seemed to rise from the pasteboards in his hands and close about him like a winding sheet.

Impulsively and for no definite reason he could think of at the moment he swept the cards together, jammed them into the ivory box and placed the box in his pocket. Puzzled at his action, yet lacking the will-power to change it, he took up his hat and coat and went out.

An hour later he was back in his Bloomsbury rooms, nervously downing a glass of brandy. The liquor quieted him somewhat, and he slumped into a chair, picked up a book and tried to read.

But the print swam before his eyes. Questions unanswerable hammered at him. Knave, queen, king. In all his experience at card playing, never had Sargent seen those three cards turn up in such chronological succession. It was weird!

He stirred restlessly. A curious chill, seeming to emanate from the ceiling above, filled the room.

Could it be possible that there was any significance in those cards? Did, for example, the queen represent Inez, the king Doctor Losada, and the knave himself? But no, such a thought was absurd.

At length Sargent tossed his book aside, undressed and went to bed.

It seemed he had but fallen asleep when he awoke, sat bolt upright, trembling in every nerve and muscle. The room was black as pitch, and there was no sound save the far-away rumble of a distant tram-car. He listened.

Faintly there came to his ears a low rustling, a scraping as of objects brushing against each other in frantic haste. It grew louder, died away.

Sargent leaped out of bed, snapped on the wall switch, flooding the room with light.

There was no one before him. The room was empty. And then, with a start, he found himself staring down at the table.

Ripped from its hinges as if by some internal force, the cover of the ivory box lay open. And Losada's deck of cards! They were arranged on the table in a partly completed game of solitaire. More than that, a chair was drawn up, though Sargent was positive none had been there before.

It was as if everything had been prepared for him to play.

Slowly he moved forward. The corner cards were queens.

Three corners had been built to the trey, but the last was still vacant.

Once again that overpowering urge swept over him. A definite psychic power drew him into the chair, moved his hands irresistibly toward the cards.

He began to move through the deck, playing slowly. The game wore on, and a vague horror began to rise within him.

The king! It was his unseen opponent. Like a hunted thing, jeering at his efforts, it remained unattainable in the discard pile.

Suddenly the telephone rang. Sargent lifted the instrument.

"Yes?"

A voice filled with triumph and mockery came over the wire. "This is Doctor Losada. Listen carefully, for what I have to say will be of interest to you.

"Please do not think our recent meeting was a matter of chance. I have known you, watched you for the past four months. I sought you out, not because of your reputation as a gambler— but because of my wife.

"My wife, yes. Did you think your intrigue with her could escape me unnoticed? Ah no, *Señor*. Doctor Losada is not that much of a fool. You have robbed me of the thing I prize most, and I have planned my revenge.

"Are you listening? You are now seated at a table, playing cards. My cards. It is not an ordinary deck, as you have perhaps guessed. It was fashioned by a Spanish sorcerer in the Fourteenth Century.

"Play your game of solitaire, *Señor*. Play with all the skill you possess. The card which represents you in the deck is the knave of snakes. The queen is Inez, my wife. *The king is myself.*

"Watch the king. Your only salvation is to defeat it with your knave. *Adios, Señor.*"

The phone clicked, and Sargent sat there, staring. Slowly he forked the instrument, picked up the cards. The words that had come over the wire were etched like fire in his brain.

But suddenly he laughed. Knave was he? Very well, as knave he would steal the queen and laugh in the king's face. With trembling fingers he began to move through the deck. Upon the trey he played in quick succession the four, the five, the six. The discard pile was lessening.

On and on he played. Cold sweat broke out on his forehead as he marshaled his forces. He was closing in on the king, and he was utilizing all of his skill to accomplish it.

A hiss of satisfaction came to his lips. Remained but one card to be played, and he would win.

And then a wave of horror billowed over him. The king card was moving, rising of its own accord from the discard pile. And as it moved, the card beneath slid out and fell upon the table directly beneath Sargent's gaze.

The joker!

He had forgotten it. Now as he sat staring at that leering death's-head that same horrible sense of suffocation seized him. His throat closed tight; his eyes bulged. It was as though an invisible poisonous miasma was floating from that painted skull, crawling into his lungs like a bulbous thing alive. He was choking. Choking . . .

He screamed and lurched to his feet. Gasping, he tore at his throat.

The joker card seemed to leave the table, to float before his eyes. He clawed at the rug, sucked wildly for air.

But gradually and relentlessly blackness closed in on him, and he felt his life ebb away.

The *London Morning Post* carried the following item the next day:

> An unfortunate tragedy occurred last night in a room of a Bloomsbury hotel. Mr. Basil Sargent, who won lasting fame by his unusual winnings at Baccarat at Monte Carlo, was found dead, apparently of asphyxiation.
>
> Investigation showed that the room's gas fixture had been left turned on.
>
> Police place no credence in the rumor that a man dressed in a black rain-cape stole into the hotel and entered the dead man's room some time after he retired.

Cosmic Teletype

Joseph Rane was not a scientist in any sense of the word, neither was he a highly educated man, though the villagers at Granite Point generally considered him so. Five years before, when he was finishing his sophomore year at the University of Minnesota, he had accidentally driven his car through the bridge rail at Hastings, and as a result had been forced to end his studies.

Physicians, patching him together, had accomplished what the newspapers termed a miracle. It had been found necessary to remove a section of his brain from the cranial cavity and substitute a piece of silver plate for it. During his convalescence fear was expressed that he would never be mentally normal, but on the day of his discharge a final examination plainly showed this not to be the case.

Rane had been warned, however, to avoid all nervous tension in the future. He might read, but he must read only light novels. He could work, but he must do nothing which would require any serious thought or heavy mental activity. In other words he was sane only by an act of Providence, and any strain to his brain, which had suffered a severe shock, might be fatal.

For two years the young man abided by these warnings. Then, tiring of his enforced inactivity, he promptly forgot the past and plunged into study so intense his physician would have been appalled had he been made aware of it.

I have said Rane was no scientist, that he was not a highly educated man. He had, however, those attributes which are the foundation of both: a strong desire to learn and, above all, an almost feverish obsession to experiment.

Then without the necessary background, and without any single fixed objective, he began to study anything which might reasonably fall under the classification of "scientific." For three months he labored at mathematics, advancing by short-cut routes of his own creation, to higher calculus and theoretical physics. Then, tiring of the abstract, he turned his attention to the vibratory scale.

Finally, as the equipment in his private laboratory began to grow in abundance, he purchased a small house near the town of Granite Point, where his experiments could be continued unhampered.

The house was a comfortable one, surrounded by a large apple orchard. In the first month at his new residence Rane both puzzled and shocked the citizens of Granite Point by blowing up every tree of this orchard with some kind of explosive. His exact method of accomplishing this was never quite known, for when his housekeeper repeated to the villagers what her employer had told her, it was thought she was more than slightly mad.

According to the housekeeper, Rane had wired each individual tree with something that was in sympathetic vibration with the wings of a bee. When the trees burst into their spring bloom and the bees came, the explosions followed.

Subsequent to the orchard incident, Rane was seen to construct a square wooden platform in the yard before his house, upon which swiftly took form a weird machine. The tax-collector who called upon him during the month of June described it as "a mess of insulators and wheels with a dial panel that looked like a powerhouse switchboard." Asked the purpose of this machine, Rane delivered the astounding statement that he didn't know yet. He had simply made it and was going to see what it would do.

Such events were bound to impress the citizens of Granite Point. The climax of it all came when the local radio station was found insolvent and decided to dispose of its studio and control room fixtures at public auction. Rane, driving up in his Model T Ford was the only bidder for two teletype machines with which the station had received for its listeners *News Flashes of the World*.

Loading the two heavy teletypes in his car, Rane broke all speed records driving back to his house. And after that for a period of more than two months little was seen of the man.

In his house, however, he was a dynamo of activity. First he mounted the two teletypes on a wooden bench, side by side.

There to the casual observer the instruments resembled two ordinary typewriters, with the twin paper-rolls in readiness, as if they were waiting to receive a telegraphic message. He next turned his attention to his cosmic radio.

He called it that for want of a better term. The earlier developments of this machine were lost in a frenzy of experimentation. Starting with a study of atomic power, Rane had developed a miniature atom-smasher; later he elaborated his instrument into a device of which he himself stood a little in awe.

"You see," he said one day to his housekeeper, "this machine as it now stands is based on a concept of the relation between time and space. It will project a ray through the fourth dimensional continuum. In other words, when turned to full power, it will cause a disruption of the space-time coordinates, a channel so to speak which leads from our own three-dimensional world into the fourth dimension. I am convinced that such a channel is being utilized by beings of other planets as a means of communication."

Rane then connected the two teletypes to the machine, with a loading-coil between each. He pulled the switch, set the dynamos in action and awaited results.

Results were cataclysmic. There was a blinding flash of light, a thunderous report which shattered twelve windows in Granite Point and a hiss of flame that swept through three rooms of the house. Rane himself escaped with only burns about the face and arms, but his housekeeper rose up in righteous wrath and promptly gave notice.

May I repeat myself when I say that Rane had the brain—or at least the partial brain—of a true scientist. One failure did not disturb him in the slightest. In fact, he had rather expected it. And he fell to work at once, repairing damaged cables and connections and rewiring his entire machine.

The newly-finished product was quite different from the original version. It was, if possible, more complicated in its control panel. There was added for no definite reason a huge antenna in the outer yard which stretched from the house to a mast some hundred and fifty feet away.

Again he connected his teletypes. And on the night of the first of August everything was in readiness for his second test. I mention the date, for it was the date of the worst electrical and wind storm that had struck Granite Point in twenty years. Outside the copper antenna and counterpoise were swaying madly in the gale. Lightning tore across the heavens to the accompaniment of an artillery of thunder.

Inside his laboratory Rane was oblivious to the storm. For two hours he had sat before the instrument panel, turning and twisting the dials. Above him a huge hourglass-shaped tube glowed orange and cherry red at intervals, but a deathlike silence hung over the two teletypes. There was only the low whine of the dynamos.

And then abruptly one of the typewriter keys of the teletype trembled and rose halfway. Feverishly, Rane readjusted the paper, turned the dials.

A moment later, with a rush and a clatter, the keys began to pound in and out, the carriage swept from right to left, and the following message came into creation on the rolled paper:

qtsf wuxz24 hkOOvey w3llmcbq bvcskha oorhg rivslyztuln kklmnwlf rywbsqv 3.2 ddcupj.

tcaw 5

Rane stared at these cryptic words as a wild gleam of triumph entered his eyes. Palms wet, heart pounding, he stood there, scarcely daring to breathe, but no further message was printed. Vainly he worked at the dials.

At twenty minutes past four A.M. the teletype moved into action again. But this time, though Rane was wild with excitement, its results were a bit disappointing. The same message was repeated word for word, or rather letter for letter. And thereafter silence.

Exhausted at last, Rane fell into a deep slumber. At dawn he was up again at his machine. What possibly could have been the source of that strange message he had, of course, no way of knowing. But that the events of the night before had been no dream was positively demonstrated by the paper in the roll which still showed its meaningless jumble of letters and figures.

All day he attempted to decipher that message. He put into play the "predominant E solution" of Poe and Doyle, as the only methods he had at his disposal. Neither worked. But that night again at five minutes past twelve and again at twenty minutes past four the first teletype resumed its clatter.

> qtsf wuxz24 hkOOvey w3llmcbq yvers chtq oorhg tfc aijbfw dpiuzqaz ywgfd bvcxzasdf wertyu.
>
> tcaw 5

Here was a different combination of letters and figures. The first, second, third, fourth words and the seventh word were the same as in the first message, as was the last word, which seemed to be a signature of some sort.

And then Rane had an idea. Suppose, he told himself, suppose he had in actuality contacted another planet, a planet which biologically, or at least psychologically, was on a parallel with the earth. And suppose the inhabitants of this planet were utilizing the fourth dimension as a means of communication. Surely even an Einstein would agree this was but an elementary supposition.

Very well, why then would messages come through twice in rotation at five minutes past twelve and twenty minutes past four? He glanced at his own radio, and the answer came abruptly. Weather reports!

His brain swung into this channel with a rush as other thoughts followed. Since the postulated planet might—in all probability, was—beyond our Solar System, its system of keeping time would be different. There would be other suns to betoken the noon hour. A night or a day very probably might fall into the intervening time between five minutes past twelve and twenty minutes past four.

Now was he to assume that the message he had received could be transposed into English words? Such an assumption seemed impossible, and the fact that numerals as well as letters had been used seemed to indicate another means of communication entirely.

Fortified by two cups of strong coffee Rane struggled with his solution. Using the single word *weather* as a key word in as many terrestrial languages as he could call to arm, he wrote and rewrote the messages again and again.

By morning Rane had it. It was in English or an equivalent of English. It was little more than a cryptogram, with letters and groups of letters having different meanings. Apparently the unknown operator was transmitting in a language that had English as a basis, but had phonetically changed it to suit his own conditions.

Decoded, the first message now read:

> Vome, Lirius. Weather forecast. Winds abating. Atmospheric coronium content 3.2. Warmer.
>
> Unit A.

The second message took Rane only a moment to transpose.

> Vome, Lirius. Weather forecast. Northwest winds and warmer. Possible light meteorite shower.
>
> Unit A.

Rane at this point was in a state of nervous frenzy. Sheer exhaustion forced him to go to his bed, where he remained dead to the world for six hours. But as the sun sank and darkness came, he awakened automatically to begin a new vigil at his machine.

The 12:05 message that night was very similar to previous messages, merely a weather prediction. But the 4:20 message was different.

> Vome, Lirius. General emergency report. Dromeda, daughter of Calian and most beautiful woman in all Lirius, was kidnapped early today by a man thought to be Tarana, son of the King of Uranus. It is believed Tarana arrived secretly on Lirius on a space ship, traveling out of patrolled space-lanes. A council of war will be held immediately.
>
> Unit A.

Swift on the heels of this breath-taking message, the cosmic teletype broke into action again. The keys pounded over the paper with weird rapidity.

Vome, Lirius. Report of the council of war to all peoples of Lirius. An ultimatum has been sent to the government of the planet, Uranus, demanding the return of Dromeda, plus a full indemnity. If this demand is disregarded, conscription of all able-bodied males of Lirius will begin tomorrow.

Unit A.

Barely had these words made their inked impression on the paper when another astounding event occurred. Joseph Rane, by now beyond all borders of amazement, reached quickly for the dials and adjusted them as best he could. The second teletype, silent until now, was responding to outer galactic stimuli. Slowly, as if under weight of serious consideration, the keys tapped off the message:

Geharla, Uranus. The King of Uranus informs the government of Lirius that Dromeda, betrothed by right of conquest, will be married in state to Prince Tarana in a wedding to be held tomorrow night in the light of our four moons. Any attitude other than friendly by the government of Lirius will be taken as a step toward war. In which case, we, of Uranus, will not hesitate to train our cosmic radiation towers on Lirius and annihilate her.

It was now two o'clock terrestrial time, and Joseph Rane was living on nervous energy alone. The hours that followed found the twin teletypes working almost continuously. There were threats and counterthreats between the two planets. There was a mass order for immediate mobilization on Lirius. There was a call to defense on Uranus. At three A.M. came the single insolent flash from Geharla that Prince Tarana had been married to Dromeda.

More messages while Joseph Rane's brain reeled to their potentialities. An expedition of war was leaving Lirius in space-dreadnoughts for Uranus. All threats of the cosmic radiation towers were regarded as bluff. Lirius would have its beautiful Dromeda back or perish trying.

But Rane's already over-strained brain demanded rest at this point. The scientist pulled the switch of his machine, stopping the dynamos, ate a little food and went to bed.

During the following day the teletypes were silent. He occupied his time by cutting the rolled paper messages into sheets and pasting them in a scrapbook. He worked indifferently, toying with an idea which had been growing with him for some time.

If he could receive messages from another world, why couldn't he send them in return? As matters stood now, he knew one of the planets was Uranus, and he assumed that since the inhabitants referred to it with the same name as the people of Earth, those inhabitants must (a) have originated from Earth, or (b) be constantly aware of the scientific developments on Earth through a method known only to themselves.

At 12:05 the following flash came over the first teletype:

> Vome, Lirius. The attack expedition, consisting of 25 space dreadnoughts, 6 space gun-ships, and 3 patrol discs has reached Oberon, one of the four moons of Uranus. Landing on Uranus so far has been an impossibility, due to the cosmic radiation towers, which have been found to be an actuality. The war is now in a state of siege.

Rane frowned. Weird and bizarre as this all was, he had a feeling deep within him that it was somehow familiar. Somewhere, long ago, he was sure he had heard of the same facts, and the same conditions. And yet such a thought was impossible.

As for two-way communication, even granting that he might be able to contact either one of the two planets, using the same code, it was doubtful whether or not he would receive a reply, due to the very great excitement there.

His sympathy, he found mounting steadily in the direction of Lirius, which he guessed was the smaller planet of the two, and which, though on the offensive, had a righteous cause for indignation.

Abruptly a memory of his old school studies struck him hard—the Trojan War of Greek mythology. This was comparable to the capture of Helen of Troy, wife of Menelaus by Paris and the classical incident of the wooden horse, which had so excited his boyhood imagination.

Joseph Rane sat down before the first teletype, threw over the switch and adjusted a control knob. An instant later he began pounding out a message.

> To Vome, Lirius. From Joseph Rane, Granite Point, Earth. Have received all messages pertaining to your war with Uranus on machine of my own construction. Exact parallel of your trouble occurred here in past ages. Can advise means of attack. Crude but can be revised to suit your conditions. Answer.

For five endless minutes the teletype remained in frozen silence. Then with a rush of type the reply came:

> Our observations led us to believe all life ceased to exist on Earth a hundred or more years ago. If you have suggestion pertaining to our war, gratitude of people of Lirius would be great. We await your reply.

Rane drew a long breath and smiled grimly. To a scientist the wooden horse of Troy was anything but scientific, but to a scholar it had stood through the ages as a classical means of deception. His hands began to move over the keys as he typed out peculiar word combinations.

Rane was no dabbler in words, no writer, no scribe, but he did himself royally at that last and final message. He called to arm all the mythology he knew, and he described the wooden horse incident with great enthusiasm. Could not, he queried, a similar trick be attempted on Uranus? He clicked out his name with a flourish.

Three hours passed. The would-be scientist smoked cigarettes chain-fashion. He drank two cups of black coffee. The teletypes stood silent. Outside, rain of a dying storm lashed itself against the windows. Another hour passed and another, and then . . .

> Vome, Lirius. General announcement to all peoples of Lirius. We are victorious. Dromeda is back, and the defeat

of Uranus is an actuality. No indemnity will be demanded, but Lirian transports will hereafter have unrestricted rights in the spaceways. Defeat of Uranus came about in the following manner:

At 29:18, Lirius time, a message was received by the Unit A operator at Vome, purporting to come from Earth and suggesting a means of attack, which, though crude, struck a responsive chord with the commandant of the Lirian Expeditionary Force.

The suggestion involved the use of a wooden horse, hollow and large enough to secrete a number of Lirian soldiers. It was believed the word, "horse," referred to higher form of animal life which was evolved on Earth during that planet's Quaternary or Post Tertiary geologic period. This object was to be landed on Uranus, where, arousing curiosity, it would be taken within the walls. Under cover of Uranian night the concealed soldiers were to leave their hiding place and demolish the cosmic radiation towers, which heretofore had made attack impossible. This plan was immediately set into operation, a life-size image of a Voldadon, that herbivorous monster of the Lirian polar jungles being substituted for a "horse."

With such favorable results we can only express our full gratitude and appreciation to the Earth operator. The Interplanetary Diplomatic Council is now in session, outlining a plan of appreciation.

For the first time in many hours Rane permitted himself to sink back in his chair and relax slightly. What he had done, he told himself, was no more than any man in similar circumstances would have done. What was important was that a machine of his own making was successful beyond his most remote dreams, opening an unlimited path to the future.

He smoked a cigarette quietly, enjoying the atmosphere of rest and quiet that now flowed about him. Across on the far wall the hands of an electric clock moved slowly around the dial.

Suddenly the teletype began again. And as Rane read and decoded the message his heart leaped within him.

Vome, Lirius. To Joseph Rane, Granite Point, Earth. This is to notify you that a good-will expedition will leave from this planet to your world via one of our super-space transports. Dromeda, the most beautiful woman of Lirius, will be one of the passengers. Advise you to increase signal strength and broadcast power tone at intervals of five minutes, Earth-time, as guide beacon. Without this it is doubtful if we could find our way through uncharted space. Do not broadcast these facts as we wish to make our visit a complete surprise. Will inform you when to begin power tone on moment of departure.

Unit A.

Rane sat there stupefied, his eyes blank, his jaw slowly dropping open. Seconds passed, and there was no sound save the wind as it moaned around the outside corners of the house. Then with a leap he was out of his chair and across to the rheostat control. They needed more power, did they? Well he had an auxiliary dynamo at his disposal, and he would give it to them. His hand trembled as it grasped the knob, began slowly to turn it to the right.

The motor hum increased to a high-frequency drone that seemed to tremble the very foundations of the house. The hour-glass tube changed from cherry red to a gleaming crimson. Louder roared the dynamos, as the control panel vibrated to a whitish blur.

He returned to the teletype and waited. Presently messages began to come in in swift succession. There was an announcement to all peoples of Lirius that preparations for the interplanetary expedition were already on the verge of completion. There was a statement by the King of Lirius, bidding good fortune and success. And there was a long statement, signed by the ten members of the Lirian Diplomatic Council, expressing appreciation to the Earth operator in the warmest terms.

Rane frowned slightly. The inhabitants of the other world were overdoing it a bit, he thought. After all, he had only sent them a suggestion. Somehow there seemed a lack of sincerity in the various communications he had received.

But abruptly the teletype clicked off the following:

> Vome, Lirius. Transport now leaving. Begin power tone.
> We will contact you at intervals.
>
> Unit A.

Rane tripped a switch, disconnecting the keyboard, and pressed a small contact button. A low, droning roar filled the room. Holding the power tone steadily, he took out his watch and laid it down before him. Intermittently at exact five-minute intervals his hand pushed down on the button. Between those intervals he switched the teletype back in, ready for any message that might be transmitted by the transport en route.

A message did come, rattling off the keys at terrific speed, but this time Rane stared at it with puzzled eyes.

> 3inqv mysyel mc8qux uu3nef qb ucaekch. gclmwuebd rsnioc
> 3inqv mj xvop lkjhg. zxc utos qb dawquipmn.

This was odd. The key which he had applied to all previous messages and which in the last few hours he had learned practically by heart, failed absolutely to decipher the message. The grouped letters and numerals seemed to have been formed in another language-cipher entirely.

"Some military code, no doubt," Rane mused aloud. "They're giving orders regarding the defeated planet, Uranus."

But his eyes darkened perceptibly, and when after three more five-minute intervals of sending the power tone, a second message, likewise undecipherable, came through, he turned the teletype over to transmission and went to work on the keyboard.

> Unable to read your last two communications. What are
> you saying?
>
> Rane.

No reply came to this interrogation. Puzzled, Rane took up paper and pencil, placed the strange messages before him and attempted to decode them. But he had no key word to work with this time, and he failed in each attempt.

Try though he would to disregard it, a lurking suspicion began to enter a far corner of his brain. Why should the Lirians suddenly begin to send messages in a cipher which they knew he could not understand? Obviously, because they did not want him to know what they were saying. But why?

Abruptly he stumbled upon a clue by accident. A single word, 3inqv, he noted, had been repeated several times, and contained a similar number of characters as the word *Earth*. Hazarding a wild guess, he substituted "Earth" for this combination, following with the other letters and words in a trial and error method. He worked rapidly in between intervals of sending the power tone. Completed, the message bewildered him:

> Earth power signal coming in clearly. Advancing toward Earth under full speed. All guns in readiness.

He read that last sentence three times while his lips tightened, and a queer glitter entered his eyes. The second communication in the new cipher was even stranger:

> Reinforcements now leaving Lirius to aid you. 26 space dreadnoughts, three speed cruisers. Proceed with utmost caution. Attack immediately on arrival.

It was then that Rane jerked out of his chair, voicing a startled oath. He saw it all now, saw it clearly. And the cunning audacity, the treachery of it cut into him like a knife. This was no good-will expedition the Lirians were speeding through space. All statements to that effect had been a blind, tricking him into aiding them.

Drunk with power from their recent conquest of Uranus, the Lirians now planned to subjugate the Earth. For years they had been aware of developments on Earth, but through some error in calculations or observations they had come to believe that terrestrial life had ceased to exist. Made aware of their mistake, they now intended to utilize their advantage of the situation.

The cold-blooded deceit of it staggered Rane. One outstanding fact overwhelmed him with its significance: it was his actions alone that were responsible for this trouble. He alone could stop it. He must do so!

The watch showed that the five-minute time when the power-tone was to be sent was overdue. Even as he raced across the room to shut off the dynamos, the keys of the teletype swung into action.

No power tone. Send immediately.

He stood there, galvanized to immobility. Would the simple discontinuance of his signal beacon be sufficient to halt the invaders before they reached their destination? He didn't know.

Demand power tone be sent at once. If not, dire consequences await you. Answer.

Still he made no move. Was this all some mad dream, some nightmare from which he would awake to laugh at his fears? The stark reality of the room, the humming dynamos, the printed words on the rolled paper told him only too clearly it wasn't. In his mind's eye he saw huge battle-craft from outer galaxies, armed with strange weapons, landing to spread fearful havoc. He saw cities and towns annihilated by forces the inhabitants could neither see nor understand. He saw—

Rane, Granite Point, Earth. Give you two minutes to send power tone. Reception vital or we cannot proceed. If you do not reply at the end of that time we will blast you through our four-dimensional teleray. Remember we are in wave-length contact with you. You are no doubt aware by now that this is an expedition of war. In this respect we promise you complete safety to yourself. We are desirous only of complete conquest of Earth, which will then be placed under our government as a planetary possession. We did not lie when we stated that Dromeda, the most beautiful woman in Lirius, is aboard this transport as a passenger. If you obey all instructions and do as we order, we promise you her hand in marriage, also high position in Lirian court circle plus large share of loot. Give you two minutes to send power tone. If not heard at the end of that interval, we discharge teleray into your station. You cannot escape.

Rane stood there like a man in a daze. His fists clenched slowly; he could feel a pulse pounding at his temple. On the instrument table the watch ticked away the seconds.

One minute dragged by. Every detail of the room seemed to stand forth with stereoscopic clarity now. The two silent teletypes squatted there on the wooden bench, mocking instruments of destruction. The drone of the dynamos sang a threnody of death.

Twice Rane attempted to rush to the door and escape the house. Each time a peculiar bluish spark spat across the binding posts on the instrument panel, and he felt a magnetic attraction radiate from it to thwart his will. Realization came to him that this time the Lirians meant what they said. They were still in contact with him, and they were exerting an unknown power to prevent his escape. It was a physical impossibility for him to leave the room.

Thirty—fifteen seconds more. He stared at the watch, glanced at the control-button and smiled grimly. He slid slowly into the chair before the instrument desk. How simple it would be! A turn of a switch, a pressure on a rubber knob, and his own life would be saved. And yet—

Two minutes slipped by. His mind made up, Rane sat rigid. He made no move to send the power tone.

And then it happened! A terrific, grinding roar belched forth from the bowels of the machine. A huge cloud of greenish black smoke shot upward, and a span of white fire arced across the cables to envelop the scientist in a shroud of flame.

Like some monstrous gatling gun the thunderous crashes pounded through the room. The fire rose higher to lick hungrily at the ceiling. Then it died, to reveal a mass of twisted smoking metal with the body of Rane lifeless beside it.

On August 5th the *New York Times* carried the following small article on the bottom of its third page:

What was thought to be a new dark star of unknown

origin was wrapped in mystery today after Professor Howard K. Althra, eminent astronomer of Mount Wilson Observatory, revealed his observations of the past two nights had ended in failure.

Two nights ago Professor Althra, aided by almost perfect atmospheric conditions, sighted a dark point moving out of the constellation Gemini, between Saturn and Neptune, and heading toward the Earth at terrific speed. Professor Althra was able to chart the course of this body through space by its frequent and unexplainable variations of course, but he was unable to determine definitely whether it was a large body seen at a great distance or a small body close to Earth.

"At the time of the last observation," Professor Althra stated, "it almost seemed as if it faltered there in space, then turned about and headed back for the constellation Gemini. This, of course, is impossible, and I am unable to state definitely what the nature of the object was."

A Pair of Swords

We had lingered and passed through the Egyptian Room, the Jade Room, and the chambers of the French and Italian Renaissance. Before that there had been many others, hundreds of others, it seemed, on either side of the long statue-lined halls with their floors of polished parquet. Curious how easily one forgets. Curious, rather, what the mind chooses to remember. A mummy or two, a necklace more delicate than the others, a wine cabinet which I childishly fancied and longed to have in my study, and a rare old candle chandelier, said to have illuminated the table of the Spanish Philip II.

The drone of the guide's voice, low-pitched and endless, seemed to emerge from somewhere behind the Flemish hangings that covered the walls. It went on and on without the slightest inflection, and I caught myself wondering whether he talked the same when the day was over and he had left the gallery.

"One of the early works of Jean Baptiste Monnoyer, late Seventeenth Century. Formerly of the Fielding collection. Note the peculiar shadow-work in the background. . . . That will be all in this room, ladies and gentlemen. Next we have the weapon gallery, said to be the most complete in all Europe. This way, please."

I was the last of the group to pass through the intervening doorway, noting with some relief that we had reached the final point of the tour. It was five o'clock, and I must hurry if I wished to make that appointment with Luella. An interesting chamber, this. It looked like the armor of a mediaeval castle. The art of killing a person has certainly developed. I munched another orange lozenge and moved across to where the guide was standing.

"This is the last executioner's sword used in France before the introduction of the guillotine. The blade is thirty-three inches long. All the blades on this wall are either Spanish or Spanish-owned. The carved saber on the right was presented by the Duke of Savoy to Philip III in 1603. Observe the graceful hilt. The smaller one next to it is a Persian sword, Sixteenth Century, probably brought from Tunis by Charles V."

Pistols next, from the earliest hand-cannon down, and the guide continued his litany like the hum of a lazy fly.

"A pair of holster pistols, Lazarino Cominazzo, mounts in chiseled steel. Probably the most perfect arms ever fashioned by the hand of man. An early Italian snaphance, a Kuchenreuter dueling-pistol with double leaf sight. Here we have an early Seventeenth Century arquebus, lock engraved with hunting scene. . . ."

Some one had tapped me on the shoulder, and I turned abruptly. For a moment I stared, chewed hard on my lozenge, then restrained a smile. Two men stood just beyond the last of the curious gallery crowd, two men dressed in a most unusual manner.

Rich blue velvet doublets, white and black satin knee-breeches, flowing lace cuffs, swords at their sides, and large hats with flowing plumes. I smiled again. Silly idea this, masquerading the gallery guards as old French musketeers.

"Pardon, *M'sieu*, but would you be kind enough to step into the next room and help two gentlemen of France settle an affair of honor?"

"Would I—?" I surveyed them coldly as refusal rose to my lips. But the words died without being spoken. For some queer reason the room with its glinting array of yatagans, colichemardes and historic blades seemed to reach far out into the background and blend with the two curiously arrayed figures before me. As I stood there, the guide's voice continuing its monotonous drone, the atmosphere slightly touched with dust pressing close at my nostrils, my first start of surprise gradually passed away, and I received the man's question as if it had not been unusual at all.

No other word was spoken. The two men, taking my silence for consent, led the way through a little doorway on the right and into a larger chamber, unfurnished save for an enormous painting of Cardinal Richelieu on the farther side.

The light from the two arched windows was better here, and I studied with interest the features of the two outlandishly dressed strangers. One, slightly the taller, was fair as a young girl, with a blond waxed mustache and blue pleasant eyes. The other, older and more at ease, was dark, smooth-shaven and thin-lipped. Both strode forward with a haughty fearless air.

"Sir," said the blond man to me, "you must be second for both of us. Should my opponent be fortunate enough to dispatch me, you will please give proper notice of my death. I am—"

"Zounds!" cried the other. "What matter who you are? Once you are dead, you are dead, and that is the end. For rest assured I am going to teach you a lesson, and when I do there will be none to despoil my claim to the hand of Lady Constance. Sir, on guard!"

There was a ring of steel, and two swords glistened in the slanting sunlight. I stepped back and stared at the two as they parried, thrust, and sought to pierce each other's guard. Back and forth, in and out, they moved, blades gyrating with the skill of masters.

"You fight well, sir," muttered the darker man through his teeth. "'Twill be a shame to take such a blade from the king."

"Love inspires strength," breathed the other. "I fight for the most beautiful woman in the world, one whom your hands shall never touch."

The dark man curled his lip in a sneer. "Fool!" he said. "She loves me, not you. Did she not hang this locket round my neck to keep with me always, a token of her love? You are but a boy and her plaything. Behind your back she laughs at you. Look at this locket, I say. See the seal of her house upon it? You are a twice-born fool!"

Slowly the face of the blond youth paled. "She gave you that?" he cried.

"Even now she laughs at the thought of you," taunted the dark man. "Put up your sword, fellow, and I will let you live and forget."

The blue eyes were glinting like agate now, the blond hair trembling in the double shaft of sunlight.

"Then you shall wear it to your death, *M'sieu*," he said. "Do you hear? That seal shall lock your lips for ever."

It happened then in the wink of an eyelash. The blond youth feinted, dropped back, and shot his rapier straight for the throat of his opponent where the golden disk hung suspended from a silken chain. Too late the dark man strove to parry. The blade struck the locket, pierced its center and passed through the man's throat. With a gurgling cry he sank upon one knee and fell to the floor.

Perhaps I closed my eyes for an instant after that as a wave of vertigo rushed through my head. Perhaps a cloud momentarily shut off the golden sunlight that streamed through the windows. But when once again I looked out before me, the scene had changed. I was standing back in the weapon gallery with the queer arms on all sides. The last of the curious crowd was passing through the exit, and the guide was following them a few steps behind.

"One moment," I said as he was about to step across the sill. "One moment, please. What are these two swords mounted here on this wall? Is there a history attached to them?"

The guide frowned. "Weren't you listening, sir?" he asked. "I explained that only a moment before. Those blades are the least interesting in the entire room. They are here only because they represent a type. Musketeers' swords. Once owned by guardsmen of Louis XIII. Why do you ask?"

Before the man could stop me, I had reached up and lifted the right-hand sword from the wall.

The guide suddenly hissed an exclamation over my shoulder, then snatched away the blade and scrutinized it closely. When he spoke there was a tone of anger in his voice.

"Damme, if some one hasn't had the nerve to take a locket from Tray Six in the Jewelry Room and stick it here on the blade!" he bemoaned. "Say, won't the superintendent be furious! Utterly ruined the thing, and for no reason at all. That locket was valuable too. Belonged to an old French noble family once. Look, sir, you can see the coat of arms just where the blade passed through."

A Study in Darkness

It lacked twenty minutes of midnight when I locked the door of my apartment and raced down the steps to the waiting cab. A heavy rain, driven by a howling wind, swirled across the pavement.

"Sixteen Monroe Street," I snapped to the driver. "Oak Square. And drive like hell!"

The cab jerked forward, roared north into Monte Curve and turned east toward Carter. I leaned back then and prayed for a clear way through the night traffic. But even with the best of luck I knew I was treading on counted time.

Only a scant few minutes before, I had been in bed asleep. Then had come that urgent telephone call with that familiar voice over the wire.

"Dr. Haxton? Dr. James Haxton? This is your old friend, Stephen Fay. Can you come immediately? Something terrible has happened, and I'm in need of medical help. Hurry, man!"

The voice had ended in a gasp and a moan, and the connection had been severed with a crash.

Fay—Stephen Fay. I had known the man for a matter of ten years. We had worked side by side, in fact, as struggling students with adjoining laboratories. A huge man with a frank, open face, an engaging smile and an uncontrollable desire to probe deeper into the mysteries of science.

Down Carter we sped, windshield gray with drooling rain, across St. Clair, and into Monroe. Stephen Fay's residence was a forlorn pile of red brick, three stories in height, with a narrow, uninviting doorway.

A girl answered my ring, and as I hesitated, staring at her, she grasped my arm and drew me quickly inside.

"Thank God, you've come, Doctor," she said. "My uncle—Mr. Fay—is in the library. He's bleeding badly."

Even in the excitement of the moment I found myself noting the exquisite beauty of the white-faced girl as we paced silently down the corridor. Then she thrust a connecting door open, and I found myself face to face with my old friend.

He lay stretched full length on a divan, face contorted in agony. His coat and shirt had been ripped to shreds, as if by the repeated slashes of a razor-edged knife, and the exposed flesh was striped and cross-striped with deep gashes and incisions. A bath towel, red with blood, had been pressed against his throat. Removing it, I saw that he was bleeding profusely from a wound a scant inch from the jugular.

Fay rose up as I slid out of my coat.

"Leave the room, Jane," he gasped. "Dr. Haxton will take care of me."

It was a hospital job, one that required four stitches and possibly a local anesthetic, but I knew Fay's wonderful strength and his hatred for any undue commotion. So without further word I set to work.

Half an hour later he was resting easily, weak from loss of blood, but still amazingly calm and composed.

"Haxton," he said as I tried to keep him from talking, "Haxton, I want you to stay here tonight. Can you arrange it? I—I need someone to help me protect that girl. It—it may come again."

I started to give him a bromide, thought better of it, and closed my case with a snap.

"What may come again?" I asked. "In heaven's name, what's wrong here?"

Fay swallowed painfully. "I'll tell you," he said. "I'll tell you what was wrong. It's a rat!"

I saw that he was in deadly earnest and that he was awaiting my reaction with almost feverish anxiety. His hands opened and closed convulsively, and his eyes regarded me with set pupils.

"A *what?*" I stammered.

He rose from the divan and lurched across to the great flat-topped desk and stood in the center of the room. He seized something like a paper weight from its surface and handed it to me.

"Look at it. I don't think you've ever seen anything quite like it before."

The thing was made of wood, mounted on a flat base, and from top to bottom measured no more than six inches. A small carving it was, with agate eyes, protruding teeth, and a long, curved tail, crudely fashioned to resemble a life-size rat.

Placed on the desk where it belonged, it would hardly have attracted a second glance, but leering up at me as it was now from my cupped hands, it was a thing of inanimate horror. There was something repulsive in that squat gray form, something utterly loathsome in the way it crouched there on its black mounting, poised as though ready to leap at my throat.

I shuddered slightly. "Not very pretty."

Fay sat down in a chair and closed his eyes.

"I found that in an Arab shop," he began, "in the native quarter of Macassar, in the Celebes. Bought it for a few pennies simply because it caught my eye. I didn't find out what it was until I came back to the States and showed it to my friend, Henderson, of the Chicago School of Anthropology. That carving is not a fetish or an ornament, but an image, a native object of worship."

I said nothing. There was a story coming, but I had associated with Fay long enough to know that he would start at the beginning, reserving any climax there might be for the last.

"North of New Guinea, almost on the equator, in longitude one hundred and forty-two degrees," he continued, "there is an island known as Wuvulu, a tiny pinpoint of land near the Moluccas. Henderson tells me the aborigines of this island have one of the lowest forms of religion in the Indies. They worship the rat! This image is one of the few that has found its way into the outside world.

"When Jane, my niece, came to live with me, she refused to let the ugly thing repose on my desk openly and insisted that I cover it. I dropped an old piece of black cloth over it, and it has remained there in that manner until tonight—until five minutes before I telephoned you. Then"—Fay braced himself and leaned far forward—"then it came alive!"

The man sat there, scrutinizing me intently, watching my every facial move. He must have seen the incredulity in my eyes, for he rose slowly like a figure on clockwork.

"You don't believe, Haxton? You think I'm joking? Come, and I'll show you the proof!"

He moved to the door, still weak from loss of blood, and I followed a few steps behind. At the threshold two people entered the room to meet us—the girl who had admitted me to this house, and a tall, thin man clad in a rubberized raincoat.

Fay waved his hand in introduction.

"My niece, Jane Barron, Haxton. I've already explained to her that my accident was caused by the breaking of a glass acid vat in the laboratory."

He nodded significantly, and I understood at once that he desired to keep the truth from the girl for the present.

"And this," he went on, "is Corelli, my laboratory assistant and helper."

The Italian bowed low. Apparently he had been out and had returned to the house only a few moments before the accident, whatever it was, had occurred.

"Are you all right, Uncle?" the girl cried. "You look so weak and pale." Then to me: "You must tell him to be more careful with his experiments, Doctor."

Fay patted her gently. "I'll be all right, child, but it's so late I've asked Dr. Haxton to stay the rest of the night. Will you arrange the guest room?"

Corelli looked at his employer with concern. "I trust the wounds are not too painful, Signor," he said. "If you wish, I will—"

Fay nodded absently. "Go to bed, Corelli. Dr. Haxton and I are going to stay up awhile. I'm going to show him my color-music machine."

The Italian bowed once more and left the room. Jane disappeared up a staircase that led to the floor above, and a moment later I found myself pacing down an ill-lighted corridor by the side of the wounded man.

We came at length to a large high-ceilinged room, lined with racks of apparatus.

"My laboratory," Fay said.

My attention was attracted to a ponderous machine in the center, which at the moment seemed only a confusing mass of wheels, tubes, reflectors and dials.

Fay led the way past this instrument, and stopped abruptly,

pointing to a spot near the floor. There was a large ragged hole there, reaching from the bottom of the baseboard to a point some distance up the wall. From the hole, leading across the parquet floor, were a series of sharp scratches, marks that had penetrated the varnish.

To the left a small zinc-covered table was overturned on its side, with a mass of apparatus thrown in wild confusion. Still wet and dripping over the latter was a large clot of blood and a tuft of what I saw on closer inspection to be short gray fur.

I rose to my feet slowly. Fay moved across the room to one of several chairs.

"I told you that rat image came to life tonight. You thought I was crazy when I said it. Believe me, Haxton, I never was more sane in my life.

"I've been working hard the last month or so, perfecting an experiment with what is known as color-music. Tonight Jane insisted I take the evening off and go with her to a movie. Accordingly I told Corelli, my assistant, to get everything ready for a final test in the morning before he left for the evening. We returned early. Jane went to her room, and I went immediately to the laboratory.

"All the way I was conscious of some kind of danger ahead. Then I pushed open the laboratory door and stepped inside. It happened before I could move. By the light of the night lamp in the corridor I had a glimpse of a gray shape and a head with red eyes and white gleaming teeth. The thing was utterly huge, large as a dog, and it threw itself straight at my throat, clawing like mad.

"I screamed, I believe. Then I managed to twist free, reach out and switch on the light.

"With the room lit, I saw it. It stood there a moment, eyes blinking in the sudden glare. Then as if the light were its only fear, it turned, raced across the floor, upset that table and made for that hole which it had gnawed in the wall. But before it reached it, I had sufficiently collected my wits to seize a heavy knife from the stand by the door, hurl it and catch the thing a full blow on the back. It let out a terrible shriek, then disappeared through the wall."

Fay paused, gripped the chair arm tightly.

"And unquestionably that rat was a gigantic incarnation of the image on my desk in the library!"

I sat there stupidly. "It all sounds impossible," I said. "Mad—insane in every detail. But why do you say that the rat was an incarnation of that wooden image?"

Fay leaned back. "Because," he said huskily, "the thing was no real rat, no natural creature of a living order. I know that. It was a hideous caricature, a deformed monstrosity with the same exaggerated lines and detail of that wooden god. The head was rectangular rather than round. The eyes were far out of proportion, and the teeth—were long white fangs. God, it was horrible!"

For a long time after that, while a clock high up on the wall ticked off the passing seconds, we sat in silence. At length I voiced my thoughts.

"Whatever the thing is, supernatural or otherwise, it's real enough to cause flesh-and-blood wounds and to be wounded itself. We can't stand by and let it come and go as it wills. Where does that hole in the wall lead?"

Fay shook his head. "This is an old house," he said, "and there are unusually large spaces between the walls. I found that out when I tapped them for several of my experiments. That rat has the run of the entire structure. It must have been only chance that led it to choose the laboratory for a point to gnaw its way to freedom."

We used two heavy boards and a piece of sheet-iron to cover the opening. Along the baseboard on each of the four walls we ran an uncovered piece of copper wire, electrically charged with a high voltage from Fay's laboratory current. It meant that a second attempt on the part of the horror to enter the room would result in its instant electrocution. It meant that—if the thing were not invulnerable to such a mundane defense.

"No one knows about what happened tonight, save me?" I asked then.

Fay shook his head. "No one. I didn't choose to frighten my niece, and Corelli was out at the time."

"Corelli has been with you long?"

"About a year. He's an odd sort of person but harmless, I think.

Never says much except when he talks about his color theory. Then he babbles incessantly. The man has a mad way of mixing spiritualism with science. Believes that white is the essence of all that is good and black is the lair of evil, or some such rot. He even showed me a thesis on this which he had written. Aside from that however, he's really a capable laboratory assistant. . . ."

A strange bed to me, whatever the surroundings, is always the same. Tonight, with my mind milling over the story that had been related to me, I found sleep almost impossible. Hours passed before I dozed off.

But at three o'clock by the radium clock on the dresser, I found myself sitting upright in bed. Something, some foreign noise had wakened me.

I got up, crossed to the door and looked out into the corridor. Blackness met my eyes. Then a sound reached me from the far end of the hall, and I stole stealthily forward. The sound came louder. It was *swish-swish* of liquid being brushed on a hard surface, the sound of a man painting.

I pressed my body close to the wall, muffling the noise of my breathing through the cloth of my pajama tops. Footsteps then, receding footsteps. Carefully keeping my distance I moved on, and at the turn of the hall stopped abruptly.

The door of the bedchamber there—Jane's bedchamber—stood out in the blackness like a panel of silver fire. It had been painted with some kind of luminous paint. The brush marks were still wet and sticky.

I twisted the latch and peered into the room. The faint glow from the window revealed the girl sleeping peacefully in the bed.

Nodding with relief, I moved on again down the corridor. At the staircase I heard the library door on the floor below click shut. I descended slowly and waited at the foot of the stairs for an eternity, listening.

At length I pushed boldly into the library. Corelli was sitting at the desk, a trail of smoke rising from his cigarette, an open book before him. He looked up as if in surprise.

"Couldn't sleep," I said shortly. "Thought I'd come down here and read a spell. You seem to have had the same idea."

He stared at me, then broke into a short laugh.

"I do more than read, Signor. I study. I am busy days, so I have only nights to work on my theory."

"Ah, yes," I replied. "Mr. Fay spoke to me about it. Something about color, isn't it, and the qualities of black and white?"

A gleam of interest sprang into his eyes.

"The Signor is interested in color, yes?"

"Some. Stephen Fay is my friend, and I have worked with him on many of his experiments."

The Italian nodded and pointed a finger toward his book.

"I am reading LaFlarge," he said. "A brilliant mind, but a fool. They are all fools, these scientists. They see only the physical facts. They see only things which exist materially before their eyes. They claim there is nothing psychic."

I crossed to a chair and sat down.

"Tell me," I said, "what has the psychic to do with color?"

"Everything, Signor. Fay—all scientists—will tell you that color is a phenomenon that occurs when daylight passes through a quartz prism. The rays from the sun are decomposed and form what the eyes see as the spectrum band, red at one end, violet at the other. That is elementary, of course.

"A body, a piece of blue cloth, for example, illuminated by daylight, appears colored because it absorbs red and yellow and throws back blue. In other words color in an object is produced by absorption. Is that clear?"

"I know all that," I said.

"Black, which of course is the absence of all color, is seen as black because it is the absorption of all and the reflection of none. One might liken it to a lake of pitch in the midst of the jungle. It takes everything into itself and allows nothing to escape. It is iniquity, the essence of all evil.

"Has it never occurred to you that even the ancients recognized this fact? We have Satan as the prince of blackness; the worshipping ceremonial to him is the black mass; we have black art and black magic. Throughout the ages black has always been synonymous for everything that is evil."

"I see," I said slowly.

"My theory then," Corelli went on, "lies in the exploration of black, not only physically but psychically. Let us say we have a room entirely painted black. Those walls are then the absorption of all wave lengths of light. Any photographer will tell you that an object—a book, a chair, a table—is seen only as a result of that object refracting wave lengths of light into the retina of the human eye.

"Is it not reasonable to suppose, therefore, that in this room of which I speak, any object or the refracted psychic equivalent of it will find itself likewise absorbed into the black walls?

"You begin to perceive, Signor? Where there is blackness, there is always fear. A child cries out when it enters a dark room. We reason with the child, tell it there is nothing there. Might we not be wrong? Might not the child's clean mind sense something which we in our more complex lives do not see nor understand?"

Corelli leaned back in his chair and lit another cigarette.

"Granting all that," I said slowly, "why would it necessarily follow that in black we would find only evil. Since black, as you say, is the absorption of everything, it must absorb the good as well, and the former has always been acknowledged to be the stronger of the two."

The Italian's eyes did not change.

"Think a moment, Signor," he said, "and you will see that only evil can live where there is utter blackness. Anything else would be smothered like a flower away from its precious sunlight. I—"

His voice clipped off, and I stiffened in my chair. From the floor above had come a girl's scream. Hollow and muffled by the intervening walls, the cry filtered through the house, filled with fear and stark terror.

With a single leap I was across the room and racing up the stairs. In the corridor above I switched on the lights as Stephen Fay emerged from his room and, white-faced, began to run toward me.

I reached the freshly-painted door of Jane's room, ripped it open and burst inside. The girl was huddled on the bed, eyes wide with terror.

"Miss Barron, are you hurt?"

She gave a low moan and buried her head in her hands, sobbing.

"It was horrible!" she gasped. "A monster! A rat! A rat twenty times the ordinary size! It came out of that hole in the wall next to my dressing table and—and leaped onto the bed. Then it crouched, staring at me. Then—"

The girl sobbed hysterically. . . .

It was a grim group that stood in the gray light of the library next morning. Jane Barron was still white and trembling, though I had administered a slight sedative a few minutes before. Corelli smoked nervously, throwing away cigarettes and lighting fresh ones before they were half consumed.

"I'm warning each of you," Fay said, "to move about the house with the greatest of caution. Something is loose in these walls, something we can't understand. Besides that, during the night the door of Jane's room was for some unexplainable reason coated with a paint containing calcium sulphide, making it appear luminous in the dark. Also someone entered my laboratory and tampered with my color-music machine.

"Haxton"—Fay nodded toward me—"I'm placing my niece's protection in your hands. Later perhaps it may be necessary to call the police."

After that I was alone in the library.

For some reason I had chosen not to reveal to Fay that it was the Italian who had smeared paint on the girl's room. Until further developments I meant to keep that fact to myself.

I picked up the thing then, which Fay claimed was at the bottom of the whole affair; the wooden carving of the rat. Again as I stared down upon its ugly body and curiously deformed head, an inner sense of horror welled over me.

Yet I told myself that was absurd. The image was only a manufactured god, representing a fanatic religion.

But an instant later I sat quite still as an insane idea began to clamor for recognition far back in a corner of my brain! An insane idea, yes, and yet one which fitted the conditions and which offered a method of combat! I leaped to my feet and headed for the laboratory.

Fay was there, as I had expected, and his composed manner quieted me for a moment.

"I can't understand it," he was saying. "The instrument was quite all right yesterday evening when I left for the movie. Corelli claims not to have touched it, and anyway he would have no reason at all for doing so. Yet the entire slide containing the color plates has been removed and this wooden frame inserted in its place."

I stared at the device. "It looks like a projection machine," I said.

Fay nodded. "It is. The instrument is constructed to throw upon a screen a rapidly changing circle of colors. It will be synchronized with an organ in such a way that when a piece of music is played, each note of sound will be accompanied by a corresponding color on the screen. There are seven notes, and there are seven primary colors. Thus in a rendition of a sonata we will both see and hear the composition. I—"

He broke off as the door burst open and Corelli lurched into the room.

"The rat, Signors!" he whispered. "It has come again! I saw it in the corridor."

But the corridor was empty. We traversed its length from one end to the other. Then we continued our search through the entire house. Deep into the many shadows of that ancient structure we probed. The rooms were silent and empty. Those on the third floor were closed off and barren of furniture. We found nothing.

At the foot of the stairs I suddenly whirled upon Fay.

"This new machine of yours," I said. "It uses artificial light to produce its colors?"

"Of course," he replied. "A carbon arc at present. Later an incandescent of some kind."

"And with the color plates removed as they are, the only thing that would appear on the screen would be a circle of white light. Is that right?"

"Not exactly," Fay explained. "Artificial light differs from daylight in that there is a deficiency of blue. Strictly speaking, the instrument would throw a shaft of yellow light."

"But could it be made pure white light?" I persisted.

He thought a moment. "Yes," he said, "it could. I have a Sheringham improved daylight lamp. Its light is the nearest man-made parallel to the rays of the sun. What are you driving at?"

"Fay," I said, "if you value your life, if you value the life of your niece, listen to me! Insert that lamp in your machine and arrange the projector so that it can be moved in a complete arc. Do you understand? In a complete arc!"

At half-past ten that night I stood once again before the frowning door of 16 Monroe Street. The intervening hours I had spent in a hurried trip to my own rooms and a brief but necessary visit to my patients in St. Mary's hospital.

Nothing had happened during my absence. Fay led me to the library, poured two glasses of brandy and then nervously packed his pipe.

"The machine is ready," he said. "What you've got in mind, I don't know, but the daylight lamp has been substituted for the carbon arc, and the projector is mounted on a swivel. What now?"

I set down my glass. "Let's have a look," I said.

In the laboratory a moment later Fay adjusted several controls and pointed the instrument toward a screen. Then, motioning me to extinguish the lights, he switched on the current.

A dazzling shaft of light leaped from the narrow tube and spread a glaring circle of effulgence on the screen. Fay moved the projector, and the light traveled slowly, stabbing each article in the room in sharp relief.

"You have casters you could mount on the instrument, making it moveable?" I asked.

Fay thought a moment. "Y-es," he slowly replied.

"Use them then and add an extension of at least twenty-five feet to the current wire."

He glared at me, but I swung about and left the room before he could voice protestations.

From eleven o'clock until eleven-thirty I prowled aimlessly about the house, glancing from time to time to time at the wall baseboards, nervously sucking a cold cigar. Finally in the library I picked up the desk phone and called Police Headquarters.

"McFee?" I said. "Dr. Haxton speaking. Yes, that's right—of St. Mary's. McFee, I'm at Mr. Stephen Fay's residence, Sixteen Monroe Street, just across from Oak Square. Can you send a man out here right away? No, no trouble yet, but I'm afraid there might be. . . . Yes, in a hurry. I'll explain later."

I forked the phone and waited. A quarter of an hour passed, and then, answering the ring at the street door, I found a lanky, hawk-faced policeman.

"Listen," I said before he could ask any questions, "I'm the physician in charge here. Your job is simply to look on, remember anything you see and prepare to sign a written report as a witness."

At ten minutes past twelve the five of us—Fay, Jane, Corelli, the patrolman and I entered the laboratory. We took positions according to my directions, the girl between Fay and me, the Italian in a chair slightly to the side.

Five feet in front of the door a connecting drop-cord was let down from the ceiling with a red-frosted electric light. Fay had wheeled the heavy color machine forward, facing the door.

"Ready, Fay?" I said, trying hard to keep my voice steady.

He nodded, and I stepped to the door, closed it halfway and extinguished the lights. We were in deep gloom now with the dim glow of the red light gleaming like an evil eye before us. And silence broken only by the hollow rumble of a far-away street car.

Suddenly Corelli leaped to his feet.

"Signors," he cried, "I refuse to sit here like a cat in the dark!"

"You'll stay where you are!" Fay snapped.

And so we waited. I could hear the ticking of my wristwatch. The Italian's breathing grew louder and more hurried, and I could feel Jane's hands open and close convulsively around the chair arm.

A quarter of an hour snailed by. I wiped a bead of perspiration from my forehead. Ten minutes more. And then we heard it!

From the outer corridor came the padding of approaching feet. Toward the laboratory door they came. I placed a warning hand on Fay's arm.

The door opened wide. A scream of horror mounted unsounded to my lips. What I saw I will never forget. A shapeless gray body with a rectangular head crouched there, eyes gleaming hellishly.

For a split second the five of us remained motionless with

horror. Then riving the silence came Jane's shriek followed by a deafening roar from the policeman's revolver. The rat braced itself and leaped into the room.

"The light!" I cried. "Fay, the white light, do you hear?"

There was a snap and a hum, and a shaft of glaring blue-white radiance shot from the mouth of the projector. But even as it formed a circle on the far wall, the horror singled out one of our number for its attack. Corelli!

The Italian went down with a scream as the rat threw itself upon him.

I heard the dull crunch and the snap of breaking bone.

Then that beam of light swept across the room under Fay's guiding hand and centered full on the thing; livid under the ghastly ray, its head twisted around, eyes twin globules of hate. With a mewling cry of rage it made for the door.

"After it!" I shouted.

Together Fay and I rolled the projector into the outer corridor. It was blind, that corridor. It ended in a blank wall, and the doors on either side beyond the laboratory were closed.

Straight down the hall we pushed the color machine. The rat was uttering queer rasping sounds now, shambling wildly from side to side as it sought to escape the hated light.

Trapped, the thing stopped, whirled, then plunged straight at Fay. Even as the scientist's cry rose up I rushed forward to aid him. A raking claw gashed its way to the bone in my left shoulder. A nauseating animal stench choked my nostrils.

Then I seized the machine's projector tube and swung it. The white glare swept upon the rat squarely, centered on the head. An instant the horror poised motionless. Then slowly it began to disintegrate. The features ran together like heated clay. The eyes and mouth fell away. Before me a lump of gray fur diminished to a thin slime, to a darkish mist that rose slowly upward. Then that, too, wavered under my gaze and disappeared. . . .

I came back to consciousness on the divan in the library with Jane Barron chafing my wrists and Stephen Fay looking on nervously.

"It's all over, Haxton," he was saying. "Corelli's dead. The rat killed him. But—but I don't understand—"

I struggled to my feet, dazedly.

"Come to the laboratory, Fay," I said, "and I'll show you."

We made our silent way to that room of apparatus where the Italian's body still lay motionless on the floor. Bending over it I searched the pockets and at length drew forth two objects. A small leather-covered notebook and a piece of black cloth, about the size of a napkin.

"Recognize it?" I asked, holding up the cloth.

Fay nodded. "Yes. It's the covering Jane gave me for the rat image on the library desk. But—"

I opened the notebook, glanced at it, then handed it to Fay. For a long time he remained silent as he scanned the pages.

When he looked up at length a strange light was in his eyes.

"You see," I said, "Corelli was in love with your niece. Didn't he at some time ask if he could marry her?"

"Yes," Fay replied. "But that was absurd, of course. I told him he was crazy and let it go at that."

"Exactly," I nodded. "And in doing so you injured his Latin pride. He became mad with secret rage, and he swore revenge against you. You know the man's color theory—that black being the absorption of everything is the lair of all evil. He saw that rat image on the library desk, and he recognized it as an artifact of devil-worship, the essence of everything satanic.

"Over the image you had draped a black cloth. According to Corelli's theory then, that cloth was the psychic equivalent of all that the image in its carved form represented. Do you understand?

"He stole the cloth, mounted it on a wooden frame and inserted it in your color-music machine. Then he reversed the mechanism, and by casting a beam of black light upon the screen caused that horrible monster to be freed from its black cloth imprisonment and endowed with physical life.

"If we accept that reasoning, then Corelli's intention was to find a way of destroying you and at the same time prove the truth of his theory. That is why he smeared the luminous paint on Jane's bedroom door. White, being the antithesis of black, was a counter-defense, and he had no desire to see your niece harmed.

"For the same reason I asked you to insert the daylight lamp in the color machine. It was the only way of fighting the thing."

Fay had listened to me in silence. A queer, bewildered look crossed his face.

"But—but you can't expect me to believe all that," he objected. "It isn't scientific. It's mad from beginning to end! The whole thing has no foundation in fact. Black—white—Good Lord, man, no scientist in the world would believe—"

"Perhaps not," I agreed. "Perhaps I'm wrong. If I am, we'll never know. Corelli is dead. But one thing I do know. I'm going to take this cloth and notebook and that image in the library, throw them into the fire and burn them."

And I did.

Mive

Carling's Marsh, some called it, but more often it was known by the name of Mive. Strange name that—Mive. And it was a strange place. Five wild, desolate miles of thick water, green masses of some kind of kelp, and violent vegetable growth. To the east the cypress trees swelled more into prominence, and this district was vaguely designated by the villagers as Flan. Again a strange name, and again I offer no explanation. A sense of depression, of isolation perhaps, which threatened to crush any buoyancy of feeling possessed by the most hardened traveler, seemed to emanate from this lonely wasteland. Was it any wonder that its observers always told of seeing it at night, before a storm, or in the spent afternoon of a dark and frowning day? And even if they had wandered upon it, say on a bright morning in June, the impression probably would have been the same, for the sun glittering upon the surface of the olive water would have lost its brilliance and become absorbed in the roily depths below. However, the presence of this huge marsh would have interested no one, had not the east road skirted for a dismal quarter-mile its melancholy shore.

The east road, avoided, being frequently impassable because of high water, was a roundabout connection between the little towns of Twellen and Lamarr. The road seemed to have been irresistibly drawn toward the Mive, for it cut a huge half-moon across the country for seemingly no reason at all. But this arc led through a wilderness of an entirely different aspect from the land surrounding the other trails. Like the rest it started among the hills, climbed the hills, and rambled down the hills, but after passing Echo Lake, that lowering tarn locked in a deep ravine, it straggled up a last hillock and swept down upon a large flat. And as one proceeded, the flat steadily sank lower, it forgot the hills, and the ground, already damp, became sodden and quivering under the feet.

And then looming up almost suddenly—Mive! ... a morass at first a bog, then a jungle of growth repulsive in its over-luxuriance, and finally a sea of kelp, an inland Sargasso.

Just why I had chosen the east road for a long walk into the country I don't really know. In fact, my reason for taking such a hike at all was rather vague. The day was certainly anything but ideal; a raw wind whipping in from the south, and a leaden sky typical of early September lent anything but an inviting aspect to those rolling Rentharpian hills. But walk I did, starting out briskly as the inexperienced all do, and gradually slowing down until four o'clock found me plodding almost mechanically along the flat. I dare say every passer-by, no matter how many times he frequented the road, always stopped at exactly the same spot I did and suffered the same feeling of awe and depression that came upon me as my eyes fell upon that wild marsh. But instead of hurrying on, instead of quickening my steps in search of the hills again, I for some unaccountable reason left the trail and plunged through oozing fungi to the water's very edge.

A wave of warm humid air, heavy with the odor of growth, swept over me as though I had suddenly opened the door of some monstrous hothouse. Great masses of vines with fat creeping tendrils hung from the cypress trees. Razor-edged reeds, marsh grass, long waving cattails, swamp vegetation of a thousand kinds flourished here with luxuriant abundance. I went on along the shore; the water lapped steadily the sodden earth at my feet, oily-looking water, grim-looking, reflecting a sullen and overcast sky.

There was something fascinating in it all, and while I am not one of those adventurous souls who revel in the unusual, I gave no thought of turning back to the road, but plodded through the soggy, clinging soil, and over rotting logs as though hurrying toward some destination. The very contrast, the voluptuousness of all the growth seemed some mighty lure, and I came to a halt only when gasping for breath from exertion.

For perhaps half an hour I stumbled forward at intervals, and then from the increasing number of cypress trees I saw that I was approaching that district known as the Flan. A large lagoon lay here, stagnant, dark, and entangled among the rip-grass and reeds, reeds that rasped against each other in a dry, unpleasant manner like some sleeper constantly clearing his throat.

All the while I had been wondering over the absolute absence of all animate life. With its dank air, its dark appeal, and its wildness, the Eden recesses of the Mive presented a glorious place for all forms of swamp life. And yet not a snake, not a toad, nor an insect had I seen. It was strange, and I looked curiously about me as I walked.

And then . . . and then as if in contradiction to my thoughts it fluttered before me.

With a gasp of amazement I found myself staring at an enormous ebony-black butterfly. Its jet coloring was magnificent, its proportions startling, for from wing tip to wing tip it measured fully fifteen inches. It approached me slowly, and as it did I saw that I was wrong in my classification. It was not a butterfly; neither was it a moth; nor did it seem to belong to the order of the *Lepidoptera* at all. As large as a bird, its great body came into prominence over the wings, disclosing a huge proboscis, ugly and repulsive.

I suppose it was instinctively that I stretched out my hand to catch the thing as it suddenly drew nearer. My fingers closed over it, but with a frightened whir it tore away, darted high in the air, and fluttered proudly into the undergrowth.

It was then that I became aware that the first two fingers and a part of my palm were lightly coated with a powdery substance that had rubbed off the delicate membrane of the insect's wings. The perspiration of my hand was fast changing this powder into a sticky bluish substance, and I noticed that this gave off a delightfully sweet odor. The odor grew heavier. It seemed to fill the air, to crowd my lungs, to create an irresistible desire to taste it. I sat down on a log; I tried to fight it off, but like a blanket it enveloped me and the desire became irresistible.

At length I could stand it no longer, and I slowly brought my fingers to my lips. A horribly bitter taste which momentarily paralyzed my entire mouth and throat was the result. It ended in a long coughing spell.

Disgusted at my lack of will-power, I turned and began to

retrace my steps toward the road. A feeling of nausea and of slug-
gishness began to steal over me, and I quickened my pace. But
at the same time I kept watch for a reappearance of that strange
butterfly. No sound now save the washing of the heavy water
against the reeds and the sucking noise of my steps.

I had gone farther than I realized, and I cursed the foolish
whim that had sent me here. As for the butterfly—whom could
I make believe the truth of its size or even of its existence? I had
nothing for proof, and . . . I stopped suddenly!

A peculiar formation of vines had attracted my attention—
and yet not vines either. The thing was oval, about five feet in
length, and appeared to be many weavings or coils of some kind
of hemp. It lay fastened securely in a lower crotch of a cypress.
One end was open, and the whole thing was a grayish color like a
cocoon: A shudder of horror swept over me.

With a cocoon as large as this, the size of the butterfly would
be enormous. In a flash I saw the reason for the absence of all
other life, in the Mive. These butterflies, developed as they were
to such proportions, must have evolved into some strange order
and became carnivorous. The fifteen-inch butterfly which had
so startled me before faded into insignificance in the presence of
this cocoon.

I seized a huge stick for defense and hurried on toward the
road. A low muttering of thunder from somewhere off to the
west added to my discomfort. Black threatening clouds, harbin-
gers of an oncoming storm, were racing in from the horizon.
The gloom blurred into a darkness, and I picked my way forward
along the shore with more and more difficulty. Suddenly the
mutterings stopped, and there came that expectant, sultry silence
that precedes the breaking of a storm.

But no storm came. The clouds all moved slowly, lava-like
toward a central formation directly above me, and there they
stopped, became utterly motionless, engraved upon the sky.
There was something ominous about that monstrous cloud
bank, and in spite of the growing feeling of nausea, I watched
it pass through a series of strange color metamorphoses, from a
black to a greenish black, and from a decided green to a yellow,
and from a yellow to a blinding, glaring red.

And then as I looked those clouds gradually opened; a ray of
light pierced through as the aperture enlarged disclosing an enormous vault-shaped cavern cut through the stratus. The whole
vision seemed to move nearer, as though magnified a thousand
times. And then towers, domes, streets, and walls took form, and
these coagulated into a city painted stereoscopically in the sky. I
forgot everything and lost myself in a weird panorama above me.

Crowds of men clothed in armor with high helmets were hurrying past in an endless procession. Regiment upon regiment of
marching humanity were retreating as if from some enemy!

And then it came, a swarm of butterflies . . . enormous, ebony-
black, carnivorous butterflies, approaching a doomed city. They
met—the men and that strange form of life. But the defensive
army and the gilded city seemed to be swallowed up.

Again a picture took form, but this time a design, gigantic,
magnificent. There with its black wings outspread was the butterfly I had sought to catch. The whole sky was covered by its
massive form.

It disappeared! The thunder mutterings now burst forth without warning in unrestrained fury. The clouds raced back again,
erasing outline and detail, and there was only the gloom of a
brooding, overcast sky.

I turned and plunged through the underbrush. Vines and
creepers lashed at my face; knife reeds and swamp grass penetrated my clothing. Streak lightning of blinding brilliance, thunder belched forth from the sky. A wind sprang up, and the reeds
and long grasses undulated before it like a thousand writhing
serpents. The sullen water of the Mive was black now and racing
in toward the shore in waves, and the thunder above swelled into
crescendo.

Suddenly I threw myself flat upon the oozing ground and
wormed my way deep into the undergrowth.

A moment later the giant butterfly raced out of the storm
toward me. I could see its sword-like proboscis, its repulsive body,
and I could hear its sucking inhalations of breath. *A thing of evil it
was, transnormal, a hybrid growth from a paludinous place of rot and
over-luxuriant vegetation.*

But I was well hidden in the reeds. The monster passed on

unseeing. In a flash I was up and lunging on again. The crashing reverberations of the storm seemed to pound against me as if trying to hold me back. A hundred times I thought I heard that terrible flapping of wings behind me. But at last the road! Without slackening speed, I ran on, away from the Mive, across the quivering flat, and on to the hills. At length exhaustion swept over me, and I fell gasping to the ground.

It seemed hours that I lay there, motionless, unheeding the driving rain on my back.

What had happened to me? And then I remembered. The fifteen-inch butterfly which had so startled me near the district of the Flan ... I had tried to catch the thing, and it had escaped, leaving in my hand only a powderish substance that I had vainly brought to my lips. What had happened after that? A feeling of nausea had set in, like the immediate effects of a powerful drug. A strange insect of an unknown order, a butterfly and yet not a butterfly. . . . Who knows what internal effect that powder would have on one? Had I been wandering in a delirium, caused by that powder from the insect's wings? And if so, where did the delirium fade into reality? The vision in the sky ... a vagary of a poisoned brain perhaps, but the monstrosity which had pursued me and the telltale cocoon. . . .

I looked back. There it lay, far below me, vague and indistinct in the deepening gloom, the black outlines of the cypress trees writhing in the night wind, silent, brooding, mysterious—the Mive.

Writing on the Wall

The idea struck Professor John Bickering in a telephone booth in a drug store on West Seventeenth Street. Bickering had been heading for a book shop where he bought most of his volumes on psychology, when he remembered he had left his electric razor connected to his hotel room current.

The razor was a gift from an aunt in Toledo. He hoped he could make contact with the hotel clerk before it would be ruined.

But once in the phone booth, Bickering noticed, absently at first, the markings on the wall. An instant later his call and the razor were forgotten.

The markings were familiar. He had seen them, or rather their counterparts, on the backs of old magazines, in book fly-leaves, wherever in fact some member of the American public found it necessary to pass time.

They were doodlings.

Bickering himself was often guilty of doodling. Whenever time was heavy on his hands, he found a scrap of paper and printed his name backwards. Then he enclosed the name in a neat square and topped the whole thing off with a heavy circle. But the marks on this wall were different. They looked like this:

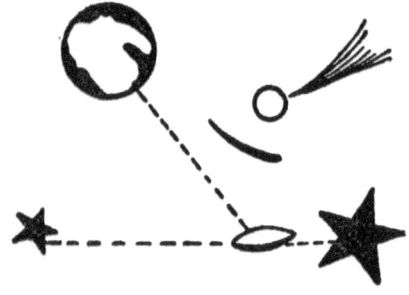

For a long time the professor stood there in the cramped quarters of the booth, staring at the hieroglyphics. His thoughts rushed back to the recently-completed last passage of the twenty-third chapter of his new book:

It is true that instincts are but tested ideas and beliefs which have been passed germwise down through the generations and with which the progeny are endowed as soon as they become mentally conscious. The workings of the subconscious mind may be exaggerated examples of this mental inheritance.

Bickering had not given any undue amount of thought to that passage when he wrote it. It but paved the way for Chapter Twenty-four which was to deal with the "subconscious mind." But the book itself represented the professor's greatest undertaking. Originally entitled *Basic Thought Reactions to Certain Stimuli and Other Manifestations of a Psychological Nature Encountered in Certain Experiments*, the name had been shortened by the publisher in the advance contract to *Thought Roots*.

Bickering had put his all into the writing of that book. He had intended it to make himself the Charles Fort of the psychological world, and he had hoped to capture the Trolheim Award.

The Trolheim Award was a tidy sum. It was offered to the man who contributed the most valuable and unusual developments in this branch of science. With the money he thus hoped to win, the professor had set his heart on buying a house and private laboratory offered for sale in West Eureka on Highway Number Seven at County Road H. For weeks now he had dreamed of emptying his cramped hotel quarters of all their apparatus and moving to that suburban home.

Bickering was convinced that the first twenty-three chapters of his book were not only "valuable," but distinctly "unusual." He had begun with the postulation that the Darwinian theory as applied to man was only partially correct; that man had not evolved entirely on this earth, but that he was undoubtedly of extra terrestrial origin; and that, therefore, the human intellect was not the result of eons of growth and development, but rather of gradual disintegration from a super-intellect of some remote age.

But Chapter Twenty-four he felt was destined to be a distinct letdown. In it he had planned to discuss the subconscious mind. As yet, however, he had not come upon a single experiment to be considered worthy of including in the book.

Now as he stood there in the telephone booth an idea suddenly struck him. Doodlings, eh? Funny, he had never thought about them before. But they were the essence of subconscious activity. And this one was the most amazing example he had ever seen.

The professor took out his notebook and carefully made a copy of the drawing on the wall. Then he opened the booth door and motioned the drug clerk.

"I don't suppose you can tell me who drew this?"

The clerk craned his neck and looked puzzled. "You from the telephone company?" he asked.

"No, I . . . I'm a detective," Bickering lied glibly. He took out a huge calabash pipe, began to fill its bowl. "I'm trying to trace someone, and I thought possibly you could . . ."

But the clerk could not tell. Everybody scribbled in telephone booths. The only thing he could say for certain was that the marks had not been there three weeks ago, for at that time the booth had been freshly painted.

Bickering realized that if he wanted to find the person who had made those marks—and to develop his idea for Chapter Twenty-four it was absolutely essential to find the doodler—he must find a more recent copy of them.

There was one factor in his favor. Doodlers always wrote the same words or made the same designs.

The professor made a thorough job of his search. He started on West Seventeenth Street and walked to Grant. From Grant to Aldrich, Aldrich to Oak, and Oak back to Seventeenth. At each shop and store which had a pay telephone he entered and examined the booth. He saw doodlings of a thousand different varieties, but none of the design for which he was searching.

Then in a corner cigar-store his luck returned. The telephone booth there was occupied by a perspiring heavy-set man. While talking, he was busy scribbling on the wall.

The design was the same as had caught Bickering's eye in the drug store.

Time seemed to drag interminably after that. But at length the man hung up the receiver, mopped his face and came out.

Bickering seized him by the arm.

"You drew that!" he announced.

The man backed away slowly.

"Don't be frightened," Bickering said, "I'm quite sane. I simply noticed those marks you made, and I'm wondering if you'd mind telling me why you drew them. You see, I'm a professor of psychology, and I'm writing a book called . . . well, never mind the title. Do you always draw that when you have nothing else to do?"

"Sure." The heavy-set man smiled. "Habit of mine. Don't mean a thing." He turned and headed for the door.

"Wait." Bickering ran after him. "You don't realize, sir, how important this is. I'm on the verge of a great scientific discovery, and I need your help. When my book is published, those drawings you made on the telephone booth wall may make you a fortune and win you undying fame. I can't say for certain yet, but I believe your subconscious brain, alone among thousands, is capable of spanning the infinity of time and space."

"You mean you're not selling something?" the man asked.

Impatiently Bickering shook his head and rapidly began to touch on the high points of the theory that lay behind his book. As the man listened, a spark of interest entered his eyes. At length he nodded slowly.

"Okay. I'm Mason Felspar of the Felspar Electric Company. If you really have something, I'm the guy that can be shown. Where do you live?"

Half an hour later in the cramped laboratory of his hotel apartment, the professor motioned Felspar to a chair and took out his notebook copy of the telephone drawings. Stacked about them on shelves and tables were strange pieces of apparatus, most of them Bickering's own inventions which he had used from time to time in conducting experiments.

"I'm going to analyze the marks on this drawing for you," the professor said. "You think they're meaningless because you've written the same ones thousands of times. The fact is they are a part of your subconscious brain.

"Now look closely. At the top of the drawing you drew what

is obviously a star. A little lop-sided perhaps, but still a star. And moving between the two stars is a black cigar-shaped object.

"In the middle of the drawing, between the two stars, is a small ring with a tail, flanked by a curved line. At the bottom is a circle. Or let us call it a globe."

"Just doodlings," said Felspar. "I've been doing it for years."

"Now," continued Bickering, unmindful of interruption, "let us accept these marks for what they represent. We have then two stars, a globe, a cigar-shaped object, and a smaller globe, with a tail, or to boil it down still farther: two stars, this Earth, a projectile, and a comet. Crude as it is, the ring with the tail can only represent a comet. You even have the path of the trajectory, as shown by the curved line. Do you see?"

"I . . . that is . . ." faltered Felspar.

"Now I don't know how much you know about the origin of man," continued the professor. "You may possibly have read of Mu and Atlantis. You may have read your Darwin, Heckel or Lamark. But I believe the theories of those men to be full of discrepancies. It is possible that some races or all races did not develop on Earth at all, but were originally foreign to Earth and came from somewhere in extra terrestrial space. As an elementary example, that in itself would account for the many skin pigments and the great ethnological difference found today."

Bickering paused to exhale a mouthful of tobacco smoke.

"And it is also true," he said, "that basic thoughts and ideas are handed down through the generations, a regular part of man's inheritance."

"But what are you driving at?"

Bickering stiffened. "Don't you see? I'm convinced that your drawings open the door to the past. They point conclusively to the fact that life on this Earth is not only the result of evolution but also mass migration from another planet. Looking at your drawing again.

"You have a projectile—a space ship, let us say, filled with life—leaving one planet of one star system, bound for another. Half way a comet approaches the projectile's path and comes sufficiently close to alter the projectile's trajectory. What is the result? The projectile misses its destination and comes to rest instead on Earth. And so powerful was the remembered thought of that occurrence it has continued down through thousands of years, through the brains of millions of men until it reached expression with you."

Felspar sat rigid in his chair. His eyes were wide open, and rivulets of perspiration were trickling down his face.

"I'm double damned," he said slowly.

Bickering opened a drawer in his desk, took out a sheet of paper, a pencil, and a ruler.

From a cabinet at the far wall he drew forth a concave piece of aluminum studded with tiny knobs, each of which was connected by a network of tiny wires. In the center of the top surface was a single quartz ball.

"Now," he said, "I'm going to try an experiment. I'm going to put this portable thought-amplifier on your head and leave you alone for an hour. There's nothing at all to fear. I've been using this thought-amplifier in my experiments for weeks, and it is . . . er . . . quite harmless. Unlike my brain-stimulator, it has no power connection but simply intensifies mildly the wave lengths of thought set up by your brain while in action. On this paper I want you to write anything and everything that comes to your head. Anything, do you understand? Try and give your subconscious brain free rein."

Felspar nodded. The professor gently placed the aluminum disc on the man's head and adjusted a delicate control. Then he passed through a connecting doorway leading to his sitting room and closed the door behind him.

Finally the hour was up. Bickering returned to the room to find Felspar slumped disconsolately in the chair.

"I'm afraid it didn't work," the heavy-set man said. "That blamed salad bowl only gave me a headache, and I couldn't think of a thing to write except this. I . . . I don't even know what it means, but the words seemed to come of their own accord off the pencil."

Bickering seized the paper and stared aghast. Over and over again in parallel lines Felspar had written:

FIRST WARNING. CEASE ACTIVITIES AT ONCE.

Next day after an almost sleepless night Bickering came to a conclusion.

He must probe deeper into Felspar's subconscious brain, and he must do it in such a way that the man would be unaware of what was happening. He must find other "patients" whose doodlings would be in harmony with Felspar's. Surely in a city of this size there must be other men and women whose inherited mental whims could be of significance and value. As for Felspar's written warning, that was a mystery which at present defied explanation.

The professor wrote ten pages of his Chapter Twenty-four describing his initial experiment with Felspar. He spent the afternoon making a tour of the city. By five o'clock he had discovered five other persons in different walks of life, each of whom was a highly specialized doodler.

"Flip" Talbot was a reporter on *The Evening Standard*. His subconscious markings consisted of a large round circle which Bickering accepted as the Universe. Near the center of the circle was a group of small dots which resembled the Milky Way. And off to the side was the age-old symbol of the sun, a circle bordered by many wavy lines.

The other four were of lesser importance. John Albright, a plumbing fixture salesman, drew interlocking triangles. The Halstead brothers made pyramids of squares and rectangles. And Miss Alice Reynolds, a pretty stenographer, drew a conglomeration of them all: squares, triangles, dots and circles.

By diplomatic persuasion and vague offers of potential fame Bickering succeeded in making the five agree to meet at his hotel room that evening at eight o'clock. Mason Felspar had already promised to be there.

Bickering knew of course that doodling was only done under certain conditions and that if he wanted his guests to work at the highest point of efficiency he must reproduce those conditions. He went, therefore, to the offices of the telephone company and interviewed the manager of the service department. He wanted, he said, five telephones installed on the wall of his hotel laboratory, to be ready within the hour.

The manager's jaw dropped. "Five phones!" he gasped. "What are you going to do with five phones?"

"You needn't mind connecting them," Bickering said blandly. "I simply want them mounted on the wall."

From the phone company the professor made his way to the Zephyr Music Store, where he purchased a portable electric phonograph and one record.

"We have some other nice records," the clerk said.

Bickering shook his head. "This one is quite sufficient."

By the time he had returned to his hotel apartment, he found the five phones in their places, mounted on the laboratory wall.

Bickering fastened a pencil on a string to each phone. Then he opened a large packing case and took out his brain-stimulator. This was the machine he had spoken of to Felspar, simply an enlarged and more powerful version of the aluminum thought-amplifier. It was a large box-like affair with three Micro-Welman tubes and a series of intricate dials and verniers on its panel.

The professor had designed both the stimulator and the amplifier for psychology experiments in Chapters Five, Seven, and Nine. Both machines had worked successfully, and he had almost, but not quite, sold them to a manufacturer for professional distribution. Bickering had made five samples of the amplifier, but unfortunately under tests they had removed all of the patients' hair.

The stimulator also was constructed in accordance with the theory that the brain while in the process of thought sets up a vibratory field. When tuned to the proper wave length, it received those vibrations, strengthened them, and redirected them back to the brain through the ear.

Bickering got a screwdriver and a pair of pliers and set about connecting the receivers of the five telephones to the stimulator.

It was close to eight o'clock when he finished. Felspar was the first to arrive. The others followed promptly. By eight-fifteen Bickering was ready to begin his experiment.

"You are each to select a telephone," he had told them, lift the receiver to your ear and wait. I won't tell you whether you will hear anything or not. But while you wait, do anything you wish. Scribble, write, doodle, anything. I'll return shortly."

He placed one of the aluminum amplifiers on each of his

guests' heads and then started the phonograph with the record he had purchased. It was Liszt's *Liebestraum*. There was an automatic repeat device, and the professor hoped the music would place his five guests in the proper mood. He switched on the brain stimulator, passed into the next room and shut the door.

But when he returned to the laboratory twenty minutes later, he found things different than he had expected.

"Flip" Talbot, the reporter, had turned the record on the other side. It was playing *Classics in Swing*, and Alice Reynolds, the stenographer, had pushed her amplifier rakishly far back on her head and was beating the rhythm of the music on the chair arm with the palm of her hand.

The only person who had made a mark by his telephone was Felspar. On the wall he had written in a flowing hand:

SECOND AND LAST WARNING. YOU ARE INTERFERING WITH FORCES BEYOND YOUR POWER. IF YOU VALUE YOUR LIFE YOU WILL CEASE ACTIVITIES AT ONCE.

Bickering frowned as he gnawed his pipe stem and eyed Felspar shrewdly. Was the heavy-set man pulling his leg? But no, Felspar was staring at the wall, apparently stupefied by what he had written.

The repeated warning troubled Bickering. First warning of what? Who was doing the warning? Surely not Felspar. And what was all this prattle about forces beyond his power? Apparently greater stimulus was needed to make the experiment a success.

A thought came to Bickering then, and his eyes lighted. The brain stimulator derived its power from an ordinary six-volt storage battery. But he had been talking to the hotel engineer only yesterday, and that individual had offered him the use of a small auxiliary refrigeration dynamo in the hotel engine room.

"Better not say anything about it to the manager," the engineer had said in his friendly way. "And go easy when you make your connections. The thing sets right next to the main dynamo and the elevator motor, and there's plenty of hot juice there."

Bickering took out a large coil of double insulated wire, connected one end to the brain stimulator and dropped the free end

out the window. Then he rode down the elevator to the basement. The engineer was not in sight. Impatiently the professor
opened a basement window and caught the other end of the
wire. He proceeded to connect it to the refrigeration dynamo,
working with clumsy haste and paying no heed to the fact that
the wire hung perilously close to a small sign which read:

DANGER. VOLTAGE.

Finished, he returned to his laboratory and switched on the
brain stimulator again. The tubes glowed orange, then cherry
red, and a dull drone came from the interior of the box.

The receivers of the five phones were still connected to the
machine. Bickering motioned each of his guests to an instrument
and sat down in a chair to await results.

Results were startling. Felspar picked up his telephone receiver
and uttered a howl of pain. His face contorted into an expression
of stark terror.

"Turn it off," he yelled. "Turn it off!"

But Bickering did not turn it off. He said quietly, "Don't be
frightened. I'm simply amplifying your thought processes. Try
and relax."

A wild light leaped into Felspar's eyes. Seizing the pencil, his
hand jerked to the wall, began to move rapidly. He drew first
his usual symbol: the two stars, globe, dot with a tail and cigar-
shaped object. Then he began a new design.

The professor, who had stepped to his side, stared. With
strangely artistic skill Felspar's pencil was flying back and forth,
forming outlines and background. As he watched, Bickering saw
the picture of a city take form. A city fantastic. There were two
suns in the sky. There were streets and avenues, flanked by cube-
shaped buildings. And here and there were groups of strange-
looking creatures, like nothing Bickering had ever seen before.

Wafer-shaped heads, curious elongated bodies, a dozen
appendages in the place of arms and legs—the creatures were for
the most part lying on their backs. By the drawn expression on
their faces they seemed—or did Bickering imagine this?—to be
dying of suffocation.

Felspar was working frantically now. Beads of perspiration were on his brow, and his eyes were glassy, with a far-away expression.

In the center of his drawing he began to sketch a high platform, raised above the city. The perspective and the detail were in perfect proportion. On the platform a strange cylindrical shape took form. There were fantastic insulators on its surface. On either side a network of wires and cables hung down. Workers clustered about it, gave the impression they were fighting against time to finish its construction. It was a weird, unreal drawing.

His pipe cold, the professor paced to the brain stimulator and turned the power rheostat another notch.

"Felspar," he said, "what are you drawing?"

Without hesitation the heavy-set man wrote:

"The city of Calthedra of the planet Lyra of the system, Aritorius."

Professor Bickering gulped. "What is happening on that planet?" he demanded.

"The citizens are building a titanic air preserve. The oxygen atmosphere of the planet is disappearing due to the rapid recession of the two suns. With this machine the citizens hope to capture the atmosphere of some other planet and transport it to their own."

"When is this happening?"

Like a man in a trance Felspar wrote the answer:

"Now!"

Icy fear seemed to chill Bickering's spine. He had hoped to penetrate by way of the subconscious brain the mysteries of the past. But in some inexplicable way he was not doing that at all. He was delving into the secrets of time and space at the present instant. He was seeing across thousands of light years to another world.

What was the answer? Was it cosmic telepathy? Had he, by amplifying the thought vibrations of Felspar's brain, produced a wave-length which could annihilate time and distance and receive similar vibrations across almost infinite space?

One thing was certain. When he had transferred this to the written page, his book, his Chapter Twenty-four would be a masterpiece. Unquestionably the Trolheim Award would be his.

Not until then did Bickering become aware of the other occupants of the room. John Albright and the Halstead brothers were simply standing by as onlookers. But Alice Reynolds and "Flip" Talbot were sketching on the wall beside their phones.

The reporter's writings were as yet indistinguishable, but the stenographer's, the professor saw to his amazement, included the likeness of a huge cannon mounted on a rectangular base. Shooting from the muzzle of that gun was a cigar-shaped object. A projectile!

Hands trembling, Bickering turned the power of his brain stimulator to its last notch.

He saw then that "Flip" Talbot was writing a series of statements in column form. They read:

> The chemical content of the atmosphere of the planet Earth is, with the exception of a deficiency of coronium, similar to that of Lyra.
>
> It is absolutely vital to all Lyranians that our atmosphere be replenished. Because of the cosmic recession of our two suns, heat on Lyra is diminishing, vegetation is dying, and as a result oxygen and nitrogen are escaping.
>
> Migration from Lyra to Earth is at the present time impossible. Both the size and expense of such an undertaking make it impractical. Also, as our astronomers have proved, the nearby double nebula will produce a new sun within a comparatively short period of time. This new sun will amply replace the two that are now receding into space.
>
> In our dying moments we are making a last and final attempt to capture that which is essential to our life. We are shooting a projectile to Earth. This projectile the moment it lands will automatically begin the process of capturing the Earth's atmosphere, breaking it down into its component atomic parts and storing it under pressure.
>
> As the need demands, that atomic matter will be hurled into the fourth dimensional continuum and transported through a disruption of the spacetime coordinates back to Lyra. In short, the projectile, once it is on Earth, will serve as a branch power station, replenishing our atmosphere. It will arrive . . .

Bickering leaped to the reporter's side and gripped his arm.

"Will arrive when?" he shouted. "When?"

There was a blank stare in Talbot's eyes as his pencil moved over the wall:

First January, 1944, 11 P.M., Earth time!

With a wild cry Bickering glanced at the clock. It was ten o'clock. In one hour the greatest event in the history of mankind would occur. In one hour the first projectile from an outer planet would reach this Earth. And he—John Bickering—was the first person to be aware of its passage.

He had been wrong in his analyzation of Felspar's first drawing. No comet would change the trajectory of this projectile's path, for the simple reason that there was not any comet. This event was not one which had happened in ages past. It was happening now. Felspar's first drawing had been a blind. Apparently the citizens of the planet Lyra could not prevent the transmission of their secret by way of his subconscious drawings, but they had changed the details so as to give a completely wrong impression.

The professor raced across the room to the one "good" telephone.

"I'm going to call the newspapers," he cried. "It's the story of the age."

But he got only half way. Felspar who had been standing motionless, suddenly lifted one arm above him.

"Stop!" he cried.

Bickering turned. There was a quality and a tone to Felspar's voice that was altogether foreign. The man's face was crimson now; his breathing was coming in short gasps.

"Stop," he repeated. "You are to make no move to warn the people of your race of the projectile's arrival. You are to keep the facts you have learned in this room to yourself."

"Are you mad?" Bickering demanded. And then like a flash of light he understood.

The race of that other planet whose movements he had tuned in were aware of his activities. They were acting through Felspar's brain to prevent information of their plans being broadcast. Felspar was but a robot responding to their command. He had no conscious knowledge of what he was doing.

Why? Because they knew there was not sufficient atmosphere on Earth for two planets. Once the projectile had landed and begun its operations, the population of Earth would be doomed.

Unmindful of Felspar, Bickering gave a mighty leap toward the phone.

But Felspar, equally agile in spite of his bulk, darted to the laboratory table and scooped up a bottle of acid. Poising it over his head he emitted a wild shout.

"We all die together, Bickering . . . you, myself, and the others," he cried. "They whose thoughts you have been reading have willed it so!"

Bickering could see the man's facial muscles contract as he made ready to hurl the acid. And then . . .

Then the door of the elevator somewhere on the floors below clanged harshly. Through the silence the cage began to drone up the shaft.

Simultaneously the brain stimulator machine on the table erupted into life. Bickering remembered with a start the hotel engineer's warning about the refrigeration dynamo's proximity to the main dynamo and the elevator motor. He remembered too that in his haste he had made haywire connections. The filaments of the three Micro-Welman tubes lit up like incandescents. The panel began to vibrate violently, and the dials whirled of their own accord.

The elevator reached the floor level of the outer corridor. Suddenly an arc of purplish fire shot from the brain stimulator. There was a terrific roar as the box flew into a thousand fragments. Bickering felt himself hurled across the room and bludgeoned against the far wall. A cloud of fallen plaster and debris rose up in a choking cloud, and a blaze of colored lights whirled in his vision. Then blackness, and he knew no more . . .

Hours later when Bickering opened his eyes, the white walls of a hospital were about him, and the familiar figure of Mason Felspar stood beside the bed.

"What . . . what happened?" the professor asked weakly.

"Plenty," replied Felspar. "But you're supposed to lie quiet and not talk and . . ."

"Tell me!" demanded Bickering.

"Well—" the heavy-set man touched gingerly a bulky bandage on his forehead—"I don't know exactly. I brought you here and signed you in under another name. You see the hotel manager is madder than a wet hen. The last I saw of him, he was standing on the sidewalk, looking up at a big hole in the hotel wall and wringing his hands."

"I don't care about the hotel manager," cried the professor. "What happened?"

Felspar shrugged. "All I can say is that I wasn't responsible for what I did or wrote there in your room. Once you had that salad-bowl on my head and turned on that machine, another power seemed to be in control of my thoughts. Talbot and the girl, Reynolds, said the same. By a miracle none of us was hurt, but the hotel is a wreck. If you want to get all the dope, why don't you turn on your radio? It's just about time for the noon news broadcast."

Bickering reached across the table beside his bed and turned the switch of the radio there. A man's voice was talking:

> ". . . and at a late hour authorities were still mystified as to the cause of the explosion at the Sheridan Hotel . . . Continuing our survey of world news: . . . Washington, D.C., the U. S. Navy Department reported today that Allied battleships operating in the Caribbean Sea sighted and sank what appeared to be a Nazi super-submarine of enormous size.
>
> "The mystery U-boat was discovered near Belize, British Honduras, and was apparently having engine trouble, since it made no attempt to submerge. No member of the craft's crew was in evidence at any time, but when Allied warships approached hidden weapons firing what was described as 'a powerful electric bolt' attempted to bombard them.
>
> "A communique from the Nazi capital disclaims any knowledge of such a super-sub, and stories told by witnesses at Belize of seeing a great crimson streak in the sky

and observing a black cigar-shaped object fall into the sea
have been discredited. . . . This concludes the news broadcast for today. Goodbye until tomorrow."

Bickering looked across the bed and rubbed his jaw with his
unbandaged hand.

"So it was true," he said slowly. "Do you realize, Felspar, what
this means? It means that complete destruction, complete spatial
doom was saved us by a hairsbreadth."

Felspar swallowed hard and said nothing.

"And yet I wonder," Bickering continued, "I wonder if it matters so much. After all, man has been spared annihilation from
without, but now he's left to fight and kill himself off by wars of
his own making."

The Face in the Wind

Today is Tuesday. For almost a week, or since the morning of last Wednesday when the dark significance of the strange affair was first publicly realized, my life and the quiet routine of Royalton Manor have been thrown into a miserable state of confusion. It was of course to be expected, all details considered, and I took it upon myself to answer carefully all questions and repeat again and again for each succeeding official the part I played in the prologue to the mystery. Doubtless the London press was justified in referring to the sequence of events as the Royalton Enigma; yet in so doing it aroused a morbid curiosity that has made my position even more bewildering. For the story which I told, and which I know to be true, has been termed impossible and merely the wanderings of a crazed brain.

Let me begin by saying that like my fathers before me, I have lived here at Royalton all the days of my life, and I have seen the manor dwindle from an imposing feudal estate to a few tottering buildings and a small plot of weed-choked ground. Time and times have gone hard with the house of Hampstead.

There are, or rather *were* until last Wednesday, but two of these buildings occupied. Both in a considerable state of disrepair, I had reserved the right lower wing of the one which in earlier years boasted the name, Cannon Tower, for myself and my books. The other, an ivy-covered cottage, formerly the gardener's quarters, I had given over to an old woman some four months before. Her name was Classilda Haven.

Classilda Haven was a curious individual. A hundred times I have sat at my desk watching her through the open window as she cultivated her patch of vegetables, and I have racked my brain for a reasonable excuse to remove her from my property. The woman, according to her own statement, was nearly eighty; her body was bent and weazened, and her face witch-like and ugly with the mark of age. But it was her eyes that bothered me, drew my gaze every time she came within my vision. They were black, heavily browed, and sharp and clear as a young girl's.

At intervals when I have taken my morning walk through the old grounds, along the ruined frog wall, as I still prefer to call it, and on to the edge of Royalton Heath, I have felt those eyes staring after me. It was imagination, of course; nothing more. There has already been to my mind something grotesque in senility, something repelling in the gradual wasting away of all human qualities day by day.

Classilda Haven had stumped up to my door one evening late in April and inquired in a cracked voice if I wished to let the old gardener's cottage. She was a stranger to the district, I knew, and a woman of her age hobbling about unsheltered at that season is bound to be an object of pity. I asked casually if she had no relatives, no home; to which she replied that her son, her only means of support, had been killed in a motor lorry accident in London a week before. She had taken her few savings and entrained for Royalton, where she seemed to remember a distant relative was living. Arriving in the village she had found no trace of him, and so, without money, had wandered aimlessly down the Gable-wood Pike.

There was, of course, no refusing such a plea, and much as I disliked having my solitude interrupted, I had given her the key to the cottage, loaned her a few sticks of furniture, and tried to make her comfortable. In due time, I presumed, the relative would make his appearance and the woman would go on her way.

But as the spring gradually wore into summer and these things did not happen, I began to look upon the old crone as a fixture. Not until August did the horror begin, and then I had undying reason to regret my philanthropy.

It began with Peter Woodley. Woodley was a youth of twenty, a son of merchant villagers, in whom I had taken considerable interest. The boy aspired to paint. He had no unusual talent, it is true, yet his canvases had a certain simplicity in their likeness to surrounding landscapes that had caught my eye, and I had given him two or three art volumes that had found their way into the Hampstead library.

But on this morning as he stood in my study he appeared greatly excited and upset. His hair was clawed in wild disarray, and he was breathing hard, as if he had run to the manor all the way from Royalton.

"Mr. Hampstead," he gasped, "it isn't true, is it, the story I heard in the village? You're—you're not going to change the frog wall?"

I leaned back in my chair. "The frog wall?" I repeated. "Why yes, Woodley, I'm going to have it repaired. Repaired, that's all. It's badly in need of work, and the masons are coming tomorrow. But what on earth—"

Young Woodley dropped into the chair opposite me and spread his hands flat on the desk top.

"You mustn't do it, sir. You can't. You promised me I could use it for one of my pictures."

"Why, so I did," I said smiling. "I had forgotten. But I'm not changing the entire wall—just the two sections on either side of the gate. The stones have fallen almost entirely away, and I don't want the frogs to get through. That's the only reason for the wall being there, you know, Peter. The marsh on the other side is swarming with frogs. The wall was erected by my ancestors to keep the manor grounds free from the pests and permit the Hampsteads to sleep. . . . If it's rustic settings for your paintings you want, there are plenty of places—"

"But you don't understand, sir." Woodley in his earnestness was leaning far across the desk. "You don't understand. There's something on the other side of that wall besides frogs. There's something in that marsh that will get out, that will come into the grounds if you have the wall altered. I can't say what, sir. I really don't know what. But if you'd been out there at night in the moonlight, staring at the gate as I have, trying to see how I wanted to place my painting, you'd know."

I looked at him curiously there in the morning light of my study. "The wall is already down in those two places," I replied. "If there's anything in the marsh, and I'm quite sure there isn't, it certainly could get through now."

Woodley shook his head slowly, half in negative, half in perplexity.

"It's not the physical boundary I mean," he said. "It's not the wall itself. It's the actual space and time that it's occupied all these years that you're changing. Mr. Hampstead, don't do it!"

Naturally, such vague innuendoes did not induce me to countermand my order to the masons. Yet as the hours passed, something in the memory of Woodley's disturbing attitude instilled in me an indefinable sense of nervousness. Several times I caught myself staring out of the window toward the decayed remnants of the old frog wall, wondering what the boy had meant.

I turned at length to the shelves of the Hampstead library and spent two hours among the ancient volumes there, trying to rest my curiosity. The diaries of each successive resident of the manor were still intact, and I knew they included all mention of wine-cellars, out-houses and rooms which had been added to Cannon Tower during the generations. Curiously enough, however, search as I would, I could find no allusion to the erection of the frog wall, save one and this in the last memoirs of one Lemuel Hampstead 1734, was most confusing. It read:

> The Frogg Wall, which I have ordered builded, will this day be finished, God willing, and I am now contente to departe from this world and bestowe my title and possessions upon my eldest son. There will be no more tragedyes like that which befelle my father, Charles Ulrich, and his wife, Lenore. The wall will be blessed by the church in the manner which I have planned, and there will be a Holie Bible sealed in each corner poste. I—

Here age had left its mark on the page and the writing became undecipherable. But vague and meaningless as it all was, it was enough to set me thinking hard.

I personally supervised the masons' work the following day. It was a prosaic affair. The two workers simply removed the crumbling bits of stone from the two sections of the wall flanking the gate and patched the aperture with modern bricks. But they were forced to move the gate forward a few feet because of the marshy condition of the ground.

Classilda Haven shambled up to me as I stood watching the men ply their trowels. She smiled a toothless, evil smile.

"Ye'll be changin' the frog wall, I see," she said in her rasping voice. "All of it?"

"No, just the two sections," I replied, viewing her presence with some irritation.

The aged woman nodded, and I found myself staring again into her strange eyes. They were young, those eyes, clear and piercing, and they seemed oddly incongruous there in the wrinkled, leather-like face.

She turned abruptly, hobbled forward a few steps, and, head down like a bird, stared at one of the workmen as he carefully placed his bricks in position. Gingerly she ran a veined hand along the newly mortised surface, then looked up and shrilled:

"Why don't you tear it all down?"

I forced a tolerant smile. "Don't be absurd, Classilda," I said. "If I did such a thing, the place would be overrun with frogs, your garden as well. You know that."

She made a queer reply, an answer which seemed to escape from her involuntarily.

"Frogs," she squeaked, her eyes gleaming queerly. "I like frogs. I like them better than anything in the world."

Peter Woodley came that afternoon with his easel and his box of paints. I saw him through the window of my study as he selected a position near the iron gate-door, opened his little folding camp-stool, and began to walk slowly back and forth along the side of the newly repaired wall.

His agitation, which had been so pronounced the day before, seemed to have left him, though I couldn't help feel that he looked upon the renovated stonework with resigned eyes. He moved about several times before he apparently found the angle he desired, then seated himself and began what I presumed were the charcoal outlines.

My book attracted my attention then, and I forgot the boy for perhaps an hour. But suddenly I was jerked out of my chair by an ear-splitting scream. With a lurch I was across the floor and staring through the open casement at the weed-tangled grounds.

Peter Woodley lay prone on his face by his easel, his body still as death!

I raced out of the house and across the intervening space with all the speed I could muster. A moment later, as I examined him, I breathed a sigh of relief. He was still alive, but his heart was fluttering weakly. Cold water applied to his forehead and smelling-salts administered to his nostrils brought him around five minutes later, but when his eyes blinked open and he looked up at me, a moan of terror came to his lips.

"Good God! Mr. Hampstead!" he whispered. "I saw it! It was beautiful, but it was horrible. I saw it!"

"Saw what?" I asked, chafing his wrists. "In heaven's name, Peter, what's the matter?"

He struggled to his feet then, swayed dizzily and stepped over to his easel. For a moment he stood there, staring down at the few charcoal outlines on the canvas. Then he slumped weakly into the camp-stool and buried his head in his hands.

"Mr. Hampstead," he said, looking up abruptly, "promise me you'll never let me come here again. Promise me you'll keep me away from the manor grounds, by force if necessary. I must never attempt to paint that wall again, do you understand? And you, sir, couldn't you lock this place up and move into the village? Couldn't you sir?"

There was sincere anxiety written across his face, and his eyes were still gazing far out into space with a bewildered frightened expression that was foreign to the boy's usually calm nature.

"Nonsense, Peter," I replied. "You've been working too hard. You've let your imagination run away with you, that's all. Come into the Tower, and I'll give you a bit of brandy."

He shook his head, muttered something incoherently under his breath, and then, picking up his painting equipment, turned and strode quickly through the manor grounds toward the distant Gablewood Pike.

For a while I stood there, watching his figure grow smaller and smaller in the afternoon sunlight. I was puzzled more than I cared to admit by his strange attitude, and I was deeply disturbed by his allusions to "something which he had seen." For obviously as strapping a fellow as young Woodley does not faint dead away from sheer imagination. Neither does he babble queer warnings to a man twice his age without a reason.

And then as I turned and began to walk slowly toward the door of my study, my eyes suddenly took into focus a patch of ground near the old wall. The workmen repairing this section had, in order to aid their movements, torn up the weeds and rank underbrush, which grew unmolested in this part of the property.

And there in the freshly upturned earth was the imprint of a gigantic bird-like claw.

It was ten minutes past twelve that night when I found myself sitting up in bed staring at the radium dial of the taboret clock. Cannon Tower was still as death, and there was no sound from without save the distant mournful croaking of frogs beyond the wall. Even as I listened, that bass obbligato ceased abruptly, and the world lapsed into a heavy, ringing silence.

I got up, slid into a pair of slippers and moved across to the window. Curious. If there is one thing that is a certainty in my life, it is my profound manner of sleeping. Once retired I seldom if ever awake before my usual rising hour. And yet there I was, eyes wide open, heart thumping madly with the terror and bewilderment of one who has been jerked suddenly from the macabre fantasies of a nightmare.

But I had not been sleeping. Neither, I was positive, had any unusual sound disturbed my slumbers. The manor grounds stretched below me, blue under the August moonlight like a motionless quilt, and beyond, vague and indistinct, I could see the flat, barren expanse of Royalton Heath.

A thin blanket of clouds slid over the moon then, darkening the shadows into a thick, brooding umbra and simultaneously it happened.

From the east, from somewhere deep in the recesses of the marsh that lay beyond the frog wall, there rose into the still air a horrible, soul-chilling cry. It was a cry I can never hope to forget, the scream of a bird of prey about to make its kill, a thousand times magnified, and ending in a high-pitched shriek that was strangely human.

Motionless I stood there, eyes riveted in the direction of the old wall, muscles tense as wire. For a moment I saw nothing, the blackness below me was thick and impenetrable. Then suddenly, with the quickness of a camera-shutter, the moon broke through that cloud mass once more, and the manor grounds returned to their blue silver.

The cry came again nearer. The echo thrown back from the walls of Cannon Tower passed on into the distance like the wail of a lost soul, and with a choking gasp I turned my eyes skyward.

High above me, outlined against the driven cloud, circling like a giant vulture in the night, was a bird of colossal size. Its wing-spread was enormous, a full twenty feet from tip to tip, and its head and body were curiously elongated and heavy. Even as I stood there, staring at it, my face wet with terror, it wheeled and swooped toward me.

Forward, straight toward the Tower it sped as if intent on dashing itself to pieces against the ancient masonry. Then it veered sharply and raced toward my window.

An instant I stood there, transfixed. Then, my subconscious mind had enough clarity to whip me around and send me lurching back into the room. There was a century-old percussion pistol on the right wall, mounted in its carved metal holster, and I knew it was always loaded, a feeble but comforting protection in my solitude.

In the half-darkness I seized it, pushed the hammer to full cock, leaped back to the window and fired.

There came an instantaneous violent flapping of those mighty wings, an over-powering stench of death and decay, and crashing into my ear-drums a repetition of that hideous cry. The specter disappeared.

Faintness seized me then. Spots and queer-colored lights swirled in my vision, and I sank backward to the floor. But even as I closed my eyes to unconsciousness I knew, as I know now, that what I had seen was no dream, no vagary of a sleep-drugged brain.

For gazing at me there, with its huge feathered wings and repulsive vulture body, had been the face of a beautiful woman!

A bad electrical storm came up next day after almost three weeks of sultry heat. I spent the morning pottering about my studio as usual. Outside, the thunder crashed and boomed ceaselessly.

But come afternoon I refused to be kept indoors any longer, and so, donning an old rain-jacket, I began my usual walk through the manor grounds. I was still weak and trembling from my unexplainable experience of the night before.

The rain was coming down hard from a thick, gray sky, and the weeds and undergrass flanking the little path were dripping with wet. Behind me the great vine-covered walls of Cannon Tower loomed grim and silent.

At the gate-door of the frog wall I suddenly stopped. The barrier, always locked with staple and bolt, stood wide open, revealing just beyond the wild, undulating expanse of the marsh. I moved to close it, but a moment later Classilda Haven appeared, working her way up the reed-covered incline toward me. And for some unknown reason I viewed her presence there with suspicion.

"Classilda," I snapped, "who gave you permission to go beyond the gate?"

Her clothes and her hair were dripping with rain, and the dishevelment gave to her, it seemed, a curiously repelling ornithoid appearance. It was odd, but never until that moment had I noticed how distinctly avian were the contours of her weazened body and her talon-like hands. She cocked her head to one side, looked at me, and laughed a squeaky laugh.

"I've been down in the marsh," she said. "I went to get some dirt for my garden. Those workmen, the careless fools, have trampled all over it."

I glanced at the orderly rows of lettuce and cabbages which in some places had been crushed and overturned by unobserving feet.

"Not workmen," I said. "I'm afraid it was young Woodley that did this. I shall have to tell him to be more careful. He comes here to paint, you know, at night sometimes in the moonlight, and I suppose he didn't notice where he walked. But," I added, remembering his words and firm decision which he had made following his fainting spell, "I don't think you'll be troubled with him any more. He's taken a dislike for the place, and he's staying away."

The old crone stood looking at me with those youthful, beady eyes. She smoothed some of the water from her black dress, shifted her basket of dirt to her other hand and smiled cryptically.

"Not too much of a dislike, Mr. Hampstead," she said, displaying her toothless gums. "He was here last night, painting. I spoke with him."

I stared at her. If both Classilda Haven and Peter Woodley had been awake and in the manor grounds during the night, then they too must have seen the hideous thing which had flown out of the marsh and looked in my bedchamber window. All the horror of what I had seen, all the terror of that nocturnal vision which the intervening hours had inclined to soften and pale in my memory, returned then, and I leaned weakly against the bole of a cypress tree.

"Classilda," I began slowly, "were you—did you see—"

But with a swish of her sodden skirts the old woman turned, laughed that mirthless falsetto laugh once more, and hobbled off toward her cottage.

Deeply troubled, I buttoned my jacket closer about the throat and continued my walk through the slanting rain. I was heading for the edge of Royalton Heath, where, as was my custom, I would stop a moment and gaze out over that somber stretch of wasteland which I had known for so many years. But this time my leisurely walk was destined to be interrupted.

Near the end of the manor grounds where the frog wall turned abruptly to the left and headed into the depths of the marsh, I came upon Peter Woodley. Hatless and without coat of any kind, he was sitting in the long, brown weeds, unmindful of the swirling rain and apparently oblivious of my approach. And in his hands were two impossible things.

For a full instant I stood there gazing at him, watching his hands as they worked diligently at their task. Then I cleared my throat and spoke:

"Peter," I said, "what on earth are you doing with that bow and arrow? I thought you were an artist, not a huntsman."

He started, leaped to his feet, and tried to conceal the two articles upon which he had been working. But as if through a telescope my eyes centered upon the arrow-shaft. It was the metallic arrow-head that held my gaze, a head long and slender, ending in a needle-point and made of silver.

Without answer Peter Woodley wrapped the two articles in a piece of canvas and seized a larger package from the ground, a package I had not noticed before.

"With your permission, sir," he said, "I'd like to walk back with you to the Tower. I finished my picture of the wall last night, and I'd like to hear what you think of it."

Fifteen minutes later, bent over the desk in my study, I stared down upon Woodley's newly painted canvas. The lowering clouds without had spread a premature darkness in the room, and I had lighted two of the candelabra. But even with this added illumination I could not quite believe my eyes.

For a long time I stood there, looking down at the oily brush marks, examining the background and the objects in the center. Then with a gasp of incredulity I sank into a chair.

"Peter, my boy!" I exclaimed, "did you actually paint this? It's excellent—a masterpiece!"

He looked suddenly wan and haggard as he seated himself opposite me and began to run his fingers absently along the design of the table.

"Yes," he said dully, "I did it. There are a few remaining touches to be added before it is completed, but the painting as you see it is the work of a few hours. I worked last night in your grounds by moonlight. I—I wish to God I hadn't."

"What do you mean?" I asked.

He nervously lit a cigarette and leaned forward in his chair.

"Mr. Hampstead," he said, "that painting—I simply can't realize it came from my brush, done by my own hand. I meant to paint a simple likeness of the old frog wall with the iron gate in the center. But as I worked there in the moonlight, something seemed to take hold of me. I felt as if a will other than my own were controlling my thoughts. I painted as I have never painted before, worked at terrific speed in a nervous frenzy. And when I had finished I was in a state of complete exhaustion.

"I don't understand it, sir," he went on. "Sometimes I think I've been going mad the last few days. But there's something wrong with that picture, something terribly wrong. Every time I look at it I have a dreadful feeling it never should have been brought into creation."

"Nonsense, Peter," I said, looking across the desk at the propped-up canvas. "You've done an admirable piece of work. Frankly, I didn't think you had it in you. None of your earlier efforts have displayed such unusual talent as this."

Woodley left half an hour later, but not before I had persuaded him to leave the painting in my care.

"I'd like to study it if you don't mind," I told him. "I'm planning to go to London next month, and I may want to take this along. Perhaps I can place it in a contest for you, or if not, find someone who would like to buy it."

He seemed little affected by my words. Ordinarily any compliment I might bestow upon his work would have been received with boyish enthusiasm and appreciation of my interest. But now he stood there in the doorway, hands hanging at his sides, eyes lowered as if he were oppressed by some mental cloud.

When he had gone I carefully shut all the doors to my study, returned to my desk and moved the painting a few inches farther back where there was no chance of shadow impairing my view of it. Then I trundled the heavy armchair into the center of the room to a position about four feet directly before the desk, sat down, and deliberately fastened my eyes upon the canvas.

I confess that at the moment there was nothing positive in my mind which would account for my actions. But from the first moment I had gazed down upon the picture I had realized that young Woodley's strange speech was not the result of an overwrought imagination. Quite definitely there was something wrong with the painting. Something wrong, I say, and yet I was unable to see anything in the oil presentation beyond a simple and familiar scene.

That scene had been beautifully done, it is true. There was the old frog wall and the black bulk of the huge gate-door with the blur of the marsh in the background. The coloring and effect of the mellow moonlight had been accomplished with rare artistry, and it did not seem possible that so inexperienced and untrained a youth as Peter Woodley could have wielded a brush with such finesse. And yet more and more as I stared across at it there came the impression that I was looking upon something indescribably evil.

For perhaps ten minutes I remained there, studying each brush mark in the flickering glare of the two candelabra. Then abruptly, acting on impulse, I stepped across the room and unhooked the long framed mirror which adorned the farther wall.

I placed the painting now at an angle on the right corner of the desk. And at the opposite corner, lengthwise on a parallel, I set the mirror.

Returning to my chair, I adjusted my position slightly, then looked hard at the reflection in the mirror. Beyond the fact that the glass vision thus seen was the usual reverse of the original, there was no change.

But an instant later, with a choking cry I had leaped from the chair and, face down, had pressed my eyes to the looking-glass. In God's name, what I had seen could not possibly be true! It was a trick of my thoughts, a mental image projected into the droning solitude by a still persistent and bewildered memory. But no . . .

Clearly focused in the mirror was the reflection of Peter Woodley's painting in oil. But my eyes had caught a different angle to the lines now, the perspective had changed, and where before I had seen only the likeness of the frog wall and the iron gate-door, and the marsh— in place of that was—a woman's face!

It was incredible, and it was incredibly beautiful. A woman's face returning my gaze silently—with black lustrous hair, Grecian features, and lips that were curved in a slight mocking smile; an exquisite face painted with classic loveliness but with strange piercing eyes I seemed to remember having seen once and many times before.

Many moments I remained there, staring far into the glass. Then I reached for the decanter, poured myself a strong, undiluted portion of whisky and slumped dazedly into the chair. My brain was going round and round, my heart pounding like a trip-hammer.

It would have been a most curious enigma, this optical illusion, this accidental use of the double perspective, even had I looked upon a reflected object thus that was new and foreign. But when I stopped to realize that what I saw there was not only familiar but engraved in my brain in a hideous memory of the immediate past, the whole vision became alive with horrific possibilities.

For the woman's face which looked back at me from the reflection of the looking-glass was the same face I had seen in the head of that loathsome flying monster that had peered into my bed-chamber the night before!

I ate no dinner that evening. As dusk darkened into night and the thunder and rain dwindled off, I sat by the window of my study, staring out into the dripping grounds, drawing deeply on my old Hoxton pipe. The hours passed slowly. By ten o'clock the last remaining cloud had left the sky, and the moon rode high and clear.

I roused my self then, and still smoking furiously, let myself out of Cannon Tower and through the garden exit into the manor grounds. In contrast to the gloominess of the afternoon, the way before me now was brilliant under the blue light and tessellated with curious elliptical shadows from the overhanging verdure. Off in the marsh, the frogs, still unaware no doubt of the complete cessation of the storm, were silent.

I walked slowly, head down, immersed in my thoughts. When I reached the high gate-door in the wall, I paused a moment, reflecting how perfectly young Woodley had caught the moonlit scene in his painting. Then, knowing that sleep would be impossible under the circumstances, I crossed over to an old tree-stump, wiped the rainwater from its surface with my handkerchief, and sat down.

How long I remained there in the half-darkness I don't know. The moon moved high in the heavens and began to descend toward the west. I filled and lighted my pipe several times.

But suddenly the snapping of a twig whipped me out of my reverie, and I turned to see Classilda Haven slowly advancing down the path. I watched her casually. Then I sat bolt upright, huddled farther back in the shadow, and stared with a rising feeling of perplexity.

What was the old crone doing in the grounds at this hour? And why was she skulking forward like a wary snake, looking back over her shoulder at each step to see if she were followed?

A moment later I was pressed close against the bole of a

cypress tree, muscles stiffened to attention. With a final look behind her, Classilda Haven had stepped to the iron gate-door, unlatched the staple and pin, and was swinging the barrier slowly open. One instant she hesitated, head cocked to one side, listening. Then she passed through the aperture and disappeared in the direction of the marsh.

For a quarter of an hour I held my position, waiting for her to return. Far back in a corner of my brain a vague suspicion was beginning to grow, and I sought for an answer to the woman's strange actions.

Then it happened! The iron gate opened again—slowly, and a figure stepped into the shadows. It was not Classilda Haven. It was a woman who did not resemble the old crone in any way. She was young, tall, dressed in filmy white, with long raven hair that cascaded down her back. A moment she paused there, her hand on the latch. Then she moved into the open moonlight, and I jerked electrified to attention.

That face again—divinely beautiful with a satin complexion, carmine lips, and eyes black and piercing! The same face I had seen once flying in the night and again in the changed perspective of Peter Woodley's painting! Was I going mad?

The woman seemed to glide slowly forward, to float down the path as though her feet were treading air. Presently she moved closer to the frog wall, raised one arm high over head and began to move it up and down, back and forth, in long sweeping arcs.

She was writing! Writing in chalk! I saw that as the moonlight streaming through the trees focused the crumbling masonry and the silent figure in blue relief. A foot high and carefully fashioned in curious stilted lines the characters took form.

The word completed, the woman stepped back and studied it carefully. I looked out from my hidden position behind the tree and read:

"C E L A E N O"

The chalk word seemed to gleam like white fire against the gray darkness of the old wall, and although I could not at the moment fathom its meaning, it touched a responsive chord somewhere in my memory. Celaeno. It seemed—

There was something weirdly impossible in it all. Standing there deep in the shadow of the huge cypress tree, my unlighted pipe clenched tightly between my teeth, I felt as if I were viewing the scene from the doorway of another world.

The woman moved farther down the wall to a position on the other side of the iron gate-door. Abruptly she stopped again, raised the chalk and scrawled in those same stilted letters:

"C E L A E N O"

I thought then I had unwittingly made my presence known, for the woman, upon completion of the last letter, whirled and turned those penetrating eyes straight in my direction. But it was another sound which she had heard, a sound of slow footsteps advancing down the path.

In measured pace they came on, louder and louder, like the rhythmic cadence of a muffled mallet. An instant later another figure came upon the scene, and a new wave of bewilderment swept over me.

It was Peter Woodley—Woodley clad in an old green dressing-robe, with his eyes closed and his arms stretched stiffly before him in the manner of a sleep-walker. Straight toward the woman in white he advanced, step by step.

"I'm coming, Celaeno," he whispered. "Celaeno . . . I love you, Celaeno."

As he drew nearer, a slight smile turned the woman's lips. I saw it in the moonlight. And she leaned forward, grasped the boy by the right arm and began to lead him toward the gate.

But there, as the iron door swung open of its own accord, a change came over Woodley. His eyes flickered open, his body stiffened, and a hoarse cry sounded deep in his throat. On the instant he seemed to realize what was happening. He wrenched his arm away from the woman's grasp, turned, and with a scream of terror began to run down the path toward the Gablewood Pike.

Transfixed, I stood there, looking after him. He fled like a deer, running wildly across the open patches of moonlight, the skirts of his green dressing-robe swirling after him. And when I again turned my eyes to the scene before me, three inexplicable things had happened.

The woman in white had disappeared; the iron gate-door was locked and pinioned from the outside; and the two chalk words scrawled upon the frog wall were no longer there!

Peter Woodley slammed open the door of my study next morning and strode into the room without knocking. I was thankful that he had come. There were a thousand questions I meant to ask, the whole fantastic mystery to discuss. It was time, I realized, to talk openly.

But Woodley brushed aside my preliminary remarks with a wave of his hand.

"My painting," he cried. "Where is it? I'm going to tear it apart bit by bit and throw the pieces in the fire! Give it to me!"

I stood up, walked across to the window, and answered him dully.

"It's gone," I said. "I had it locked here in the old wine cabinet. When I came down this morning I found the doors still locked but the picture gone."

He seemed on the verge of a complete collapse as he stood there swaying.

"Gone," he repeated in a far-away voice. "Gone." Then:

"It's that painting that's caused it all, Mr. Hampstead. It's a net, a spider-web that has entangled me and brought me under her power. Since I have finished it I cannot help myself. I almost succumbed last night. She was beautiful. God, how beautiful! But when I think of the condition of my arm—"

"Your arm?" I repeated. "What do you mean?"

He stared at me a moment as if hesitant to say anything further. Then, abruptly, he slipped out of his coat and pulled back the sleeve of his shirt.

"I haven't been to a doctor yet," he said slowly. "But I know medicines won't be able to do anything for me. This—this is not a physical ailment."

I took a step closer and then suddenly recoiled.

"Good God!" I whispered. "Not a physical ailment? Are you mad?"

From the elbow down, the flesh of the right arm was a horrible blackened mass, with the veins standing in livid prominence and the hand shriveled as in the last stages of gangrene.

"But Peter—yesterday!" I began in a trembling voice.

He nodded lifelessly.

"Yesterday," he replied, "that arm was all right. I found it this way when I awoke in bed this morning. Mr. Hampstead, don't you realize what we're up against? Don't you realize what it all means?"

I reached for the brandy glass and drank a little with shaking lips.

"Am I going mad, Peter?" I asked finally. "Are we both mad? None of it seems possible—like some strange dream that has become a reality."

Woodley turned abruptly and strode across to the wall of bookshelves on the farther side of the room. There he ran his eyes slowly along the stacked array of ancient volumes. At length he chose one and returned with it to the desk.

"I was here yesterday morning when you were still in bed," he explained. "I knew I could find what I was looking for in your library, and I wanted to verify my suspicions. Mr. Hampstead, when you read this, you must believe. You must help me. Together perhaps we can free ourselves."

The volume he had laid on the desk before me was significant in itself. It was a copy of Richard Verstegan's *Restitution of Decayed Intelligence*, that evil work long ago banned by God-fearing people as being inspired by Satan. Up to that moment I had never been aware that it existed in my library, but from the signature on the fly-leaf I saw it must have come into my ownership as part of the collection of Lemuel Hampstead, my ancestor of the Eighteenth Century. Woodley now opened it to a middle page, and bending lower, I read:

> And Neptune and Terra had three daughters. And their names were Celaeno, Aello, and Ocypete. But theye were offspring accursed, for theye were winged monsters with the face of a woman and the bodys of vultures. Theye emitted an infectious smell and spoiled whatever theye touched bye their filth. Theye were harpies!

With a choking cry I kicked back my chair and leaped to my feet. "Harpies!" I screamed. "God in heaven!"

Harpies! Those fabulous monsters, creatures of evil who delighted in carrying mortals from this earth to hell and everlasting torture! Harpies, winged horrors of classic mythology, sometimes with the face of a hag, sometimes with the body and face of a beautiful woman! Was it possible such fantasies were more than the mental creations of Grecian philosophers and actually existed in our own mundane world?

In a swirl of confusion the pieces of the mystery were beginning to take position in my brain. One thing I saw. Alone among my ancestors, Lemuel Hampstead had sensed the hideous danger that lurked in that ancient marsh, and under guise of keeping the frogs out of the manor grounds had erected a protecting wall. I recalled the faded passage I had read in his memoirs:

> The wall will be blessed by the church, and there will be a
> Holie Bible sealed in each corner poste . . .

Now I understood why the two manor residents previous to Lemuel Hampstead, Charles Ulrich and his wife, Lenore, had come to such dark and horrible ends, the woman dying from "a strange maladie whiche caused her face and hands to blacken and rot away," and the body of the man "to be found in the depths of the slough with his eyes torn from their sockets and his head slashed with the mark of claws."

An idea struck me, and I whirled upon Peter Woodley. "Classilda Haven!" I cried. "Classilda Haven, it is she—"

He nodded. "I've suspected so for a long time," he said. "But there are two more. Always three. They are the spirit of the storm winds. Their homing-place is said to be in Crete, but they can move about the world with the speed of light. They are the personification of classic evil, created perhaps by mass mental imagery long ago and still existing, a throw-back from another age."

"Classilda!" I repeated dazedly. "I'm going to her cottage and—"

Woodley shook his head slowly. "You wouldn't find her now," he said. "But even if you did, nothing can harm them while in human form. No, we must wait." He turned on his heel, left the room a moment and returned with a long tube of rolled canvas.

Opening it and removing its contents, I saw that he was holding the long bow and arrow which I had seen him working on in the grounds the day before.

"They're finished, sir," he said; "the only method I know of fighting them. A bow and an arrow with a silver head. I've made two arrows. What good they'd do even if they struck, I don't know. But we can try."

For a moment as the clock pounded its ticks through the silence of the room we sat staring at each other. Woodley's face was tight and drawn, his eyes were glassy, his hands shaking.

"Tonight," he said suddenly, "in a few hours the horror will begin. God help us!"

Midnight, and the wind was screaming over the grounds with the mournful whine of an Eolian harp. I lay stretched at full length in a clump of underbrush, waiting . . . waiting for I knew not what. At my side, within arm's reach, lay Woodley's bow and his two silver-headed arrows. In my pocket was a metal bottle with the crucifix emblazoned on its sides.

There was water in that bottle, holy water from the little church in Royalton, obtained by Woodley early in the afternoon as part of our feeble and blind defense. What its Christian effect would be against these nightmares of another theology I did not know, but in case of any emergency I meant to use it.

We had made hurried plans there in my study before darkness closed in. Woodley was to remain in the Tower, all lights turned off, while I, armed with those strange weapons, kept watch near the wall. Not unless I called out for help was he to show himself, and then only with the utmost caution. I had argued hard before Woodley grudgingly consented to this arrangement.

"It's youth they want, Peter," I told him. "They want you because you're young. They care nothing about me. I'm a middle-aged man with a life half spent."

Time snailed by as I crouched there. Up above, the moon shone at intervals through rents in a flotilla of velvet clouds.

And then the garden door of the Tower creaked open, and I saw Peter Woodley step out and advance down the path. He had removed his hat and coat, and his face shone white as death.

Unable to understand his appearance, I hissed a warning at him there in the shadows.

"You fool!" I cried. "Go back! I didn't call."

My words had no effect. Slowly, stiffly, with the same mechanical sleep-walking pace that had marked his entrance to the grounds the night the harpy-woman wrote her name in chalk, he passed me and continued parallel to the wall. Straight to the iron gate-door he moved, then stopped motionless.

"Celaeno!" he called softly. "Where are you?"

For a moment there was silence, broken only by the moaning of the wind. Then mounting into the night air, wavering and hideous, came once again that wailing scream. From the other side of the frog wall it sounded, rushing nearer.

An instant later I had leaped to my feet and was staring above me. In the gloom, high over the manor grounds, circled that mighty shape—a giant, vulture-like bird with great pointed black wings *and the head and breast of a woman. A harpy!*

I watched it hover there, carried back and forth by the raging wind. Then my eyes turned farther to the left, and I jerked back with a shriek of horror. There were two more of the loathsome creatures, and those two were swooping down straight toward me.

I caught a glimpse of female faces with exquisite features, long, streaming black hair and crimson, evil lips. Then a sharp claw ripped across my chest and tore my coat. I struck out madly, felt my fists pound deep into the feathery wings, struck again and went down, overwhelmed by their bodies.

I fought with every ounce of strength I possessed, with terror striking deep into my very soul. I rolled over and over, sought frantically to free my right hand and draw forth the bottle of holy water.

A stench of death and decay seared into my nostrils. My face and body were bleeding from a hundred places, and I was fast losing my strength. But suddenly one of those razor claws yielded to my frenzied blows and with a lunge I whipped my hand sideward, grasped the bottle, uncorked its spout and showered the water out before me.

The harpies leaped back and stood gazing at me, women faces

twisted in expressions of stark hate. Again I whirled the bottle, this time spilling part of the contents into their eyes.

There was a double shriek of rage. The monsters ran clumsily backward, then swooped into the air and fled.

I leaned gasping against the trunk of a tree. Then as the realization that the horror still was not finished filtered into my bewildered senses, I turned, seized the bow and silver-headed arrows and ran on into the grounds.

Near the end of the property, far beyond the gate, I saw them again. They were flying high above me, three huge shapes etched black against the moonlit sky. And in the claws of one of them, held by his hair, dangled the body of Peter Woodley.

With shaking hands I fitted an arrow to the bow-string and pointed it upward. Back until the bow was bent almost double I pulled, then released it. It whined upward, shot past one of the monsters—and missed.

Panting, mumbling a prayer aloud, I seized the second shaft and made ready to fire again. But the harpies had sensed their danger, ceased their circling and with enraged cries were heading high toward the frog wall and the distant marsh.

I gave a last frenzied look above me, took quick aim and let fly that last arrow. Upward it sped, a gleaming streak in the moonlight.

And suddenly the night was hideous with the cries and shrieks of the wounded monster. The creature fluttered and spun like a top. It opened its claws as it wobbled off toward the marsh, and the body of Woodley, released, dropped downward, fell like a meteor straight onto the jagged top of the frog wall.

An instant later I was at the boy's side, bending over his broken and blood-covered body. He rose up as I lifted his head in my arms.

"Thanks, Mr. Hampstead," he whispered. "It was—it was the only way."

He fell back with a sigh, and I was alone with the corpse of Peter Woodley.

There is little more to tell. No one believes me. The villagers stare curiously at my whitened hair and shrink away shuddering as I meet their gaze. The district doctor feels of my pulse, looks into the cornea of my eye and shakes his head perplexedly. And the police continue to search the countryside for some trace of Classilda Haven.

Fools! I have taken them to the gardener's cottage and shown them the empty black silk dress, nailed as it is to the center of the floor by a silver-headed arrow. I have led them to that section of the frog wall near the iron gate-door and traced slowly, letter for letter, the faint, almost obliterated lines that one moonlight night spelt so clearly the word "Celaeno." And I have placed on the table the wall mirror and Woodley's painting, which had been found somewhere in the depths of the marsh—placed them at their proper angles and pointed out the strange woman face that looked back silently from the changed perspective.

But in each case they only look at me sadly and murmur: "Poor man, there is nothing there."

Rails of the Yellow Skull

There was thunder in the air as Frank North stepped into the smoky gloom of the Denver depot train shed. He guided the girl at his side through a crowd of disembarking passengers to the last coach of the Coast Express.

"This is it, darling," he said. "Brooks Delfield's private car. We ride in style tonight."

Madge Lane jerked nervously at the collar of her trim traveling suit. "I wish we weren't going, Frank. I . . . I wish we could stay here at least until tomorrow."

North nodded. Yesterday they had looked forward to taking this train. Tonight, with the trip changed from a carefree honeymoon to a serious business mission, death loomed before them.

Inside the private car a sweet, sickish odor assailed their nostrils. The smell of new varnish and new furnishings, perhaps, it made North clear his throat. He felt somehow as though he had entered a coffin—a coffin on wheels that was waiting to carry him to doom and destruction.

"Nerves," he growled. "Dammit, this thing is getting me down."

Two persons were in the car. Marc Delfield, hollow-cheeked son of the president of the Colorado, North & Western, leered back at them through horn-rimmed spectacles. At his side sat a smallish man with patent leather hair and a cream fedora hat.

"You're early," Marc said thickly. "The rest of the gang won't be here for fifteen minutes."

Unconsciously North felt a chill course down his spine as he answered the second man's gaze. Armand Guise was the fawning suitor of Garnet Delfield, the president's daughter. There was something about the Frenchman's womanish face and beady eyes that reminded one of a harpy, poised, ready to strike.

Nodding and striding to the end of the car, North tossed down his pigskin bag.

"Can I get you something?"

Madge shook her head. "Frank, I'm afraid. I have a premonition something's going to happen this trip."

He smiled slowly. "Nothing's going to happen, sweetheart. You're tired, that's all."

But his voice sounded without emphasis. Even now he wasn't sure why he was here. He guessed, of course, that Brooks Delfield had decided at the last moment to look over that proposed right-of-way to Rock River, up near the Wyoming line. Information had come through that a government dam was to be erected there as part of a federal project. The influx of traffic which would follow would make the laying of trackage to the mountain town a worthwhile investment.

As chief detective-investigator for the C.N.&W., North would be in charge of the policing of this spur construction-job. He had worked for the railroad for three years now. And during that time his friendship for Madge Lane, Delfield's private secretary, had grown into a deep love.

He drew a pipe from his pocket. "Going out for a smoke," he told Madge. "Back in a moment."

He paced down the aisle, swung open the rear door and stepped out on the observation platform. He wanted to be alone, to collect his black thoughts. Dropping into a chair, he lit his pipe and sucked smoke savagely.

The whole thing went back to those damnable cards. There had been ten of them, and Madge Lane had found one each morning along with Delfield's mail it was her duty to open and sort. Ten postcards, grey in color, the address neatly typed, each bearing that design.

On the reverse side, like a macabre coat of arms, a death-head was engraved in yellow ink!

Delfield had sworn good-naturedly at first and muttered something about the work of a crank. But the cards kept coming.

Yesterday the routine was broken; *two* cards arrived. Madge had uttered a short, terrified cry as she saw that one was addressed to Frank North, the man she was going to marry.

Delfield's card bore writing this time. Above the death-head was scrawled:

YOU ARE THE FIRST. YOU HAVE FORTY-EIGHT HOURS TO LIVE. THE YELLOW SKULL IS CLOSING IN ON YOU.

The president of the C.N.&W. was not a man to be frightened by unsigned correspondence. But he had turned the cards over to North.

"If there's something behind it," Delfield had said, "you figure it out. As a railroad bull, it may be a little out of your line, but you always did have a flair for things out of the ordinary."

The thunder was crashing louder now. North turned his gaze out over the train shed. Abruptly he stiffened.

Thirty feet away a baggage-cart was standing, piled high at one end with labeled trunks and gripsacks. A man, garbed in company overalls, was spraying that baggage with an automatic force-pump, shooting a thick mist out before him.

It was *Dustneer*, North's own invention, a chemical he had devised to protect the passengers' luggage from grime and grit while traveling. Only recently placed on the market, the product was already bringing him good returns.

But the man with the spray gun didn't act like a company employee. He kept well to the side of the baggage cart. From time to time he looked furtively toward the depot proper.

Abruptly the man's head twisted about, and North's eyes jerked wide. He was gaping at a face that was a horrible expanse of featureless flesh. The eyes were black, oblong holes. A drooling hole, without lips or teeth, formed the mouth. The skin was wrinkled like parchment, colored a gleaming yellow.

The yellow skull! North jerked to his feet. Before he could throw himself over the railing to the platform a locomotive far down the track screeched its whistle. Simultaneously through the iron gate of the train shed a tall man with a cane appeared. Behind him came two other men and a young woman.

The figure with the spray gun leaped into action. Thrusting the nozzle up, he sent a jet of thick vapor shooting forward.

North, lunging forward, shrieked a warning: "Delfield! Look out!"

His words were drowned in an ear-searing hiss. Ahead a blinding sheet of flame appeared, issuing from the mouth of the spray gun. A river of red, that flame lashed across sixty feet of space toward the advancing railroad president.

In the split second before North reached the baggage cart, hell broke loose. He heard screams, terrified shouts. Then his outstretched hands reached one end of the cart. He vaulted over it and rammed into the overall-clad figure.

He sent a hard blow into the squat neck. A startled oath blasted from the skull-faced man's throat. With a snarl he swung, swiveling the flame gun. North grasped the man's wrists, fought to turn the liquid blaze aside.

There was but a split second to act. The detective lunged down, slammed headlong into his opponent's legs. The man reeled. The spray gun shot from his hand and crashed to the platform. He twisted, raced for the depot.

"Stop him!" North, stumbling to his feet, kicked the flaming nozzle into the lower level between the tracks and lunged in pursuit. Ahead he saw horrified passengers open a lane before them.

"Stop him!"

The man with the skull face zigzagged, ran in long leaping strides. He reached the gate, wheeled. Whipping out a revolver he sent three shots thundering through the train shed.

Something hot thudded into North's shoulder. He ran on faster. But when he reached the gate he saw only a huddle of paralyzed men and women. Madly he charged into the brighter light of the waiting room. At the street entrance he stopped, a moan of defeat on his lips.

The man with the yellow face had disappeared!

For two minutes North stood there, leaning weakly against the wall. A moment later he saw Conrad Kyle, the C.N.&W.'s construction engineer, approach.

"He got away," Kyle panted. "I chased him into the Street. He vanished in thin air."

North nodded, swayed. Gripping the engineer's arm, he gasped, "Delfield! Was . . . was he hurt?"

Kyle shook his head. "Not a blister. All four of us—Delfield, the old man's daughter, Doctor Gage, and myself—would have been burned to a cinder if it hadn't been for you. But . . . by the Lord Harry, you've been shot! Come out here. I'll get Gage!"

Supported by Kyle, North let himself be guided back into the train shed. The pain had left his shoulder now, but his arm felt numb and feverish. His legs stumbled beneath him.

On the platform all was confusion. Passengers talked excitedly in strained voices. Two depot guards fired a steady stream of questions.

And then North saw a blond figure run forward to throw herself in his arms.

"Oh, Frank, you've been hurt!"

He shook his head weakly. "It's nothing, Madge. I'll be all right."

Spots swirled before his eyes. Vaguely he felt supporting hands lift him, heard Doctor Gage, Delfield's physician, give a command.

Then blackness came, and he knew no more.

CHAPTER II

The Voice of the Yellow Skull

The steady staccato of the wheels over the rail joints was drumming in North's ears when he returned to consciousness. He was lying on a couch in Brooks Delfield's private car, and Madge Lane was bending over him.

"Frank"—her voice was filled with latent fear—"I saw it from the car. In heaven's name, what was it?"

For a moment he lay there, fighting to collect his strength. Abruptly he sat erect.

They were all there, standing in a huddled, terrified group. Brooks Delfield chewed a cold cigar savagely. Marc, his son, was pale and trembling. Garnet Delfield, the president's daughter, leaned against Armand Guise, her rouged cheeks glowing like fever-spots. Conrad Kyle, the company engineer, stood stiffly erect, staring like a man who did not believe what he had seen. Of them all, Doctor Gage seemed unmoved.

"You'll have to take it easy for a time," Doctor Gage warned.

"That bullet went through the fleshy part of your arm, but it took quite a lot of blood."

North gnawed his lips. "That man," he said huskily, "used one of my *Dustneer* spray guns. But he had it filled with some inflammable chemical. When he ignited it, it changed to a wall of flame. Practically the same as liquid fire used during the war. If he . . ."

"If you hadn't acted when you did," Brooks Delfield said, "we wouldn't be here now. We're grateful, North. I'll see that you're repaid for this."

North stepped forth unsteadily and peered out a window. The train was roaring through the night. Outside the bark of the locomotive's exhaust mingled with the snarl of thunder. Slanting rain swished through the panes.

"Where are we?" he demanded.

Delfield sank into a chair. "Somewhere between Bald Canyon and Deerhorn," he answered. "We stay with the Coast Express as far as Harmony. The local waits for us there, and we take a special engine to Benton. We'll spend the night in Benton. It's the nearest point on rails to Rock River."

The president of the C.N.&W. twisted about. "Have you found anything?" he asked. "Know what all this means, North?"

North frowned. "I haven't learned much. Those cards were mailed from different parts of the city. They bore no finger prints, and the addressing in each case was done by a different typewriter. I've got a man checking up on all engravers to see about that yellow skull. If he finds anything he'll wire me."

In the chair opposite, Madge Lane sat, hands opening and closing convulsively.

The roar of the storm and the clatter of the speeding train surged louder to drown further conversation. North swept his eyes across the car, scowled as his gaze centered on Armand Guise. The Frenchman, he knew, had a double reason in worming himself into the Delfield graces. He too was a construction engineer, with wide experience on the Continent. Disgraced in France because of faulty bridge planning, he had asked Delfield to place him in charge of the proposed Rock River spur. So far the railroad president had refused.

As for Doctor Gage, North admitted he didn't like him either.

He was hawk-featured, and there was an unmistakable leer in his eyes when he looked at Madge Lane.

A lull came momentarily in the storm. North stiffened, listening.

Then he relaxed, smiling grimly. He had heard only the wailing scream of the locomotive whistle.

But a moment later he was sitting rigid, staring at the varnished ceiling of the car. Vaguely he realized the others had sensed it too. A ninth presence was in the car. The air was suddenly thick with an aura of brooding evil.

North's eyes trailed across the ceiling, past two lighting fixtures to an oblong panel directly overhead. That panel was a ventilator opening, and the cover was ajar now, letting in a draft of air.

Stereoscopically, like a picture slowly brought into focus, something moved in that opening. And then Garnet Delfield threw back her head and uttered a jangling scream of terror.

"My God!" she gasped. "Look!"

It was a face, leering down at them, the face of a yellow skull, hideously without expression, without detail. The same face North had seen on the man with the spray gun. Then it was gone, leaving a blank square of onyx sky.

North lunged to his feet, raced for the rear door, and charged onto the platform. Cold rain slapped his face. The night was like pitch save for zig-zag lightning streaks that cut across the eastern sky.

By the light of those flashes he climbed over the rail, clawed for the grab-iron ladder that led to the top of the car.

On the roof he saw nothing. The wind shrieked at him, tore at his clothes. On hands and knees he crawled to the ventilator panel. A span of light filtered through the aperture. North peered inside, braced himself as the train swung into a curve.

And suddenly from the blackness about him a sound rose over the roar. Low-pitched, it was a voice speaking in a low chanting cadence.

THIS IS THE YELLOW SKULL SPEAKING. I AM CLOSING IN ON YOU. THIS IS THE YELLOW SKULL SPEAKING. I AM CLOSING IN ON YOU . . .

Again and again the words were intoned. Abruptly the voice stopped. In its place, dying away into a hideous diminuendo, came a burst of savage laughter.

CHAPTER III

A Scream in the Dark

A slow shudder swept over North. He remained rigid for a moment, then forced his way on past the ventilator panel to the end of the car. But he saw nothing. It was as if that voice had been carried by the wind. Only a dull patch of red broke the murk, the glow from the engine's fire box far ahead.

The train roared on westward. Telegraph poles like gaunt one-legged monsters raced by.

Clothing soaked, North retraced his steps. He had reached the ladder and was climbing down when the jolt came. There was the grinding of brake-shoes, the screech as couplings took up the play. The train was slowing down.

North swung onto the platform, wrenched open the door and re-entered the private car. Brooks Delfield turned to meet him.

"Why are we stopping here?" he demanded. "We're thirty miles between stations. We've got a meet order with the way freight at Solaris."

North scowled, made fists of his hands. "There must be something wrong in the cab. . . . Where's Guise?"

Garnet Delfield looked up languidly from a chair. "Armand and Marc went into the smoking car," she said. "Mr. Kyle went with them."

There was a final jolt, and the train ground to a halt. Silence, broken only by the wail of the storm, swooped down upon the car. Stiffly North strode to the vestibule door, twisted the latch. His eyes widened.

"It's locked," he said dully.

Her composure vanished, Garnet Delfield pushed slowly out of her chair. Then North was shoving past them, pacing down the aisle to the rear door. Again a locked latch resisted his efforts.

"Frank"—Madge Lane came forward, swaying. "Frank, take me out of here. I'm . . . Oh God, I'm frightened."

He patted her shoulder gently. "Brace up, pal. After all, it takes human figures to lock a door, and if it's human we can fight it." He yanked open a wall cabinet, pulled out an emergency fire-ax. A glance at Brooks Delfield told him his proposed action had the president's consent. He raised the ax, swung.

With a splintering crash the door panel jerked outward. North reached through, twisted the knob, slammed the door wide.

An instant later he was running along the ties toward the front of the train. The wind howled, lashed at him like so many restraining hands. Save for a dim glow, the galley light in a dining car, the Pullman coaches were in darkness.

Midway past the fourth coach North drew up; in the gloom ahead heavy dragging footsteps grated. The advancing figure stopped, stood there in sinister silence.

Then lightning flashed, and Conrad Kyle strode forward. North gave a gasp of relief, yet even in the momentary light he could see the engineer's eyes were wide and gaping.

Kyle reached out, gripped North convulsively. "I was up forward in the cab," he whispered. "Good God, there's hell to pay there! The engineer's laid out cold, and the fireman . . ."

North stared at him. "Dead?"

Kyle nodded. "Decapitated."

Pandemonium broke loose as they stood there. Trainmen with lanterns ran back and forth in the darkness. The shrill, terrified voice of the conductor vibrated between bursts of thunder.

Abruptly North snapped harshly, "About this boy, Marc Delfield. Do you know of any bad feeling between him and his father?"

Conrad Kyle wiped a smear of sweat from his face, gave a hollow laugh. "Marc? You're crazy if you think that sap had anything to do with this. Delfield himself thinks the boy's a fool. When the old man dies, Garnet, the daughter, will be sole heir."

The detective nodded dully. "I'll take a look in the cab," he said. "You go back to the car, quiet the others." He moved on down the roadbed toward the front of the train. A brakeman rushed past him, yelling something. Opposite the tender, North suddenly halted dead in his tracks. Behind, hollow and muffled, a sound had risen up, wavering through the blackness.

Again it came, a woman's scream, laden with terror and agony.

Like a crazed man North wheeled, lunged back toward the private car. His legs seemed dead things holding him back.

He threw himself up the steps to the platform, ripped open the door. A harsh cry welled to his lips as he stared inward.

In the narrow aisle between the double row of easy chairs Brooks Delfield lay sprawled full length. His legs were doubled curiously upward. At the far end of the car Doctor Gage leaned weakly against a chair back. Across the physician Garnet Delfield stood like a propped-up image.

But Madge Lane was gone!

CHAPTER IV

Death Pounds the Key

For the fifth time in twenty minutes the night operator at Caxton City paced to the door of his station and looked out. It was a dirty night. Thunder cannonaded in an opaque sky. Rain swept across the platform to drive against the drooling wall of the freight shed.

The operator lit a cigarette nervously. For more than an hour now, without reason, an inner feeling of unease had been slowly stealing over him.

He closed the door and went back to his chair. On the instrument desk a clock said 12:23. In twenty minutes the Eastbound way freight would be due at Solaris, thirty miles west on the canyon rim. The freight would wait there, giving right of track to the Coast Express.

A stronger gust of wind tore past the station with a sullen whine, and the operator shivered. A quarter of an hour snailed by. At 12:38 the train-wire sounder jumped into life for a brief moment. Hill Junction reported to the despatcher. The way freight was "by" there.

The clock on the desk ticked steadily. The operator paced

across the room to a water-stand, spilled water in a glass. And then at 12:58 his every muscle became rigid.

The message-wire sounder suddenly broke into a chattering staccato. Hammering the familiar Caxton City call-letters, it vibrated over the roar of the storm, clamoring in insistence.

"CC—CC—CC—CC—CC"

Slowly the operator slid forward in his chair.

"CC—CC—CC"

There was something wrong. The call was unsigned. The touch to the brass was strange, different from any regular station along the line. Opening the switch, the operator reached for his key.

"I—I," he answered. "CC."

A moment's hesitation. Then in slow, jerky Morse the sounder began to spell out its message:

THIS IS THE YELLOW SKULL. YOUR HOUR IS AT HAND. WITHIN TEN MINUTES AFTER YOU READ THIS YOU WILL BE DEAD. TEN MINUTES! THIS IS THE YELLOW SKULL . . . THE YELLOW SKULL . . . THE YELLOW . . .

Like a man in a trance the operator stared down at the scrawled sentences he had automatically written. A hoarse dry laugh came to his lips. An instant later, he was pounding the key, demanding that the message be repeated.

But there was no reply. The operator kicked back his chair, groped to his feet. "The yellow skull," he muttered. "Am I going nuts . . . ?"

Only the storm answered him, the thunder rumbling, the wind moaning like a creature in agony.

Sweat broke out on his forehead. He paced to the door, swung it open. For a long moment he stood there, staring out before him. Suddenly his eyes accustomed themselves to the gloom . . .

Ahead where the passing track merged with the main-line a switchlight shined vaguely. But that switchlight was no longer green. It was yellow, a gleaming yellow, and it was shaped like a human skull. The operator stiffened. His hands jerked upward.

Slowly the skull-light advanced toward him. Black cavernous

eyes leered at him hypnotically. A gibbering laugh issued from formless lips.

A scream rose to the operator's lips. He clawed for the door. But with a final forward movement the yellow skull slithered across the intervening space and closed in.

CHAPTER V

Combat with the Monster

In the private car of the Coast Express Frank North stood stunned. Vaguely he was aware of Conrad Kyle pushing through the door at his side, halting with a sucking inhalation of breath, then rushing forward to the prone figure of Brooks Delfield.

North clamped his jaws together and stumbled down the aisle to confront Doctor Gage.

"Miss Lane!" he demanded. "Where is she?"

The physician shuddered. "She's gone! Gone! It came and it took her. Oh God!"

"Gone where? Answer, damn you, or I'll . . ."

"The yellow skull. The thing wasn't human, I tell you."

Terror, like an icy hand, clutched at North. He turned, paraded stiffly down the aisle to the door. A moment later in the storm-swept darkness he was stumbling toward the front of the train.

"Madge!" he screamed. "Madge!"

The wind tore away his voice, swallowed it in a wail of mockery. Sobbing, he sloshed on. The train was a place of confusion now. Lights gleamed in windows. Passengers, clad in night attire, stood staring in vestibule doorways.

"Madge!"

Nothing. A trainman with a lantern lurched out of the gloom, strode past him.

And then abruptly North halted. Flanking the right-of-way here was a flat expanse of plain, strewn with massive rocks and boulders. In the lightning flash something black and indistinct was outlined, running away from the train.

North lunged forward. The rain had blurred his vision, but the electrical flare had been sufficient to reveal a girl's body thrown sack-like over the figure's shoulder. Leaping across a drainage ditch, North ran as he had never run before.

The figure was gaining. They plunged down a low incline, entered a shallow gully. And then suddenly the thing was down, stumbling, dropping its burden.

A driving juggernaut, North closed in. It was a fiend that turned to face him. Steel-like fingers clawed up, tore at his eyes. They exchanged blows. North rocked backward as a fist grounded into his abdomen. Back and forth they surged, pounding each other mercilessly.

And then the figure twisted free, bent down. It whipped something high over its head.

North sensed his danger a split second too late. A jagged rock hurtled through space to strike with sickening impact against his temple.

Blackness swooped down upon him, and he felt himself falling . . .

How long he lay there he didn't know. Even after consciousness returned, he gaped up into the gloom, physically unable to move. The rain revived him at last. Pawing erect, he stared frantically about him.

"Madge!"

He saw the girl stretched prone beside an outthrust of granite. He gathered her in his arms and stumbled back to the train.

The six others were all there as he entered the private car. Lowering the girl to the couch, he massaged her wrists, breathed a sigh of relief as she opened her eyes.

"It's gone, darling. You're all right now."

Slowly he stood up, surveyed the fear-stricken faces before him. Slumped in a chair, Brooks Delfield held a crimson handkerchief to a gash in his forehead. His face was taut, his lips quivering. Beside him stood his son, Marc, and his daughter, Garnet. Armand Guise and Doctor Gage were talking in low tones.

The conductor entered the car, strode forward to Delfield.

"We're ready to go on now, sir," he said. "One of the brakemen will fire until we reach Solaris. I'll wire ahead for a new crew to meet us there when we reach Caxton City."

Delfield nodded silently. Two minutes later the train was once again boring into the night.

Abruptly North swung about, faced Conrad Kyle.

"We'd better make a thorough search of the train," he said to the engineer. "It won't do any good, but we . . . we can't stay here like rats in a cage without raising a finger."

Kyle's eyes showed too much white. He nodded and led the way through the vestibule door. Through five Pullmans they marched slowly, looking to either side, ready for instant action. The cars were silent, curtain-lined tunnels of gloom. The occupants had returned to their berths. They crossed a diner, entered more Pullmans.

At length they found themselves in the smoker. Here four men sat playing cards over an upturned suitcase. North gaped into their faces, turned away with a scowl. He paced to the far end of the car, yanked open the wash-room door, peered inside.

But their search was futile. Save for a black-faced porter who babbled hysterically to himself, they found nothing.

"No use, Kyle," North said finally. "We can't wake every person on the train and cross-examine them. We haven't the authority."

The engineer nodded. "I'll go back to the car," he said. "We're coming into a station in a moment."

Outside a green switchlight swirled by. Up ahead the whistle shrieked, and the train slowed to a rattling crawl. Hollowly the voice of the conductor sounded, "Caxton City, Caxton City."

North strode into the vestibule, waited until the train stopped, then swung down the steps. He crossed the little platform to the door of the station, pushed the barrier open. On the threshold he froze rigid.

The Caxton City telegraph operator sat motionless in his chair. His hands were resting on the instrument desk before him; his eyes were opened wide.

A piece of wire had been lashed around the man's throat, twisted to cut off life from the body!

CHAPTER VI

The Death Coach

For two terror-ridden minutes North stood there. Then:

"Dead!" It was the conductor who had followed him to the door who spoke. "He's been murdered!"

North's fists clenched. "Murdered, yes!" He paced slowly across the room to the dead man's side, automatically dropped his hand downward and felt for a pulse. But life had left the operator long before.

Then North saw the paper. The pad containing the operator's last words before the horror had struck. Reading slowly, the detective went over each word, mouthing them aloud.

The yellow skull! With a hand that shook despite his efforts to control it, North began to search the station's interior. Unrewarded at the end of five minutes he turned to the waiting conductor.

"This is a matter for the police. Leave everything the way it stands and make a complete report when you reach Solaris. Now let's get out of here."

He placed the message in his pocket, strode across the room. On the platform again, he closed the station door, glanced toward the train. As he looked four persons descended the steps of the private car and advanced toward him.

North scowled as the leader, Marc Delfield, lurched within speaking distance. "Well," the detective demanded, "what's the idea?"

The road president's son sent a furtive glance over his shoulder. "The idea is," he snarled, "we're leaving. Getting out of here, do you understand? We're going to wait for the local and go back to Denver."

Behind him, nodding in agreement, were Garnet Delfield, Armand Guise and Doctor Gage.

"Dad can be a stubborn fool, if he wants to," the president's daughter said. "He can go on in the face of death. We . . . I can't stand it."

For a moment North looked at them blankly. After what had happened, he didn't care much whether these four stayed on or not. Individually and collectively he disliked all of them. On the other hand he could not but admire Brooks Delfield, who, in spite of all odds, was determined to combat the unseen forces.

Suddenly a thought whipped the detective around.

"Madge! . . . Is she . . . ?"

Doctor Gage nodded. "Back in the car, yes. She's all right."

The physician's voice was drowned in a sudden sound. Rising over the rumble of thunder came the grating of steel, the reap of flanges over rails. North wheeled.

He saw nothing for an instant. Then his muscles jerked rigid, and a wave of horror swept over him.

Ahead where the private car joined with the next coach of the train an aperture of yawning space was slowly widening. A steep downgrade descended to the east from the Caxton City station. Down that grade the private car was moving—alone! It had been uncoupled from the Coast Express and was rolling backward—without control!

North's body seemed clamped in a vice. Madge Lane was in that car! Even as he watched, the car trucks, feeling the effect of the grade, increased their speed.

The conductor's shout of warning snapped him into action. He sucked in his breath, hurtled forward. Across the platform he raced, onto the cinder roadbed. The car was moving faster, drawing away from him steadily. Suddenly from its interior a woman's scream tocsined out into the darkness.

Terror probing into him, North ran like a madman. He threw himself forward, clawed for the hand-rail by the steps. Breath burning down his lungs he clung there. Slowly he moved up the steps and pushed the door open.

He stood rigid.

He was gaping into the bore of a revolver. Inside a death-like figure stood, holding the weapon. The face was hidden by a low-hanging mask of yellow silk.

"So you are here, Frank North. Well, you have been expected. Your reception has been carefully planned for you."

North swayed. Five feet beyond he could see the motionless

figure of Madge Lane, lying prone on the couch. In the chair opposite Brooks Delfield sat like a wooden image, hands lashed behind him, ankles securely bound. The road president's face was twisted in terror.

An icy chill shot over North as he looked at the figure in the mask. "Who . . . who are you?" he gasped.

"I am the yellow skull. I am he who is going to kill you."

As the figure spoke Madge Lane stirred on the couch.

"Oh, Frank!"

Mad fury seized North then. With a side-swiveling lunge he threw himself forward, clawed for the revolver. But he got only half way.

Like a cat the figure leaped back. It whipped forth a length of rope and sent a noose coiling forward. The thong dropped around the detective's throat, jerked tight. Strangling pressure jammed against his larynx.

An instant later he felt himself seized, flung backward to the car wall. When the pressure was eased, he was lashed helpless to a floor-bracketed chair.

The car was racing faster now. Over the howl of the storm the wheels rumbled and roared as they felt the full effect of the downgrade. The figure in the mask uttered a low laugh.

"You are a fool, Frank North. Your heroics may be appreciated by your sweetheart here, but they will avail you nothing. In five minutes the car will reach the end of this downgrade. It will lessen its speed for a mile as it drifts along a straightaway. I plan to get off there.

"But five minutes after I have left the car it will enter the outer reaches of Deerhorn canyon. I think you know the rest. The grade there is even greater. And if the car does keep to the rails, there's another train, a freight, just beyond."

"But who—" A half-stifled moan welled to North's lips as he struggled frantically. "Who are you?"

"You will never know who I am. I am sending you to your death only because you have persisted in interfering with my plans. It is you"— the masked figure swung about to face the road president—"you, Brooks Delfield, that I want. With you dead the Colorado, North & Western will discard its plans to lay trackage to Rock River. That right-of-way is rightfully mine. I have planned such a project, dreamed about it for years."

Swaying with the movements of the car, the figure suddenly whipped about. Madge Lane had left the couch and was moving towards North's revolver on the floor of the car. The masked figure seized her, slapped its open fist into her face and flung her back on the couch.

North's brain spun as he watched. He tore at his bonds.

"For two years I have known the federal government planned to erect a dam to the Rock River site. There is only one passable right-of-way to the town, the one which the Colorado, North & Western plans to use. Do you think I intend to let a fortune slide between my fingers when it is so close?"

The figure glanced out the window. "We are approaching the straightaway. If you thought to stop the car after I get off, put it out of your mind. I shall damage the brake wheel beyond use."

He turned, strode down the aisle to the observation door. The car was plunging into the night like an insane thing now. Wheels over the fish-plates thundered a pounding death-dirge. Brooks Delfield sat like a man of stone, staring blankly before him.

And then hope swept through North. His hands, lashed tight to the arm of the chair, were but inches from his open vest. Across that vest stretched his watch-chain, and from one end of the chain hung a silver monogrammed pocket knife.

Twisting, North jammed his body sideways, reached for the chain, tore it loose. His fingers dug the knife blade open, began to saw at his hands.

Like members of another body his hands worked. And then . . .

The ropes parted! He lurched erect, raced down the aisle toward the masked figure still bent over the brake wheel on the observation platform. A hiss of surprise came from the figure's lips as it turned to meet the attack.

They struck. Fists pounding in and out, North fought to reach that yellow mask. The revolver was in the figure's hand now. North seized the gun wrist, sent the weapon clattering to the platform.

They stumbled to the rail. Cold hands clamped about North's throat, bent him slowly backward into space. He forced himself up, strove frantically to break that death grip.

And then he found an opening. The car shot into a curve, heeled to the tangent. Off-balance, the figure staggered back.

North slammed his right fist forward with every ounce of strength he possessed. The figure uttered a hollow cry, stiffened and slumped downward. The yellow mask was ripped away, revealing a man's face in the light spilling out the car door.

It was the face of Conrad Kyle!

The events that followed remain in Frank North's brain only as a swirl of confusion. Moving as in some strange dream, he stopped the car—Kyle had only partially damaged the brake wheel—waited for what seemed interminable hours, and finally flagged the oncoming freight.

A long time later they arrived back at Caxton City. There they joined the Coast Express, continued to Solaris. And at Solaris police came aboard and took charge.

Conrad Kyle was completely broken in spirit as he saw the failure of his plans. Cross-questioned, he finally broke down and confessed.

It was a confession fantastic. Thirsting for more wealth he had in some way obtained advance information of the proposed federal dam and had foreseen the huge possibilities of railroad communication with the site. He had realized that if he could prevent the Colorado, North & Western from acting he could obtain an option on the property and sell for a high price to any of a dozen rival roads.

The rest was a matter of carefully laid plans. From the attempted murder of Brooks Delfield in the Denver depot by means of the flame liquid in North's own *Dustneer* gun to the uncoupling of the private car at Caxton City, all had proceeded on a prearranged schedule. The mysterious voice which North had heard on the roof of the car was found to have come from a miniature phonograph, cleverly concealed in the ventilator opening. The yellow skull face that appeared in the aperture was a mask, worked by the same mechanism.

Kyle had accomplices to aid him. Underworld characters whom he knew from earlier contacts had tapped the telegraph wires, sent the mysterious messages, attempted to kidnap Madge

Lane and killed the operator at Caxton City. The whole thing was worked out on a huge scale to prevent the slightest slip-up.

But now all that is past. The last spike has been driven on the Colorado, North & Western spur-track to Rock River. Frank North and Madge Lane are married and live in a small town near Denver.

Yet there are times when North is gone and the screech of an eastbound train wails up the valley that Madge stops and shudders. She still remembers the terror of that night on the Coast Express.

Acknowledgments

Revelations in Black, copyright 1933, by the Popular Fiction Publishing Company, for *Weird Tales*, April 1933.

Phantom Brass, copyright 1934, by the Frank A. Munsey Company, for *Railroad Stories*, August 1934.

The Cane, copyright 1934, by the Popular Fiction Publishing Company, for *Weird Tales*, April 1934; copyright 1944, by August Derleth for *Sleep No More*.

The Coach on the Ring, copyright *The Haunted Ring* 1932, by Good Story Magazine Company, Inc., for *Ghost Stories*, December-January 1932.

The Kite, copyright *Satan's Kite* 1937, by Beacon Magazines, Inc., for *Thrilling Mystery*, June 1937.

Canal, copyright 1944, by Better Publications, Inc., for *Startling Stories*, Spring 1944.

The Satanic Piano, copyright 1934, by the Popular Fiction Publishing Company, for *Weird Tales*, May 1934.

The Last Drive, copyright 1933, by the Popular Fiction Publishing Company, for *Weird Tales*, June 1933.

The Spectral Pistol, copyright *The Phantom Pistol* 1941, by Weird Tales, for *Weird Tales*, May 1941.

Sagasta's Last, copyright 1939, by Better Publications, Inc., for *Strange Stories*, August 1939.

The Tomb from Beyond, copyright 1932, by Stellar Publishing Corporation, for *Wonder Stories*, November 1933.

The Digging at Pistol Key, copyright 1947 by Weird Tales for *Weird Tales*, July 1947.

Moss Island, copyright 1932, by Teck Publishing Corporation, for *Amazing Stories Quarterly*, Winter 1932.

Carnaby's Fish, copyright 1945, by Weird Tales, for *Weird Tales*, July 1945.